Praise for Arlene James

"This is a terrifically lovely story."

—*RT Book Reviews* on *Anna Meets Her Match*

"James' story touches the heart and brings tears to the eyes."

—*RT Book Reviews* on *A Match Made in Texas*

"A warm, loving and engaging story."

—*RT Book Reviews* on *His Small-Time Girl*

"[An] incredibly tender, solid and very satisfying story."

—*RT Book Reviews* on *Mommy in Mind*

HEARTS IN TEXAS

Arlene James

Previously published as *Anna Meets Her Match* & *A Match Made in Texas*

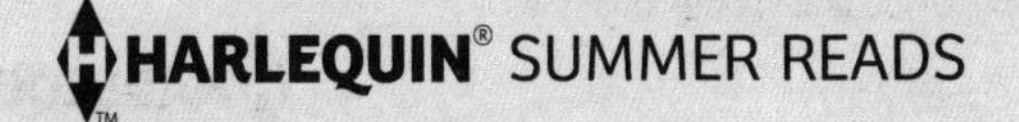

ISBN-13: 978-1-335-00526-7

Recycling programs for this product may not exist in your area.

This edition published by arrangement with Harlequin Books S.A.

For questions and comments about the quality of this book, please contact us at CustomerService@Harlequin.com.

Printed in U.S.A.

CONTENTS

Anna Meets Her Match 7

A Match Made in Texas 243

Arlene James has been publishing steadily for nearly four decades and is a charter member of RWA. She is married to an acclaimed artist, and together they have traveled extensively. After growing up in Oklahoma, Arlene lived thirty-four years in Texas and now abides in beautiful northwest Arkansas, near two of the world's three loveliest, smartest, most talented granddaughters. She is heavily involved in her family, church and community.

Books by Arlene James

Love Inspired

The Prodigal Ranch

The Rancher's Homecoming

Chatam House

Anna Meets Her Match
A Match Made in Texas
Baby Makes a Match
An Unlikely Match
Second Chance Match

Eden, OK

His Small-Town Girl
Her Small-Town Hero
Their Small-Town Love

Visit the Author Profile page at Harlequin.com for more titles.

ANNA MEETS HER MATCH

Therefore, there is now no condemnation for those who are in Christ Jesus.

–*Romans* 8:1

I am often asked why, after all these years, I continue to write romance. The answer is very simple. I've been happily married for all this time to the same increasingly wonderful man.

No wife has ever been more blessed in her husband, and no husband has ever given his wife more inspiration!

Thank you, sweetheart.
DAR

Chapter One

"Da-a-a-dy!" Gilli's muffled voice called from the backseat of the silver sedan as Reeves Leland lifted the last of the suitcases from the trunk. "Out!" Gilli demanded, rattling the disabled door handle.

He had parked the car beneath the porte cochere on the west side of the massive antebellum mansion known as Chatam House, where he and his daughter had come seeking sanctuary. "In a minute, Gilli," he said, closing the trunk lid.

Since turning three six months earlier, his daughter had grown increasingly difficult, as if he didn't have enough problems. He thought of the letter that he'd recently received from his ex-wife. The divorce had been final for nearly a year, but she had suddenly decided that he hadn't treated her fairly in the settlement. He shook his head, more pressing concerns crowding his mind. The most immediate had to do with housing.

Honeybees had driven him and his daughter out of their home. Honeybees!

Pausing in stunned contemplation Reeves felt the gray chill of an early February breeze permeate the camel-tan wool of his tailored overcoat. It rattled the dried leaves of the enormous magnolia tree on the west lawn like old bones, adding to the strangeness of the morning.

Father in heaven, I'm so confused, he thought. *Honeybees?*

Whatever God was doing in his life, he knew that he need not worry about his welcome here. He hadn't even called ahead, so certain was he of that welcome, and he gave himself a moment now to bask in that certainty, his gaze wandering over stately fluted columns, white-painted stone walls and graceful redbrick steps leading to the deep porch and the vibrant yellow, paneled side door with its so proper black framing. Terracotta pots flanked this side entry. In the springtime, he knew, flowers would spill over their edges, presenting a colorful welcome that would echo throughout the fifteen-acre estate.

Reeves had always loved this grand old house. The picturesque antebellum mansion and its grounds belonged to his aunts, the Chatam triplets, elder sisters of his mother. None of the aunties had ever married, but they were the first ones of whom Reeves had thought when the full weight of his situation had become clear to him.

"Da-a-dy!" Gilli bellowed.

"I'm coming. Hold on."

He took one step toward the side of the car before the sound of tires on gravel at the front of the house halted him. Turning away from his impatient daughter, he trudged to the corner of the building. A battered, foreign-made coupe pulled up at the front of the mansion. Reeves stared in appreciation at the slender blonde in dark clothing who hopped out. Lithe and energetic, with a cap of soft, wispy hair, she moved with unconscious grace. As if sensing his regard, she looked up, and shock reverberated through him. Recognizing Anna Miranda Burdett, his old childhood nemesis, Reeves frowned.

Well, that was all this day needed. Back during their school days she had done everything in her power to make his life miserable, which was why they hadn't spoken in years, though her grandmother Tansy was a friend of his aunties. Her pranks were legendary, and he'd once had the dubious honor of being her favorite target. She'd made a travesty of his senior year, his young male pride taking a regular beating at her hands. Given his current problems, he had no patience for dealing with Anna Miranda today.

He comforted himself with the thought that she was most likely just picking up her grandmother. He couldn't imagine any other reason why she would be here at Chatam House. Hopefully, they would depart before he met with his aunts.

"Da-a-a-dy!"

He turned back toward his daughter, his footsteps crunching in the gravel as he hurried over to let her out of the car.

"I want out!" she complained, sliding down to the ground, her caramel-blond curls mingling with the fake fur on the hood of her pink nylon coat. She looked up at him, an accusing expression on her face.

A perfect combination of her mother and himself, with his rust-brown eyes and dimpled chin and Marissa's hair and winged brows, Gilli looked like every father's dream child. Unfortunately, this child whom he had wanted so much seemed terribly unhappy with him. Whatever was he going to do without Nanny?

Gilli bolted across the gravel toward the porch.

"Watch it!" he barked. Even before the warning left his mouth, she skidded and, predictably, tumbled down.

She fell to her knees, howling. Reeves reached her in two long strides and was lifting her to her feet when that yellow door opened, revealing the concerned countenance of Chester Worth. Sturdy, pale and balding, Chester and his wife, Hilda, along with her sister Carol, had served as household staff for the Chatam sisters for more than two decades. Wearing nothing more than a cardigan sweater over a plain white shirt, suspenders and slacks, Chester stepped out into the February cold, his bushy brows drawn together over his half-glasses.

Gilli's wails shut off abruptly. "H'lo, Chester," she greeted brightly.

"Miss Gilli, Mister Reeves, good to see y'all. Can I help?"

Reeves tugged Gilli forward, saying to Chester, "Could you get Gilli to the kitchen and ask Hilda to give her some lunch while I bring in the luggage?"

"Luggage, you say?" Chester asked, taking Gilli by the hand.

"We've come for a stay," Reeves replied, adding wearily, "It's been quite a morning, Chester."

"We got bees," Gilli announced, "lots and lots."

"I'll explain after I've seen the aunties," Reeves went on. "Where are they?"

"All three are in the front parlor, Mr. Reeves," Chester answered. "You just leave those bags and go let them know you're here. I'll take care of everything soon as Miss Gilli's settled. The east suite should do nicely. Bees, is it?"

"Lots and lots," Gilli confirmed.

"Thank you, Chester. I'll leave the bags inside the door."

Reeves returned to the rear of the car as the older man coaxed Gilli away. He carried the luggage into the small side entry then removed his overcoat, folding it over one arm. Smoothing his dark brown suit jacket, he headed off down a long narrow hallway, past the kitchen, butler's pantry and family parlor, toward the center of the house.

The scents of lemony furniture polish and gingerbread sparred with the musty odor of antique upholstery and the mellow perfume of aged rosewood, all familiar, all welcome and calming. Running through this house as a child with his cousins, Reeves had considered it his personal playground and more home than whichever parent's house he'd currently been living in. It had always been his one true sanctuary.

Feeling lighter than he had for some time, Reeves paused at the intersection of the "back" hall and the so-called "west" hall that flanked the magnificent curving staircase, which anchored the grand foyer at the front of the house. He lifted his eyes toward the high, pale blue ceiling, where faded feathers wafted among faint, billowy clouds framed by ornate crown moldings, and prayed silently.

It's good to be here, Lord. Maybe that's why You've allowed us to be driven from our own home. You seem to have deemed Chatam House a shelter for me in times of deepest trouble, so this must be Your way of taking care of me and Gilli. The aunties are a good influence on her, and I thank You for them and this big old house. I trust that You'll have a new nanny prepared for us by the time we go back to our place.

Wincing, he realized that he had just betrayed reluctance to be at his own home alone with his own daughter. Abruptly he felt the millstone of failure about his neck.

Forgive me for my failings, Lord, he prayed, *and please, please make me a better father. Amen.*

Turning right, Reeves walked past the formal dining room and study on one side and the quaint cloak and "withdrawing rooms" on the other, to the formal front entry, where he left his coat draped over the curved banister at the bottom of the stairs. The "east" hall, which flanked the other side of the staircase, would have taken him past the cloak and restrooms again, as well as the library and ballroom. Both of the latter received a surprising amount of use because of the many charities and clubs in which the aunties were involved. The spacious front parlor, however, was definitely the busiest room in the house. Reeves headed there, unsurprised to find the doors wide open.

He heard the aunties' voices, Hypatia's well-modulated drawl, followed by Magnolia's gruffer reply and Odelia's twitter. Just the sound of them made him smile. He paid no attention to the words themselves. Pausing to take a look inside, he swept his gaze over groupings of antique furniture, pots of well-tended plants and a wealth of bric-a-brac. Seeing none but the aunties, he relaxed and strode into the room.

Three identical pairs of light, amber-brown eyes turned his way at once. That was pretty much where the similarities ended for the casual observer, although those sweetly rounded faces, from the delicate brows, aristocratic noses, prim mouths and gently cleft chins, were very nearly interchangeable.

Hypatia, as usual, appeared the epitome of Southern

gentility in her neat lilac suit with her silver hair curled into a sleek figure-eight chignon at the nape of her neck and pearls at her throat. Magnolia, on the other hand, wore a drab shirtwaist dress decades out of style beneath an oversized cardigan sweater that had undoubtedly belonged to Grandpa Hub, dead these past ten years. Her steel-gray braid hung down her back, and she wore run-down slippers rather than the rubber boots she preferred for puttering around the flowerbeds and hothouse. Lovingly referred to as "Aunt Mags" by her many nieces and nephews, she hid a tender heart beneath a gruff, mannish manner.

Odelia, affectionately but all too aptly known as Auntie Od, was all ruffles and gathers and eye-popping prints, her white hair curling softly about her ears, which currently sported enamel daisies the size of teacups. Auntie Od was known for her outlandish earrings and her sweetness. The latter imbued both her smile and her eyes as her gaze lit on the newcomer.

"Reeves!"

He could not help laughing at her delight, a patent condition for the old dear.

"Hello, Aunt Odelia." Going at once to kiss her temple, he held out a hand to Mags, who sat beside her sister on the prized Chesterfield settee that Grandma Augusta had brought back from her honeymoon trip to London back in 1932.

"Surprised to see you here this time of day," Mags stated.

Swiveling, Reeves bussed her forehead, bemused by the strength of her grip on his fingers. "Honeybees," he offered succinctly.

"What about them, dear?" Hypatia inquired calmly

from her seat in the high-backed Victorian armchair facing the door through which he had entered. Its twin sat facing her, with its back to that door.

He leaned across the piecrust table to kiss her cool cheek, Mags still squeezing his hand. "They've invaded my attic."

He quickly gave them the details, how the nanny had phoned in a panic that morning, shrieking that she and Gilli were under attack by "killer bees." Racing home from his job as vice president of a national shipping company, he had found both of them locked into the nanny's car in the drive. Inside the house, a dozen or more honeybees had buzzed angrily. Nanny had climbed up on a stool to investigate a stain on the kitchen ceiling. Hearing a strange hum, she'd poked at it. Something sticky had plopped onto the counter, and bees had swarmed through the newly formed hole in the Sheetrock.

Reeves had called an exterminator, who had refused even to come out. Instead, he'd been referred to a local "bee handler," who had arrived outfitted head-to-toe in strange gear to tell him more than he'd ever wanted to know about the habits of the Texas honeybee. A quick inspection had revealed that thousands, perhaps millions, of the tiny creatures had infested his attic. It was going to take days to remove them all, and then his entire ceiling, which was saturated with honey, all of the insulation and much of the supporting structure of his roof would have to be torn out and replaced.

"Oh, my!" Odelia exclaimed, gasping. "The bees must have frightened Gilli."

He spared her a smile before turning back to Hypatia, the undisputed authority at Chatam House. "Hardly. She wanted to know if she could keep them as pets."

Gilli had been begging for a pet since her birthday, but he didn't have time to take care of a pet and so had staunchly refused.

"What can we do?" Hypatia asked, as pragmatic as ever.

"What you always do," he told her, smiling. "Provide sanctuary. I'm afraid we're moving in on you."

"Well, of course, you are," she said with a satisfied smile.

"It could be weeks," he warned, "months, even."

She waved that away with one elegant motion of her hand. She knew as well as he did that checking into a hotel with a three-year-old as rambunctious as Gilli would have been sure disaster, but he'd have chosen that option before moving in with his father, second stepmother and their daughter, his baby sister, who would soon turn four.

"There is another problem," he went on. "Nanny quit. She'd been complaining that Gilli was too much for her." Actually, she'd been complaining that he did not spend enough time with Gilli, but he was a single father with a demanding job. Besides, he paid a generous salary. "I guess the bees were the final straw. She just walked out."

"That seems to be a habit where you're concerned," drawled an unexpected voice. "Women walking out."

Reeves whirled to find a familiar figure in slim jeans and a brown turtleneck sweater slouching in the chair opposite Hypatia. A piquant face topped with a wispy fringe of medium gold bangs beamed a cheeky grin at him. His spirits dropped like a stone in a well, even as a new realization shook him. This was not the Anna Miranda of old. This Anna Miranda was a startlingly attractive version, as attractive in her way as Marissa was in hers. Oh, no, this was not the same old brat. This was worse. Much worse.

"Hello, Stick," Anna Miranda said. "You haven't changed a bit."

"I'm so sorry, dear," Hypatia cooed. "We forgot our manners in all the excitement. Reeves, you know Anna Miranda."

Reeves frowned as if he'd just discovered the keys to his beloved first car glued to his locker door. Again. Anna smiled, remembering how she'd punished him for refusing her a ride in that car. Foolishly, she'd pined for his attention from the day that she'd first met him right here in this house soon after his parents had divorced. Even at ten, he'd had no use for an unhappy rebellious girl, especially one four years younger, and she had punished him for it, all the way through her freshman and his senior year in high school. While she'd agonized through her unrequited crush, he had pierced her hardened heart with his disdain. High school hadn't been the same after he'd graduated. Despite his coolness, she had felt oddly abandoned.

In the twelve or thirteen years since, she had caught numerous glimpses of Reeves Leland around town. Buffalo Creek simply wasn't a big enough town that they could miss each other forever. Besides, they were members of the same church, though she confined her participation to substituting occasionally in the children's Sunday school. In all those years, they had never exchanged so much as a word, and suddenly, sitting here in his aunts' parlor, she hadn't been able to bear it a moment longer.

Reeves put on a thin smile, greeting her with a flat version of the name his much younger self had often chanted in a provoking, exasperated singsong. “Anna Miranda.”

Irrational hurt flashed through her, and she did the first thing that came to mind. She stuck out her tongue. He shook his head.

“Still the brat, I see.”

The superior tone evoked an all too familiar urge in her. To counter it, she grinned and crossed her legs, wagging a booted foot. “Better that than a humorless stick-in-the-mud, if you ask me.”

“Has anyone ever?” he retorted. “Asked your opinion, I mean.”

His response stinging, she let her gaze drop away nonchalantly, but Reeves had always been able to read her to a certain extent.

“Sorry,” he muttered.

Before Anna had to say anything, Odelia chirped in with a reply to Reeves's tacky question. “Why, yes, of course,” Odelia declared gaily, waving a lace hanky she'd produced from somewhere. “We were just asking Anna Miranda's opinion on the announcements for the spring scholarship auction. Weren't we, sisters?”

“Invitations,” Hypatia corrected pointedly. “An announcement implies that we are compelling attendance rather than soliciting it.”

Anna's mouth quirked up at one corner. As if the Chatam triplets did not command Buffalo Creek society, such society as a city of thirty thousand residents could provide, anyway. With Dallas just forty-five miles to the north, Buffalo Creek's once great cotton center had disappeared, reducing the city to little more than a bedroom community of the greater Dallas/Fort Worth Metroplex. Yet, the city retained enough of its unique culture to bear pride in it, and as a daughter of the area's wealthiest family Hypatia Chatam, while personally one of the humblest individuals Anna had ever known, bore that community pride especially well.

"This spring," Hypatia said with a slight tilt of her head, "instead of holding the dinner and auction at the college, as in years past, we are opening the house instead."

This seemed no surprise to Reeves. "Ah."

Everyone knew that Buffalo Creek Bible College, or BCBC, was one of his aunts' favorite charities. Every spring, they underwrote a dinner and silent auction to raise scholarship funds. This year the event was to acquire a somewhat higher tone, moving from the drafty library hall at BCBC to the Chatam House ballroom. In keeping with the intended elegance of the occasion, they had contacted the only privately owned print shop in town for help with the necessary printed paper goods. Anna just happened to work at the print shop. Given her grandmother's friendship with the Chatam triplets, they had requested that Anna call upon them. Her boss, Dennis, had grudgingly allowed it.

"Anna Miranda is helping us figure out what we need printed," Mags explained. "You know, invitations, menus, advertisements…"

"Oh, and bid sheets," Hypatia said to Anna Miranda, one slender, manicured forefinger popping up.

Anna Miranda sat forward, asking, "Have you thought of printed napkins and coasters? Those might add a nice touch."

"Hmm." Hypatia tapped the cleft in her Chatam chin.

Reeves looked at Anna Miranda. "What are you, a paper salesman, er, person?"

She tried to fry him with her glare. "I am a graphic artist, for your information."

"Huh." He said it as if he couldn't believe she had an ounce of talent for anything.

"We'll go with linen napkins," Hypatia decided, sending Reeves a quelling look.

He bowed his head, a tiny muscle flexing in the hollow of his jaw.

"Magnolia, remember to tell Hilda to speak to the caterer about the linens, will you, dear?" Hypatia went on.

"If I don't do it now I'll just forget," Magnolia complained, heaving herself up off the settee. She patted Reeves affectionately on the shoulder, reaching far up to do so, as she lumbered from the room. Suddenly Anna felt conspicuously out of place in the midst of this loving family.

"I should be going, too," she said, clutching her leather-bound notebook as she rose. "If I'm not back in the shop soon, Dennis will think I'm goofing off."

Hypatia stood, a study in dignity and grace. She smiled warmly at Anna Miranda. Reeves stepped away, taking up a spot in front of the plastered fireplace on the far wall where even now a modern gas jet sponsored a cheery, warming flame.

"I'll see you out," Hypatia said to Anna, and they moved toward the foyer. "Thank you for coming by. The college press is just too busy to accommodate us this year."

"Well, their loss is our gain," Anna replied cheerfully. "I should have some estimates for you soon. Say, have you thought about creating a logo design for the fundraiser? I could come up with something unique for it."

"What a lovely idea," Hypatia said, nodding as they strolled side by side toward the front door. "I'll discuss that with my sisters."

"Great."

Anna picked up her coat from the long, narrow, marble-topped table occupying one wall of the opulent foyer and shrugged into it. She glanced back toward the parlor and caught sight of Reeves. Frowning thoughtfully, he seemed very alone in that moment. Instantly Anna regretted that crack about women abandoning him.

As usual, she'd spoken without thinking, purely from pique because he'd so effectively ignored her to that point. It was as if they were teenagers again, so when he'd made that remark about the nanny walking out, Anna had put that together with what she'd heard about his ex simply hopping onto the back of a motorcycle and splitting town with her boyfriend. Now Anna wished she hadn't thrown that up to him. Now that the harm was done.

Reeves leaned a shoulder against the mantel, watching as Hypatia waved farewell to Anna Miranda. He didn't like what was happening here, didn't trust Anna Miranda to give this matter the attention and importance that it deserved. In fact, he wouldn't put it past her to turn this into some huge joke at his aunts' expense. He still smarted inwardly from that opening salvo, but while she could make cracks about him all she wanted, he would not put up with her wielding her malicious sense of humor against his beloved aunties. He decided to stop in at the print shop and have a private chat with her.

"Lovely. Just lovely," Odelia said from the settee, snagging his attention. "What color is it, do you think?"

"I beg your pardon?"

"Antique gold. Yes, that's it. Antique gold." She made a swirling motion around her plump face with the lace hanky. "I wish I could wear mine that short."

Reeves felt at a loss, but then he often did with Auntie Od. Adding Anna Miranda to the mix hadn't helped. He walked toward the settee. "What about antique gold?"

The hanky swirled again. "Anna Miranda's hair. Wouldn't you say that perfectly describes the color of Anna Miranda's hair?"

Antique gold. Yes, he supposed that did describe the color of Anna Miranda's short, lustrous hair. It used to be lighter, he recalled, the brassy color of newly minted gold. She'd worn it cropped at chin length as a girl. Now it seemed darker, richer, as if burnished with age, and the style seemed at once wistful and sophisticated.

Unfortunately, while she'd changed on the outside—in some rather interesting ways, he admitted—she appeared not to have done so on the inside. She seemed to be the same cheeky brat who had tried to make his life one long joke. Reeves's thoughtful gaze went back to the foyer door, through which Hypatia returned just that instant.

"She's so very lovely," Odelia prattled on, "and such a sweet girl, too, no matter what Tansy says."

"Tansy would do better to say less all around, I think," Hypatia remarked, "but then we are not to judge." She lowered herself into her chair once more and smiled up at Reeves. "Honeybees," she said. "I've never heard of such a thing."

He shrugged. "According to the bee handler, we humans and the true killer bees coming up from the south are driving the poor honeybees out of their natural habitat, so they're adapting by invading every quiet, sheltered space they can find, including attics, hollow walls, even abandoned cars."

The sisters traded looks. Odelia said what they were both thinking.

"We should have Chester check out the house."

"I think, according to what the bee handler told me, the attics here would be too high for them," Reeves assured her.

"We'll have Chester check, just to be sure," Hypatia decided.

A crash sounded from the depths of the great old house, followed by a familiar wail, distant and faint but audible. Reeves sighed. "I'll start looking for another nanny tomorrow."

Hypatia smiled sympathetically. "It's all right, dear. I'm sure we'll manage until you're ready to go back to your own home."

Reeves closed his eyes with relief. Finding another nanny was one difficult, time-consuming chore he would gladly put on the back burner for now. He had enough to contend with. He wondered if he should contact his lawyer about Marissa. Just then Mags trundled into the room, huffing for breath.

"No harm done, but Gilli's not apt to calm down until you go to her."

Nodding grimly, Reeves strode from the room and headed for the kitchen. The sobs grew louder with every step, but it was a sound Reeves knew only too well. Not hurt and not frightened, rather they were demanding sobs, willful sobs, angry sobs and as hopeless as any tears could ever be. Deep down, even Gilli knew that he could do nothing. He could not make Marissa love them. He could not mend their broken family.

God help us both, he prayed. But perhaps He already had, honeybees and all.

The sanctuary of Chatam House, along with the wise, loving support of the aunties, was the best thing that had happened to them in more than a year. Pray God that it would be enough to help them, finally, find their way

"Poor Reeves," Odelia said as his hurried footsteps faded.

"Poor Gilli," Mags snorted. "That boy is deaf, dumb and blind where she's concerned, though he means well, I'm sure."

"Yes, of course," Hypatia said, her gaze seeing back through the years. "Reeves always means well, but how could he know what to do with Gilli? Children learn by example, and while I love our baby sister, Dorinda hasn't always done best by her oldest two. And that says nothing of their father."

"Melinda has done well," Odelia pointed out, referring to Reeves's one full sibling. He had five half siblings, including twin sisters and a brother, all younger than him.

"True," Hypatia acknowledged, "but I wonder if Melinda's happy marriage hasn't made Reeves's divorce more difficult for him. He's a man of faith, though, and he loves his daughter. He'll learn to deal with Gilli eventually."

Mags arched an eyebrow. "What that man needs is someone to help him understand what Gilli's going through and how to handle her."

"If anyone can understand Gilli, it's Anna Miranda," Odelia gushed.

Hypatia's eyes widened. "You're exactly right about that, dear." She tapped the small cleft in her chin. Everyone in the family had one to some degree, but Hypatia wasn't thinking of that now. She was thinking of Anna Miranda's childhood. "I believe," she said, eyes narrowing, "that Anna Miranda is going to be even more help to us than we'd assumed and in more ways than we'd realized."

Mags sat up straight, both brows rising. After a moment, she slowly grinned. Odelia, however, frowned in puzzlement.

"Do you think she'll volunteer for one of the committees?" Odelia asked.

"Oh, I think her talents are best used with the printing," Hypatia mused. "She's suggested that the fundraiser should have its own unique logo, and I concur, but designing it will probably require a good deal of her time. After all, we have to pick just the right design."

"Exactly the right design," Magnolia agreed.

"Yes," Hypatia went on, smiling broadly, "I do think that best suits our needs."

"Ours," Magnolia purred suggestively, "and Reeves's."

"And Gilli's!" Odelia added brightly, finally seeing the wisdom of this decision.

Hypatia smiled. How perfect was the timing of God and how mysterious His ways. Honeybees, indeed.

Chapter Two

The back door of the shop had barely closed behind Anna before her boss's voice assaulted her ear. "Took you long enough!"

Dropping her notebook on the front counter, she turned toward his open office door. "I'll skip lunch to make up for the time."

She'd been late to work that morning. It happened all too frequently, despite her best efforts, and Dennis despised tardiness. He rose from behind his desk and stalked around it, his big belly leading the way. Looking down his nose at her, his sandy brown mustache quivered with suppressed anger. Her coworker Howard gave her a pitying shake of his graying head before turning back to his task. Dragging up a smile, Anna faced her employer with more aplomb than she truly felt, but that was the story of her life. She had made an art of putting up the careless, heedless front while inwardly cringing.

"They want a lot of stuff," she told him cheerfully, "and they're interested in a special logo, something unique to the fund-raiser. I'll just draw up some designs and get together some estimates."

"They better be good," Dennis warned.

"Of course," she quipped. "Good is my middle name. Isn't that why you keep me around?"

"Miranda is your middle name," he pointed out, shaking his head in confusion.

Howard sent her a chiding look. He was right. Dennis was the most sadly humorless man she'd ever known. All attempts at levity were lost on him.

The chime that signaled the opening of the front door sounded. Smile in place, Anna turned to greet a potential customer, only to freeze. Correction. Dennis was the second most humorless man she'd ever known.

"Well, if it isn't Reeves Leland." Twice in an hour's time. Some day this was turning out to be. She bucked up her smile and tossed off a flippant line. "Playing errand boy for your aunties?"

"Something like that." Reeves opened the front of his tan wool overcoat, revealing the expensive suit that clearly marked him as executive material.

Howard shook his head and turned away, as if to say she'd blundered again. Anna admired Howard. Despite his thickset build, he appeared fit for a man nearing sixty. He and his wife were devoted to one another and led quiet, settled lives, the sort that Anna could never seem to manage. Her parents had died just months after her birth in a drug-fueled automobile accident, leaving her to the oppressive care of her grandmother. Anna had rebelled early against Tansy's overbearing control, and at twenty-six, she continued to do so.

"Can I help you?" Dennis asked Reeves, elbowing Anna out of the way as he bellied up to the counter.

Reeves barely glanced at the big, blustery man.

"Thank you, no. I need to speak to Anna Miranda. About my aunts and the BCBC fund-raiser."

Trembling inwardly, Anna pulled out her most professional demeanor. Reeves Leland had come to speak with her, and she couldn't imagine that was good. *Please, God,* she prayed silently, *don't let him be here to cancel the order.* Dennis would blame her for certain. She waved toward her desk around the corner. Whatever Reeves wanted, it was best dealt with in private.

"Take a seat."

She tucked her notepad under one arm and followed. Reeves glanced around at the illustrations pinned to the walls, his expression just shy of forbidding. *Be still my foolish heart,* she thought. But it was no joke. To her disgust, Reeves Leland, with his sinewy strength, cleft chin and dark hair, still had the power to send her pulse racing.

Dropping her notebook on the desk, Anna parked her hands at her waist and cut to the chase. "What's up?"

Reeves just looked at her before folding himself down onto the thinly padded steel-framed chair beside her utilitarian desk. He made himself comfortable, stretching out his long legs and crossing his ankles. All righty then. She'd play. Pulling out her armless chair, she turned it sideways and sat down, facing him.

"Okay. First guess. You're going to pay the print costs for the fund-raiser. Sky's the limit, right? Oh, joy," she deadpanned, waving her hands. "My job's secure."

"Is that what you're trying to do," he asked, "secure your job at my aunts' expense?"

She blinked at that. "Hey. They called us. I didn't call them."

Reeves folded his hands over his belt buckle, appearing to relax. "Okay, so maybe you didn't solicit their business, but that doesn't mean you don't have a secret agenda."

"Like what?"

"You tell me."

Suddenly angry, she snapped her fingers. "I never could pull anything over on you, could I, Stick? After all these years I've finally found a way to get you back for not asking me to the homecoming dance."

Ack! Had she said that out loud? It wasn't as if she'd ever actually expected him to ask her to the homecoming dance. But she'd hoped. Oh, how she'd hoped. Not that he'd believe it. He smiled thinly and sat forward, one forearm braced against the corner of her desk.

"I'm warning you, Anna Miranda," he rumbled in a low voice. "You better not make my aunts the object of one of your pranks."

Pranks? Anna goggled. She hadn't pulled a prank in years, since high school, at least. She'd been much too busy trying to feed and house herself.

"And to think," she hissed, "that I was feeling sorry for that crack I made. I heard about your wife, how she took off, and I felt bad about saying women made a habit of leaving you. Now I'm thinking maybe they got it right."

The color drained from his face. For an instant, raw pain dulled his copper-brown gaze, and once more regret slammed her. "Reeves, I'm sorry. I didn't mean that."

"My aunts," he said in a strangled voice, climbing to his feet. "I'm watching you, Anna Miranda Burdett. If you hurt or disappoint them..." Shaking his head, he started to turn away.

Desperate to convince him of her sincere regret, she

reached for his arm. They jerked apart as if zapped by electricity.

"Never," she vowed, gazing up at him repentantly, her tingling hand clenched at her side. "I would never hurt your aunts. They've always been kind to me. I have the greatest respect for them, and I'll give them my very best work. You have my word."

"I haven't always found your word trustworthy," he reminded her quietly, "like the day you swore you hadn't seen my keys."

Anna flushed. "Oh, that."

What was it with men and their precious cars? She'd been fourteen, for pity's sake, just a kid caught in the throes of an unrequited crush. She wasn't about to apologize for something that had happened twelve years ago.

Reeves nodded sharply. "Yeah, that." After staring at her for several seconds, he whirled and strode away.

Anna slumped against her chair, feeling more alone than usual, though why that should be the case, she couldn't say. She'd always been alone, after all. Obviously, that was how God intended her to be. But at least she could show Reeves Leland that he was wrong about some things. She did have talent, and she wasn't afraid to use it.

As she'd promised Reeves, she would give the Chatams her very best effort, if for no other reason than to secure her job. She'd only been here a few months. After a long string of pointless, temporary positions, she'd finally found work that she enjoyed, even if the boss was difficult. She would hate to lose that, especially since her grandmother expected her to. Also because she had to pay the rent.

The tiny one-bedroom apartment where she had lived

since the age of eighteen in no way compared to the two-story, gingerbread-Victorian house where she had grown up, but Anna would crawl across glass on a daily basis to keep from moving back in with Tansy. She would do worse, she realized suddenly, to raise Reeves Leland's poor opinion of her, and that's exactly what she feared she would do. Worse.

Nevertheless, for the remainder of the week, she concentrated on showing up for work early and giving the BCBC job her best. She contacted the university and got permission to incorporate their insignia into her designs, then she experimented with fonts, illustrations and document styles until she had a handful of satisfactory possibilities to offer for consideration, along with detailed estimates for those items already discussed. She was ready by midmorning on the following Monday to meet with Reeves's aunts once again. Dennis elected to make the call informing them of that. Afterward, he told her that she had a four o'clock appointment at Chatam House. She blinked as Dennis shook a finger in her face.

"And don't think you're going to cut out at five o'clock, either. You stay until those old ladies are satisfied, or I'll wash my hands of you!"

"Be easier to wash me out of your hair," Anna quipped, eyeing the thin strands covering his poor crown. The instant the words were out, she wished them back. Dennis literally snarled at her until she muttered, "Sorry. Won't let you down. Promise."

Dennis turned away, leaving Anna to ponder whether Reeves would be there or if he would, as in years past, go out of his way to avoid her. He'd said he would be watching, but she didn't take that literally, especially as he'd shown such a marked disdain for her company. It shouldn't have bothered her so much—she had made a career, after all, of earning disapproval, especially that of her grandmother—but Reeves Leland's attitude had always wounded her. Only when she was tweaking that handsome, aristocratic nose of his had he deigned to look her way. Even then, he had only seen "the brat." Apparently that was all he saw now, too.

What hurt most was that he had always seemed unfailingly polite and kind to everyone else. Indeed, Reeves Leland had a reputation for being a fine Christian man, which was why the town had been so shocked when his wife had left him.

Pushing him out of mind, she concentrated instead on getting through the day. Howard, the dear, made sure that she got away from the office in plenty of time for her appointment. In fact, when she pulled up in front of Chatam House the dashboard clock of her old car told her that she had nearly ten minutes to spare.

Gathering her materials, she stepped out into the cold February air, tucking her chin into the rainbow-striped muffler wound about her throat inside the collar of her bright orange corduroy coat. The instant she straightened a whirling dervish came out of nowhere and knocked her on her behind. Anna instinctively put out a hand and grabbed hold. Simultaneously Carol Petty, one of the Chatams' household staff, huffed into view, her dark slacks and bulky sweater dusted with white powder, her light brown hair slipping free of the clasp at her nape. While Carol gasped for breath, the little tornado who had knocked Anna down screeched.

"Gilli Leland, stop it!" Carol scolded, stomping forward across the deep gravel to take hold of the girl. "You are going to have a bath, and that's that."

Anna hauled herself to her feet and picked up her portfolio, thankful she'd had the foresight to zip it closed as that was not always the case. Dusting off her jeans, she turned to take in the girl who had flattened her.

So this was Reeves Leland's daughter. Pretty little thing, with all that curly hair, provided one disregarded the wailing and white powder. What was that stuff covering her anyway? Talcum? Chancing a sniff, Anna leaned forward, only to draw back in surprise. The kid had coated herself in flour. Hopefully, no one planned to pan fry her, though given Carol's exasperation, Anna wouldn't have been surprised.

"I wanna make cookies!" the girl sobbed.

"Hilda is saving the cookies until you get cleaned up," Carol told the distraught child. She cast an apologetic look at Anna. "I'm sorry, Miss Burdett. A mishap in the kitchen. The misses are expecting you."

"Uh-huh, and Mr. Leland?" Anna glanced around, expecting Reeves to arrive at any moment to take his wayward offspring in hand.

Carol shook her head. "He's not in from work yet." Glancing at Gilli, she muttered, "Works too much, if you ask me."

"Hmm. Well. I'll, uh, just ring the bell, I guess."

"If you don't mind," Carol said, dragging Gilli back the way they had come.

Gilli stopped howling long enough to glance back at Anna, who impulsively stuck out her tongue and crossed her eyes. Gilli first looked surprised, but then she giggled, causing Carol to pause and look down at her. Grinning, Anna climbed the shallow brick steps and rang the bell. Odelia let her in, swinging black onyx chandeliers from her earlobes and chattering gaily about how excited they all were to see her designs.

Excited they might have been, but see her designs they did not. Neither were they interested in her estimates. Instead, Hypatia presented her with a "more complete list," of the items they would be needing: place cards, menu cards, table assignment cards, letterheads, donation forms, receipts, a spiral-bound auction catalog, name tags, item tags, signs… The list seemed endless.

While Anna tried to take in the expanding size of the order, the sisters chatted about their various ideas for the final logo design, all three at the same time. Anna mentally tossed everything she'd done to this point and quickly jotted down ideas as the sisters shot them to her. At one point she put her hand to her hair, just trying to take it all in. Hypatia reached over then to lay her manicured hand on Anna's shoulder.

"How would it be," Hypatia asked, "if you worked up designs for each of us?"

"Using your individual ideas, you mean?" Anna raised a mental eyebrow at Miss Magnolia's "nature" theme, Miss Odelia's "lace and satin" and Miss Hypatia's "biblical" motif. "I can do that." Along with a new idea of her own, she decided, suddenly picturing the fluted, Roman Doric columns of Chatam House topped with an elegant swag of flowers intertwined with the BCBC emblem, which itself contained a Bible.

"You just let us know when you're ready to meet again," Mags said. "We'll have the teapot simmering."

"That's very nice of you," Anna returned, a thought occurring. "So you'll be wanting me to continue coming *here?*"

"Is there a problem with that?" Hypatia asked.

"No, no. Not so far as I'm concerned. Dennis may not always go for it, though."

Hypatia just smiled. "Oh, he seems perfectly willing to indulge three old ladies who like their creature comforts too well."

Anna laughed. "Well, I certainly can't argue that the print shop compares in any way to Chatam House."

"What does?" a smooth male voiced asked.

Anna looked up as Reeves strolled into the room, dispensing kisses and smiles on everyone but her. At last, he turned a cool nod in her direction. "Anna Miranda."

Anna grit her teeth. She hated her full name. Hated it. Sometimes the chants of children's voices rang in her dreams. *Anna Miranda the brat. Anna Miranda the brat...*

She couldn't blame them really. They'd had parents and siblings, and she had resented that fact greatly. Of course, as children do, they had picked up on her envy. Accordingly, they had sneered, and she had made their lives miserable in every way she could imagine. Eventually she'd learned to channel her animosity into jokes, earning herself a few friends and the designation of class clown. Reeves had never thought her the least bit funny, though. She faced him and returned his greeting in kind.

"Reeves Kyle."

He lifted an eyebrow before turning his back on her. "More printing?" he asked his aunts.

Anna bit her tongue, literally.

While the aunts gushed about everything they had discussed, Anna secured her notes, reminding herself that this was business between her and the Chatam sisters. Reeves's opinion did not matter, and she had been foolish to think for a moment that it did. Or that it might ever change.

"Aunt Hypatia," Reeves asked, having listened carefully for some minutes, "are you certain that this printer is the right one for the job?"

He'd thought about it a lot. Actually, to be completely honest with himself, he'd thought about Anna Miranda, almost constantly. For some reason, he couldn't seem to get her off his mind. He kept picturing her contrite face as she'd made her apology last week, and somehow he now felt in the wrong.

She'd always done that to him. She made his life miserable and one way or another he always felt to blame. How did she do that, and why did she have to turn up again after all these years? What was God trying to tell him? That his life could be worse? That was exactly what he was trying to avoid and not just for himself. Having seen the print shop and knowing his aunts' expansive plans, Reeves truly felt that they would be better off taking their business elsewhere. Yet, because of one thing or another—primarily the complaining emails he'd been receiving daily from Marissa—he'd put off making the argument until now.

Hypatia smiled her serene smile, the one that could make a troubled ten-year-old feel that all might actually one day be right with his world, and answered him. "Absolutely certain. Why do you ask, dear?"

Why? Because he didn't trust Anna Miranda. No matter what she said, there would surely be a shocking message buried in a letterhead or something else inappropriate. His aunts had always defended her, however, telling him that he didn't understand her situation. The opposite seemed true to him. At least she hadn't shuttled back and forth between her warring parents throughout her childhood as he had, never quite belonging either place. Maybe her grandmother, Tansy, was a bit difficult and not the warmest person, but at least she'd provided Anna Miranda with a stable home.

"A larger shop would be better able to handle a job this size," he argued, "and with Dallas just up the road—"

"In other words, you think our shop will do shoddy work," Anna interrupted hotly. "Or is it just *my* abilities that you doubt?"

Reeves clenched his jaw. He had studiously avoided making eye contact with her, but now he leveled a stare at her face. "I didn't say that. I just don't want my aunts to be embarrassed. This scholarship fund is important to them."

Odelia laughed, her pendulous earrings wriggling. "Oh, sweetie," she chuckled. "We're embarrassed all the time."

"Not that Anna Miranda has or would embarrass us," Mags put in quickly.

"Anna Miranda is a very gifted artist, Reeves," Hypatia told him, "and she's a very dear girl."

Very dear? Not the Anna Miranda he remembered. And no girl, either, he thought, not anymore. How, he wondered, did she manage to appear so casually polished and smirk at the same time? She looked...womanly, innately female, right down to that twisted little smile.

"Besides," Anna Miranda said, "there are a surprising number of items needed, but not so many copies of each that a larger printer would find it worthwhile."

Reeves opened his mouth to argue with that, but just then Gilli came sliding into the room in her stocking feet, her hair wet, her T-shirt and pants twisted.

"Daddy, I had a aksident and Carol made me take a bath!" she complained.

Automatically, he demanded, "What did you do?"

Mags and Auntie Od reached out to Gilli, clucking and quickly righting her clothes, while Hypatia explained that they'd had a little incident involving homemade cookies and an open bag of flour. Groaning inwardly, Reeves folded his arms.

"And just how did that bag of flour tip over, Gilli?"

Poking out her bottom lip, Gilli shrugged. "I don't know."

He doubted that, but she just stood there staring up at him with those wide eyes. Anna cleared her throat. Suddenly mortified that she, of all people, should witness this, Reeves made a snap decision. His daughter would not lack discipline as Anna Miranda evidently had. He would not have a brat of his own.

"Go to your room, Gilli," he ordered, "and do not come out again until you're called down for dinner." Wailing, Gilli tore out of the parlor. Avoiding all gazes, especially Anna's, Reeves said, "I apologize. I'll make sure she's in her room, then I think I'll go out for a run."

"We'll keep an eye on her," Magnolia offered gently.

"Try to enjoy your run, dear," Ophelia told him, pity in her voice.

Some days his runs were all he did enjoy. Casting around a wan smile, Reeves strode out after his daughter. Tonight, he desperately wanted to run away from his troubles. Of late, those troubles all seemed female in nature. First Marissa had reminded him that she held joint custody of their daughter in a veiled attempted to make him renegotiate their divorce settlement. Then he returned to his one sanctuary to find Anna Miranda there and Gilli upsetting the household. All together, it was enough to add miles to his regular routine.

Of all his problems, however, Anna Miranda was the one he couldn't get off his mind. She had once seemed intent on making his life miserable, and now she was at it again. He knew, as he had known even way back in school, that the best way to deal with her was to ignore her. Unfortunately, he didn't seem able to do it now, which made no sense at all.

Then again, what in his life did?

The aunts exchanged worried glances as they settled for evening prayers.

Odelia pulled her hot pink robe tighter as she snuggled into the corner of the well-used sofa. Several dozen pink foam curlers covered her head. "It's too bad Reeves had to work this evening," she commented sadly. "Gilli missed him."

Reeves had returned from his run with only enough time to hurriedly shower before sliding into his seat at the dinner table. After the meal, he'd spent the evening in his room on his laptop, while Gilli played glumly in the shared private sitting room of the aunties' suite. Grumpy and sullen, the child had whined and fussed until Reeves had come and taken her off to bed. It had become painfully obvious that Reeves avoided the child, which was why she acted out.

"Remind you of anyone?" Hypatia asked from her chair beside the fireplace.

"Just Anna Miranda," Mags said, dropping down beside Odelia.

"Oh, but Tansy didn't ignore Anna Miranda," Odelia protested.

Mags snorted. "She criticized her daylight to dark, you mean."

"Do you remember that time Tansy scolded little Anna Miranda for plucking roses off her front bushes?" Odelia asked with a giggle.

Hypatia nodded, a smile tugging at her lips. "As I recall, Anna Miranda used a pair of sewing scissors to snip off every one of Tansy's prized blossoms. The result was a bumper crop the next year."

All three chuckled, but then Mags sobered. "If anyone can understand Gilli, it is Anna Miranda," she insisted.

"Well, it's certainly not Reeves," Hypatia said with a sigh. "I've tried speaking to him about it myself a time or two, but he always seems so hurt by the slightest criticism." They all knew who was responsible for that. Marissa had destroyed Reeves's hard-won self-esteem. "I suppose we must simply pray that God will somehow reach him."

Was it possible, she wondered silently, that Anna Miranda might be God's tool in this? Might she be the one to help Reeves stop hiding his heart and learn how to deal with his little girl? It occurred to her suddenly that their Heavenly Father might have something more in mind than they had yet considered.

"Oh, sisters," she said, her eyes wide, "I fear we've been going about this all wrong. Think about it. What Reeves and Gilli really need is a wife and mother."

"Someone to understand Gilli," Magnolia murmured,

comprehension beginning to glow in her eyes, "and someone to lighten Reeves's heavy spirit."

"Someone like Anna Miranda!" Odelia chirped.

Hypatia smiled, praising God in her heart, for He always had more in mind for His children than they themselves sometimes dared to dream. And if in this case He didn't, well, it wouldn't hurt to pray about the matter, would it?

Chapter Three

Sitting at her usual table in the little coffee shop across from the BCBC campus, Anna huddled over her steaming mug and yawned, trying to shake the cobwebs from her mind. She'd worked late into the night, prompted by a phone call from her grandmother, who had only just learned from some committee member that Anna was handling the BCBC fund-raiser account. As usual, Tansy had displayed no faith whatsoever in Anna's abilities, lecturing her on the importance of the assignment and her responsibilities to her employer and the cause. Anna had hung up on her, not an uncommon occurrence, and set to work. Now she had two good reasons for wanting to do her best. To her surprise, the first appeared at her elbow.

"Hard night?"

She looked up at the handsome face of Reeves Leland, handsome but somewhat haggard despite being cleanly shaved. "I could ask the same of you."

"Or you could just ask me to sit down."

She looked around, saw that the other tables were full

and nodded. He sprawled across the chair with a sigh, hanging an elbow on the edge of the tabletop.

"I haven't seen you in here before."

He slugged back coffee from the disposable cup in his hand, wincing at the heat. "I usually wait and get my caffeine at the office, but this morning I need a little extra fortification just to get there. Figured I might as well order a hot roll while I was at it." He glanced at the counter. "Does it usually take this long?"

"Mornings are busy," she said. "So why the extra fortification?"

He grimaced. "I worked all night, and Gilli was on a tear this morning." He shook his head and sucked up more brew.

"Well, that makes two of us," she said, "working late, that is." He lifted an eyebrow. "What? You don't think I ever put in long hours?"

"Did I say that?"

"You didn't have to." She cut her gaze away, muttering, "And here I thought you'd come to cry peace."

He straightened in his chair and set his cup on the table, folding his arms behind it. "I think that's a very good idea, actually." She shot him a startled, wary glance, and he lifted a hand in a gesture of openness. "It wasn't what I had in mind when I was looking around for an empty seat, but now that you mention it…" He rolled his shoulders beneath his overcoat. "I don't see why we should be enemies over stuff that happened ages ago."

Recalling some of that "stuff," Anna grinned. "That's very generous of you, Stick. You mean you forgive me for busting up your baseball bat?"

His forehead furrowed. "How did you do that? I've always wondered."

"Nothing to it. I just carried it down to the tracks and waited for a train to come by, then tossed the pieces back in your yard."

He shook his head, one corner of his mouth curling up. "Guess we should've let you play, huh? I almost did, but the other guys never would've let me forget it."

"I didn't think about that."

"Why am I not surprised?"

She stuck her tongue out at him, and he laughed, his eyes crinkling up around the edges. "There's that brat again."

It was perhaps the first time he'd ever actually laughed at her. Picking at her napkin, she tried not to read too much into it, but she couldn't help asking, "So, you ever going to forgive me for gluing your car keys to your locker door?"

"Not a chance." He wagged a finger at her. "Do you have any idea what that cost? I had to replace the ignition module to get a working key for the car, not to mention the locker door."

She jerked up onto the edge of her seat. "They made you replace the locker door?"

He suddenly seemed uncomfortable. "They didn't *make me* exactly."

"But you did it anyway," she surmised, shocked. "You must have because they didn't make me do it." She'd sat in two weeks of detention, but nothing had been said about financial reparation.

For several seconds Reeves sat very still. Then he tilted his head slightly and confessed, "It wouldn't have hurt me to give you a ride that day. I never figured you'd walk all the way to school in the rain. I just thought your grandmother would take you."

"She wasn't there that morning," Anna told him. "One of her committee meetings or something." He closed his eyes and shook his head. She instantly took pity on him, saying, "Look, it's not your fault. I could have called someone else, but after you said no, I was so mad I just struck out on foot. Later, when you dropped your keys, well, I couldn't resist."

He shook his head, saying softly, "Kids do stupid things."

"Yeah, well, I think I probably did more than my fair share."

He looked up from beneath the crag of his brow. "I think you probably did, too."

She tried for outrage but wound up spluttering laughter. He joined in, and it was perhaps the first moment of real camaraderie they'd ever shared.

"So," she asked, making small talk, "what were you up all night working on?"

"Aw, we've got this big negotiation with a new fuel provider. I was putting together the figures, trying to estimate their costs and our—" He broke off suddenly, his eyes going wide. "The figures!" He smacked himself in the forehead with the heel of his palm. "They're in my laptop, which I left at the house! Oh, man." On his feet before he'd finished speaking, he started for the door.

"What about your roll?"

"Uh, you eat it. I've gotta run. Sorry. I'll, uh, be seeing you."

"Right. Later. Maybe," she said, her voice waning as he rushed out the door.

After a moment she turned back to contemplate the coffee in her mug, wondering what had just happened. Had she and Reeves Leland actually taken a step toward putting the past behind them? If so, then what else might be possible?

She was afraid even to contemplate the answer to that question.

Irritated, Reeves quietly let himself into the house via the front entry hall. He never left his laptop behind, but he'd just been so frazzled this morning. If only Gilli hadn't awakened in the same petulant mood that she'd gone to sleep in, he might not have forgotten the thing. Sneaking about made him cringe, but he took care to walk softly just the same. The last thing he wanted was for Gilli to see him and pitch another fit for him to stay home—as if he could! He had almost passed by the open door of the front parlor when the sound of his own name brought him to an abrupt halt.

"Reeves is perfect!"

Well, that was nice to hear, but what followed knocked the breath out of him.

"He's perfect for Anna Miranda! I can't believe I didn't think of this earlier."

"Now, Tansy," Aunt Hypatia said, an edge to her voice that none of her nephews or nieces would dare to ignore, "don't get carried away. It's just a thought, a matter for prayer. Odelia was simply mentioning a possibility in passing, one she would have done better to keep to herself, obviously."

"There must be something I can do," Tansy went on, ignoring Hypatia. "Anna never has more than a few dates with a fellow. If I leave it to her, she'll never marry."

Reeves had his doubts about that. Plenty of men were bound to be interested in a woman as attractive and clever as Anna Miranda. Just not him. True, he'd seen a different side of her this morning, a compelling side, but she had demonstrated that the brat was ready and willing to reemerge at a moment's notice, and he had no intention of dealing with that. Best to nip the idiotic notion in the bud right now. Sucking in a deep breath, he strode through the doorway.

Hypatia winced as Odelia exclaimed with innocent delight. "Reeves! We were just talking about you." Red enamel hoops a good two inches wide dangled from her earlobes.

"So I heard."

Mags asked warily, "Shouldn't you be at work?"

Reeves gave her a frown. "Yes, and I would be if I hadn't left my laptop in my room." He settled a narrow look on Tansy Burdett, adding, "Fortunately."

"Reeves, dear," Hypatia began apologetically, "please don't think—"

"No, no," Tansy interrupted, getting to her feet. "*Do* think about it. You need a wife. My granddaughter needs a husband."

Reeling from that pronouncement, Reeves watched as she drew herself up to her full height, which must have been all of five feet, including the tall thick heels of her brown pumps and the helmet-like perfection of her chin-length, pale yellow hair. Slight and angular, with sharp features and faded blue eyes, she wore a white cotton blouse and a straight skirt beneath a boxy jacket.

"And that's all there is to it?" he scoffed, incredulous.

Lifting her chin, Tansy met him eye to eye and proclaimed, "You're a good Christian man with a sound head on your shoulders, despite the mistake you made the first time around. Besides, Anna Miranda's always had a thing for you."

Now *that* was absurd. Anna Miranda had a thing for him, all right. He'd always been her favorite target, a butt for jokes, a subject for pranks, an object of ridicule.

"I have no intention of marrying again," Reeves said to Tansy, exasperated, "and certainly not to—" He couldn't even say it. Anna Miranda Burdett and *him?* Instead, he turned on his aunties, focusing on Hypatia. "Surely you do not believe that she…we…. Tell me you haven't been matchmaking."

"Now, Reeves," Hypatia said calmly, "it was nothing more than idle chatter. We merely agreed to pray about it, that's all."

"Pray as you like, Aunt Hypatia," he grit out, "but leave my private life to me!" He hadn't meant to raise his voice, but he had done just that, which was why he winced and said, "Sorry."

"No offense taken, dear," Hypatia remarked meekly. "It's just that we're so concerned for you and Gilli."

"She needs a mother, dear," Odelia put in.

"She *has* a mother," he snapped, knowing that in Marissa's case it was little more than a title, despite the allusions and veiled threats of late.

Marissa continued to complain of financial difficulty, and lately she'd started mentioning that she missed Gilli. For their daughter's sake, he wished that were so, but he knew better. Marissa had no more desire to see Gilli than she'd had to give birth to her. He regretted offering her joint custody now, but at the time he'd hoped she would actually use it to be part of their daughter's life, not browbeat him for money.

And they thought they could convince him to marry again!

All three of the aunties bowed their heads in contrition. Tansy merely flattened her mouth and tugged at the hem of her jacket, sharp chin aloft, before dropping back down into her chair with a huff.

Reeves pinched the bridge of his nose, eyes closed, and counted to ten before carefully saying, "Look, I appreciate your concern, but I don't want any more talk about matchmaking, not with Anna Miranda, not with anyone. Is that clear?" The aunts gave him nods and wan smiles. "Now, if you'll excuse me," he managed, "I have to get to the office." Turning on his heel, he swiftly left the room and headed for the stairs.

Behind him, he heard Odelia say, "Poor Reeves."

"No more matchmaking talk," Hypatia instructed quickly.

Poor Reeves. How pathetic. The thought of the aunties meddling in his life both shocked and hurt, but he knew that he really had no one to blame except himself. He had mucked it all up. Sighing, he hurried up the stairs, intent on getting that laptop and out of the house before anything else could happen to delay him.

But he could not get over the thought of Anna Miranda and him as a couple.

Wherever would the aunts get such a preposterous idea? Anna Miranda Burdett and him! He wondered how long it would be before he could get that ridiculous notion out of his head.

Anna's determination to show Reeves that his aunts were right to trust her with this project only grew after their meeting in the coffee shop. That resolve turned a couple days of work into four, but excitement gripped her as she waited at the sunny yellow, black-framed door at the front of the enormous house late that next Friday afternoon. Chester Worth, the Chatam's long-time driver and houseman, opened it for her.

"Miss Anna, come on in here out of the cold."

"Thank you, Chester." She held a soft spot for Chester, who had never in her memory referred to her as anything but Miss Anna. "I called ahead. The Chatams should be expecting me."

"They surely are. Miss Hypatia and Miss Odelia are in the parlor, and Miss Magnolia will join y'all shortly. I'll bring in the tea soon as she shows up."

Anna smiled. "I'll let the others know."

Chester went on his way, and Anna walked into the spacious, elegant front parlor. Odelia hopped up and hurried forward to hug her, chains of orange crystals hanging from her earlobes. She wore a long, multi-colored, gathered skirt with a melon pink blouse, wide black belt and purple vest. Hypatia, in contrast, looked the picture of prim wealth in a tailored, moss-green pantsuit and pearls. She, too, rose and came to meet Anna with a smile and handclasp.

They were still exchanging greetings when Mags trundled into the room, smelling of loam and flowers. She seemed to own only one dress, or else they all looked alike. This one she wore with a pair of brown slacks, a moth-eaten gray cardigan and red-rimmed black galoshes. Anna managed not to laugh. Mags beamed back at her and plopped down on the settee.

Anna quickly extracted three copies of four designs from her portfolio, passing them to the sisters. They were still exclaiming over her nature design when Chester arrived with the tea tray. A quarter-hour later, they sat balancing delicate, steaming Limoges teacups on matching saucers while Anna explained the second design to them. Odelia, predictably, gushed, but Mags screwed up her face at the ribbons and lace, while Hypatia made the sort of nice comments that one made when complimenting a beaming bride in a particularly heinous gown. She was obviously better pleased with the "biblical" design that followed.

Finally, Anna introduced the fourth rendering. "This," she said neutrally, "is something of a combination of the other three in what I like to think of as the definitive Chatam House spirit."

The effect was immediate, gasps, clattering of cups and saucers, oohs of pleasure.

"Anna Miranda," Hypatia exclaimed, holding out the sheet to gaze at it, "this is..."

"Gorgeous!" Odelia finished for her.

Mags actually sniffed. "Those are magnolias in the swag, aren't they?"

"Seemed apt," Anna told her with a fond, pleased smile.

Hypatia placed the sheet of paper reverently atop the piecrust tea table and folded her hands. "Well, I think it's obvious—"

Suddenly Odelia interjected herself. "Oh, but the romantic one is so...romantic."

Mags sat up straight. "What are you talking about?"

"Now, I know you prefer the nature one," Odelia cut in, "but this is an important decision. It needs time." Ophelia tapped the little watch pendant pinned to her blouse and waved obliquely toward the door.

Mags stared at her for a moment then her eyebrows shot up. "But he said—"

"Talk," Odelia interrupted hurriedly. "No more *talk*. E-except about the design."

Mags blinked at that then she cleared her throat. "Ah. Well, it's just that m-my idea is the best. Uh, the way Anna Miranda has designed it, that is."

"Now, sisters," Hypatia began sternly, but once more Odelia charged in.

"You don't agree that we should *talk* about the designs a little more?"

Hypatia seemed uncomfortable. She actually fidgeted, shifting her trim weight side to side. Anna sat fascinated, not at all certain what was going on but entranced by the sisterly byplay. She said not a word as Odelia and Magnolia entered into a spirited debate of their individual preferences.

Some minutes later, Chester entered to remove the tea tray. Bending over it, he looked straight at Odelia and announced, "Mr. Reeves is home."

With that, he straightened and exited the room. Odelia popped up and scuttled after him as far as the doorway. At the same time, footsteps could be heard in the back of the central hallway. Odelia produced a lace-edged hanky, which she began waving.

"Yoo-hoo! Reeves, dear! Can you help us please?"

Several heartbeats passed, during which the only sound was that of Hypatia softly moaning. Finally, Reeves said, "Of course."

Anna twisted in her chair and leaned over the arm to watch Odelia grasp his elbow and pull him bodily into the parlor.

"We just can't decide," she trilled, tugging him forward. "Anna Miranda's done such a marvelous job for us, but we just can't agree. Give us your opinion, won't you?"

She hauled him over to the table, where Magnolia

laid out the four options for him. Reeves slid a hooded glance at Anna before quickly bending over the table. Anna held her breath. After a moment, he turned a look in her direction, surprised appreciation in his copper-brown eyes.

"These are quite good."

She managed a blasé nod and a dry, "Thanks."

He went back to the designs, tapping the fourth with the tip of one forefinger. "This one's the best."

Anna stifled a crow of delight.

"Well," Hypatia said, sounding relieved, "that's that."

Odelia jerked, all but physically throwing herself back into the fray. "Oh, but…what about the staff?"

"The staff?" Mags echoed.

"They ought to have a say in this. We'll be depending on them, after all, to keep everything running smoothly the night of the auction."

"Odelia," Hypatia said wearily, pressing her fingertips to her temples.

Undetered, Odelia began gathering up the designs. "I know, we'll take these back to the kitchen." She nudged her sisters to their feet. "We'll each make our case, and see what Chester, Hilda and Carol have to say. That seems fair, doesn't it?"

Hypatia sighed and sent an apologetic look to Reeves, who lifted a hand to the back of his neck. Absolutely no one, including Anna, was surprised when Odelia turned to him and instructed, "Now, Reeves, dear, you'll entertain Anna Miranda for us for a few minutes, won't you?" She began pushing and shooing her sisters from the room. "So rude to leave her sitting here on her own, you know."

Anna watched the whole thing in bemused fascination, especially the part where Odelia winked at Reeves then pinched her thumb and forefinger together and drew them across her lips in a zipping motion.

"Yeah, thanks for that," he said wryly.

Anna waited until their footsteps receded before favoring him with a direct look, her elbows braced against the arms of the chair. "What on earth is that about?"

"Don't ask," he grumbled, sliding his hands into the pockets of his slacks. "Just let this be a lesson to you. Be very, very exact when dealing with my aunts."

"They can be a little…scattered."

He snorted. "That's one word for it."

"Actually, I think they're very sweet."

"Well, of course, they're sweet!" he exclaimed. "That's half the problem."

"What problem?" she shot back, stung. "I wasn't aware there was a problem, unless having to give your opinion has strained your brain."

"Ha-ha. Very funny. I hope you didn't pull a muscle coming up with that one."

"Oh, for pity's sake!" Anna shot to her feet and sidestepped the table. Why did he have to be so difficult, anyway? She thought they'd gotten past this.

Just then, Anna caught a muffled roaring sound, followed swiftly by a shrill, elongated scream. The next instant, Gilli burst into the room, wailing like a police siren, and shot across the floor on, of all things, roller skates, the cheap plastic sort that strapped over the soles of the shoes. She headed straight for the antique Empire breakfront in the corner. Reeves leapt forward to snatch up a priceless Tiffany lamp, while Anna lunged with outstretched arms for Gilli.

The pair of them went down in a tangle of limbs. Fortunately, they missed the tall Federal table in the center of the floor and the enormous flower arrangement atop it. A small elbow landed in Anna's midsection, knocking the air out of her in a painful rush. For one long moment, all was silent and still. Then a sigh gusted forth, and Reeves's handsome head, paired up nicely with a stained glass lampshade, appeared above her.

"And so," he muttered, "goes my life."

Anna laughed. The look on his face, the droll tone of his voice, the memory of Gilli's flailing arms as she flew across the floor, even the collision that had Anna on her back—again—gazing up at his resigned, hangdog expression, it all suddenly seemed like something out of an old slapstick comedy. Oh, how little he appreciated that, but his frowns merely made her laugh that much harder. It had been a long time since she'd had this much fun. Too long. She pushed up onto her elbows, Gilli sprawled all over her, and as was too often the case, said the first thing that came to mind.

"You know something, Stick? I've missed you."

He couldn't have looked more appalled if she'd decorated him with her lunch, but that didn't change a thing. She had missed him. She had missed him every single day since he'd graduated from high school, and some part of her always would.

She had missed him.

The idea warmed, shocked and alarmed Reeves all at the same time. He recognized the glow in the corner of his heart with disgust. Was he so desperate to be loved that even an offhanded quip from a girl who had all but tortured him could produce such a reaction? Or was it Tansy and the aunties who had put that into his mind?

Groaning, he decided that God must be punishing him. That had to be the case. Yet, had Solomon not written that the Lord disciplines those He loves?

But does it have to be her, Lord? he asked in silent prayer. *Isn't Gilli enough?*

Horrified that he'd thought of his own child as punishment, Reeves reached down a hand to help as Gilli began struggling up onto her knees. It was Anna Miranda's hand that found his, however, and with his other still clutching the Tiffany lamp, he had little choice but to haul her up. She came to her feet with a little hop and a cheeky smile. Gilli collapsed upon the hardwood floor and began to wail as if she'd broken all four limbs.

Tamping down his impatience with such melodrama, Reeves turned to set aside the lamp so he could help his daughter up, but when he turned back, she was already on her feet, thanks to Anna Miranda. Gilli abruptly yanked away from her, and threw herself at Reeves with a cry of outrage, her skates slipping and sliding as she clamped her arms around his thighs. Reeves sent an embarrassed look at Anna Miranda before grasping Gilli by the shoulders and holding her far enough away that he could look down into her face. He saw more petulance there than pain or fear.

"Cut it out," he ordered over the din of phony sobs.

"I fell down!" she defended hotly.

The last tenuous thread of Reeves's patience snapped. "I said to cut it out!" he roared. As he rarely raised his voice to her, Gilli was shocked into frozen silence.

Not so Anna Miranda, who brought her hands to her slender hips and snapped, "*You* cut it out. It's all your own fault, you know."

Exasperated, Reeves glared at her. "*My* fault? I didn't come flying in here on skates."

"No, but you might have taught her to skate properly before this," Anna reasoned.

Gilli immediately seized on that notion. "Yes, Daddy! Teach me! Please, please!"

He ignored her, focusing on the one who'd opened this can of worms. "And how am I supposed to do that?" he demanded. "Look at her. She's not old enough for that."

"I am!" Gilli insisted, her tears suddenly dried.

"Of course she is," Anna Miranda agreed, folding her arms.

"I think I know my daughter better than you do, thank you very much. Besides, I don't even own a pair of skates myself, let alone all the necessary safety equipment for the two of us."

"So get some," Anna Miranda retorted.

"I got skates!" Gilli interjected desperately. "Real skates. My mama brought them at Christmas."

"Sent them," Reeves corrected distractedly. "She *sent* you a pair of roller skates, but they're too big for you." Gilli had waited with breathless anticipation for her mother to arrive for Christmas as Marissa had promised during her one visit some six months ago, but all that had arrived was a crumpled card and a pair of roller skates with hard pink-and-purple plastic boots two sizes too large.

"They're not too big!" Gilli insisted. "And I'm old. I am!"

Reeves pinched the bridge of his nose. "Gilli, I'm not going to argue about this. All I need is you flailing around here on skates. You'll break a leg. Or worse."

"All the more reason to teach her," Anna Miranda insisted.

It was the last straw for Reeves. Lifting Gilli by her upper arms, he sat her in a nearby Victorian lyre-back chair and began stripping off the cheap demi-skates, which consisted of nothing more than rollers attached to a platform that belted to shoes with fasteners. He'd thought to placate her with them when she'd discovered that she couldn't wear the "real" skates that her mother had sent, but he hadn't realized she could get the demi ones on by herself, which was why he hadn't refused when she'd insisted on bringing both pairs with her to Chatam House.

"When you become a parent," he told Anna Miranda coldly, "maybe your opinion will matter."

"You know what your problem is, Stick?" she shot back. "Your problem is that you were never a child."

Straightening, he whirled. "That's rich coming from someone who has obviously never grown up!"

"And who never wants to, if growing up means achieving pure stupidity."

"Stupid would be teaching my daughter to do something so dangerous as skating!"

"As opposed to letting her teach herself, I suppose."

"As opposed to dropping these in the nearest trash can!" he yelled, holding up the skates by their plastic straps.

Gilli threw herself off the chair and pelted from the room, yowling her outrage at the top of her lungs. Reeves sighed, slumping dejectedly. Wow, he'd handled that well. Once more, he'd let the brat get to him, and he didn't mean his daughter. What was it about Anna Miranda Burdett that turned him into a crude adolescent? And why could he never hit the right note with his daughter?

Father, forgive me, he prayed, squeezing his eyes shut. *I fail at every turn, and I'm as tired of me as You must be. In the name of Christ Jesus, please help me do better!*

He sucked in a deep breath and grated out an apology. "I didn't mean to shout."

"Well, you sure do plenty of it" was Anna Miranda's droll reply. She glared at him from behind folded arms.

Suddenly, Reeves craved a run with every fiber of his being. Maybe some exercise and a long, private talk with God would give him the serenity and clarity to deal with this latest insanity. Loosening his tie, he said to Anna Miranda in what he felt was a very reasonable tone, "Please tell my aunts that I've gone for a run before dinner."

Some seconds ticked by before she reluctantly nodded. Reeves headed for his room and the numb exhaustion of a hard run in the February cold, more heartsick than angry now and helpless to do a thing about any of it.

Intellectually, he knew that Gilli's behavior had to do with her mother's abandonment. Marissa hadn't even said goodbye to Gilli before she'd slammed out of the house and run down the drive to jump onto the back of her boyfriend's motorcycle, which made her recent communication all the more absurd. Marissa had been a pitiful mother, but Gilli couldn't know that. All she knew was that her mother had walked out, and she seemed to blame him. It hurt far more than he would ever let on. In fact, nothing in his life had ever made Reeves feel like such a failure as Gilli's resentment of him, which was undoubtedly why he had been so rude to Anna Miranda just now. For some reason, it embarrassed him to have her know in how little regard his own daughter held him.

That, of course, was no excuse. As he changed into his jogging outfit, he apologized to God once again for his behavior and attitude. He would do better, he vowed. He would do better with Gilli and, God help him, with Anna Miranda, too. Somehow.

Chapter Four

It seemed to Anna that Reeves needed to be taught a lesson. He needed to learn that his daughter could, indeed, learn to skate—and behave—given enough time, attention, patience and praise. Surely, once she showed up with all the requisite gear, he'd have to let her try; otherwise, Gilli would never forgive him. Maybe he wouldn't be happy about it, but, oh, well. Anna would not even consider that he might be right about Gilli being too young. She'd get Gilli rolling if it killed her. Then let the big goof tell her what an immature idiot she was.

Reeves wasn't the only reason Anna wanted to do this, though. She felt for Gilli, recognized the yawning, unknowing need in her. What that poor kid really wanted was attention and reassurance, not constant criticism and impatient, domineering control.

The Chatam triplets returned to declare the "classic Chatam House" motif their choice. They seemed deflated at finding her alone in the parlor, but Anna merely smiled, delivered Reeves's message and promised to return tomorrow with samples of the motif printed on various papers.

The next day was Saturday and Valentine's Day, to boot, but Anna saw no reason to delay, especially considering what she had in mind for Gilli. She swung by the shop to pick up sample papers, then as soon as she got home pulled down her old in-line skates from the top shelf of her bedroom closet. Next, she went to work on the mock-ups. Once her personal printer had spit out those, Anna set about designing a pair of hand-drawn Valentines, one for the triplets, using the Chatam House theme, to thank them for their business and unfailing kindness, and a glittery one for Gilli, featuring a curly-haired little girl pirouetting on roller skates while wearing a pink tutu, muffler and mittens.

After a quick dinner, Anna made a run to the local discount store and bought protective gear for Gilli, stuffing it into a big, pink paper bag with red tissue paper, confident that she would have put Reeves Leland firmly in his place by noon the next day. As she slipped into bed that night, she told herself that, for once, Valentine's Day promised to be sweet, indeed.

Hypatia answered the front door at Chatam House the next morning. Dressed in a lovely soldier blue, cowl-neck knit sheath and buckled pumps dyed to match, with pearls at her throat and her silver hair twisted into its usual smooth chignon at her nape, she looked fit to meet the Queen of England over tea; her smile could not have been more gracious if she had been.

"Good morning, dear," she all but sang. The gray morning seemed to brighten.

"Good morning!"

"Come in, please." Anna stepped into the spacious entry hall and set aside her portfolio and the gift bag to shrug out of her coat while Hypatia continued to speak. "What is that you have there, dear?"

Anna turned to smile over one shoulder. "Just a little something for a little someone. And the paper samples, of course."

"Of course. How very prompt you are, and how kind of you to think of Gilli. It's very timely. She's in a bit of a snit because her father had to go in to work this morning."

Anna's spirits dimmed. She had been strangely looking forward to butting heads with Reeves again. This way was probably better, though.

"Maybe I can brighten Gilli's mood a bit," Anna said. "We had a little, er, skating altercation yesterday, and I thought I might give her a lesson. My gear's in the car."

"I'm sure she'll be delighted. We're still nursing our morning tea out in the sunroom. Won't you join us?"

"Yes, thank you."

Anna took up her leather portfolio and the gift bag to follow along behind Hypatia. Reeves would undoubtedly disapprove of her plans for Gilli. They might even argue about it after the fact. The possibility made Anna smile. She had forgotten what fun it was to argue with Reeves. His quick wit easily matched hers, and she found his innate sense of outrage deliciously ridiculous. She couldn't help feeling disappointed that she wouldn't see him this morning. The sunroom lifted her spirits significantly, however.

Two glass walls, numerous plants and groupings of comfortable bamboo furnishings upholstered in colorful fabric printed with oversized flowers gave the space an airy, tropical feel that bravely defied the gray Texas winter. Anna found the other two sisters lounging on matched chaises. A small table between them held teacups and saucers. Magnolia, she noted, wore her usual garb, while Odelia's red plaid jumper and yellow silk blouse warred violently with the upholstery upon which she reclined. The red enamel hearts clipped to her earlobes were the size of drink coasters. It was Gilli, however, who drew Anna's interest. Wearing jeans and a purple turtleneck, she sprawled half on, half off a deeply padded chair, her bottom lip sticking out in a pout.

"Looks like someone woke up on the wrong side of the bed this morning," Anna remarked lightly, sinking down onto the plush chair that Hypatia indicated with a wave.

Magnolia sighed. "Reeves had to go in to work today. He's having some issues with an important negotiation."

"It's really not his fault," Odelia put in, glancing at Gilli, who made a rude sound and curled into a ball on the seat of the chair, covering her head with her arms.

Anna smiled to herself and placed the paper bag on the floor nearby. "What a shame," she said with a sigh. "I guess that means Gilli won't be interested in what I've brought her." Anna pulled the two handcrafted Valentine cards from her portfolio.

Gilli's arms relaxed, and her little chin with its tiny cleft lifted as she attempted to peer in Anna's direction without being too obvious about it. Anna passed one of the cards to Hypatia, saying, "This is for the three of you. Happy Valentine's Day."

Odelia clapped her hands as Hypatia extracted the card from its envelope.

"How lovely. Thank you, dear," Hypatia said, showing the front of the card to her sisters. She quickly read the sentiment penned inside and passed the card to Magnolia.

Magnolia passed the card to Odelia, smiling at Anna. "You do such good work, Anna Miranda, but what's in the bag, dear?"

"Oh," Anna said, "that goes with this second card, the one I'd hoped to give to a certain little girl."

Gilli sat up, her curiosity getting the better of her. "I'm a little girl," she said.

Anna bit back a chuckle. "So you are. The very little girl I had in mind, actually."

Gilli slid off her chair and went straight to the bag, but Hypatia forestalled her. "Card first, Gilli."

The girl paused, eyes wide. Smoothly, Anna offered the card to Gilli. "Happy Valentine's Day, sweetie."

Gilli's brow puckered. "What's Balertine?"

"It's a day for sweethearts," Odelia supplied, smiling beatifically, "when people who love each other exchange gifts."

Gilli stared at Anna, speculation lighting her copper-brown eyes. They were so like Reeves's that Anna's heart flipped over inside her chest. Gilli's gaze switched to the envelope. Anna carefully removed the card and held it out. Gilli pounced.

"Pretty!"

"Let us see," Odelia urged. Gilli ran to her great aunt, trailing glitter. Odelia gushed over the card, opening it and reading the sentiment inside. "Happy Valentine's Day to a roller-skating ballerina."

Gilli tilted her head, caramel-colored curls bouncing. "What's balaringa?"

Odelia tapped the drawing on the front of the card. "This is a ballerina. See her pretty dress?"

Gasping, Gilli ran to the bag. "Is it balaringa dress?"

"Nope," Anna replied as Gilli pulled the helmet from the bag. "It's what you need to learn to skate."

The girl instantly deflated, dropping the helmet and slumping her shoulders. "Daddy won't teach me."

"I will," Anna told her, reaching into the bag to remove the knee and elbow pads.

Gilli gasped and immediately turned pleading eyes on Hypatia, wheedling, "Can I? Pleeease, pleeeease? I'm old to skate."

Anna said nothing. Was it her fault if Reeves hadn't made his opinion on the matter clear to his aunts?

Hypatia exchanged glances with her sisters before saying, "I think some exercise would do you a world of good, Gilli. Thank you, Anna. Gilli, run upstairs to get your skates."

Gilli began to bounce up and down. "Skates! Skates! Skates!"

"I'll go with her," Odelia volunteered, swinging her legs off the chaise.

"And I'll get her coat from the cloakroom," Magnolia added.

"Bring extra pairs of thick socks, too," Anna said to Odelia, who had risen and taken Gilli by the hand. "The skates may be a little large for her."

"The extra socks will keep her warm," Hypatia noted.

"Skates! Skates! Skates!" Gilli chanted, hopping along beside Odelia as the older woman led her from the room, Magnolia on their heels.

"How thoughtful you are, Anna Miranda," Hypatia said with a gentle smile.

Anna shrugged and confessed, "I have an ulterior motive. I think Reeves needs to pay his daughter more attention, and I hope this shows him that she's old enough to reason with and not just scold."

Hypatia's smile widened. "You are answered prayer, my dear."

Taken aback by that, Anna passed the older woman her portfolio, babbling, "The…the samples…for you to look at."

"Ah," Hypatia purred, drawing the portfolio into her lap. "We'll talk again later."

Nodding, Anna shoved the pads and helmet back into the bag, then quickly excused herself and escaped to fetch her gear from the car. She left the bag at the foot of the stairs and returned moments later to find an excited Gilli with her helmet on backward, trying to tear her pads from their packaging. While Odelia clucked and Magnolia held Gilli's coat, Anna laughed to see Gilli so excited. She sat down on the stairs to help the girl properly don her new safety gear then put on her own before working the extra socks onto Gilli's feet.

"We'll put on our skates outside," she instructed.

"How come?"

"So we don't damage the floors or break any of your aunts' valuable antiques."

Gilli blinked at her then quickly gathered up her hard plastic skates, hugging them to her chest. Anna slung her own over one shoulder by the carry strap, while Odelia and Magnolia together managed to get Gilli into her coat.

With Gilli's great-aunts waving fondly, Anna ushered the girl out of the house and across the porch to the brick steps. It took several minutes to get skates on both of them. Anna donned her own first, and then buckled Gilli tightly into the pink-and-purple skates. They were a bit large as well as a little too tall, but they would do.

"Okey-doke, let's get out to the sidewalk."

That proved a major undertaking. Gilli literally threw herself toward the street, only to wind up sprawled facedown on the gravel drive. Though she wailed for a minute, she wasn't hurt. The gravel was very deep and served to cushion Gilli's fall; it also provided a perfect base for Gilli to learn to stand and walk in her skates. By the time they'd made their way down the drive to the edge of the property, Anna had almost convinced herself that she actually could accomplish her goal and teach Gilli to skate. Sort of. She hoped.

They reached the massive wrought-iron gate, which stood open, and used it to work their way past the grate between drive and street to the sidewalk beyond. A harrowing half hour followed, during which they both took several spills. Thankfully, neither suffered more than bruises, and gradually Anna found herself merely tense rather than terrified. Then, suddenly, everything seemed to click and Gilli was skating, or waddling on wheels, anyway. Gilli couldn't have been more thrilled.

Relieved, Anna's fatigue disappeared, and she began to instruct Gilli on technique, confident of success. She forgot all about tweaking Reeves and got swept up, instead, in the pride and joy on Gilli's sweet little face. They were both exhausted but laughing as they skated slowly, hand in hand and noses rosy, back toward the estate gate over an hour later. They had almost reached it when a late model, silver, domestic sedan turned into the drive and stopped. The driver's door opened, and Reeves Leland got out, staring at them over the top of the car.

"Daddy!" Gilli called, waving. "Look! Look!"

Anna held her breath, suddenly wishing she'd gone about this whole thing differently. Why hadn't she realized that she might be overstepping? Gilli was his daughter; he had authority over her, not his aunts. He might be not just irritated but very angry with Anna. That did not seem like such a fun thing all of a sudden.

"I'm skating!" Gilli cried needlessly.

"So you are," Reeves said after a moment, and to Anna's everlasting relief, he smiled. His gaze shifted to Anna then, and the smile froze, looking a tad strained around the edges.

For the first time, no quip sprang to her tongue, no goading put-down, no clever crack or blistering boast. Instead, Anna drew Gilli to a halt at the edge of the drive and smiled tentatively, aware that Gilli babbled at her side about the morning's adventure. Reeves switched his attention back to his daughter, smiling down at her and nodding.

Finally, Gilli drew breath enough for Reeves to speak. "I guess you've grown into those skates, after all."

"They're actually a little large still," Anna confessed. "She's got on extra socks."

A shaft of sunlight broke through the clouds just then, lighting his face so that his eyes glinted like new pennies. "Guess it's a good thing it's winter."

"True." An awkward silence followed, and Anna felt

a great urge to fill it. "Maybe by summer she'll truly have grown into them."

"Maybe," he said, looking down at Gilli. "If you'd like to take off your skates you can ride up to the house with me."

Gilli dropped Anna's hand and plopped down onto the cold sidewalk. Reeves came around to crouch beside her and help her remove the skates. He tapped a knuckle against her pink-and-purple helmet, asking, "Where did you get this?"

Gilli tilted her head back, looking up at Anna. "She got it."

Reeves looked up at Anna, his forearms balanced atop his knees. "That was very nice of her."

Anna muttered that it was nothing. She had never felt so off-kilter in her life. It was weird. This was not what she expected of Reeves. He was actually being nice to her.

He rose to open the back door of the car and drop the skates onto the floorboard while Gilli scrambled inside. Reeves got her into her safety seat, closed the door and turned to Anna. "How about you?"

"Huh?" The question made no sense to Anna, so she stood there gaping at him like a landed fish.

"Want a ride?"

"Oh! No, I'll just—" She almost bit her tongue off, realizing only belatedly what she'd said. Why had she refused a ride up to the house? Tired and beginning to feel chilled, she dreaded that deep gravel, but it was as if her brain had gone into hibernation. Before she could bully it to full wakefulness, Reeves got in behind the steering wheel.

An instant later, the car engine started. She watched

the car move up the long drive and sighed before beginning the slog up to the house.

Things weren't turning out quite as she'd planned for some reason, but what could she do except trudge forward?

Gilli chattered happily all the way up the drive, something about ballerinas, as far as Reeves could tell. She casually mentioned falling down, as if it was no big deal, and actually laughed about "bonking" her head and how much she liked her helmet. Reeves marveled that this was the same kid who howled like she was being beaten with a whip if he so much as shook a finger in her face, not that he'd ever laid a hand on her in anger. His stepmother, Layla, often counseled him to spank Gilli, but he'd noticed that Layla never followed her own advice with his baby sister, Myra, though in fairness Myra did tend to behave better than Gilli. Reeves knew instinctively that was his fault; he just didn't know what to do about it.

"And now I can skate!" Gilli announced, pride in every syllable. "But not in the house," she went on, barely drawing breath. "No, no, not in the house, because of the val'ble antikies."

"Antiques," Reeves corrected with a smile.

"What's antiks?"

"Furniture and things like that. Very old furniture and things. The aunties' house is full of them."

"If they're old, how come they don't throw them away," she wanted to know, "like you threw away my shirt?"

"Because, unlike old shirts, antiques are very rare.

That means they cost a lot of money. That's why we have to be very careful with the aunties' things."

"Oh." She sounded surprised but also informed, as if she'd just made a discovery.

Reeves shook his head, wondering why he hadn't thought to explain that to her before. Anna Miranda obviously had, at least to a point. He glanced into the side mirror, watching Anna Miranda struggle up the graveled drive.

He hadn't been able to believe his eyes when he'd first seen Gilli and Anna Miranda skating toward him, holding hands. At first, he'd been angry enough to spit. Then, once he'd accepted the fact that Gilli had obviously learned to skate, he'd felt a flash of resentment because Anna Know-It-All Miranda had been right. Remembering his promise to God the evening before, he'd said a quick prayer and tried to analyze the situation clearly.

What he had seen after that was the triumphant smile on his daughter's face and, to his surprise, the wary expression on Anna Miranda's. He'd expected her to be smug, self-satisfied, perhaps even disdainful, but she had looked genuinely guarded, almost worried. With good reason. He hadn't exactly given her the benefit of the doubt since they'd become reacquainted. Just the opposite, in fact.

From the beginning, he had assumed that she was up to no good, entertaining herself at his expense. Yet, there sat Gilli in safety gear that perfectly matched her skates, beaming and chattering like the happiest of little girls. He had to admit that, whatever Anna Miranda's intentions, she had made his little girl very happy today.

It stung that he hadn't been the one to do that for his

daughter. It even stung a bit than Anna Miranda had refused to ride up to the house with him, but he pushed that aside, determined to concentrate on the good she had done for Gilli. And him. His daughter obviously could respond to instruction if properly given.

He brought the sedan to a halt behind Anna Miranda's battered coupe, noting that she'd pasted a bumper sticker that said "Imagine Art" over a scratch on the trunk lid and covered a hole in her taillight with red plastic tape. He wondered if she couldn't afford better. The idea surprised him, for the Burdetts, while not in the same league as the Chatams, were known to be well-off.

After climbing out of the car, he went for Gilli. She reached up, and because she was in her stocking feet, he pulled her into his arms and carried her toward the steps. It occurred to him that he hadn't actually held her in a long time, and he was surprised by how much she had grown, how much she had changed. Her little muscles felt strong and lean. She wasn't a baby anymore, and the realization clutched at his heart.

"Want to see my balaringa?" she asked hopefully.

"I think you mean ballerina, yes?"

Gilli nodded eagerly. "Her dress is so pretty. It sparkles, too. Wanna see?"

"Okay. Where is it?"

"Auntie 'Patia gots it, and she got one, too, but it is the house on it, and no sparkles." She slashed a hand downward, emphasizing the sad lack of sparkles.

"Ah."

He had no idea what she was talking about, not even when she said, "Anna did it."

"Is that so?"

Gilli nodded enthusiastically. Reeves glanced down

the drive. Anna Miranda was finally drawing near, huffing and puffing with the effort. He felt Gilli's arm slip around his neck, and a love so strong and poignant seized him that it constricted his throat. He looked at her and saw the undiluted pride and joy in her eyes. It broke open something inside his chest, something cold and hard that he hadn't even known existed. It hurt, ached, but he felt an odd sense of relief, too, as if a boil had been lanced.

Anna Miranda drew up at last, leaning against the rear fender of his car. Reeves hefted Gilli a little higher against his chest and asked her, "Have you thanked Anna Miranda for your new things and teaching you to skate?"

Gilli leaned toward Anna Miranda and shouted, "Thank you!" Apparently in her world volume added weight to gratitude.

Before Reeves could scold her, Anna Miranda laughed and shouted back. "You're welcome!"

Gilli giggled behind her hands. For several seconds he could do nothing but revel in his daughter's sweet laughter, glad that he hadn't prevented it with his scolding. Finally, he turned and carried her up the steps.

"Go tell the aunties how well you're skating now," Reeves instructed, opening the front door and setting her on her feet in the foyer. "I'll bring your skates in after I speak with Anna Miranda."

Gilli waved at Anna Miranda and ran down the hallway, yelling, "I can skate! For real! I can skate!"

Reeves pulled the door closed and turned to address Anna Miranda. He didn't quite know how to behave with her. They'd been at loggerheads for so long, despite the years without contact. Those few minutes in the coffee shop were his only frame of reference for dealing with her on a normal basis. She lifted her helmet off her head, holding it against her hip with one hand while ruffling her hair with the other. She looked tired and mussed and perfectly adorable.

Adorable?

Shaking his head, Reeves descended the shallow steps and simply said, "Thanks."

Her delicate brows rose, her light, pure blue eyes widening. A smile tugged at her lips. "And?"

Of course, she would have her pound of flesh. Ah, well, in this case she deserved it. "And," he said slowly, "you were right."

Anna laid her head back against the roof of his car, her gaze moving back and forth. "Excuse me while I check to see if the sky is falling."

He fought a sudden smile. "Very funny. But, really, you shouldn't have done it."

Her gaze sharpened, instantly defensive. "Your aunts gave me permission."

"I didn't mean *that*."

"Well, what did you mean, then?" she snapped. "That I'm not a capable teacher? I think events prove otherwise."

Reeves sucked in air and counted to ten. He would not, would *not,* let her spike his temper. Again. "I meant that you shouldn't have spent your money on Gilli. I'll reimburse you the cost of the helmet and pads."

"No, you won't." She pushed away from the car and made her way to the steps, where she sat and began removing her skates.

Reeves swallowed the argument that wanted to batter its way out of his mouth and changed the subject, asking, "What's this about a ballerina? And something about the house?"

Anna Miranda looked up at him, smiling crookedly. "I made Valentine cards for Gilli and your aunts last night."

Reeves's mouth dropped open an instant before he pressed both palms to his temples. "This is the fourteenth! It's Valentine's Day!" And he had nothing for his daughter or aunts. Anna dropped one brow. Her expression seemed to say that he was the biggest idiot in creation. He couldn't disagree. "Oh, man. I completely forgot! There's this negotiation at work, and my house is all torn apart, and..."

Why even bother explaining? She'd still think he was an abysmal failure as a father and nephew, and she would be right. His aunts and daughter didn't have to know that he'd forgotten about them, though. He shoved aside his overcoat and dug his hand into the pockets of his pants for his keys.

"I—I have to go. J-just say I'll be back in a minute, would you? Please, Anna Miranda."

"Okay," she said, and he pivoted to leave, but then she added, "provided..."

Reeves froze then slowly turned back. "Provided what?" he asked sharply.

She looked him square in the eye. "Provided you stop calling me Anna Miranda."

Of all the things she could have said, that was the last one he might have expected. "What else would I call you?"

"Anna!" she exclaimed, as if it ought to somehow be obvious. "Just Anna. It is my first name, you know."

"B-but," he sputtered, "you've always been—"

"Anna Miranda was a child," she interrupted hotly.

"Anna is an adult. Surely you've noticed that I am an adult."

Oh, he had noticed, all right. He was noticing at that very moment, and it made him want to run fast in the opposite direction. But he owed her. Heaven help him, he owed Anna Mir—uh, Anna Burdett.

"I, um, won't be long," he said, easing back a step. "Anna."

Going back to her skates, she him cut a sly look from the corners of her eyes. "Should I tell Gilli that you'll have a surprise for her?"

"Um, okay." Except… Surprise? He'd thought a card, something appropriately girlie. That suddenly seemed laughably inadequate now. He had the feeling that Anna Mir—make that just plain Anna—would have a suggestion. Not quite believing that he was doing this, he asked, "What sort of surprise would you recommend?"

A smile came and went on her face. "There's a reason chocolate is a traditional Valentine's Day gift. Females love it, females of every age."

Was that a hint? he wondered. Surely not, but… "Will you be here when I get back?"

"Maybe. I have some stuff to go over with your aunts."

"I won't be long," Reeves promised again, hurrying around to drop down behind the steering wheel of his sedan.

He probably ought to have his head examined for what he was about to do, but he couldn't see any other option. He couldn't very well give his aunts and Gilli gifts in front of Anna Miranda. Rather, *Anna.* Besides, he owed her for teaching Gilli to skate. He would just have to pick up something for *Anna,* too. The idea made him distinctly nervous, but then he thought of a way to blunt the impact, so to speak. He'd also buy small gifts for the household staff. It was only fair. Hilda, Carol and Chester looked after Gilli as much as his aunts did, and they took care of him, too. Yes, he definitely ought to demonstrate his gratitude to the staff of Chatam House.

"Thank You for the reminder, Lord, and thank You again for the sanctuary of Chatam House," he whispered as he started the car and made the loop in the driveway that would take him back to the street. "I'm trying to take advantage of this opportunity that You've given me to do better with my daughter." He drew a deep breath before adding, "And thank You for Anna. I'm trying to do better with her, too."

Who knew? They might even wind up friends.

Now, wouldn't that be a kick in the head?

Chapter Five

"How wonderful," Hypatia said in reply to Gilli's exuberant account of her adventure in skating.

Gilli's head bobbed like a bouncing rubber ball, and all the while she chattered. "They aren't too big for extra socks. My nose got cold, but not my toes, and not my hands and not my head. And it didn't even hurt when I fell down." She glanced around, then asked, "Where's Daddy?"

"He'll be in soon," Anna told her, "with a surprise."

Gilli gasped.

"You must be hungry after all that exercise," Magnolia said, getting to her feet. "Hilda ought to have something special to eat in the kitchen."

"Excellent," Hypatia said as Magnolia trundled off. "Now about the samples..."

Gilli got up to hang over the arm of Anna's chair, but she quickly grew tired of the conversation and began to whine until Magnolia came in bearing a tray crowded with the paraphernalia of a proper tea, including a platter of heart-shaped cookies with red icing. Moments later, when Reeves came in, a big bag in one hand and

Gilli's skates in the other, Gilli was sitting on the floor at the end of the coffee table, drinking milk from a cup with a chip on the bottom rim and munching on cookies. Hypatia rescued the teacup when Gilli leaped up and literally threw herself at her father.

"Now, now," Reeves admonished mildly, working his way around the table. "Patience." He sat on the floor with Gilli. Mags jumped up to go for another cup, but he forestalled her. "Wait! I have something for you to take to the kitchen with you."

"What is it? What is it?" Gilli screeched, bouncing on her knees.

He held her off with one hand while he delved into the bag with the other, pulling out at least a half-dozen envelopes and a like number of small heart-shaped candy boxes, which he placed on the top of the coffee table. Gilli squealed with delight as he matched the cards to the boxes and passed them out.

"This is for you," he said, handing his daughter the pink box and envelope. While she shredded the envelope to get at the card inside, he simultaneously placed a red box and white envelope in Hypatia's lap and a flowered box and purple envelope in Odelia's.

"My favorite!" Odelia exclaimed, clutching the box of chocolate-covered cherries.

"And mine," Hypatia said, over the box of solid chocolates in her lap.

Magnolia got chocolate-covered pecan pralines, to her laughing delight, and a bright green envelope. He handed over two more cards and boxes, one of the latter larger than the other.

"These are for Carol and Hilda and Chester," Reeves

told. "I didn't think I ought to buy Chester his own box. What do you think?"

"I'd say not," Mags told him, pointing to the white satin box and pale blue envelope left on the table, "but then who is that for?"

Anna's heart sped up when Reeves's gaze met hers. *For me?* she thought, swallowing a gasp.

"To thank you," he said, as if he'd read her mind.

Odelia squeaked like a mouse. Magnolia shot her sister an oddly triumphant glance as she turned away, laden with goodies for the kitchen. It was Hypatia's calm, warm smile that helped Anna reach forward with trembling fingers to gather in the box of assorted chocolates and the card.

"H-happy Valentine's," she managed just as Gilli, who had dispensed with her card and been busily tearing the cellophane off her box, spilled pieces of candy across her father's lap.

"Whoa!" he said, frowning, but then Gilli threw her arms around his neck, her mouth stuffed with the one piece of chocolate she'd managed to get her hands on. His expression froze, but the poignancy that shone from his brown eyes squeezed Anna's foolish heart.

Suddenly, she felt like that needy little girl again, the one who would do anything to be noticed, to prove that she was wanted. Slightly panicked and feeling terribly conspicuous, Anna shot to her feet, juggling her portfolio with Reeves's shocking gift. She hadn't even read the card yet. Curiosity all but burned a hole in her brain, but she could not bring herself to open that envelope in company.

"I—I have to run. It's been..." For one horrible moment, her mind went totally blank, but then Reeves dropped his gaze, beginning to help Gilli pick up the candy pieces and return them to the box. As if released from some invisible grip, Anna's thoughts began to whir again. "It's been quite a morning."

"Oh, don't hurry off, Anna Miranda dear," Odelia urged.

"Actually," Reeves put in, his gaze carefully averted, "I think she prefers to be called just plain Anna these days." His eyes met hers then. "Isn't that so, Anna?"

For some insane reason she said, "All my best friends do. C-call me Anna, that is." She could have kicked herself for saying such an inane thing. "I—I really have to go."

"I'll walk you out," Hypatia said, starting to rise.

"No, no." Anna moved swiftly toward the entry hall. "I know the way. Enjoy your tea before it gets cold. I'll be in touch."

She practically ran from the room, relieved that Hypatia sank back down into her chair. As she made her escape, one crazy notion kept circulating through Anna's mind. Reeves Leland had bought her a Valentine's Day gift. *Reeves Leland* had bought her a Valentine's Day gift.

Her heart pounding, she rushed home to her apartment and feverishly let herself inside. Tossing her keys into a bowl atop a plant stand near the door, she dumped the portfolio in the single chair that comprised her living room furniture before carrying the card and candy box to the drawing board that took up the majority of the space. Carefully, Anna peeled back the flap of the envelope and pulled the card free.

It was a thank-you card.

Tamping down her disappointment, she peeled the

cellophane from the candy box and lifted off the lid. She popped a chocolate piece into her mouth. As orange cream melted on her tongue, she mused that at least the card had a heart of pink lace and a bouquet of yellow and blue flowers on the front. Plus, to be fair, the sentiment was appropriate. She opened the card and read it aloud around the remnants of the chocolate.

"You did a thoughtful thing when you didn't have to, and your efforts are greatly appreciated. God bless you." It was signed, "Reeves Kyle Leland."

The doofus had signed it with his full name, as if there might have been another Reeves in the room. Why were men so stupid? Every man she had ever known was clueless, not that she'd known very many.

Anna picked another candy from the box and let her thumb sink into its middle, cracking the chocolate shell to reveal the pink cream inside. The faint aroma of strawberries teased her nose. She slipped the candy into her mouth, taste buds exploding with chocolate and strawberry, and looked around at the cramped little apartment, which was all she could afford on her meager salary.

With a living room turned studio, despite the sagging, slipcovered chair in the corner, and a kitchen the size of a linen closet, she mostly lived in her bedroom, which made entertaining problematic, not that she had much company. Most of her women friends were married now and starting families, and she made sure to keep the few men she dated well away from here.

Pensively sucking the tip of her thumb clean, Anna folded the card and slid it back into its envelope. As she picked another chocolate from the box, she told herself that it did not matter that the card lacked any romantic sentiment. The days when Reeves Kyle Leland had been a hero to her were long gone. Now he was just an acquaintance, an oblivious father with a little girl too much like herself. If the yawning pit of longing inside her felt unhappily reminiscent of high school, well, Anna knew better than to expect that to have changed. It would be enough, she told herself, if they could just be friends. It would, in fact, be more than she had any reason to hope for.

Reeves pushed away his plate and sat back in his chair, his gaze going to his daughter, seated opposite him next to Odelia. Aunt Mags occupied the chair beside him, while Hypatia, naturally, sat at the head of the massive Renaissance Revival table, leaving the foot and six more chairs empty. Running a finger along the gadrooned edge of the table, Reeves tried not to listen to the *clunk, clunk, clunk* of Gilli's shoes against the stylized Corinthian column that supported the dark, parquet top. She had been a perfect little darling all through dinner, and he hated to upset the applecart by reprimanding her for kicking the table leg with her rubber-toed tennies. It wasn't as if she was doing damage to the table. For some reason, though, his nerves had been on edge all evening, as if the world had unexpectedly shifted on its axis and thrown everything off balance.

He had felt this way once before. That had been the day when Marissa had announced that she was not ready for a child, despite the fact that she was pregnant. She had proposed that they "put off" parenthood. In one horrific moment, he had realized how fundamentally selfish his wife was and that his feelings for her had irrevocably changed. Why he should think of that now, though, he couldn't imagine. It wasn't as if anything had really changed today. Sure, Gilli had learned to skate, but why should that rock his world? Yet, something was different. It was as if a cavern had opened in the floor of the ocean, sucked up all the water and spewed it out again in another direction.

He stared at his daughter, trying to figure out what had happened. She looked up from her plate and smiled, her mouth full of buttered brioche. He thought about correcting her table manners but didn't.

"I have dessert now, Daddy?"

He sat forward and made a show of assessing her plate, which had been picked almost clean despite the cookies and chocolate on which she had dined earlier. "Okay."

"You did very well," Odelia praised her.

Gilli beamed. "I get one piece, don't I, Daddy?"

Nodding, he watched as Hypatia produced that one piece of airy chocolate and crisp rice. Gilli gobbled it down.

"What do you say?" Reeves coached automatically.

To his surprise, she ran around the table and threw herself against him, crying, "Thank you!"

All the water in the ocean rushed back into that undersea cavern. He felt as helpless against it as a piece of flotsam wafting to the ocean floor, waiting to be thrown willy-nilly in a direction it had never traveled before.

Awkwardly, he patted his daughter's back, suggesting, "Why don't you go play until bath time, hmm?"

She ran out of the room without another word or a backward glance.

"I knew Anna Miranda would be good for her," Odelia gushed.

Whoosh! The tide spewed and flung him blindly out

to sea. He cleared his throat, shifted in his seat and tried to keep his voice level and casual. "Learning to skate certainly seems to have given Gilli a sense of accomplishment."

"And it's Anna, dear," Hypatia reminded her sister gently.

"Oh. Yes. Amazing what a little time and patient instruction can accomplish with one so young," Odelia went on. "Who'd have thought it? *Anna* was just brilliant with Gilli today. Don't you agree, Reeves?"

He opened his mouth but couldn't find a thing to say that wouldn't drown him, so he closed it again and tilted his head in what might have been construed as a nod. But how, he wondered, could Anna Miranda Burdett be a good influence on his impressionable daughter? Okay, she'd been right about it being time to teach Gilli to skate, though Reeves still privately marveled that anyone could get Gilli to concentrate long enough to do something as physically complicated as skating. That did not mean that Anna knew more about his daughter than he. Did it?

Odelia apparently thought so. "If ever a woman was born to understand a child," she pressed on, "it's Anna Miranda and Gilli." No one corrected her use of Anna's full name this time.

Reeves felt as if he was choking. "Excuse me," he said, dropping his napkin onto his plate. "I'd better check on Gilli."

He left the dining room as sedately as he could manage, despite feeling as if he was being dragged down into that undersea cavern again. Only God knew when and where the unmanageable sea of difficulties that was his life would spit him up next time, but he had the unsettling feeling that wherever that new shore might be, Anna Miranda Burdett would be there waiting. Worse, he feared that Odelia just might be right about her. But, if Anna was actually good for his daughter, then what did that make him?

The problem, he decided. That made him the problem. Just as Marissa had said.

Maybe, he told himself bleakly, it would be best if Marissa did take over raising their daughter. If only he could convince himself that Marissa really cared for Gilli and not whatever financial support might come with her. He just didn't know what was best anymore, and he wasn't sure now that he ever had.

"Nooooo!" Gilli twisted and pulled, trying to free herself of Reeves's hold as he divested her of her coat.

"Cut it out now," Reeves scolded, keeping his voice pitched low. "You know you have to go to Sunday school."

"I don't want to!"

Somehow he'd expected her good behavior to carry over from the day before, but she'd been fighting him all morning, first over what to eat for breakfast and then over getting dressed. Gilli insisted that she hated the dark green velvet and black satin dress that Aunt Mags had given her for Christmas, but it was a cold-weather dress that was already too small, and Reeves figured that if she didn't wear it now, she wouldn't get to wear it at all, which would undoubtedly hurt Magnolia's feelings. After he'd gotten Gilli outfitted in black tights, black patent leather shoes and the abhorred dress, he'd had to badger her into the very coat that she didn't want to take off now. He simply could not fathom what her problem was today.

Glancing around at the families passing through the hallway of the children's education wing, Reeves wondered why his daughter had to be the only one to balk at going into her class. She had done so almost since she'd been promoted to the three-year-old room six weeks ago. To calm her, he released his grip on her coat but blocked her flight with his body, trapping her against the wall.

"Gilli, you have to go in."

"I wanna stay with you."

Frustration boiled up in him. "You're just being silly," he told her sharply. "I'm sure you'll have fun. Now get in there and enjoy yourself!"

A derisive chuckle had him turning his head. Anna Miranda—rather, *Anna*—stood with arms folded not a yard away. "You figure that's going to work, Stick?"

Overwhelmed and disappointed by the events of the morning, he used his most repressive tone, the one that made his subordinates gulp. "Excuse me?"

Clearly unimpressed, Anna dropped her arms and sauntered closer. "In my experience, you can't just order someone to enjoy themselves."

He felt his face heat. Okay, technically, she was right, but she didn't understand what he'd been through that morning or the resulting level of his frustration. Where had all the amity between him and his daughter gone? Dredging up his driest tone, he drawled, "No? Really? So good of you to share that. Considering you don't have a clue about what's going on here."

"No?"

"No."

Anna parked her hands on her hips, and suddenly he

realized that she wore a sweater dress the exact color of blue as her eyes, as well as a pair of tall, sleek black boots. Both left just her shapely knees bare. That dress, modest as it was, left no doubt as to her womanly shape, and Reeves found that it required conscious effort to resist the alarming impulse to step closer.

Something of his thoughts must have shown in his expression, for she instantly bristled. "What's your problem?"

Reeves tried to cover his disturbing fascination with a frown. "I don't have one, other than my daughter not wanting to go into her Sunday school class."

Gilli, who had been staring through the window behind them into the busy, colorful room beyond, tugged on his sleeve. "Daddy, I wanna stay with *you*."

"Gilli, you know that's not going to happen!" he snapped, at the end of his patience, especially with Anna standing there rolling her eyes.

"And you say I'm the one without a clue," Anna drawled.

Very deliberately, she looked around him and through the large window at the state-of-the-art play area. Over the years, the church had expanded into all of one whole block of the downtown square surrounding the historic county courthouse. On Sunday, it literally took over the downtown area. The one-hundred-and-thirty-year-old sanctuary and the circa 1930s facade on the rest of the buildings in the church plant might have historic significance, but the rabbit warren of rooms in the sprawling complex included easily reconfigurable spaces and all the modern amenities.

Going down on one knee, Anna beckoned Gilli closer

and whispered into her ear. Gilli nodded, and Anna whispered again.

"It will?" Gilli asked.

"Mmm-hmm. I bet the other kids will laugh," Anna said, "and everybody likes to laugh, don't you think?"

Giggling, Gilli nodded, then she ran to the half-door and knocked at it. A teacher appeared, smiling down at her. Too relieved to question this about-face, Reeves rushed over to facilitate the process of signing her in. Seconds later, he was waving goodbye to his daughter. Stepping aside, he turned back to Anna with as much annoyance as amazement. How could she manage Gilli when he couldn't?

"I don't know what that was all about, but thanks."

Anna shrugged, her lips curving into a wry smile. "You just have to know what bothers a kid and how to have a little fun with it."

"This morning everything has bothered Gilli," Reeves grumbled.

Anna spread her hands. "So you stuck her in that tight, uncomfortable dress as punishment?"

"No!" Stung, Reeves glared and told her stiffly, "For your information, Aunt Mags bought Gilli that dress for Christmas." He heard giggles from the room behind him but ignored them.

"That doesn't make the dress any more comfortable, you know," Anna argued.

"Well, Gilli seems perfectly happy with it now," he pointed out smartly.

Anna smirked. "Sure she is. I told her what a dress like that is good for."

"And that is?"

"Showing off. Getting people to notice. Especially upside down."

Confused, Reeves shook his head. "Upside down?"

Anna gestured toward the window. "They've got the equivalent of a jungle gym in there, you know."

Reeves whirled around and with very little effort caught sight of his daughter—hanging upside down by her knees from a crossbar on the play station, her skirt covering her face, her ruffled bottom exposed. A crowd of children had gathered around her, laughing and pointing. Horrified, he rounded on Anna.

"You told her to do that?"

Thankfully, the hall had emptied of all but an older gentleman doing duty as a greeter at a side door some distance away. Nevertheless, Reeves lowered his voice, stepping closer to make himself heard. "What were you thinking, telling her to do that?"

"I was thinking," Anna retorted, meeting him nose to nose, "that you wanted her to go into that room without pitching a fit."

Her eyelashes, he noticed, were as bright as brass beneath a thin layer of brown mascara, and why he should find that so infuriatingly intriguing he could not imagine.

"I didn't want her to expose herself in front of the whole class!" Reeves hissed, dropping his gaze and reaching for the doorknob.

Anna intercepted his hand. He jerked back, feeling scorched.

"Will you calm down?" Anna gritted out. "She's three, for pity's sake, and all she's exposed is her ruffled tights. Besides, the teacher's already taken care of it."

He peered through the window again in time to see

a woman setting Gilli on her feet and brushing down her skirt. As he watched, a set of blonde, freckle-faced twin girls bracketed Gilli, laughing behind their hands. The teacher shepherded them, chattering animatedly, toward a circle forming around another woman with a storybook.

"And look," Anna said, "she's made a couple of friends."

It suddenly occurred to Reeves that he did not know any of these kids, which meant that Gilli probably didn't know any of them, either. Now that he thought about it, he realized that only Gilli and one or two others had been old enough to move up at the beginning of the year. No wonder she had balked at going in. She probably didn't have any friends there. Knowing Gilli, she'd most likely been sitting in a corner all these weeks with her arms folded and her bottom lip stuck out, a sullen, silent, unhappy little stranger. He watched Gilli whisper to her new friends, a gleam in her eye, and sighed inwardly. Turning, he stared down at Anna.

Why was it that he was always the clueless one and Anna always had to be right where *his* daughter was concerned? Still, to tempt Gilli to hang by her knees in Sunday school while wearing a dress.... It was just so *Anna Miranda* and did not seem to bode well for the future.

"She won't always be three, you know," he pointed out.

"But you won't have to drag her kicking and screaming into class next week," Anna rebutted smugly.

Considering how happy Gilli seemed, Reeves imagined that Anna was right about that, too. Still... "And when she's fourteen and desperate to be popular, do I advise her, in your considered opinion, to show her bottom and play the class clown?"

Anna waved that away with a flick of one wrist. "Oh, please. It was just about having a little fun. That's what kids do."

"Is that what you were doing all those years?" he challenged, folding his arms. "Having a little fun at everyone else's expense?"

All expression left Anna's face, but then she lifted her chin and narrowed her eyes at him. "Shouldn't you be in a class somewhere, too?"

He started slightly, remembering time and place. "Yes. And so should you. We can continue this conversation after worship."

"Don't hold your breath waiting for that," Anna said, dancing away, that old cocky insouciance in place once more. "I have a class of six-year-olds to manage, then I'm off to brunch."

"You teach the six-year-olds?" he asked skeptically.

Walking backward, she explained, "Every now and then I substitute for a friend. Why? Don't you think I can handle a six-year-old as well as a three-year-old?"

"Well, yes, but that's not the point."

"Then what is?"

"It's just that I never see you in worship."

"I don't go."

"You teach Sunday school, but you don't stay for worship?"

"Never."

Reeves could not resist following her. "Why not?"

Anna grinned and baldly admitted, "Because it would give my grandmother entirely too much pleasure." She moved on down the hall, winked at the greeter and pushed through a door into a classroom.

Reeves stood where he was, wondering how could she

be so right and so wrong at the same time. She dutifully taught children's Sunday school but wouldn't stay for worship because it would please her grandmother. She convinced Gilli to happily go into class and at the same time coached her to make a spectacle of herself. What kind of sense did that make? None, Reeves concluded, which just proved that Anna had never completely grown up. In some ways, he realized, heading toward the men's Bible study class, some part of her would always be a brat, and that made the woman a maddening puzzle, one moment clever and kind, the next irrational and immature. So that meant that one minute the aunties might be right about Anna being a good for Gilli, and the next the opposite might true. Now how was he supposed to deal with that?

He simply did not know what to think of Anna Burdett or how to feel about her. He did know this much: By letting Tansy drive her away from the worship service, Anna was as good as cutting off her nose to spite her face. Everyone needed a healthy personal relationship with God Almighty through Jesus Christ, and that meant regularly being in worship. Someone had to make Anna see that.

Of course, he was not that someone. Why, he was the last person for the job.

But if not me, then who? he wondered.

Shaking his head, Reeves told himself that God would bring the right person along. He just didn't want to think that maybe He already had.

Smoothing the ruffled edge of a pink skirt with the tip of one finger, Anna tilted her head to study the drawing, her toe tapping along with the lively beat of a favorite rock song. She loved working with pastels, but it had been weeks since she'd last pulled them out. Her encounter that morning with Reeves and Gilli had left her feeling oddly unsettled, so it was inevitable that she should turn to her secret passion as a way to center herself. She strove to tell a story with each picture, imagining how other fertile imaginations might interpret her drawings.

A knock at the door had her first looking up in surprise then checking the time via the digital display on the small, inexpensive stereo system atop the cheap shelving unit tucked into a corner next to the tiny bar that separated the tiny kitchen from the tiny living/studio area. As it was just past noon, the hour at which Downtown Bible Church turned out, Anna had a hunch that Tansy knocked at her door. Sighing, she got up and went to find out. It was too late, with music pumping out of the stereo, to pretend to be gone. Sure enough, her grandmother pushed into the room the instant that the door cracked open, her patent leather handbag dangling by the strap from one elbow.

"Well, hi there, Tansy," Anna deadpanned, taking on a dual role. "Hello, Anna. Won't you come in, Tansy? Why, thank you, Anna. How nice of you to ask."

Tansy ignored this completely, just stood there in heavy pumps that, naturally, matched the handbag. The navy patent leather seemed a bit much with the casual style of her dark blue knit pants and flowered rayon blouse, but it was quintessential Tansy. Turning in a circle, Tansy's critical gaze swept the tightly confined space. Even strict organization could not keep it from appearing cluttered and messy, but Anna would not defend herself on that or any point.

"Ginger Elkanor had her baby last night," Tansy announced baldly. "Girl. Thought you'd want to know."

"Thanks," Anna said drily. "I'm aware." Actually, it was for Ginger that Anna had substituted that morning, not that she wanted her grandmother to know about that.

"Since it's the second child, there won't be a shower," Tansy went on, "but that doesn't mean her friends shouldn't take over a gift."

As if Anna could not decipher that for herself. She glanced at the illustration on her drawing board, murmuring, "I thought I'd frame one of my drawings. That would at least be unique."

"Unique," Tansy huffed, a familiar expression of disapproval on her face. "Unique is overrated. Besides, what would an infant need with a drawing? Buy her a bag of disposable diapers. Now that's useful."

"Useful but boring."

Tansy rolled her eyes. "That's the trouble with you, Anna Miranda. You think life ought to be entertaining, fun. When are you going to act responsibly, settle down and have a family of your own?"

Now that Tansy's excuse for this visit was out of the way, Anna mused, the old girl could get about her real business of running Anna's life, or trying to. Anna had to give it to Tansy. She never quit, a trait she shared with her granddaughter.

"And give up all this?" Anna quipped, holding out her hands. "What makes you think I want a family, anyway? All family's ever been to me is a pain."

"You want to talk about pain? What about the pain of losing my only son?"

"He's been dead for over twenty-five years," Anna pointed out softly.

"And his father for ten years before that, but do you ever think about the pain I've suffered because of it? What about the pain and embarrassment you've caused with your behavior?" Tansy went on. "All I've ever wanted is what's best for you."

"That and to control my every breath," Anna sniped.

"Will you be serious for once!" Tansy demanded. "And if you're going to listen to that ridiculous music, at least turn it down!"

Anna went straight to the stereo and turned up the volume a notch.

Tansy marched over and punched the power button on the stereo as if Anna was ten and they did not stand in *her* home. Anna glared through the silence that followed.

"You're going to ruin your hearing," Tansy said defensively.

"It's *my* hearing. I'll ruin it if I want to," Anna snapped, aware that she was reverting to her sixteen-year-old self but unable to stop. "You have no right to touch things in *my* apartment!"

Tansy frowned sourly. Stomping to the door, she muttered, "Just once I'd like to have a normal conversation with you. Just once!"

As Tansy went out, Anna spun around and slapped the power button on the stereo with one hand, wrenching up the volume with the other. Anna was still heaving in angry breaths when the neighbors next door began to beat on the wall. Instantly, Anna lashed out by spinning the volume knob all the way up. Then, for some reason, Reeves came to mind. In a flash, she imagined him watching from afar, like God on high peering down from lofty realms. Anna turned down the volume, feeling foolish and immature and…sad.

After a moment, her raging heartbeat slowed, but the sick feeling in the pit of her stomach remained. She sat down at her drawing table and began ruthlessly "correcting" her work. After a long while, she sat back to take a critical view. It came as no surprise that the little girl in that ruffled pink skirt bore a decided resemblance to Gilli Leland.

Chapter Six

"Anna was at church this morning?" Odelia asked breathlessly, clapping her hands together. She barely missed catching the tips of her long, dangling earrings. They looked like bunches of grapes swaying above the dining table. "How wonderful! I'm sorry I missed her."

Reeves forked a bite of omelet into his mouth—the aunties ate so-called "simple fare" on Sundays—and shook his head. "She didn't stay for worship. She was just there to substitute for a teacher in the six-year-old department."

Her fork poised in midair, Hypatia sighed. "I worry about that girl."

"What girl?" Gilli asked, butter all over her face from the triangle of toast in her hand. "I know two girls, Elizbet and Mogumry." She scrunched up her face, adding, "But I don't know what one they are."

Reeves smiled. "You must mean the twins I saw this morning." Obviously, Gilli couldn't tell them apart. Their mother surely had not named them Elizabeth and Montgomery, though. Had she?

"I meant Anna, dear," Hypatia clarified for the child,

adding mildly, “Don’t wipe your mouth on your sleeve. You’ll ruin your pretty blouse.”

“It gots ruffles,” Gilli announced proudly, holding out her arms.

“Say, ‘Yes, ma’am,’” Reeves coached, fixing her with a level look.

Defiantly, she bit off a huge chunk of bread instead, replacing the butter that she’d just wiped off her face with her sleeve. Reeves counted to ten, tamping down his temper as Gilli chewed, as soon as she swallowed, he leaned forward and removed the remaining bread from her plate.

“Yes, ma’am. Or we trade the ruffles for a plain T-shirt.”

Ruffles suddenly had taken on a monumental importance in Gilli’s life. Since this morning’s escapade, she had talked ruffles almost nonstop. She’d even insisted on wearing that white blouse when Reeves had helped her change out of her church clothes before lunch.

“Yes, ma’am,” she muttered.

Apparently hanging upside down by her knees to show off the ruffled bottoms of her tights had made her a minor celebrity with the three-year-old set, and so ruffles must now be the predominant feature of her wardrobe. Reeves still was not thrilled about that episode, but Gilli had been so happy since then that he couldn’t bring himself to lecture her on the subject. Besides, he reasoned, Anna was to blame, not Gilli.

“About Anna,” Odelia said thoughtfully, picking up the thread of the conversation. “I wonder why she doesn’t attend worship.”

Reeves put the bread back on Gilli’s plate. She snatched it up and took another big bite. “I believe it has to do with her grandmother," Reeves revealed absently. "Anna said it would please Tansy too much if she went to worship."

Hypatia frowned. "Surely she didn't mean that."

"Surely she did," Mags muttered, "and who could blame her? You know how Tansy is. Let her think she's won on one issue, she'll try to run everything."

"Well, it's not right," Hypatia pointed out. Reeves had thought the same thing, but he wisely kept his mouth closed. He was glad of it when Hypatia said, "Someone has to speak to Anna about this."

"Not that she would listen to us," Odelia said innocently. "Why would a girl, er, young woman like her care what three old biddies like us might say?"

"I take issue with being called an old biddy," Hypatia sniffed, "but you're entirely right about the other. She needs to hear it from someone nearer her own age."

Reeves shifted in his chair, uncomfortably aware where this was headed.

Mags pointed her knife at him. "Maybe you should do it, nephew. Maybe you could make Anna see what a mistake she's making by not attending worship."

Just because he had known it was coming didn't mean he had to like it.

"Me?" he asked indignantly. "What makes you think she'd listen to me? Why should I be the one?"

Mags went back to cutting a slice of tomato with a steak knife. "If not you," she asked, stabbing him straight through the conscience, "then who?"

Reeves stared at her for a good ten seconds as his own thought from that morning returned to pour salt into the wound. Bowing his head, he surrendered in silence. God didn't have to crack his skull with a two-by-four. Ruffles and a steak knife were quite enough. He would say something as soon as the right moment presented itself. Now if only Anna would listen, but why should she?

He hadn't exactly been amiable and personable with her. Most of the time he'd been downright rude. He was going to have to mend his ways, make friends with her, if that was possible. At the very least, he was going to have to be polite.

Okay, Lord, if that's what You want, then You're going to have to help me. Big time.

Pleased with the new fuel contract that he had just successfully negotiated, Reeves stepped up into the charming little bistro with the Director of Operations at his side. Their hard work had been rewarded with nice bonuses, and they'd decided to celebrate at Buffalo Creek's most popular café. Considering that the morning had started with a telephone call from his ex, the day had definitely improved; yet, he couldn't quite get that call off his mind.

Marissa had taken up residence in San Antonio and wanted, she'd said, to give him her new address. She had complained that she wasn't earning enough to make ends meet and insisted that they needed to "rethink their divorce agreement." Otherwise, she had said, she'd have to find another way to "make an adequate home for Gilli." He had pointed out that she'd never stated any intention of making any sort of home for Gilli before, to which she had retorted, "Things change."

He knew a threat when he heard one, but his ready cash was tied up in house repairs and would be until the last of the insurance came through. If he'd had the bonus money then, he might have given that to her, though it was just as well she did not have the means to hire an attorney or open court proceedings, not that he seriously thought she would do so. Every time she reached out, though, he was forcibly reminded of his inadequacies and failures. But not today, he decided. Today he was going to hold this one small triumph close and forget about all the rest.

That proved easier than he'd expected when he spied Anna at a table with an older couple across the way. The man looked vaguely familiar, but he knew that he'd never seen the woman before. She said something, and Anna laughed, putting her head back to let the sound roll up out of her throat in a rich, musical flow. The instant that she saw him, the laughter stopped. Reminded forcefully of his conversation with God on Sunday past, he put on a smile and was rewarded with a look of genuine welcome. He found that welcoming expression compelling, so as the waitress showed him and his companion to their table, he excused himself to briefly detour in Anna's direction.

The vibrant yellow-orange walls, painted with trailing vines and birds nesting in tree branches, provided a fetching backdrop for Anna's golden beauty, Reeves mused as he walked across the black-and-white checkerboard floor. Once he arrived at the table, however, he found himself appallingly bereft of conversation beyond, "Hello."

Anna, fortunately, had no such problem. "Come here often?"

It sounded like the worst of pickup lines, and he almost laughed, as she no doubt intended. Instead, he cleared his throat. "Not really, no."

"Special occasion then?"

"Business thing," he said, nodding.

Both of Anna's eyebrows lifted. "The negotiations must have gone well."

"You knew about that?"

"Your aunts mentioned something about it." Effectively changing the subject, she looked to the couple with her. "You may not remember Howard from the print shop."

"But I do," Reeves said, shaking hands with the older man.

"And this is his wife, Lois."

"Ma'am."

"They have a special occasion, too," Anna announced.

Lois, whose slate brown, shoulder-length hair was sprinkled with silver, hunched her plump shoulders and cast a loving gaze on her husband. "Twenty-eight years."

"Your wedding anniversary?" Reeves surmised.

Leaning sideways, she linked her arm with her husband's. "Yes. Anna's treating us to lunch in celebration."

"Congratulations. That's quite an accomplishment."

Harold smiled and patted his wife's hand. "Sadly, these days it is, but then there aren't many like my Lois."

"Oh, you shameless old flirt," Lois teased. She winked at Anna and quipped, "He just keeps me around because I make him laugh."

"Hey, a man with a sense of humor is a rare find," Anna returned. "Take it from me. I would know. Right, Stick?"

He didn't know what to say to that, so he just smiled. "Well, I don't want to keep my friend waiting." He nodded to Howard and Lois. "Nice to meet you folks. Anna."

"Enjoy your lunch."

"Thanks. You, too." He started to turn away, but then

he stopped, remembering that he had a mission where Anna was concerned. For a moment, he was unsure what to do. He didn't think it wise to say that he wanted to talk to her about church. Then he remembered something. "Actually," he said, "I meant to tell you that Gilli's been asking about you."

Anna brightened. "Oh?"

Relieved in a way that he couldn't quite identify, Reeves smiled and nodded. Gilli *had* asked when Anna would come and skate with her again, prompting Reeves to walk out onto the back patio with her to watch her demonstrate her newly acquired skating skills. She hadn't asked after Anna since. Indeed, that simple gesture on his part had seemed to have pleased his little girl mightily, which had, in turn, humbled him. He was beginning to realize how much he'd left to the nanny, more than he should have. Much more. In some ways, he was only now getting to know his daughter.

"She'd like it if you stopped by to say hello sometime," he went on carefully.

"I'll make a point of it," Anna said. "I have to call on your aunts soon, anyway."

"We'll look forward to it." The seed of a future conversation planted, Reeves seemed to have run out of words for this one again. He flipped a wave and walked away, leaving Anna smiling as if he'd given her something precious, something more than just a friendly word. It made him feel small to think that he might have given her that at any point in the past.

He could not remember when he'd taken an early weekend, Reeves thought, turning the sedan into the drive of Chatam House that following Friday a good three hours before his usual quitting time. The gate, featuring a large copperplate *C* at its center, stood open in welcome as usual. He could count on one hand the number occasions, in his memory, that it had been closed. Perhaps that perpetual welcome was one reason why he so looked forward to coming home. God knew that Chatam House felt more like home to him now than the house that he had shared with Marissa ever had.

He pushed away thoughts of her and her increasingly shrill demands, steering the sedan around to the west side of the house. Strangely unsurprised to find Anna's battered old coupe parked beneath the porte cochere there, he parked next to it and got out. He *was* surprised to find Anna and Gilli sitting cross-legged on the ground at the edge of the drive tossing pebbles at the massive magnolia tree on the west lawn. The waxy, palm-sized, evergreen leaves had turned brown around the edges due to the cold, but Reeves knew that they would not fall from the stems until new foliage appeared in the spring, unless they were knocked free by, for example, flying gravel.

He walked toward them, pleased when Gilli smiled and waved at him. Anna glanced his way, then picked a small stone from the edge of the drive and tossed it into the tree. What fell to the dirt was not a large, leathery leaf, as expected, but a scrawny gray cat, yowling in surprised protest. Gilli gasped, and for a second the entire tableau froze. Then, suddenly, both Anna and Gilli burst out laughing. An instant later, the cat streaked around the converted carriage house, where the staff lived, and out of sight.

"It was a cat!" Gilli exclaimed needlessly. "We got a cat, Daddy!"

He didn't bother correcting her. The cat was long gone, after all.

Sobered, Anna said, "I hope I didn't hurt it."

"It looked okay to me, just surprised."

"No more surprised than us," she replied with a chuckle.

"Anna knocked off a cat!" Gilli exclaimed, laughing. Suddenly she looked up at him. "I can knock off leaves, Daddy. Watch!"

Anna sent him a telling glance, even as she too reached for a pebble—from behind Gilli. "Slow and easy," she counseled, glancing up at him again, this time with a conspiratorial look in her eyes.

Gilli took aim, holding her pebble no higher than her nose. Then suddenly her arm shot up, and she threw it. At the same time, Anna flung her stone up from the ground and over Gilli's head. Gilli's pebble traveled about ten feet, plopping silently and unseen, by her at least, to the right. Anna's sailed into the tree about midway up, and a pair of leaves rattled slowly to the ground beneath.

"I got two! I got two!" Gilli crowed.

"Beans!" Anna complained. "That makes you the winner."

Gilli radiated delight even as she comforted Anna with a pat on her knee. "Uh-uh. You knocked off the cat. 'Member?"

Anna snorted. It sounded suspiciously like a strangled laugh.

Abruptly, Reeves wanted to reach down and scoop them both into his arms. He wanted to savor the whole moment, including the mute byplay with Anna. He had known, somehow, what she was planning, what she had been doing, for Gilli all along, and it warmed his heart, especially when Gilli seemed so pleased with her supposed pebble-tossing prowess. Rattled by these unexpected emotions, he nevertheless wanted Anna to know how grateful he was, despite his doubts sometimes about her methods and the sudden envy that he felt because Gilli never laughed so easily with him. That, he knew, was his own fault, and he meant, somehow, to remedy the situation.

Anna pushed up from the ground, her long, slender legs straightening to show off the snug, easy fit of her nut-brown corduroy jeans, which she wore with a quilted tan jacket and long, colorful striped wool scarf.

"I better get a move on," she said, and the sound of her voice made him realize that he'd been staring. Quickly, he dropped his gaze, nodding.

"Don't go, Anna," Gilli pleaded. "Stay and knock off leaves with us."

"I can't, sweetie," Anna said. "I still haven't seen your aunts, and I need to get back to work soon. Unfortunately."

Reeves seized on that. "Don't you like your job?"

She grimaced. "I like the work, at least."

"You should. You're quite good at it."

Her eyebrows lifted. A moment later, she bowed her head as if trying to hide the smile that curled her lips. "Yeah, well, to tell you the truth, my boss is a bit of a bear. Kind of takes the fun out of things, you know, but I like working with Howard."

"He seems very nice."

"He is, and that makes dealing with Dennis easier."

Reeves found himself reaching for some way to help

her. "Maybe you ought to consider changing jobs anyway. There are bound to be opportunities in Dallas."

She shook her head, already moving away. "I wouldn't know how to even begin looking."

He didn't want her to leave. That nonsensical, rather alarming thought took him by surprise. He immediately rationalized it. How was he supposed to talk to her about getting back into the habit of attending worship service if they never spent any time together? Before he could think of a way to make that happen, she called out, "Gotta go. See you guys later."

Gilli folded her arms, pout in full force, but then she turned a beseeching face up at him. "Wanna play? Wanna knock off leaves with me, Daddy? Please? Pleeease."

Gilli had never asked him to play before. Maybe she hadn't realized that adults could play, or maybe that was just one more essential that he'd left to the nanny. He looked back over his shoulder, watching Anna disappear around the corner of the house, then he carefully lowered himself to the ground. Gilli's happy laughter curled around him like tendrils of incense. Was this how God felt about the happiness of His children? Reeves hoped so.

"I wonder if I can knock off a dog," he teased, reaching back to pick up a handful of pebbles.

Gilli giggled. "Daaady! Dogs don't go in trees!"

"No? Hmm. We'll see." He let loose with the pebble in his hand. It sailed high into the tree, but the leaf that he knocked free failed to make it to the ground, caught somewhere in the jumble of limbs.

Gilli couldn't believe it. Her elbows braced on her knees, she turned up her palms. Then she gasped and wonder lit her face as she whispered, “Maybe the dog gots it!”

Grinning, Reeves looked back to the tree, calling, “Hey, pooch! Fetch me my leaf.” Without Gilli realizing it, he threw another pebble, aiming for the middle limbs this time, and a single leaf fell straight to the ground. Gilli’s eyes popped big as saucers. “Good, pooch,” Reeves said, winking.

“Daaady!”

She fell against him, laughing, and when he put his arm around her, joy suffused him. He almost felt sorry for Marissa. Despite all of her declarations about making a home for Gilli, she hadn’t even asked how their daughter was or said anything about arranging a visit. All she’d talked about was needing money. She had no idea what she was really missing.

It occurred to him that Anna was nothing like Marissa. She obviously didn’t have much, and she just as obviously didn’t expect much. For another thing, she was good with Gilli, better than any nanny he had ever hired. She actually seemed to like his daughter and spending time with her. The aunties were right. Not only did she seem to understand Gilli better than her own mother did, Anna seemed to understand Gilli better than her father. That was the saddest thing of all. Anna Miranda was a better parent than him or Marissa.

But he was trying, and maybe someday he could change that, once God was through with him, had *fixed* him somehow, made him a better man, a better Christian. Maybe, with the right woman… He dared not ask himself if Anna could be that woman. Yet, she had indisputably given him insight into his daughter, and he thought that perhaps he was a bit better as a father because of it.

The thought occurred to him that he ought to do something for Anna in gratitude. An idea began to form in the back of his mind. But first things first.

"Your turn," he told Gilli, surreptitiously picking up another pebble from the edge of the drive.

Once more, she took careful aim, and a tiny rock plopped into the grass, but she saw only the rusty green leaf that tumbled to the ground as she crowed in celebration.

They spent a good quarter-hour tossing pebbles at the magnolia tree. Later, while she napped, he slipped off on a long run. When he returned to the mansion, she complained about having awakened and found him gone, so he consented to watch a video with her after dinner. As it was Friday, he even allowed her to stay up later than usual. Eventually, she drifted off to sleep, cuddled up next to him on the comfy cream white leather sofa before the fireplace in their suite.

Carrying her to bed, he felt that lately they had made progress. Being at Chatam House helped. His aunties and their faith permeated the place with peace and comfort. Not having the nanny around to take care of things like getting Gilli dressed and bathed had made a big difference, too, more than he could have guessed, but he knew that the lion's share of the credit went to Anna.

She had shown him that Gilli was more than a fussy, irrational baby. Anna had shown him how important it was to pay attention to Gilli and have a little fun with her. As a result, Gilli laughed more, shone more and behaved better. Reeves realized that he'd secretly feared that his daughter hated him, but that was not the case.

She needed him; she might even love him. Life wasn't without its frustrations where Gilli was concerned, but he certainly enjoyed her more.

"Thank You, Lord," he whispered, lowering her onto her pillow. He brushed her curls from her forehead and pulled up the downy blanket to tuck it around her. He spent a long time in prayer that night, just being thankful, and he asked for something that had never occurred to him before. He asked to forget the pain of his failed marriage, realizing that it had caused him to ignore in so many ways the one good thing to have come from that catastrophe, his daughter.

They slept in on Saturday then enjoyed a light, simple breakfast together in their suite. Reeves went downstairs and put it together himself, Hilda having moved on to other chores. Gilli was thrilled to discover that he'd sent it up in the old dumbwaiter that opened onto the landing. Later, when he had errands to run, she begged to go along. Despite fearing that she would tire before he had accomplished what he must, he gave in.

Their first stop was the dry cleaners, where he picked up a week's worth of shirts and his tuxedo. He'd dropped off his tux as soon as the aunties had made it clear that this year's fund-raiser was to be a gala affair. He had worn the thing exactly twice in his life, once at his sister's wedding and again at his own. Might as well get some good out of it when he could.

After that, he drove over to the pharmacy to replenish their supply of vitamins. There Gilli demanded a candy bar, but he deflected a confrontation by offering lunch at her favorite pizza place instead, a small concession since he'd planned to eat out anyway. Taking Gilli into the local home improvement store next probably wasn't the smartest move he could have made, which was why he gave up trying to pick out a new light fixture for the kitchen midway through the project. He still had time, he told the beleaguered salesman, who was undoubtedly relieved that he'd gotten rid of them before something ended up broken. Lunch became a rather long, drawn out, fractious affair, but Reeves was pleased that he managed to keep his cool, even though Gilli couldn't seem to sit still in the booth for three minutes running.

Their final stop was their own house, where he inspected the new rafters. While he was up in the attic, Gilli went to her bedroom where she pulled out half a dozen more toys that she wanted to take back to the mansion with her.

"Please, Daddy, please."

Reeves shook his head. "You have plenty of toys at the aunties' house now. Besides we'll be moving back here soon."

She looked positively stricken for a moment, then she did something he hadn't expected. She pitched a crying, screaming fit. "I don't want to! I want my toys! I want my toys!"

Stunned and exasperated, Reeves resorted to the only method that he knew of to cope. He pulled her up and sternly marched her outside to the car, wailing like a banshee. Saddened that their day out had come to this, Reeves drove back to Chatam House in pained silence, letting her wail and rage until, exhausted, she calmed to mere snuffles.

No sooner did he set her feet on the graveled drive, however, than she bolted, wailing anew. The aunties finally managed to calm her. Reeves knew this because some time after he left them to it, her cries finally faded, and at dinner she, like his aunts, was glum and quiet.

It tore at Reeves heart to think that they had not made as much progress as he had believed, so much so that he actually thought about calling up Anna to discuss it with her. But no, that was the sort of thing one discussed with a wife and partner or, at the very least, a trusted friend and advisor. He would figure this out on his own, somehow, God willing. But how? Oh, Father in heaven, how?

Chapter Seven

Sunday brought little of the angst and frustration that Reeves expected. Gilli morosely donned the dress that he chose for her without serious complaint, though she bemoaned the lack of ruffles on her tights. For his part, he made sure that the dress fit comfortably. He had to bite his tongue to keep from admonishing her not to repeat that upside down business, but in the end it did not seem necessary as the twins were waiting for her when she trudged sullenly through her Sunday school room door. He stood outside the window and watched her for a few minutes, turning away only when she giggled at something one of her new friends said.

He turned half expecting Anna to be there with some sarcastic quip on the tip of her tongue, but he was alone in the hallway except for a couple dropping off their child at the six-year-olds' classroom. He moved that way before he even realized what he was doing. At the door, he heard himself asking if Anna Burdett was teaching today.

"No, she's not part of our team," a young woman told him. "We trade off, every other Sunday, except for the directors. Would you like me to ask them where you could find her?"

He shook his head, already moving away. "It's not important. I'll catch up with her later. Thanks."

Why, he wondered suddenly, instead of looking for the right moment to speak to her about attending worship had he not simply invited her to come to church with him and Gilli? What a simple solution that would have been! On the other hand, inviting Anna to church might presage more than mere Christian concern. He was afraid that he was coming to like her too much.

With a sudden rush of insight, he saw all the ways he had employed to keep from thinking of her. The errands, the meals, television, even arguing with Gilli. He had abdicated a sacred responsibility out of selfish fear.

Guilt swamped him. He owed Anna; not only that, he owed God. The two felt inextricably intwined.

That thought stayed with him throughout the remainder of the day and on into the next morning. Recalling their conversation about her dissatisfaction with her job, he took the time to do some research online concerning opportunities for graphic artists. What he found surprised him, but he wasn't sure what to do with the information, even when he returned to Chatam House that evening to again find Anna's vehicle parked in the drive.

The rich, meaty aroma of Hilda's roast beef welcomed him as he entered, as usual, through the side door. Inhaling deeply, he whispered a prayer of thanksgiving for the feast to come and moved on toward the central hall. Even before he reached the intersection, he could hear Gilli giggling in the sunroom. Making a sharp left, he went straight there.

The aunties occupied their usual seats, Mags and Od

on identical chaises, Hypatia in the chair across the way. Next to Hypatia, on her right, sat Anna. Gilli lay draped belly down across Anna's lap.

"Oh! Here's your daddy now," Odelia said, beaming up at Reeves.

Today's earrings glittered like the moon and stars. Actually, on closer inspection, they *were* moons and stars, blue and silver, radiating outward in small, spiral galaxies. The colors perfectly matched her denim jumper and the silvery satin blouse beneath it. Reeves grinned. Auntie Od never failed to delight, bless her.

"Hi, Daddy," Gilli greeted offhandedly. Sliding off Anna's lap to loop an arm around Anna's neck, she announced, "Anna stayin' for dinner."

"Is she?" He forced a smile, feeling a bit off kilter. His heart seemed to be beating too hard. "Someone must have told her that Hilda's serving a roast for dinner tonight."

Anna chuckled. "Let's just say that my nose works perfectly, so no one had to ask me twice."

Hypatia tilted her head back to look up at him. "You have time to change if you'd like, dear."

"I think I'll do that," he decided.

The women went back to their conversation, and he made a quick escape up the stairs, where he traded his suit for jeans and a burgundy pullover. Anna, it seemed, was becoming a fixture around here. Not even the aunties were immune to her quirky charm. He froze, a sense of déjà vu coming over him.

Suddenly he was back in high school, listening to everyone laugh at Anna Miranda's latest nonsense—and secretly burning up with envy. He could never be that clever, that careless, that uninhibited. He could only be stolid, responsible…confused. His mother had once called him "self-contained," as if that was a good thing and did not separate him somehow from everyone else.

He was heartily sick of being contained within himself, bored beyond bearing with the passionless existence he'd created. It was, he realized, how he had protected himself from the chaos of his childhood and the reason he had chosen Marissa, a creature of excessive passions. And wasn't Anna the same?

No, he decided, she wasn't. Her behavior with Gilli demonstrated that, as did her willingness to toil at a job where she was not appreciated, drive a battered old jalopy and accommodate three adorably eccentric old women. Perhaps she was stubborn and clever and glib, but she was also generous and principled in a way that he had never expected.

After stomping into a comfortable pair of old loafers, he hurried back down the stairs to plop into a chair placed at an angle to Anna's. Gilli had stretched out next to Mags on the chaise in the interim and was in the midst of a long story about "her" cat, claiming that it lived in the magnolia tree and a hole in the hedge that rimmed the property on three sides. Mags said that she had seen the thin gray cat around the place several times lately. Hypatia, who had an aversion to cats, shuddered.

Carol came in to announce that dinner was ready, and they all trooped in to take seats at the massive dining table. They made a motley crew, Mags in her scruffy usual, Od at her outrageous best, Hypatia fit for a diplomatic mission in her pearls and elegant suit, him in his jeans and Gilli in a long-sleeved T-shirt and baggy, faded pink pants just a tad too short despite the ruffles around the hems. Anna looked wonderful in black boots, a long, slender black skirt and a black suede vest worn over a soft white blouse with voluminous sleeves cuffed at the wrists. She proved not only a lovely dinner companion but also a very amiable one.

"Thanks to you three and your fund-raiser, my stock has quite risen at the print shop," she said in reply to a question from Hypatia concerning her job. "Why, I suspect that if I hadn't spilled coffee on Dennis's estimates for a new project today I would be enjoying unprecedented job security just now." Cocking her head, she narrowed her eyes. "No, wait, if it's intentional, that's *pouring,* isn't it?" Grinning, she added, "Spilling is *accidental.*"

Odelia twittered behind her hand then asked, "Was it really intentional?"

"Absolutely," Anna said without the least regret. "It was either that, watch a client get unintentionally hosed, or attempt to point out Dennis's glaring mistakes to him."

"Attempt?" Reeves echoed.

She lifted an eyebrow at him. "Hard to see a mistake when you cannot be wrong."

"Ah. I see. You shouldn't have to put up with that."

"Must be tough when it's the boss who's like that," Mags surmised.

Anna shrugged. "Howard and I worked out a system to deal with him."

"Who's Howard?" Mags asked.

"Coworker," she answered succinctly, spearing a piece of browned potato. "I spill—or rather, pour—and when Dennis roars, Howard runs in with a fresh estimate sheet. Dennis rarely even notices the corrections." She ate the potato, musing, "I look at my job like a cat and mouse game. Unfortunately I keep on winding up as the mouse."

"What's cat-n-moufe game?" Gilli wanted to know, concentrating, as usual, on the bread, in this case, hot, fluffy yeast rolls.

Anna shifted slightly to address her. "You know, cartoon stuff, where the cat's always chasing the mouse, and the mouse always manages to get away."

Gilli nodded, laughing. "Oh, yeah. That."

"Hey, did you ever see the one about the skillets?" Anna asked.

She went on to give them a hilarious blow-by-blow account. It went on for a good ten minutes, and no sooner had the laughter died down than Gilli asked, in all innocence, "What's a skillet?"

Anna traded a look with Reeves, a silent communication that felt oddly intimate. He felt the strangest impulse to reach out and take her hand beneath the table, but then, eyes sparkling, she tucked her chin to hide her silent laughter while Hypatia calmly answered.

"It's a pan for cooking in, and much too heavy for a real cat or mouse to lift."

Gilli nodded, offering sagely, "Cartoons is just pretend."

"Indeed, they are," Hypatia replied while everyone else continued to hide smiles.

"What are your favorite cartoons?" Anna asked Gilli, getting a mangled mishmash of description and titles in return. The aunties were lost.

Anna, who seemed quite well informed on the subject, went on to explain and describe each and every one of Gilli's favorite programs. It became apparent to Reeves that the nanny had allowed Gilli to view much more television than he'd have preferred. He made a mental note to police her viewing habits more carefully. A few moments later he noticed that she was nodding over her plate. They had stayed at the table far longer than normal, but it was not yet Gilli's bedtime.

"She refused to take a nap today," Hypatia informed him softly.

"Sat out on the kitchen doorstep with a bowl of milk all day long waiting for that cat," Odelia explained.

"Nearly caught it, too," Mags added proudly.

Reeves got to her feet. "I'd better take her up now."

Gilli roused at that, mumbling, "Anna come."

Reeves looked to Anna. Without even the slightest hesitation, she pushed back her chair, dropping her napkin beside her plate.

"Thank you for a lovely dinner," Anna said to the aunties. "I'll say good-night now, but I'll see you soon. I'll bring the other print goods over as they are finished." She followed him around the table toward Gilli. Bending, he scooped Gilli into his arms. She wrapped all four limbs around him, laying her head on his shoulder.

"Good night, dears," Hypatia said. "Reeves, I trust you'll see Anna out?"

"Uh, sure."

More matchmaking? he wondered, carrying Gilli toward the central hall. He didn't mind as much as he might have.

Anna fell into step beside him. They climbed the stairs side by side, then Reeves led the way along the landing to the open door of the suite. There he motioned Anna to go ahead, knowing that the modern amenities of the suite in this house of antiques would be something of a surprise to her. She didn't try to hide her curiosity or appreciation as she looked around the comfortable sitting room with its cream walls, puffy matching leather couch, thick burgundy rugs and flat screen television hanging over the mantel of the ornate fireplace, all accented with touches of spring green and gold.

He carried Gilli into her bedchamber. As in his own bedroom at the opposite end of the sitting room, the burgundy carried over into the carpeting and drapes here with pale French Provincial furniture and muted spring green linens softening the effect. Only the stuffed animals on the bed, toys scattered around the room in various containers and stacks of books on the dresser identified this as a child's room.

He sat Gilli on the side of the tall bed then went to pull her pajamas from the dresser. Anna moved in and began to undress the weary child. Once she was suitably garbed for bed, Reeves urged her into the small private bath. Freshly washed and brushed, Gilli made no protest as Reeves lifted her up and laid her on the pillows, but as soon as the covers were folded beneath her chin, she began to plead for a story.

"Aw, Gilli, you're exhausted," he argued. "Let's just say our prayers and get to sleep."

"Pleeease, Daddy. Anna will read. Won't you, Anna?"

"I have a better idea," Anna said, going to the dresser to quickly rifle through the books. Finding one she liked, she returned to sit against the headboard and gather Gilli against her. "Let's make up a story." She opened the book and showed Gilli the first picture. "Hmm," she said, "this bunny looks lost to me. Where do you think she was going? A birthday party, maybe?"

Gilli's eyes lit up. "Yeah, a birthday!"

"I wonder where she'll wind up," Anna murmured, turning the page.

Reeves stood there, listening to the two of them spin a simple story based on the pictures alone. It was nothing like the actual story, which Gilli knew by heart. Why, she could practically recite it, and for that reason he had steadfastly refused to read the thing for days. Now here was Anna patiently, happily breathing new life into one of Gilli's favorite books, and all it took was a little time, attention and imagination.

Gulping, Reeves realized that he normally rushed through the bedtime routine, his mind on the instant when he could take his own ease in private. Yet, what did he do as soon as he closed the door to this room? Too often, he began to dwell on the problems awaiting him at work or rehashed his many failures. Alone and lonely, he routinely cried out to God, begging to be made a better father, nephew, boss, employee, servant, whatever, never facing the fact until now that he failed because he hurried through the most important moments.

Forgive me, Lord, he thought. Then he sat down on the other side of the bed and joined in the story.

Gilli finally giggled herself to a happy ending. Anna closed the book and, following Reeves's example, dropped a kiss on the little curly-top's head. Gilli immediately folded her hands and started to pray.

"God is great, and God is good," the girl began. Anna smiled, for Gilli had begun the mealtime blessing. With a nudge from her father, she started over. "Now I lay me down to sleep..."

After the usual rhyme, Gilli began to thank God. Her list was long, including her daddy, the aunties, grandparents, cousins, many other family members, toys, dolls, skates, books… Eventually she got to the whole earth, sun, sky, trees and so forth. At the very end, she shook Anna to the core.

"And thank You for Anna 'cause You love her, too, and she's my goodest friend. Amen."

"Amen," Reeves echoed, but Anna found that she couldn't speak around the lump in her throat.

Silently, she watched Gilli snuggle down and close her eyes. Slipping from the room, she keenly felt Reeves on her heels. It was as if Gilli's prayer had awakened a new and sharper awareness of him in Anna. She stood, lost, in the sumptuous sitting room while he quietly pulled the door to Gilli's room closed. Then he completely destroyed her with a casual touch, lightly sliding his hands over the knobs of her shoulders and down her arms about midway to the elbow. Those few inches of contact warmed, stunned and scared her. She felt fourteen again, craving his attention and understanding. She wanted him to like her, to approve of her, to love her.

Thank You for Anna 'cause You love her, too, and she's my goodest friend.

Anna knew intellectually that God loved everyone, but she had never *felt* loved. Why, she wondered, was that, and how pathetic was it that her "goodest" friend these days was a three-year-old child? On Sunday, Anna had dropped by the Elkanors' place with gifts, a small framed drawing and a bag of disposable diapers, for the new baby. She'd been gratified by the drawing's reception. The proud parents had both exclaimed over it and carefully examined every detail, but watching them with their baby, Anna had felt very much as if she were on the outside looking in, as usual.

Somehow, at this moment she felt even more isolated than ever, isolated by a yearning for the impossible. Every moment at dinner she had been aware that she was not a true part of the family that gathered around the table, so she had done what she always did. She had teased and joked and showed off. She'd cast surreptitious glances at the man beside her like the lovesick fourteen-year-old she had once been and tried to read the answers to her hopes in every word and gesture.

She stood there in that lovely sitting room and admitted that her foolish heart had long ago set itself on something that could never be hers, and the pain of that suddenly threatened to overwhelm her. It was always best, Anna had found, to get as far away from disappointment as quickly as possible, but the instant she took a step through the door onto the broad central landing, Reeves spoke.

"I'll walk you down."

"Oh." She half turned. "You don't have to do that. I'm sure you're tired and—"

"I told Aunt Hypatia that I would see you out," he insisted, taking her by the arm.

Making a smile, Anna let him steer her along the landing to the top of the stairs. As they were descending the broad curving steps, he spoke again. "Can I ask you something?"

"You just did," she cracked.

He went on as if he hadn't even heard her. "Don't you miss going to church? Worship, I mean."

The question took her so off guard that she blurted the first thing that came into her head. "Why should I?"

He measured her with a sidelong glance. "How else do you expect to maintain a healthy relationship with God?"

In light of her recent thoughts, that rocked her back enough that she had to actually consider her answer. "There are other ways to maintain a healthy relationship with God."

"Such as?"

"Well, reading the Bible, praying."

"Do you? Regularly? Routinely?"

She tried, but invariably she let it slide or simply forgot. Too embarrassed to admit that, she said, "There are other ways to worship besides in church, you know. Haven't you ever praised God in a quiet meadow or forest glade?"

"Sure. Are you telling me that you take a nature hike every Sunday morning to worship God?"

Anna bowed her head. "No, of course not, but there's always the TV."

"Televised services are a godsend for shut-ins and others who can't travel to a church," he conceded, "but for everyone else just getting up and getting to church is an act of worship in obedience. Don't you think God values that?"

They reached the foot of the staircase before she had formulated a reply. It was an honest one; she couldn't seem to find another. "Yes, but in my case I wouldn't be worshiping. I'd be too aggravated by how much I had pleased my grandmother just by being there."

Reeves bowed his head, pondering that. "So," he said carefully, "she controls even your ability to worship God."

Anna almost dropped where she stood. She caught hold of the curved mahogany railing to steady herself, her heart pounding painfully as his conclusion sank in.

The deep breath that she sucked in hurt almost as much as the truth.

"I've never understood you," he told her bluntly, not that it was anything she didn't already know. His puzzlement furrowed his brow, and she quelled the urge to brush back his streaky brown hair. "When my parents split, they actually broke up my home. It was so hard, trying to live in two different places. God knows I never wanted that for my own daughter. You, on the other hand, always lived with your wealthy grandmother, who seemed to give you everything you needed."

"Except approval," Anna said.

He stood there for several seconds, before murmuring, "So you worked to earn her disapproval instead. And you still are."

That stung, sharply enough to make her retort, "Which is why I'm so concerned for Gilli."

His coppery eyes narrowed. "What do you mean?"

Determined to make him understand, she grasped his forearm with both hands. "In the beginning, rebellion may be just a way to get attention, but over time it can become…punishment for those who hurt o-or disappoint you. Worse, it gets to be a habit."

She could almost see him replaying things in his mind and would have given her next breath to know what they were. She desperately wanted to make him see, for Gilli. And for herself.

After several moments, he nodded. "I get it. Yes." To her absolute shock, he took her hands in his. "Thank you. Thank you for sharing that and for caring about my daughter," he said, his molten copper gaze holding hers. "Thank you especially for spending time with her. It's made a difference, all of it."

Several heartbeats ticked by before Anna realized that she was standing there with her jaw flapping in the breeze. Snapping her mouth shut, she managed a nod.

Reeves tucked one of her hands into the curve of his arm and stepped off across the foyer. Somehow, she kept pace with him, despite feeling a step behind.

"I just have one more question," he said companionably, drawing up in front of the yellow door. "How is that rebellion thing working for you nowadays?"

Bleakly, Anna realized what he was telling her, that she'd been stuck in that rut too long; yet, she couldn't imagine how to get out of it. Any softening on her part would be seen by Tansy as a tacit admission of defeat. But wasn't that the problem? This ongoing war of theirs had been at a stalemate for…how long now?

"Isn't it time," Reeves asked softly, "for you to start thinking about what is best for you instead of what makes your grandmother unhappy? They aren't always mutually exclusive, you know."

Anna blinked up at him. "When did you get so smart?" she whispered.

Reeves chuckled. "I could ask you the same thing. Taken us some time, though, hasn't it?" He sighed. "Maybe we're just a pair of slow learners, Anna." He shook his head, one corner of his mouth crooking up. "Better late than never, though, huh?"

She smiled. "That's what I hear."

His smile matching hers, he reached for her hand and squeezed it. For one heart-stopping moment their gazes held, and she actually thought, wondered, hoped… He leaned forward slightly—and pressed a kiss to her forehead before dropping her hand and stepping back.

"Drive safely."

"I—I will."

He opened the door, and she stumbled through it, her head reeling. "Good night."

"Good night."

He waited until she moved across the porch and down the steps to her car before closing the door behind her. Anna stood in the dark, staring up at the big, silent house. It was, perhaps, the loneliest moment of her life.

Chapter Eight

Reeves had given her much to think about, and Anna did not shirk the task, going over and over in her mind all that had been said between them and much that had not. The guilt came unexpectedly. For the first time, Anna realized that she had allowed her anger at her grandmother to keep her from doing much that she should have done, even from worshiping God. She had been so fixated on her resentment of Tansy and her treasured independence that she had blocked out everything else. Or did it go deeper than that? Had she been secretly angry with God all this time?

Surely, He could have seen to it that one of her parents had been around to love her and make her feel wanted. He could have made her life a heaven on earth, if He'd wanted to. Except there was no such thing. Heaven was heaven. This life was...problematic. She wondered why that was. Suddenly she wondered about so much and was shocked by how few answers she seemed to have, despite a childhood spent in church. She knew, admitted, that she needed to be in God's house, really be in

God's house, on a regular basis, but oh, how the idea of pleasing Tansy chafed.

Feeling uncharacteristically tentative and pensive, she went into work on Tuesday morning a bit late without even realizing it. Apparently, she was quieter than usual after the regular dressing down by Dennis, for Howard came to her corner to ask if she was okay.

"I'm fine. Didn't sleep much last night, that's all."

"I hear you. Sometimes, for no reason at all, you just can't shut it down."

She nodded, pondered, and said, "Howard, you and Lois go to church."

He stared at her for several moments through his too-large glasses. "That's right."

"Where exactly?"

He told her, then, "You looking for someplace to go, Anna?"

She sat there for a long time trying to nod, but finally she shook her head, knowing that she wouldn't go anywhere but to Downtown Bible. She wished that was not the case, but she knew that it was. Downtown Bible Church was home even if she hadn't attended a service there in years. "No, I just wondered."

He stood there for a moment longer, then her phone rang, and he walked away. She lifted the receiver and cradled it between her ear and shoulder.

"Print Shop. This is Anna. How can I help you?"

Hypatia Chatam spoke to her from the other end of the line, asking that she drop by that evening. "It's a minor thing, dear. We'll discuss it when you get here, say, half past five?"

"Sure."

"So good of you. We won't keep you long. Have a blessed day."

Anna hung up, wondering less what that was about than if she would see Reeves and Gilli. Just that she wondered made her queasy. She'd felt a slowly growing sense of unease since that moment after Gilli's prayer, and it was becoming more and more difficult to ignore.

Work became her cover. She crawled beneath it, buried herself with it, so that when the end of the day came she could only wonder where the time had gone. With equal parts dread and eagerness, she took her leave of Dennis and Harold and drove over to Chatam House.

Odelia came to the door wearing electric blue lace and stick people earrings, a pink female, a blue male. Anna looked at that little blue stickman and blurted out what was on her mind.

"Is Reeves here?"

She could've strangled herself.

"Not yet. He had to stop by his house for a word with his builder."

"Ah." Because she felt so deflated, Anna naturally acted pleased. "In that case, what can I do for you?"

"In here," Odelia directed, waving her toward the front parlor.

Anna followed and was soon going through a box of forms, one pad of which had a smudge in one portion of the design. "I don't know what that is," she said. "It could be something as simple as someone bumping into the printer during the process. Ink, unfortunately, smears. But it's not on any of the other pads. I'll replace this one and make sure it doesn't happen again."

"Oh, no, dear," Hypatia said, taking the offending pad from her hand. "It won't be necessary to replace this. We just wanted to call your attention to the matter in case it could become a larger problem."

"I don't think that's likely to happen."

"Ah. Just what we wanted to hear."

Anna smiled. Odelia asked how her day had gone.

"Oh, fine."

Unusually chatty, Magnolia wanted to know what she had actually done, explaining, "We find your work so fascinating."

Bemused, Anna gave her a brief overview of her day, if only to prove that nothing about it was fascinating. Hypatia offered her tea, which she declined, thinking it too close to the dinner hour. She noticed that Mags sent Odelia a troubled glance, but she didn't think too much about that. What went on in the minds of these triplets one never knew. Though they were dear old things, they were each a bit of a trip.

She got up to go, saying, "I'll see myself out."

They gave each other helpless looks, then smiled and nodded. Partly mystified and partly amused, Anna strode out into foyer.

A movement in the shadows in the back of the hallway snagged her attention. Peering closely, she spied Gilli sitting with her back against the wall, her chin propped atop her drawn-up knees.

"Hello, there, goodest friend," Anna ventured.

"'Lo."

Anna knew a sulk when she heard one. She ambled closer, studying the child who sat forlornly on the floor in the darkness of the shadows of dusk. "Something wrong?"

Gilli hitched up a shoulder in a shrug. Anna pinched the creases of her loose, olive-green slacks and slid down the wall to sit by the girl. She tugged her snug, cowl-necked ivory sweater into place and straightened the buckle of her wide brown belt, drawing up her knees so that the soles of her brown flats met the floor. Draping her forearms over her knees, she studied her companion.

"Want to tell me about it?"

Gilli shook her head. Anna tried another tack. Thinking of what Odelia had mentioned about Reeves meeting with his builder, she said, "I bet you'll be glad to get back home."

Gilli's knees dropped like rocks. Slinging her hands as if to rid them of something unpleasant, she cried, "I don't wanna go back there!"

Anna felt her brows leap upward. "No? Why not?"

"It's better *here,*" Gilli insisted, folding her arms.

Anna let that settle, considering things from Gilli's point of view. "More fun, I guess."

Gilli shrugged again, muttering, "I don't wanna go back and be by myself."

"But you won't be alone," Anna pointed out. "Your daddy will be there with you."

Gilli looked at her helplessly and began to cry. "I don't wanna go back there. A nanny will come and Daddy will go to work."

Anna slung an arm around her and hugged her to her side. "It's all right. Your daddy won't forget about you. He loves you."

Sniffing, Gilli asked in a trembling voice, "How you know?"

For a moment, Anna was too taken aback to speak, but then she tried to answer in a way Gilli would understand. "Why, it's obvious. He lives with you, doesn't he? Lots of daddies don't live with their kids, but he tucks you in at night and sees to it that you eat well and have pretty clothes. He teaches you to be polite and how to behave. He even prays with you and takes you to church. All in all, I'd say he's a wonderful father, a wonderful man, even. Why, I wanted a daddy just like him when I was a girl, a daddy who would take me home to live with him."

Gilli blinked at her, clearly shocked. "You didn't live with your daddy?"

Anna shook her head. "Nope. Not my daddy or my mommy. I had to live with my grandmother."

Gilli frowned, a troubled look on her face. Then she whispered, "My mommy went away."

Anna beat back the tears that sprang to her eyes and tightened her arm about the child. "Some mommies," she explained carefully, "do go away. It's very sad, I know, but let me tell you something, Gilli Leland. I feel sorry for your mommy because she doesn't get to see you every day. She doesn't know what a bright, fun, beautiful girl you are." She laid her check atop Gilli's curly head, whispering, "If I had a little girl, I'd want her to be just like you."

"Oh, there's just one Gilli," said a voice out of the darkness at the far end of the hall, startling them both.

"Daddy!"

Gilli sprang up and ran down the hall to meet him, giving Anna time to gather her composure and get to her own feet. "Hello, sugar," she heard him say.

For one wild moment, Anna considered making a dash for the door, but then she heard him walking toward her. He materialized out of the deep shadow at the end of the hall, carrying Gilli on his hip, his tan overcoat hanging open over his suit. Her arms about his neck, Gilli hugged him tightly.

"Anna," he said, his warm gaze sweeping over her.

"I—I didn't hear you come in."

"I know." He smiled at her. "You're looking very pretty today. I especially like the sweater."

She gurgled out a "Thank you," wondering just how long he'd been standing there in the shadows. She waved lamely toward the front door. "Gotta go."

"No," he said, "not yet. I need to speak to you. Just give me a minute."

Anna meekly followed at a distance as Reeves carried his daughter to the stairs.

"Come here," he said, standing her on the third step up from the floor. "I want to talk to you, too."

He sat down, and Gilli sat down next to him, hunching her shoulders. "Anna's right," he said, sweeping a hand over her adorable curls. "You are a bright, fun, beautiful little girl, and I'm sorry if I've let you be lonely sometimes. I didn't mean to. I hope you know that, because Anna's right about something else. I love you very much, and I'll never let you be lonely again, not ever."

Blinking back tears, Anna covered her mouth with her hand. Gilli launched herself up onto her knees and threw her arms around his neck, squeezing tightly.

"I love you bery mush, too, Daddy."

He laughed. Sort of. That was quite a chokehold she had on him. When she finally loosened her grip, he patted her and instructed, "Go tell our aunties that I'm home. Okay?"

"Yes, *please,*" she said, displaying her manners if not quite correctly.

Reeves pressed a finger to his lips, one hand holding

her in place. "Excuse me," he said solemnly. "*Please* go tell the aunties that I'm home."

She popped up and bounced down the stairs, little legs pumping. "Okay! You're welcome!"

"Thank you," he said belatedly and shook his head, grinning. She disappeared into the drawing room, crying, "Daddy's home!"

Reeves sighed, but he didn't get up right away. Instead, he beckoned to Anna. She moved toward him tentatively. He held out his hand, and she placed her own in it, allowing him to pull her down to sit next to him. He started to speak to her, but then he bowed his head and began to pray.

"Thank You, Lord. I see You answering my prayers. Every day You draw me a little closer to You and to my daughter, to the Christian father and man I want to be. Thank You. Thank You so much." He sat for a moment longer, squeezing Anna's hand so tightly that her fingers ached. Finally, he looked up, tears sparkling in his eyes. "Thank you, Anna. What you said back there means more to me than you know." Then he slid his free hand into the hair at the back of her head and pulled her toward him, bringing her lips to his.

Stunned, Anna froze. Yet somewhere in the back of her mind she was counting.

Thousand one, thousand two, thousand three, thousand four.

Those were perhaps the most wonderful four seconds of her life, and then it was over. Suddenly she was staring into his copper eyes, her heart hammering with painful hope. Gratitude, she reminded herself, jumping to her feet. Just gratitude. Nothing more.

"Uh, go," she babbled. "I—I have to..." She gestured behind her.

He nodded, just once. Anna ran to grab her things from the table in the foyer, suddenly desperate to get out the door.

"Don't," she told herself, throwing on her coat and hurrying across the porch. "Don't think it. Don't dream it. Don't even want it."

But she did. Oh, she did.

Dennis printed the invitations to the gala auction on Monday morning. Anna examined each one by hand and found them perfect. She even crosschecked every name and address on the accompanying envelopes against the voluminous mailing list. All that remained was for the envelopes to be stuffed and dropped into the mail.

When Anna called to set a time for the delivery, she was a bit surprised to be told once again to come at the end of the day. She had expected to conduct an immediate transport, given the eagerness of the Chatam sisters to get their hands on the invitations. They had called several times during the past week to check on the progress, and she couldn't blame them for being anxious. March had arrived the day before, not that the weather had changed one iota. It was, however, that much closer to the date of the fund-raiser.

Intending to drop off the invitations and go, Anna stood shivering inside her cowboy boots, leggings and oversize, dark red sweater on the veranda of Chatam House at precisely five o'clock that afternoon. She rang the bell with her elbow, the box of invitations secure in her arms, her keys dangling from her teeth. The keys hit the deck when Reeves opened that yellow door.

She truly had not expected to see him, had counted on not doing so, in fact. Given what had happened between them the last time they'd met, she had figured he would be as wary of seeing her again as she was of meeting up with him. Yet, there he stood wearing a huge grin, along with comfortable jeans, athletic shoes and a long-sleeved rusty orange T-shirt.

"Oops," he said. Bending, he swept up the keys and backed out of the doorway so she could enter. "Trade you," he said, reaching for the box.

She pocketed the keys somewhat warily. "I didn't expect to see you here."

"I'm trying to cut back on my hours a bit, spend a little more time with Gilli."

"Ah. She must be pleased."

"Not pleased enough to miss a fast-food dinner and playdate, I'm afraid. She's with my stepmother and baby sister. My father had a business dinner, so it seemed like a good time to get the girls together. I'm just the drop-off and pickup service today."

"That's all right," Anna told him. "At least you're here to do it. That's what matters, believe me."

The sharp planes of his face softened. "I believe you."

Suddenly her heartbeat doubled. Good sense told her that it was stupid to be here yearning for what she'd already accepted would never be hers. She should go. She'd done her job and done it well. The invitations had been delivered; she knew they were perfect, so the Chatams could have no complaint. No one in her right mind would keep opening the same wormy can, but here she was, just as helplessly dim-witted as she'd been way back at the beginning of high school. Lest she doubt it, when Reeves beckoned, she followed him.

He spoke to her over his shoulder as he led the way, not into the parlor but down the hallway to the right of the sweeping staircase, where she had never ventured. "The aunties are cracking the whip in the ballroom. They've set up something of a production line. I suspect they'll have these in the mail within the hour."

They walked past a sumptuously appointed library that would have made many small towns envious before they came to a small, closed door.

"What's in there?" she asked, her curiosity temporarily overriding everything else.

"Music room," he told her, walking on toward the nearest of two sets of broad pocket doors. "Sections of one wall slide apart so that it opens into the ballroom."

Music rooms, cloakrooms, ballrooms… Despite the number of times she'd been in this house, it was hard to believe anyone lived this way. She suddenly felt as if she'd fallen down the rabbit hole.

Reeves turned right and disappeared. Anna followed, coming to an abrupt halt as the cavernous space beyond those pocket doors revealed itself. That rabbit hole turned out not to be far off the mark. It was like something right out of a fairy tale: marble and gilt and burnished oak with ceiling-to-floor windows draped in muted blue and yellow, crystal and a coffered ceiling overhead. Anna stared, unabashedly taking in every detail, while Reeves carried the box to a table set up at the near end of the room.

The exclamations of the aunties, as Reeves called them, and their "production line" pulled Anna's attention back to the matter at hand.

"Oh, Anna Miranda, they're wonderful!" Odelia gushed, hurrying across the floor to hug her. Fortunately, given the older woman's penchant for big jewelry, fur dangled from her earlobes, big balls of white fluff that perfectly matched the cuffs and collar of her purple-and-white windowpane-check dress, not to mention the pompoms on her shoes, which looked suspiciously like white bedroom slippers. Anna grinned with delight.

"I'm so glad you're pleased."

Odelia linked arms with her and towed her across the room, where Hypatia was calling her babbling troops to order.

"Ladies, ladies. Your attention, please." Her hands folded at her waist, Hypatia announced importantly, "Our graphic designer, Anna Burdett."

A wave of delicate applause followed. Anna knew all but a couple of the faces around that table. She was surprised but relieved not to see her grandmother's among them, even as she did the polite thing.

"Thank you. That's very kind but not at all necessary."

"It definitely is," Reeves refuted, examining one of the invitations that the ladies were now eagerly removing from the box. "You've captured the spirit of the thing exactly, an excellent job."

Anna was so nonplussed by his praise that she didn't even manage a thank-you this time.

Hypatia waved a hand dismissively, ordering, "Now run along, the two of you. We have work to do."

Winking, Reeves caught Anna's hand in his, and she found herself once again being towed across that marble floor.

"I have something for you," he told her, "something I think you'll find interesting. I didn't know what to do with it, at first. Then I hit on the idea of a database."

Puzzled, Anna allowed herself to be swept back along the hall and into the library.

"Sit," he directed, waving toward a pair of black leather armchairs positioned at slight angles to a most unusual rectangular table. Atop it lay an orange binder. "Relax," he invited, moving to an oddly shaped cabinet standing against one wall. "Get comfortable."

Anna did neither. She was too busy wondering how he could behave so casually. Didn't he remember that he'd kissed her? To cover her agitation, she ran her hand over the glossy, coppery wood.

"I've never seen a table like this. What is it?" she asked, examining the unique diamond-shaped marquetry on the side and legs.

Reeves glanced back over his shoulder. "It's a Henredon. We know that because it's signed underneath. I believe the style is called Chinese Chippendale."

Anna fought the urge to drop to all fours to check out that signature, not that she had any idea who Henredon might be. "What kind of wood?"

"Light red mahogany, I believe. Grandpa Hub was especially proud of that piece."

"I can imagine."

"What'll you have?" he asked, opening the upper doors of the cabinet to reveal a beverage bar, complete with a small sink, a row of empty crystal decanters and a silver ice bucket, along with various sodas, bottled water, a box of powdered drinks and an electric teapot. "We've got tea, coffee, tea, apple cider, tea, cocoa and, of course, tea." Tossing her a grin, he opened a lower door and took out a mug. "I'm going for the cider myself." She watched him tear open a packet, dump the contents into the mug and pour in hot water. "There's ice if you'd prefer a cold drink."

"Uh." She waved a hand. "Whatever. So long as it's hot."

"Okay, cider it is."

He went through the process again, stirred both cups and carried them to the table. She winced when he set the steaming drinks on that lovely wood. He folded down into the chair facing hers, picked up one of the mugs and sat back to sip.

"Mmm, not bad."

He looked at her over the rim of his mug, and Anna's every nerve ending quivered. She snatched up the other mug and stuck her nose in it.

"Very nice. Uh, you…you said something about a database?"

"Mmm." Leaning forward, he set aside the mug and reached for the binder on the table. "I ran across some interesting info recently, and I thought you might like to see it."

"Info," she parroted uncertainly.

"About the many applications of your particular expertise."

"Expertise?" She shook her head, feeling particularly idiotic. "I don't understand."

He laid the folder in her lap, picked up his mug and leaned back. "I was surprised, frankly, by how many industries and processes require graphic artists. Many are work-from-home positions."

Anna stared at him uncomprehendingly for long seconds, until he dropped his gaze, saying tentatively, "You seem unhappy with your current employment. I thought this might help."

It hit her then, like a sledgehammer to the back of the skull. He'd put this together, or had it put together, because of what she'd said about Dennis and her job. She got her mug back onto the table without spilling her drink and opened the binder.

Page after page after page of job descriptions, business perspectives, website addresses, even names and contacts, all for graphic artists. All for her. Something lurched and stretched inside of her, like a sleeper awakened from a long, unknowing slumber. It thrilled and terrified her all at the same time.

"Why?" was the only thing she could think to say.

"To thank you," Reeves said, sounding earnest and fond. "You've been so kind to Gilli and the aunties. I know they can be demanding, time-consuming and—"

"No! Oh, no," she cut in. "Gilli's a delight, and your aunts, well, they've been utterly charming to work with."

He smiled knowingly. "Charming is their stock-in-trade, as I'm sure you know. It's how they get exactly what they want."

"And you obviously learned at their knees," she muttered, thinking better of it only when it was too late. As usual.

He opened his mouth as if to reply but then said not a word. Quickly she tucked the binder beneath her arm and rose, her cheeks heating. How blatant could she be, for pity's sake?

"It's very thoughtful of you to, er, think of me." She edged away from the chair, babbling, "Sorry I have to run. Tell Gilli…" Her brain stuttering, she pasted on a fatuous smile and finished lamely with, "You know. And, um… Bye."

He was still sitting there impersonating a cod when

she turned her back and all but ran, that binder clutched to her chest. She knew that she was going to treasure the silly thing for the rest of her days simply because he had put it together for her.

"To thank you," he'd said. For being kind, no less. For failing to live up to his worst expectations of the brat, more like.

Yes, she would treasure the folder and the effort that it represented, but that was it. Period. End of story. End of dream. End of foolishness. Gratitude, however well meant, would never be enough for her, and that's all she could ever realistically expect from him. So this, then, was also the end of hope.

It was better that way, she decided, for hope invariably brought the pain of disappointment.

Chapter Nine

Charm! Reeves stared into the mug of cooling cider and looked for some element of truth in the undissolved powder that settled on the bottom of the cup. They must have different definitions of the term. First, he'd given her a hard time, followed by a meaningless box of chocolates and a thank-you card, for Valentine's, no less. Then he'd given her a database of job prospects and a cup of powdered apple cider.

Yeah, he was smooth, all right.

Marissa had not found him charming, at least not once they'd wed. She had called him dull and cold and unimaginative, while explaining that she needed a "real" man to make her feel like a woman.

What did Anna need? he wondered. What did Anna want? He was pretty sure about one thing. She did not seem to look at his Chatam connections and see dollar signs.

He suspected that was the only reason Marissa had married him. She had been so disappointed to realize that he would likely never see a nickel of the Chatam millions. He suspected that his own mother had blown her inheritance ages ago, and even if she had not, he had three siblings in direct line for that money. As for the aunties, so far they had five nephews, seven nieces and seven greats of one gender or the other. He would be foolish in the extreme to count on inheriting anything from them. Why should he? He made a good living, but that hadn't been enough for Marissa.

He sat there shaking his head and listening to the grandfather clock in the corner tick off the seconds until it was time to go after Gilli. Rising, he carried both barely touched mugs to the sink. Without a word to anyone, he got his brown leather jacket and went out to his car.

Little more than fifteen minutes later, he walked through the fast-food restaurant toward the indoor playground. He opened the glass door that segregated the children's space from a restaurant full of strangers and walked into earsplitting chaos. Surveying the crowd of parents and children for his daughter, he spied instead the long auburn hair of his stepmother, Layla, his father's third wife.

All of five years his senior, Layla had been his father's legal secretary and was now the mother of his nearly four-year-old baby sister, Myra, whom Reeves saw next. Myra wore a pink-and-white polka-dot bow in the sleek auburn hair that she had inherited from her mother. Her knit pantsuit matched the bow, as did the bows on her black Mary Janes. She looked like she'd just stepped out of a picture book. Beside her, in head-to-toe maroon suede, Layla just looked angry. It was only when Layla shook her finger in Gilli's face that he finally found his daughter.

Gilli was sobbing. Her curly hair stuck out in a dozen

places, as if she'd been pulled headfirst through the towering maze of crawling tubes. Bedraggled and dirty, she looked like a street urchin next to Myra. Sighing, Reeves made his way through the churning bodies and din to their table, arriving in time to hear Layla yell, "Never again!"

"Never again what?" he asked loudly.

Layla turned on him, her otherwise attractive face twisted into a disapproving mask. She thrust a perfectly manicured finger at Gilli. "That child is incorrigible! She attacked Myra!"

Gilli wailed even louder. Standing there in the midst of the madness, Reeves felt as if his head would explode, but for once he was going to give Gilli the benefit of the doubt. Seizing each of the girls by a hand, he turned and hauled them through the crowd and out the door, leaving Layla to gather their things and follow as she saw fit. The instant the din of the playroom dimmed behind them, Gilli's sobs waned, too. She was mostly gasping and shuddering by the time he found a quiet corner booth and parked her and Myra on opposite sides of it.

"What's this about?" he asked as Layla came huffing up behind him. He went down on his haunches, keeping his voice low. "Gilli, I want you to tell me why you hit Myra."

Gilli's head came up, and she wailed, "Myra pull my hair!"

Reeves turned to his baby sister, whose chin now rested on her chest, and asked, "Myra, why did you pull Gilli's hair?"

Myra looked up, her dark eyes sparkling with tears. After a moment, she whispered, "Gilli wins. Ever time we race, she always wins."

Reeves knew instantly what had happened. They were racing around the climbing structure to see who could get on the ladder next, and Gilli had been in the lead. "Did you grab her hair on purpose?" To her credit, Myra nodded glumly. "So you yanked her hair and Gilli punched you in retaliation," he clarified, making sure Layla heard every word.

"I didn't see that," Layla said crisply. "I just saw Gilli hit Myra."

Reeves heart wrung. How many times had he just assumed that Gilli was the lone culprit? He cleared his throat and calmly went on.

"So you're both to blame, which means that you have something to say to each other, doesn't it?"

Myra sank a little lower on the bench before muttering, "I'm sorry I pulled your hair, Gilli."

Gilli straightened and wiped at her glimmering eyes, leaving dirty smears on her face. "Sorry, too."

"All right," Reeves said, smiling, "I think we're done here. Time to go."

He twisted up and out of the booth, reaching for Gilli's coat. As she slid to the floor, he shook out the coat then began helping her into it. Gilli looked up at him, gratitude shining in her eyes, and her little hand crept into his. Pride swelled in him.

Turning to his stepmother, he quietly said, "Next time, get the full story." She nodded curtly, her gaze averted. "Say goodbye, girls," he instructed.

They exchanged waves and overly cheery "Byes."

Reeves squeezed Gilli's hand, and together they walked out to the car. As he was lifting her into her seat, he thought he ought to clarify a few things while he was still in her good graces.

"Gilli," he said, "no matter what someone else does to you, it's not okay to hit or pull hair. You know that, don't you?"

"Yes, Daddy."

"I expect you and Myra to behave better next time. Understand?"

"Yes, Daddy."

"Good. Let's get you buckled in."

"No!"

Shocked by her sudden vehemence, he opened his mouth to scold, but she threw her arms around his neck and squeezed tight, whispering, "Love you, Daddy."

Gulping, he wrapped his long arms around her. "I love you, too, sugar." Drawing back, he cupped her face in his big hands and studied it. What he saw took his breath away. "You're a happier girl now, aren't you, my Gilli?"

She nodded. He wasn't sure she really understood the question, but she was eager to give him whatever answer he wanted, and that was more than answer enough.

"I'm a happier daddy, too," he told her, bending to kiss her forehead.

She grinned just as if she knew that she was the reason, and of course she was, but it wasn't just her.

He knew who got the credit for this unexpected turn of events. First, God Almighty, Who had commanded the honeybees to drive them out of their house, and second, the aunties with their calm, charming, interfering faith and the warm sanctuary of Chatam House. And finally, Anna.

So much for which to be thankful. So many reasons to praise his Lord.

"Sweet Jesus," he whispered, standing beside his car

there in the cold parking lot, his happy child safely buckled inside. "Sweet, sweet Jesus. Thank You."

His soul brimming with praise, he couldn't think of any other words to say until they fell out of his mouth.

"Let there be a happier Anna, too."

Anna had never felt so hopeless. She didn't know why. Nothing had changed. She'd never believed, not even as a fourteen-year-old with a killer crush, that she could have the sort of life that everyone else seemed to. In all honesty, she'd never found much to like about herself, and that probably would not be any different if her parents had lived. The only thing she found to value was her independence, however tenuous. As a whole, she was a disappointment, barely able to pay her bills, hold her controlling grandmother at bay—or form a private, more personal relationship.

In truth, she'd never imagined herself romantically involved with anyone except Reeves, but he remained as unattainable as ever. A successful, stalwart Christian like Reeves Leland could never have any genuine personal interest in her. Gilli liked her, and he felt grateful to her, but that was all it amounted to, all it *could* amount to. Anna could do nothing about that, but she could do something about her relationship with God.

She kept hearing Reeves ask when she had last worshipped. God deserved worship. She had forgotten that in her battle for independence from her grandmother. What God must think of her! No doubt, she was as much a disappointment to Him as everyone else, so she got down on her knees and confessed. With tears rolling down her face, she apologized to God for failing to worship Him, for allowing her resentments and stubbornness to keep her from giving Him His due. Then she made up her mind to do better.

It wasn't easy. She already knew that she couldn't, was not supposed to, go anywhere but to the Downtown Bible Church. That meant facing not only her grandmother but Reeves and the Chatam sisters, everyone who had wondered why she was not in church and everyone who had invited her to join them over the years. So many had made polite inquiries and invitations, and she had blown off every one of them without a qualm. It seemed fitting then that she do this alone.

She rose early on Sunday morning and donned, ugh, pantyhose and a long-sleeved mauve shift belted at the waist with four-inch-wide purple suede leather perfectly matched to the only pair of heels that she owned. Despite taking pains with her appearance, she arrived early in the arched foyer of the sanctuary. She walked alone across an expanse of dark gold carpet to the tall, arched double door with its heavy black wrought iron hardware. Inside the sanctuary, a full dozen chandeliers hanging high overhead echoed the black wrought iron theme. They, along with their heavy, draping chains, added a Southwest flavor to the stately interior.

Little had changed in the years since Anna had last been here, but the few changes were startling. As always, milk-white, plastered walls stood punctuated by tall, elaborate, stained glass windows and soaring beamed arches leading to sumptuous gold leaf high overhead. Familiar, pale polished wood lay underfoot, softened now by strategically placed runners of gold carpet. Row upon row of long pews, now padded in startling turquoise velvet, still led to the massive altar and the railed apse with its raised, carpeted platform, throne-like chairs and pulpit. The glass baptistery at the very front stood flanked by the golden pipes of an ancient organ, the console of which was hidden in the loft positioned above the foyer, but two large video screens had been added, one high on either side and just in front of the apse. Both sat at an angle that did not distract from the dramatic tableau below. Neither did the railed spaces on either side of the wide aisle before the altar where a full orchestra and choir were already beginning to gather.

Anna had forgotten how much she loved this grand space, how it quieted the soul and set the mind on God and His glories. Walking swiftly to the far end of the nearest pew, she sat down closest to the wall and bowed her head, hoping that her grandmother would not venture in before the spaces around her filled with enough people to provide her with camouflage. As she sat there, stillness filled her. Even her troubled thoughts dissolved, and she felt her breaths come and go with peaceful ease.

After some time, the organ began to play, the music softly soaring and rippling. Soon the buzz of people finding their seats and greeting their brethren overlay the music, but Anna kept her head down. The pew rocked slightly as someone else dropped down onto it, and a shoulder bumped hers.

"Well, well, just who I most wanted to see here."

A thrill of satisfaction shot through her, but she tamped it down before tilting her head. Reeves grinned at her, and she suddenly felt terribly conspicuous. Glancing around the now bustling room, she lifted a hand to the fringe of hair at her nape, telling herself that his delight stemmed from nothing more than Christian concern.

To cover both her discomfort and her pleasure, she asked, "Where's Gilli?"

Crossing his legs, Reeves pinched the crease in the cuff covering the ankle that he balanced atop the opposite knee. "On her way to Children's Church."

Anna smiled. "No fuss?"

"None at all. Pardon me if I brag, but she's been a perfect delight lately." He grinned again, and goodness, was he attractive like this. "That is, if you don't mind having stray cats and dirt dragged into the house."

Anna's eyes went wide as she imagined what must have happened. "Oh, no."

He chuckled. "Yep, she finally caught that skinny gray cat that *you* knocked out of the tree that day. Poor Hypatia." Reeves sighed gustily, stretching an arm along the back of the pew behind her. "The sweet old dear is exercising a great deal of patience with us, I'm afraid."

Anna could just imagine Hypatia's reaction…all those priceless antiques and spotless floors. "You didn't blame me, did you?"

Reeves turned a face of purest innocence to her. "Of course, I did."

"Reeves!"

Laughing, he moved his arm to her shoulders and curled it tight. "I'm nobody's fool, sweetheart. They adore you, and I'm using that for all it's worth."

What protest could she make to such a pronouncement? Provided, that was, she could have gotten a word past the sudden constriction of her throat. Sweetheart. He had called her sweetheart.

Meaningless, she told herself. *Utterly meaningless.* Goofball would have served as well. She wished he'd called her that, anything that didn't make her wonder if he might actually *like* her. Good grief, was this going to be high school all over again?

At the front of the sanctuary, a man moved to a microphone and lifted a hand. The organ music stopped, and the man began welcoming one and all before calling their attention to the announcements now slowly scrolling across the video screens. The organ began to play again, very softly this time, and stillness once more settled over the room.

A woman stepped up to the microphone and asked the congregation to prepare themselves for worship. Reeves removed his arm from about Anna's shoulders and leaned forward, bowing his head. Surprised that he didn't rise and slip out to join his aunts or friends, she quickly followed suit. Closing her eyes, she reached for some sense of God in this place. And found it. When the formal call to worship came, spoken in reverent tones by the woman at the microphone, Anna was in silent prayer.

Dear Lord, I'm here, just as I promised, but please don't let my grandmother make a scene, and please don't let me embarrass myself. Most of all, please don't let me get all caught up in Reeves again when I know that could never work out. Amen.

The orchestra joined the organ, and the choir began a beautiful song based on Psalm 118. The congregation rose and joined in on the next selection. No hymnals. Instead, the words were projected onto the video screens. This was not a familiar hymn to Anna, and she felt lost. Beside her Reeves sang in a low, quiet bass, competent but with perhaps a limited range. She rather liked that tiny flaw in him. Later songs proved more familiar, but by that time Anna was content to simply let the music flow around her. She had forgotten, if she'd ever known, how sacred music could lift the spirit.

When the pastor stepped up into the pulpit, Anna

tried not to regret the end of the music portion of the service. He began with a few joking remarks, but then he got down to business with a Scripture reading. The passage, Romans 8:1-8, flashed up onto the video screens, but Anna noticed that Reeves followed along in his Bible. She divided her attention between him and the video screen, until the sixth verse smacked her right between the eyes.

"The mind of sinful man is death," the pastor read, "but the mind controlled by the Spirit is life and peace."

Life and peace, Anna thought, staring at those words on the screen. Suddenly she knew that she desperately needed that. For years now, she'd been existing in some kind of solitary limbo, and in all that time she could not recall more than mere moments of peace. The satisfaction that she occasionally derived from displeasing her grandmother in no way offset the long, lonely days and nights, the emptiness and grief that she felt every time she thought of her parents, the uncertainty of her job, not to mention the general hopelessness of her life. Was that all she had to look forward to? Irritating Tansy, wondering about her parents, dragging herself into the shop every day and back to her dreary apartment again in the evening, alone? That did not seem like life to her. It certainly was not peace.

While she listened to the pastor, she watched Reeves make notes on a slip of paper that he'd drawn from inside the cover of his Bible. At one point, he underlined something in the Bible itself, and she wondered what it was in that passage that could apply to him. Looking back up to the screen, she decided that it must be the first verse.

Therefore, there is now no condemnation for those who are in Christ Jesus.

She had always known, never doubted, that Reeves was a Christian. Certainly, he did not live "according to the sinful nature." Somehow, even when he most irritated her and was most irritated by her, she had always realized that he lived by an inviolate code of conduct that she could only admire.

After a brief invitation, during which the pastor and others prayed with several individuals who came forward, the service moved toward a close. Anna snagged her handbag from the floor where she'd placed it earlier, nodded silently at Reeves and slipped out of the pew to hurry through those double doors—only to find Tansy waiting for her in the foyer.

"I can't believe my eyes!" her grandmother exclaimed, rushing toward her. "Why didn't you tell me you were going to be here?"

Anna made for the nearest exit, replying with her customary bluntness, "Because I didn't want you to know."

Tansy stepped in front of her. "Just tell me what's brought this about?"

"You wouldn't understand," Anna said, attempting to move around her. Tansy made an ungainly sideways hop to block her, and Anna panicked, looking around blindly for an escape. A long, square-palmed hand closed around her forearm.

"This way," Reeves said. Anna stared at him in confusion. "Children's Church," he went on, watching Tansy, "it's this way. Better hurry if we want to beat the crowd."

Gratefully, Anna followed, rushing to keep up as his long legs led her away from Tansy and through a doorway across the foyer into a hall. They were well out of sight when he turned into yet another long hallway.

She finally drew up. Her feet, in shoes meant for nothing more demanding than a short, sedate saunter, were killing her. Reeves stopped and strolled back to where she slumped against the wall.

"Thank you."

He shrugged. "I assumed you didn't want a scene."

"You're right. I don't."

He lifted an eyebrow at that. "I can remember a time when you'd have relished one, done your best to embarrass Tansy."

Anna smiled wanly. "So can I."

He tilted his head. "Looks like the brat's grown up, after all. And yet, I suspect you're about to make a liar out of me."

"What do you mean?"

"I implied that we have plans."

"Which we don't."

"Not if you refuse to join us for Sunday dinner," he conceded pointedly. Anna blinked at him. "Mind you, the aunties eat 'simple' on Sundays," he hastened to add, "simple but ample. I'm sure they'd be delighted for you to join us. I know Gilli would."

Anna noticed that he didn't say anything about himself, but then she didn't expect him to. Why then was she disappointed?

"Let me add a little more incentive," he went on, stepping closer. "I doubt Tansy would follow you to Chatam House."

Anna widened her eyes in horror. "But she would trail me back to my place." Smiling, she quipped, "You sure know how to convince a girl, Stick."

"Charm," he said with a wink. "I learned it at the knees of my aunties, you know."

Anna shook her head. Not only had he rescued her from an ugly public scene, he'd found the perfect way to diminish her embarrassing gaffe of the day before. Always one to value a good joke, she retorted, "Baloney. It's genetic, bred into your very bones."

"Like the cleft chin."

They both laughed, and then he asked in an entirely conversational tone, "Where is your place anyway? I don't think I even know where you live."

"Cherry Hill Apartments."

"Ah, yes. The complex in that low spot out there by the highway."

She snickered. "That's right. The one with no cherry trees."

"Hmm, I'd have thought you were more the Peach Orchard type," he said, naming another apartment complex in town.

She shook her head with mock sincerity. "I don't particularly care for peaches."

"You mean they actually *have* peaches?"

"Of course not, but still..." She wrinkled her nose. "It's the principle of the thing."

"Right." His lips twitched.

"I did consider Pecan Valley," she said, just to keep the joke going.

"But?" he asked.

"They actually have pecan trees."

He arched both eyebrows. "How trite."

They laughed again.

Anna thought, *Look at us. We're having fun together!* Who would ever have believed it? The Brat and the old Stick-in-the-Mud actually enjoying each other's company. It was, she suspected, as close to having her dreams come true as she would ever get.

Chapter Ten

"See!" Gilli ran into the parlor and came to an abrupt halt directly in front of Anna. "Here she is!"

Anna bit her lips. The skinny gray-on-gray striped cat hung by the neck from the crook of Gilli's arm, its also-gray eyes staring off into space. Anna would have thought it was paralyzed or traumatized if not for the lazy curl of the tip of its tail.

"He," Reeves corrected, leaning against the doorjamb. He had removed his coat and tie and rolled back the cuffs of his shirtsleeves. "Here *he* is."

Gilli nodded and announced, "Her name's Special."

"*His* name is Special."

"Uh-huh," Gilli agreed, petting the cat's narrow head. "Do you like her collar?"

Anna looked to Reeves, waiting for his correction. He shrugged and shook his head as if to say that it was pointless. Anna cleared her throat, looked at Gilli and commented, "It's, um, pink."

"Special likes pink!" Gilli declared. "Don't you, sweetie cat goodie dear?" She peppered her endearments with kisses to the cat's ears. Other than a single twitch, the cat might have been a stuffed toy.

Hypatia showed up in the doorway beside Reeves. She sent an exasperated look at Gilli, shoulders slumping.

"Gilli dear, what are you doing with that cat *now?* Luncheon is on the table. Come along. Reeves, see Anna into the dining room, will you?"

"With pleasure," he said, straightening away from the door frame. He strolled toward Anna just as Hypatia swept Gilli and the cat from the room.

"Poor Hypatia," he remarked, "overcome by a three-year-old."

"And a cat named Special," Anna added, grinning.

"I suggested we name him Catatonic, but only the vet thought that was funny."

Anna sputtered laughter.

"You laugh," Reeves said, eyes sparkling, "but I spent a minor fortune on that critter before the veterinarian could convince Hypatia that it would make a safe house pet, although the jury's still out on its mental health."

"I adopted a baby possum once," Anna told him, still sputtering.

Reeves grinned. "Tansy must have loved that."

"She didn't know. Until it escaped. Silly thing fainted every time I got near it, or pretended to, then one day it bit me and ran."

He shook his head, still grinning. "Don't think that's going to happen in this case."

She lifted her eyebrows. "How can you say that?"

As if on cue, a high, plaintive *"mmmmrrrrrroooowwww"* began to echo through Chatam House. Reeves crooked a finger at her. "You'll see."

Curious, she accompanied him to the dining room, where Hypatia sat with her head in her hands. Gilli occupied her usual chair, her feet swinging merrily as she spoke to a pet carrier on the seat next to her.

"There, there, Special baby doll dear. I right here."

Anna went to peer into the carrier. The cat was laid out on its side, as stiff as a corpse, the only sign of life that eerie, mournful, ceaseless howl that emanated from its open mouth. Alarmed, she looked to Reeves.

"What's wrong with it?"

"Gilli's not touching it, that's what's wrong with it," Reeves said.

"I will not have an animal loose at the table," Hypatia insisted.

Magnolia and Odelia entered through the butler's pantry then, carrying a loaf of bread and a pitcher of water, respectively.

"It's not working, Hypatia," Magnolia asserted, plunking the bread platter onto the table. Odelia placed the pitcher on the sideboard and cupped her hands around the twin fruit salads clipped to her earlobes.

"Oh, all right!" Hypatia snapped. "Anything to placate that absurd—" She cast a long-suffering look at Gilli. "Special." She sighed. "Anything for Special."

Magnolia promptly marched around the table, took the furry siren from its carrier, and draped it over a delighted Gilli's lap. The yowl abruptly faded to a purr. Gilli giggled and beamed.

While Magnolia went to rinse her hands, Reeves shook out his daughter's napkin and spread it over the now contented and apparently paralyzed cat, his gaze finding Anna's. She shook her head, amazed, but wisely kept her tongue glued to the floor of her mouth. Reeves came to escort her around the table to a chair, pulling it out for her and holding it until she smiled up at him. He went to seat his aunts before returning to take the chair at Anna's side.

Hypatia scowled and looked to Reeves. "Perhaps you would say the blessing?"

"Of course." He cleared his throat, and they all bowed their heads. "Most gracious Lord God, we thank You and we praise You for this, Thy bounty, given for the nourishment of our bodies. Most of all, Father, I thank You for each woman around this table, child and adult alike, given, no doubt, for the nourishment of my heart. In the name of Christ Jesus, amen."

Anna quivered inside. Had he purposefully included her in his prayer of thanksgiving? For the nourishment of his heart? As if. What was he going to say, thanks for everyone but Anna?

Gilli patted the cat under the napkin on her lap, crooning, "You, too, sweetie Special girl."

Anna thought it as likely that the cat was included in Reeves prayer as her. Oh, no, wait. It was a male.

"Gilli," Reeves said, as if reading Anna's thoughts, "that cat really is a boy."

"I know." Gilli hunched her shoulders and crooned, "My beautiful boy sweetie."

Reeves rolled his eyes. Anna covered her mouth. Hypatia looked like she might weep. Magnolia and Odelia, on the other hand, seemed content to dish out soup and pass around the salad. Reeves and Anna shared a smile, then set to enjoying their own lunch.

The meal passed in near silence, as if the purr of the comatose cat draped over Gilli's lap blocked all conversation. It was perhaps the most physically uncomfortable hour of Anna's life. She hadn't worn this dress since the wedding for which she'd bought it, over two years ago, and she had forgotten how the belt cut grooves in the tops of her hips, the stockings itched like steel wool and the heels of her shoes made her feet swell. Plus, if there existed in this world a dish she disliked more than split pea soup, she hadn't tasted it.

Yet, somehow, she'd never been happier. Or sadder.

After lunch, Anna offered to help clean up, but Reeves could have told her that the aunties would have none of it. They practically chased Reeves, Anna and Gilli from the dining room, along with the cat, of course. He suspected, from the knowing smile that Mags and Od shared, that they were indulging in a bit of matchmaking again, but he let it go. To his surprise, he enjoyed spending time with Anna, and he'd been thinking a lot about that kiss on the stairwell.

As much as he'd tried to tell himself that it had been an impulsive expression of gratitude, he knew better. Oh, it had been impulsive, all right, and gratitude was part of it, but that kiss had been as much about him as her. He didn't want to be alone. He had never wanted to be alone, and in the deepest well of his soul, he believed that God intended him to marry, despite the mistake he had made with Marissa. If the very idea of a "him and Anna" still boggled his mind, well, at least it was a more open and informed mind than it had been.

He suggested to her that they move to the library in hopes of discussing the dossier of information that he'd given her the last time they'd been there. He truly wanted Anna to be happy, but the most he could do was encourage her to look for another job. Before he could bring up the subject, however, Gilli seized upon the opportunity for a story. Anna took down a picture book, not a child's book but a nature book of desert photos, finding a surprising picture of a lizard, snake and hare in close proximity. Soon she and Gilli, a purring Special draped over one arm, had spun a fascinating tale of animals that cooperated to find water and shelter from the sun.

Afterward, Gilli screwed up her face and asked, "What is berrow?"

"Burrow," Anna corrected, reaching for a paper and pen that someone had left on the library table earlier. Quickly, she sketched a picture of a lizard squeezing into a snake's burrow, explaining as she drew.

"O-o-oh," Gilli said. Then she wrinkled her nose. "I wouldn't want to live in the dirt. And not in the bush, either. That's where Special had to live, isn't it, dear baby sugar?" She stroked the cat as she spoke.

While listening to the story then watching Anna sketch, an idea had come to Reeves, one he wanted to explore with Anna, but just then Gilli yawned and duty called.

"Someone needs a nap."

Gilli immediately put up a howl. He just shook his head at her pleas.

"Can I help tuck you in again?" Anna asked, and that did it.

"Okay," Gilli conceded glumly.

They all went out and climbed the stairs together. Gilli carried the cat in a chokehold, but Reeves had learned from experience not to tamper with the arrangement. Whenever anyone tried to help her find a seemingly gentler way to handle it, the ridiculous animal hissed and showed its fangs. Reeves had no doubt that it would take off a finger if it sensed that anyone meant to truly separate it from Gilli. Besides, after showing her what would hurt the cat, the vet had said that the animal would teach them how it wanted to be handled. So far, the cat wanted to be handled only by Gilli, and obviously, no matter how awkward it looked, she wasn't hurting the silly thing. To her, the cat was a person, the dearest and sweetest of all beings, and she was wounded by anyone who suggested otherwise. She spoke to the animal as if she expected it to reply.

"We got to take a nap. Daddy says the world is better from a nap, but I think it's good without it. Don't you? Hmm?"

Despite hiding many a grin, they made short work of tucking in Gilli and her cat, which curled up next to her on her pillow and glared at them balefully until they left the room. They were headed back down the stairs when Reeves asked, "The library or the sunroom?"

To his disappointment, Anna grimaced. "I hate to say it, but I need to go. If I don't change my clothes soon I'll scream."

He could understand the sentiment. He felt the same way every evening when he came in from work. Still, it was a shame. She looked awfully good in that dress. And those shoes… Whoa.

"Lunch was interesting, to say the least. Will you thank your aunts for me?"

He put on a polite smile. "Sure. After I walk you to your car."

They slipped on their coats, and Reeves opened the door. Cold air and bright sunshine slapped them in equal measures. The light angled perfectly to slice beneath the overhang of the porch, which usually provided shade.

They walked across the planking on the verandah to the top of the brick steps.

"So what did you think of the sermon?" he asked. He'd been wanting to know all afternoon.

She shrugged, pausing at the very edge of the porch. "I thought it was interesting. Except I didn't quite get what he meant about peace." She waved a hand. "The control of the mind..."

"The mind *controlled by* the Spirit," Reeves corrected gently.

"Is life and peace," she finished. "But what does that mean?" The way she said the word *peace* told him a lot. He gathered his words carefully.

"I know that when I can't find any peace it's because I'm not yielded to the control of the Holy Spirit. I just don't always know how to let go of whatever's cutting me up."

"How do you find out?"

Looking down, he admitted, "The hard way, usually."

She snorted at that. "Doesn't sound like you."

"Oh, yes, it does." Sighing, he looked her straight in the face. "Sometimes I think I do everything the hard way."

She shook her head, refusing to believe it, and that pleased him so much that he smiled and said, "Lately, though, it seems to have gotten a little easier. I seem to have acquired some wisdom from somewhere."

She considered then nodded. "I can see how your aunts might contribute to that."

He looked back at her in surprise. "True. But I was talking about you."

"Me?" She laughed as if it was a joke.

He spread his hands. "Anna, I've learned more about parenting my daughter from you than anyone else, ever."

Her jaw dropped. "Why, that can't be!"

"You've helped me understand how she thinks," he insisted, tapping his temple with his forefinger. "That's helped me change how I deal with her. What I wouldn't give to be able to read her as easily as you do."

"The only thing I do easily is make mistakes!" Anna exclaimed.

A bark of laughter escaped him. "Then that makes two of us. Though I suspect it's a universal problem."

"Why is it so easy to mess up and so hard to get things right?" she wondered.

"I don't know," Reeves told her, "but I suspect it has to do with what the pastor was talking about this morning. We don't keep our minds on the things of God as much as we should. Instead, we dwell on everything that can and has gone wrong, everything we can't do or mess up ourselves." Wow. Was he talking to her or himself?

Acknowledging his words with a pensive nod, she stepped down onto the brick. Aware that she was thinking over what he'd said, he took her by the elbow and led her down the remaining steps to the walkway.

"I think you're right," she said, "and I think that was exactly the message I needed to hear this morning."

"Funny," he said, "I was thinking the same thing about myself." They stepped onto the gravel, and he dropped his hand.

When she looked up, he expected another question. Instead, she said, "Thank you for the invitation to lunch."

"You're welcome." An idea popped into his head, and before he could even think it through, it was coming out of his mouth. “Say, why don’t you come for a run with me in the morning?”

He hadn’t known her eyes could go that wide. “Running? In the morning?”

“Yeah, I’ve started running in the morning rather than the evening so I can spend more time with Gilli.” And not only was his daughter happy about it, his stress level at work had dropped precipitately.

“Oh. Um…well, what time?”

“Sixish?”

“S-s-s—” She coughed behind her fist. “Six.” Nodding, she smiled. “In the morning?”

Delighted, he grinned and followed her around the car, telling her where to meet him in Buffalo Creek’s expansive Chataugua Park.

“Maybe we can talk after,” he suggested.

“About what?”

“Oh, I don’t know. The database, if you’ve had a chance to look it over. I’ve got an idea I’d like to run by you, too.”

“A-all right,” she said, letting herself into her car. Smiling, she started up the battered little coupe and pulled away.

Pleased, Reeves waved farewell, but as he jogged back up the steps and into the house, the hard truth of Anna’s earlier words came back to him.

The only thing I do easily is make mistakes.

Man, could he ever relate to that.

Maybe he was making a mistake right now, with her.

Or maybe it was time that he took this morning’s sermon to heart, kept his mind on the things of God and allowed the Spirit to take control, for wherever God led was the right path. Suddenly he realized that his fears, doubts, assumptions and self-protective limits were just so much minutiae that he'd allowed to crowd out the things of God. No wonder he'd lost his way!

Lead me, O Lord, he thought, *and where You lead, I will follow. I want the kind of life that You want me to have. I won't try to make it happen myself this time, and I won't let the mistakes that I've made in the past hold me back from Your will. In Christ I am forgiven, and in Him I will do better, for myself, for Gilli. And for Anna.*

The database? Anna thought. He wanted to talk about that jam-packed folder of information he'd given her? After they went running at six o'clock in the blooming morning! Anna could not believe what she'd just agreed to. She couldn't get herself to work by eight, let alone haul her lazy behind out to a park by six a.m.!

"Say, why don't you come for a run with me in the morning?" she mimicked, sitting at a stop sign at the intersection of Chatam Boulevard and Main. She threw up her hands. "Sure! What time?" Banging her head on the steering wheel, she groaned. "Just kill me now."

The driver in the car behind her beeped his horn. She stomped the accelerator and winced as pain shot through her foot. That, she suspected, would soon be nothing by comparison. In the morning when she collapsed in an aching heap on the ground, Reeves would be all too aware that she was not who he evidently thought her to be.

She was nothing like him. Not only was she no spiritual giant, she couldn't run a business, couldn't run a relationship, couldn't run her own life, couldn't run, period. Maybe she could identify with Gilli, but that just made her the equivalent of a three-year-old! If she had a real brain in her head, she'd feign illness and beg off their running date before bedtime. Instead, she changed her clothes and went to buy running shoes. Then, in order to stay out of Tansy's way, she took the "dossier" to the coffee house and went through it line by line, cramming as if Reeves was going to give her an oral exam on the morrow.

Hours later, her brain clogged with data, Anna treated herself to a hearty dinner. Afterward she went straight home to bed, where she replayed over and over everything that had been said, done and read throughout the entire day, from standing before her mirror that morning until she'd crawled between the sheets. Oddly, the thing that she kept circling back around to was that morning's sermon.

"The work of Christ on the cross set us free from the law of sin and death," the pastor had said. "That law demands sacrifice for sin, and should we die in our sin, without the cleansing of sacrifice, the law condemns us to true death, an eternity separated from God."

Jesus had made Himself the sacrifice, the pastor had explained. Perfect and without sin, He sacrificed His earthly body and life, once and for all, rising again to ascend into heaven and His rightful place.

"Do you want life?" the preacher had asked. "Accept the Lord's sacrifice."

That part Anna understood, but she'd never thought about what the preacher had said later.

"Fix your mind on Christ Jesus and keep it there. Learn everything He has to teach you through His word. Dwell in His Spirit so that when difficult times come you have the strength and the certainty to face them."

She remembered Reeves saying that he didn't always

know how to let go of whatever was cutting him up. He'd termed it as not being yielded to the Holy Spirit. She wondered just what he meant by that. Did it have to do with fixing one's mind on Jesus?

She lay upon her bed and prayed as she had never prayed before, almost as if in conversation with her Lord. Her last thought as she finally slid into unconsciousness was that for the first time she didn't feel alone.

The alarm started going off at five. At half past, Anna finally hauled herself out of bed. After scrambling into her running gear, she hurried out to the car. Ten minutes later she stood within the inky shade of an immense hickory tree and watched Reeves stretch beneath the watery light of a vapor lamp perched high atop a pole beside a bench. The jogging track snaked through the trees and over the bridge that crossed the rambling creek that gave the town its name. He was already sweaty, his caramel-streaked nut brown hair darkened by perspiration, which meant that he'd been running for some time before she'd even gotten there.

"Oh, you are so out of your league," she told herself. "You're going to wind up in the emergency room." She wondered how many coronaries this track produced every year and deemed it a good thing that the hospital had been built nearby. Reeves straightened and waved. It was too late to rethink, so she picked up her feet, joining him just heartbeats later.

"Good morning," he called as she drew near.

"Morning."

A fellow with a big belly huffed by them. Obviously, she wasn't the only one out here freezing her toes off and courting a heart attack.

"Cold?" Reeves asked, and just the word spoken aloud made her shudder.

"Uh-huh."

"Let's get you warmed up then." He led her over to the bench. "Have you done this before?"

"Sure. About a decade ago in gym class. Whenever I couldn't get out of it."

Reeves chuckled. "Put your foot up on the seat and lean forward, keeping everything else straight."

She did as instructed. "Like this?"

"Looks right." He went down on his haunches and squeezed her calf. She nearly jumped over the bench. "Again," he ordered.

Her face flaming, she did as told until he decided that she'd properly loosened up her muscles. Surprisingly, she already felt warmer.

"Now what?"

"Now we walk," he answered, nodding toward the narrow track.

Anna brightened immediately. Walking she could manage.

The track was just wide enough for them to walk side by side, their shoulders occasionally touching. He asked how her evening had gone. She shrugged and said that she'd spent it at the coffee shop then blathered on about how it was one of her favorite places and what her favorite drinks were and her favorite muffins, even her favorite barista, for pity's sake.

"She can make a perfect flower right in the center of the cup with the cream. Says she learned it in Seattle."

"Imagine that," Reeves replied with a grin. "Let's pick up the pace a bit."

Two minutes later, they were jogging and five minutes after that running. Reeves had the most fluid gait. It was impossible to stay even with their arms pumping in time to their strides, so she naturally fell back a bit, all the better to enjoy the show. The man's head stayed level while he ran, his long paces steady and gliding. She tried to match him stride for stride and found, to her surprise, that she could manage. For a time. And then she couldn't. Suddenly, without warning, she could no longer keep up. Just a minute or so later, she could no longer even breathe.

He seemed to know and slowed, but for Anna nothing would do but a full stop. Bending at the waist, she gasped for air. He jogged back to her and pulled her up straight, propelling her along the track again, this time at a walk.

"Come on. Walk it out. Otherwise you're going to hurt."

"As. Opposed. To. What?" she gasped out.

"As opposed to just being sore," he told her with a chuckle, slowing the pace.

After a while, she could breathe again. "I don't think I'm cut out for this," she told him, shaking her head.

"Ah, you're a natural," he refuted with a smile. "Take it from me. You just need a bit of conditioning. It would be nice to have a running buddy."

She groaned, but inside she was doing backflips. She was a natural at something? And they were going to be running buddies! Maybe. Why couldn't they have done this in high school? If he had shown just the least bit of interest in her back then she might have scrapped her rebellious habits just to please him. Then she might not have blown her chances at college by skipping senior finals week and settling for a D average.

Water under the bridge, she told herself. Sadly, it was too late for all that. Her life had been set in stone long ago.

He put her through the stretches again, and this time she watched as he did them and tried to copy his posture. Finally, she collapsed upon the bench. Reeves reached beneath a towel on the ground and brought up two bottles of water. He tossed her one, and she broke the seal, drinking greedily.

"Thanks."

"Yep."

They sat and slowly emptied the bottles, watching the sun come up and day gradually take over. Reeves hooked his elbows over the edge of the bench.

"I've had this idea I've been meaning to talk to you about."

"Oh? Something you didn't think to put in that portfolio?"

"Yeah." He waved a hand. "Just an idea. The only way I can think of to describe it is as a book without words."

"Come again?"

"You know, for toddlers, little kids like Gilli. I mean, they can't read, right? And I got to thinking about how you take a picture and make up a story about it."

"Well, that's just because of how I draw," she said dismissively. "Every time I lay down a sketch, I'm basically drawing a story in my head. Hmm." She bit her lip, thinking about that. "Actually, I have wondered what stories other people might dream up around one of my drawings."

"There. You see? It fits. What if you could come up with a series of drawings that suggest a story."

"But don't dictate it," she muttered to herself, envisioning a series of panels based on the skating ballerina concept.

"I'm sure there are parents who lack the imagination to utilize something like that," he admitted, "but—"

"Not many kids," she stated, feeling her excitement build.

"I knew I was onto something," Reeves declared. He stood then looked down at her. "Shall we talk this out over breakfast?"

She nodded eagerly, aware that a hole had opened in the bottom of her stomach during the past few minutes. She popped up with more energy than she'd expected to find. "Where do you want to go?"

He considered. "What time do you have to be at work?"

Work! She grabbed his arm and twisted it until she could read his watch. That could *not* be the time!

"Beans!" She lurched away, crying, "I'm going to be late!"

He put his hands to his waist, calling, "I guess that means breakfast is off?"

"Breakfast, lunch, maybe even dinner if I can't shower in five minutes flat!" she yelled.

She drove off and left him there, shaking his head. Dennis was not going to be a happy camper if she was late again. Depressing the accelerator, she took a deep breath.

"Fix your mind on Jesus," she whispered. "Fix your mind on Jesus."

Chapter Eleven

Reeves came in whistling that evening. The quartet of vehicles all but blocking the drive at the front of the house told him that the aunties were holding another of their meetings. They had clearly shifted into high gear with their plans for the fund-raiser. The place was like Grand Central Station. He'd run into one committee after another last week, and this week he expected it to be a daily occurrence, but today he didn't mind.

Gilli came through the side door just as he climbed out of the car and greeted him with a cheery, "Hi, Daddy!"

When he held out his arms, she literally leaped off the top step into them and gave him a noisy kiss. How wonderful it was to be loved by his baby girl! Hugging her close, he asked, "How's my sugar?"

"Goody good."

"Where's Special?"

"Getting her milk."

"I thought the vet said to go easy on the milk."

"But she already had 'nuff cans. Chester said she couldn't have no more."

"I see." As he carried Gilli into the house and set her on her feet, he asked just how many cans of cat food she had served Special that day. She'd already proved that she could open the small pull-top tins with surprising ease.

Gilli shrugged evasively. "I dunno."

Reeves frowned. Wasn't a child who could learn to skate old enough to know better than to go into the pantry and help herself to all the cat food her schizophrenic pet wanted? "Do you remember how many the animal doctor said Special could have in a day?" Reeves asked, going down on his haunches to bring their faces level. Gilli just looked at him. He held up three fingers. "This many."

"Three," Gilli said, "like me."

Three. Old enough to be lonely without her daddy, not so old when indulging her first pet. "So how many did you give Special today?"

She held up four fingers, then five. When she got to six, she shrugged again and tucked her hands behind her. Reeves suppressed a sigh. A girl with a mommy-in-name-only could be forgiven for showering too much attention on a devoted animal. Still, there were boundaries. "From now on," he instructed, "you feed Special only what an adult gives you for her. Him."

Gilli nodded.

"The proper response is, 'Yes, sir,'" he coached.

"Yezer."

As she ran off to make sure Special had lapped up her—his!—fill of milk, Reeves made a mental note to tell Hilda to move all cat food to the top shelf of the pantry. Best make sure the milk was out of reach, too. Call it preventive parenting.

Making his way to the cloakroom, he hung up his coat before heading for the stairs. He wasn't the least surprised to find Tansy Burdett in the foyer. Naturally, he assumed that she served on one or more of his aunts' committees, but he also knew that she'd want to pump him for information about Anna, information that he was determined not to give her. Nevertheless, he smiled congenially as he started up the steps.

"Hello, Mrs. Burdett. When you see my aunts will you tell them I've gone up to change please?"

Behind him, she said, "You took my granddaughter to church."

Reeves paused, telling himself not to respond, but then he turned to look down at her. "I did not. She took herself to church."

"You had something to do with it," Tansy insisted.

"I merely asked her why she didn't attend worship."

"And what did she say?"

He considered telling Tansy that she was the reason Anna had foregone worship, but he said instead, "What's important is that Anna decided to do the right, best thing."

The skepticism in Tansy's expression offended him on Anna's behalf. "But you brought her here to lunch afterward," Tansy insisted, as if she could not bear to give her granddaughter the benefit of the doubt. "And you were also seen jogging in the park together this morning."

"So? What of it?"

"So it seems to me that you are not as uninterested in my granddaughter as you first claimed."

Irritated, Reeves managed to speak calmly. "My interest in your granddaughter, or lack of it, is really none of your business." Turning, he stepped upward.

"I'll make it worth your while to marry her."

Reeves froze, wondering if he could possibly have heard Tansy correctly. Slowly he turned, his head tilting to one side. "Did you just try to bribe me to marry your granddaughter?"

Tansy looked him square in the eye. "Everyone thinks the Chatams are made of money, and they are. But you're a Leland, and there isn't enough money to go around in that branch."

Reeves glared at her until he was sure he had his temper under control. "I earn a comfortable living, thank you very much, and even if I didn't, no one marries for money in this day and age."

"Unless I miss my guess, the first Mrs. Leland did," Tansy said smugly.

That stung, but he couldn't argue with it. Besides, that was not important. Didn't she realize that something like this could only hurt Anna? He stepped back down to the foyer floor and demanded, "Why are you doing this?"

Tansy's face set in lines as hard as those of her too-yellow hair. "I want my granddaughter happily married. What's wrong with that?"

"It's her life. That's what's wrong with that."

Tansy's nose wrinkled in a sneer. "I've seen what she's done with her life. Trapped in a dead-end job, living in a dingy, depressing apartment too small to turn around in, no real friends, a date once in a blue moon. The one saving grace is that she hasn't tried to drown herself in alcohol or snort her problems up her nose the way her parents did."

"I don't call that a small thing," Reeves stated flatly, "and neither is your interference in Anna's life."

Tansy lifted her chin, shoulders squared like a general. "Someone has to do something, and I know what's best for my granddaughter. She needs a husband. You seem to have a beneficial influence on her, and she always did have a crush on you."

"That's ridiculous."

"You really don't know?" Tansy chuckled. "I thought you were smarter than that. When she was a teenager I used to find sheets of torn notebook paper in her trash can." She mimicked handwriting. "Mrs. Reeves Leland. Anna Leland. Reeves and Anna Leland."

Reeves must have gaped at her for a full minute. Anna had had a crush on him in high school? That's what all that torment was about? Surely not. But what if that had been the case? How mortified would Anna be after keeping that secret all these years? He went straight from shock to outrage in three seconds flat. "How dare you reveal such a thing? Have you no respect for your granddaughter?"

"I thought you knew. Besides, what does it hurt? The truth is the truth."

"If it's true, then it's Anna's truth," he insisted. "She's entitled to decide if and when she reveals her secrets. In fact, she's entitled to make her own decisions about everything, period. To make such a revelation to further your own cause is cold and heartless."

Tansy jerked as if he'd struck her, bawling, "I'm not heartless. I only want what's best for my granddaughter!"

"You want what *you* want," he rebutted, his voice rising, "to the point of trying bribery! That's not just selfish, it's sick!" The sudden appearance of the aunties in the foyer was enough to forestall further explosion, but Reeves wasn't about to back down.

Tansy stood with military stoicism, shoulders back, chin up. "I know my granddaughter," she declared defensively.

"You know nothing about Anna," he told her. "You say I've been a 'beneficial influence' on her, but it's actually the other way around. Anna's the one who's had a 'beneficial influence' on me."

"I certainly see no evidence of it," Tansy snapped. The aunties gasped. Tansy's chin ratcheted up another inch or so.

"Then I'm sure you want better for Anna than me," Reeves said evenly. "Anna certainly deserves better."

"I'm more concerned with what she needs, and I'll do what I have to do to see that she gets it," Tansy vowed. With that, she executed a neat about-face and marched into the parlor. Casting worried, apologetic glances behind them, Magnolia and Odelia hurried after her.

"I'm so sorry, dear," Hypatia said to Reeves, rushing forward. "We had no idea what she was up to when she left the room, but it's all our fault, just the same. If we hadn't planted that ridiculous notion about you and Anna in her head..."

Anna Leland. Anna and Reeves Leland.

In some ways it felt as if his world had turned upside down. And in some ways it felt as if it had been turned right side up!

Hypatia wrung her hands. "Oh, poor Anna. I'm afraid we've set Tansy off on a new tangent. We have to fix this. Is it possible, do you think, to convince Tansy that this scheme of hers is hopeless?"

Reeves shook his head, still reeling. "I don't know."

"We have to try. We started this. We have to stop it. Don't you think so?"

"I—I'm not sure," Reeves admitted, barely attending. Had Tansy always been this controlling? Yes, of course, she had. In fact, she'd probably been worse. No wonder Anna had left home at the first opportunity.

"What if we got everyone together and hashed this out?" Hypatia was saying. "All of us together, we might make Tansy see reason, don't you think? It might nip Tansy's meddling in the bud. At the very least, Anna would know that she has support. It would need much prayer to work, of course. Much prayer."

Prayer. Reeves nodded absently, wearied by the weight of his anger at Tansy and a growing sense of all-too-familiar guilt.

Mrs. Reeves Leland. Anna Leland. Anna and Reeves Leland.

She had liked him. Liked him. And he'd assumed the very opposite.

Hadn't it been the same with Gilli? Every time she'd misbehaved, he'd assumed on some level that she hated him for letting her mommy leave, and all along she'd been doing everything in her power to grab his attention and hold it. He hadn't seen it until the bees had driven Nanny away and brought them here to Chatam House where they'd met Anna. Anna, who had taught him so much about his daughter—and himself. Anna whom he had treated so disdainfully in the past.

"Should I do it then?" Hypatia's voice interrupted his thoughts. He looked down at her blankly.

"Uh, whatever you think best."

She bit her lip and nodded as if still uncertain. Not really cognizant of Hypatia's concerns, Reeves let it go. Who could be more competent than Aunt Hypatia, after all? As he mounted the stairs once more, his thoughts sought heavenly counsel.

Father in heaven, I've been such a lunkhead. All those years that I judged Anna's behavior so harshly, when I had no idea what she was dealing with, no understanding of her at all, when a kind word from me might have made a difference, a ride in my car in the rain, a friendly gesture, a smile of acknowledgment... But I did none of those things. And after all of that, she still found it within her heart to take my little girl under her wing, to reach out to me in friendship and honesty. What a fool I have been.

God forgive him.

And Anna, too. If she could.

"And how are you this afternoon?" The voice of Reeves Leland traveled over the telephone line, through the receiver, into her ear and across her every nerve ending with a rush of heat.

Anna turned her back to the workroom and kept her voice low. With Dennis on the rampage again, it wouldn't do to get caught mooning over a caller.

"In hot water," she muttered.

"You're not talking about soaking away your muscle aches, I assume."

Every muscle in Anna's body had screamed when she'd crawled into the tub last night, but this morning she'd only felt a few twinges as she'd showered, dressed and headed out. She should have made it to work with minutes to spare, but no. She had to get stuck at one of the town's many railroad crossings by the longest train in history. Did that matter to Dennis, though? Not one bit.

"I feel fine. It's a work thing."

"I hope it's not this call. Some workplaces have a rule about personal calls, I know, but I tried to call you at home last night only your number's unlisted."

Personal calls. She had to quip around her heart, which had leaped up into her throat. "Yeah, I know. It infuriates Tansy that she has to stop by to harangue me."

He did not laugh, not even a chuckle. "I'll keep it brief," he said after a pause. "Are you up for a run tomorrow morning?"

Anna put her hand over her mouth to hide her pleased smile, but then she deflated. If she was late for work one more time, Dennis would can her for sure, especially with the BCBC job winding down. Should she risk it?

Reeves went on in a coaxing voice. "I was out there all by myself today. Not nearly so much fun without a buddy."

Anna grit her teeth to keep from saying yes. Maybe if they started a little earlier… Right. Like she could manage that. It took a good half hour to get her brain started in the morning.

"Oh, man. I just don't think I can do it."

For several seconds Reeves said nothing then, "Anna, if I've done anything, recently or in the past—"

"What? No, no, no." She hated to tell him that she couldn't trust herself to get to work on time. If she were more conscientious or more mature or just more of a morning person, she'd be able to manage an early run, but right now, having been late twice in a row, it was just asking for trouble. "This is on me. I'm just not, you know, cut out for early morning activity." She thought of Gilli and added, "But you, now, you need your evenings free for your daughter."

Maybe, she thought, when Dennis got off the warpath she could try again. She'd just tell Reeves that she'd changed her mind and decided that she needed to get into shape. Right then she made a plan. Starting tonight she was going to go to bed and get up an hour earlier every day, and just to be on the safe side, she'd set the clocks in the apartment forward by fifteen minutes, too. She'd train herself to get up earlier and be out on that jogging trail in a couple weeks.

"Maybe I can call you sometime anyway," Reeves said after a bit. "Just to hear an adult voice, you know? I mean, it won't be long now before we'll be back in our own place, just the two of us, Gilli and me."

"Sure," Anna answered brightly. "Anytime you need to hear an adult voice." She waited two seconds. "I can always turn on the television and lay the phone next to it."

He laughed, finally. "I'll remember that."

"Great, and do a favor for me, will you? Tell your aunts that I'll be around with the final print run tomorrow."

"They'll be happy to hear it."

"Tell them to expect me around noon," she said, thinking that it wouldn't hurt her cause with Dennis any if she made the delivery on her lunch hour rather than during the workday.

"I'll tell them," he said softly.

"Thanks." She rang off with a cheery, "Later, alligator," but then she hugged herself, wondering just how long she'd have to wait for that next call.

Reeves hung up the phone and leaned back in his desk chair, regret weighing heavily in his chest. Well, that answered that. Whether she'd had a crush on him all those years ago or not, Anna obviously didn't think of him that way any longer. If she did, she'd have accepted his invitation. Not a morning person, she'd basically said. Yet, she'd been out there once already, and she'd put forth a fine performance, too. Apparently, the company had not been worth the effort, however.

Well, what was a high school crush, anyway? They never lasted, rarely turned into anything real. Had he not been stupid as a fence post all those years ago—and all those between then and now, for that matter—he might have treated her a little more kindly. They might have come away friends, at least. Instead, in his judgmental mind they'd been enemies. He finally saw her for who and what she was, someone admirable, strong and true, clever, beautiful, giving… She saw him as…what? Unworthy of her time and effort. Never let it be said that his was not a just God.

"Okay, Lord," he prayed aloud, "if that's how You want it. You know best."

Didn't mean he liked it, of course, but he couldn't help thinking that if he'd had that attitude about Marissa, he most likely wouldn't have married her. Of course, then he wouldn't have Gilli. It occurred to him that he hadn't heard from Marissa lately. Maybe she'd finally figured out that he wasn't going to offer her money to stay away, not that he wouldn't prefer that. As long as she was Gilli's mother, though, Gilli needed to see her.

Right now he was more likely to pay Marissa to make Gilli think she cared. Of course, if he did give Marissa money, she could use it to make his life miserable by hiring a lawyer and petitioning the court for physical custody. She wouldn't win, but it would it be a huge headache, which she undoubtedly knew, one he might be willing to pay to avoid. No doubt that was her game. On the other hand…

He shook his head. What did it say, he wondered, that he'd rather fill his head with useless speculation about Marissa than admit how much it hurt for Anna to refuse to go running with him? Nothing good. He very much feared that it said nothing good. Regret, it seemed, was to be his companion, one way or another, for the rest of his days.

Sunshine as clear as glass picked out bits of green in the straw-brown lawn in front of Chatam House. The heady scent of spring kissed the slight breeze that chilled the warming air. It was about time, Anna remarked to herself, scooping the stacked boxes on the backseat of her car into her arms. In true Texas fashion, the change in the weather had actually been startling. Only two days had passed since she'd met Reeves in the park for their run, but those two days had seemed like weeks.

She carried the boxes of auction catalogs to the front door, where she managed to hit the doorbell button with an elbow. It opened almost instantly. Magnolia said not a word in greeting, just turned back into the house and called, "Anna's here!"

Anna stepped into the foyer behind her and kicked the door closed with her foot. Odelia appeared, garbed in a flowered shirtwaist and pearl white cardigan, with what looked like yellow tennis balls sprouting from her earlobes. She clasped her hands together beneath her chubby, cleft chin and cried out, "Anna Miranda, how lovely!"

Hypatia arrived on the scene next, rushing and murmuring, "Excellent. Excellent." The three of them quickly divested Anna of the boxes, which they deposited on the foyer table. "You're just in time for lunch."

"Oh, no," Anna said. She should have realized when she'd chosen to deliver the material during her lunch hour that the Chatams would have a meal waiting on her. Suddenly, Gilli flew down the hall and barreled into her, arms outstretched.

"Anna, Anna!"

She staggered back, catching the girl in a crouching hug. "Hey, munchkin."

"Do you like fishy salad?" Gilli asked excitedly.

"Tuna salad," Magnolia corrected.

Actually, Anna loathed tuna salad. Tuna itself she had no problem with, but any fish mixed up with mayonnaise and whatever else, no, thanks.

"I'm afraid I grabbed a hot dog on the way over here," she said evasively. A chili cheese dog, in fact, eaten behind the wheel of her car.

The Chatams murmured regrets, but those got lost in Gilli's announcement.

"Special loves fishy salad!"

Hypatia gasped, and Magnolia moaned as Odelia hurried down the hall and through the dining room door, screeching, "No, cat! No! Get off that table!"

Magnolia looked at Hypatia, her cheeks rather pale. "Hot dogs sound good. I wonder if Hilda has any." She quickly trundled off toward the kitchen.

Anna cleared her throat to keep from laughing, as Hypatia was clearly not amused. Hypatia looked down at Gilli and instructed smartly, "I want you to take that cat upstairs and lock it in your suite, Gilli Leland, and I don't care if it howls its head off."

Gilli's lip puffed out, and for an instant Anna feared

she was going to argue, but even a child could tell when Hypatia Chatam had reached her limit. "'Kay, Auntie 'Patia," Gilli murmured, running off to the dining room.

Hypatia sighed. "The adventures of housing a cat," she said with a strained smile.

"Sorry about lunch," Anna ventured.

"It's not lunch I'm really concerned about," Hypatia said staunchly. "We were wondering if you'd come to dinner on Friday evening?"

Anna smiled. "Of course. I'd love to. Thank you for asking."

The cat yowled, and Hypatia put a hand to her head. "We've, ah, become so fond of you," she said, "and you've done such wonderful work for us."

"It was my pleasure," Anna told her honestly, "and I was paid. You don't have to go out of your way to thank me, you know."

"Well, it's not that exactly," Hypatia began, over the sounds of scrambling from the dining room. "Although we are very grateful, you understand. It's more of a..." Odelia yelped, and Hypatia floundered. "That is, well, Reeves and..." She cast a worried glance at the dining room door.

"Reeves will be here at dinner on Friday?" Anna pressed hopefully.

Hypatia glanced at her, "Yes, yes. Didn't I just say so?"

Clearing her throat, Anna did her best not to beam. "What time should I arrive?"

Suddenly the most awful caterwauling came from the dining room. Hypatia winced and replied succinctly, "Six-thirty."

Assuming that a cat fight, in the truest sense of the

term, was about to break out, Anna reached for the scrolled doorknob. "I'll see you then."

"Wonderful," Hypatia said, turning away. "Do excuse me."

Anna danced out onto the veranda, pulling the door closed behind her. Looked like she wouldn't have to sit home indefinitely waiting for that phone call, after all. She could, in fact, just tell Reeves on Friday that she'd changed her mind about those early morning runs. What was a job compared to spending time with Reeves Leland, anyway? If she stuck to her plan, he might well get busy and never call her. It wouldn't be the first time that had happened. And who knew where those morning runs might one day lead? This, after all, was not high school any longer.

She never dreamed that she might soon wish otherwise.

Chapter Twelve

Tansy showed up on Anna's doorstep at eight o'clock the next evening.

"I just want to be sure that you understand the significance of tomorrow's dinner," she announced, practically pushing her way inside the apartment.

Puzzled, Anna closed the door and turned to stand in front of it, her arms folded. "What would you know about it?"

"I know that you need a husband, and Reeves Leland is the ideal candidate," Tansy said, lifting her chin and smiling slyly.

Anna's jaw dropped. "I don't *need* a husband!" And if she did, Reeves would not be applying for the position.

"As if your job isn't hanging by a thread this very instant," Tansy scoffed.

"I can always get another job." In fact, she'd been thumbing through that dossier Reeves had given her. There were work-from-home positions that would allow her to concentrate on a new project she'd started, a project also inspired by Reeves.

"You wouldn't need a job if you had a husband," Tansy proclaimed.

Anna gaped, boggled by this new interest in her marital status. "That's nonsense. Husbands are more than paychecks, and lots of wives work. Besides, do you think I'd marry just so I could quit my job?"

"I think you'd marry for any reason at all if the right man asked you."

"The *right* man," Anna stressed, "not *any* man who could support me."

Tansy threw up her hands. "That's what I said! Why are you always arguing about nothing? You live to argue about nothing!"

"And you live to dictate to me!" Anna shot back. She slashed her arms down angrily. "I'm not going to debate this. You don't know what you're talking about anyway. Reeves isn't interested in me like that." It pained her to say it, but it was the truth. Even if he had kissed her that one time.

Gratitude, she reminded herself. Simple gratitude.

Still, he had invited her to go running. That wasn't exactly a date, but it could change, given time—and provided Tansy didn't get involved.

"He could be," Tansy was saying, "if you played your cards right." She swept a scathing glance over Anna's comfy sweats. "Wear something feminine. Like that dress you wore to church."

Anna rolled her eyes. That day had been a special case. She'd feel like a complete fool waltzing in there Friday evening in heels and nylons. That was not her usual style, and everyone at Chatam House well knew it by now.

"And don't worry," Tansy went on. "The rest of us will be there to smooth over any gaffes."

"The rest of us?" Anna yelped. "You won't be there."

"Oh, but I will." Tansy gave her a long look. "We're in agreement on this."

"We?" Anna stared at Tansy's smug smile, feeling the blood drain out of her head.

"Me and the Chatam sisters. They agree that Reeves could be the best thing to ever happen to you."

Anna actually felt light-headed. "You got the Chatams to set this up?"

"Dinner was actually Hypatia's idea," Tansy said, looking away, "but I believe that it's a wise course of action, especially if you take my advice to heart. For pity's sake, just try to fix the man's interest, will you? I've done my best to pave the way, give you a real opportunity with him."

"Opportunity," Anna echoed, horrified.

"It's what you've always wanted, isn't it? Since high school you've been dreamy-eyed over him."

Anna gasped. *Please, God, no.* That had been her secret, her one real secret. She couldn't bear it if her grandmother knew about her idiotic crush. And yet, she seemed to.

"Opportunity?" Anna repeated in angry disbelief. "You think you've engineered an opportunity to get me and Reeves together? What you've really done is ruined it! Even if he might have one day looked at me as someone he could love, I would never give you the satisfaction of falling in with your plans!"

Tansy reared back. "You can't be so idiotic as to not take what you want just to thwart me!"

"Can't I?" Anna cried, teetering on the edge of self-control. "Thwarting you has been my lifelong ambition! Isn't that what you've always said?" She reached behind her and yanked open the door. "Get out of my apartment!"

Something flashed across Tansy's face, not disappointment precisely or even sadness but something close to both. "I thought you'd be pleased," she said in a strange voice. "For once I actually thought you'd be pleased."

Anna refused to even think about what that look and that voice meant. All she wanted was for Tansy to leave before she dissolved into blubbering tears. To her relief, Tansy did just that, trudging through the door with her head down. Anna slammed it closed behind her and threw the deadbolt for good measure, then she collapsed into the chair in the corner.

Tansy and the Chatam sisters had plotted to bring her and Reeves together? Anna had always known, of course, that the Chatams were friends with her grandmother, but she'd never dreamed that they would stoop to Tansy's level of manipulation. She thought of all those late afternoon appointments when Reeves just happened to arrive home from work. Tansy must have put the idea in their heads. Oh, good grief. Had Tansy told them about that ridiculous crush? She clapped her hands over her ears as if that alone could undo their hearing of it.

"Dear God," she whispered, "Oh, dear God, please." But she already knew.

It really was ruined. She could never show her face at Chatam House or to Reeves Leland again.

The last thing Reeves wanted to do after a long Friday at work was stop by the grocery store to pick up tea bags, but he had his reasons. For one, it was the least he could do for his poor, put-upon aunts. The cat raid on the tuna salad the previous day had resulted in banishment—for both Special and Gilli, who had adamantly refused to leave their suite without her beloved pet. Everyone had been so upset that he'd thought it best to take dinner with her and Special in their rooms last evening. Today, fortunately, had offered no repeat of the previous day's events. He'd called home half a dozen times to make sure of it.

Cars jammed the parking lot of the aunties' preferred grocery. It was rush hour at the supermarket, with everyone just off work and trying to stock up for the weekend. Reeves consoled himself with the expectation of seeing Anna again over dinner in less than two hours. He'd been disappointed to be rebuffed when he'd called to ask her to go running again, so he'd been glad to learn on his way out the door this morning that the aunties had invited her to dinner tonight.

He wasn't sure what had occasioned the invitation, but he was grateful that they'd issued it. He wanted a chance to change Anna's mind about him. An apology might even be in order, if he could manage to explain his regretful behavior without revealing Tansy's deplorable tactics. Anna would no doubt be hurt by her grandmother's thoughtless, heavy-handed actions. Hopefully tonight's dinner would give him a perfect opportunity to make amends. Therefore, stop for tea bags, he would.

If he could somehow also find time to get by his house before dinner, he'd have his whole evening free, and his meeting tomorrow morning with the remodeling contractor would go much more quickly. Then maybe he and Gilli could actually do something fun this weekend to stay out of the aunties' hair. He wondered if they might find a movie that they could both enjoy. And if Anna might want to enjoy it with them. After his dealings with Tansy, his admiration for Anna had grown. He felt strongly that she deserved whatever enjoyment he and Gilli could give her.

Reeves found a parking spot far back in the lot and hiked in. He fought his way through a crowd gathered around the carts and another at the deli counter then cut through a side aisle to the correct section of the store. Finding the right brand required some minutes. The aunties were particular about their tea, but after living in their house these past weeks, even he was beginning to note the subtle differences in blends.

Finally, with the nearly weightless packet firmly in hand, he started toward the checkout, only to find one aisle after another clogged with shoppers pushing carts. He decided to cut all the way across to the frozen food section and skirt around the busy center of the store. Passing by the ice cream, he quickly turned down the frozen food aisle—and bumped smack into Anna.

They collided hard enough to knock the frozen entrée that she was examining out of her hand, and both instantly went down to retrieve it. Reeves snagged it first, owing to his longer arms.

"Glad to have run into you," he quipped.

"Sorry," she muttered, reaching for the small cardboard carton.

"Here you go." He returned it to her with a chuckle and drew her up to her feet, his hand beneath her elbow. "Not that you need it," he told her with a grin. "I hear Hilda's cooking a pork loin for our dinner."

"*Your* dinner," Anna retorted. Turning toward the

freezer, she yanked open the glass door and practically tossed the frozen entrée inside before reaching for another.

Reeves felt a *thunk* inside his chest, and several things occurred to him at once. First, she was angry, and not because he had bumped into her. Second, she was shopping for her dinner. Third, she wouldn't even look at him. Obviously, had she ever intended to come to Chatam House that evening, it would not have been to see him. That last stood out with painful clarity, but it all culminated in one conclusion.

"You're not coming."

Mutely, she shook her head.

"Why not? I'm sure my aunts are expecting you."

She snorted. "Me and my grandmother. Did you think I would go once I found out how Tansy had manipulated everything?"

Reeves winced. "You know about that?"

Anna hung her head, muttering, "She told me last night."

He clenched his fist and brought it to the center of his forehead. What was wrong with Tansy Burdett? Did she actively seek to hurt Anna? So much for only wanting what was best for her granddaughter!

"Anna, I'm so sorry," he said, dropping his hand. "I hoped you wouldn't find out."

She gaped at him. "You were going along with it?"

"No! How could you think I'd take her money?"

"Her money? Don't you mean her granddaughter? That's what she wants, you know, to get us together."

"How could I not when she offered me money to marry you?"

Anna goggled, her eyes going impossibly wide. "You're telling me she offered you *money* to *marry me?*"

Reeves clamped a hand over his mouth. She hadn't known!

"I—I thought…when you said you knew about her manipulation…"

"Of dinner tonight! We were all supposed to eat together."

He shook his head, trying to make sense of this. "All? Wait. Tansy, too?"

"Of course, Tansy, too! They're all in it together, my grandmother and your aunts. I'm somehow supposed to, quote, fix your interest, unquote."

Reeves moaned. He couldn't say that the aunties would never do such a thing because, after all, they had already dabbled in matchmaking between him and Anna, but he was shocked that they would involve Tansy, especially after that scene at Chatam House on Monday evening.

"I can't believe…" His voice trailed off as he recalled Hypatia saying something about trying to convince Tansy that her plan was hopeless. "Wait a minute. That's not what this is about."

Anna's face set. "But my grandmother specifically said—"

"That's Tansy's agenda for tonight," Reeves interrupted firmly. "My aunts have something else entirely in mind, I'm sure of it." He tapped his temple with the tip of one forefinger, trying to recall Hypatia's exact words, something about convincing Tansy and supporting Anna. "It was after I blasted Tansy for mentioning the crush."

Anna gasped. "She…she told you?"

"What?"

"She told you!" Anna warbled, tears filling her eyes. Before he could ask her to explain, she dropped the frozen entrée and ran.

"Anna!"

Ignoring him, she disappeared around the corner. Stunned, Reeves looked at the flimsy packet of tea bags in his hand. Then he simply tossed it and went after her.

Anna ran blindly through the supermarket, stumbling into people and careening around carts and displays in a desperate bid to get away from the mortifying truth. Her grandmother had tried to bribe a man to marry her, and of course it had to be the only man she'd ever cared about! Even worse, Reeves knew how she'd pined for him, how she'd hoped and prayed and dreamed that he would look her way and finally truly see her. The humiliation was worse than anything Anna had ever imagined.

She got to her car and reached for the door handle before realizing that the keys were still in the pocket of her jeans. She was trying to dig them out when a hand clamped down on her shoulder and spun her around.

"I'm sorry."

She shook her head. What did he have to be sorry about? It was all Tansy's fault. It was always Tansy's fault. Capturing her with his hands, he splayed his fingers in her hair, his palms covering her ears.

"I'm sorry I hurt you. I didn't know. I didn't understand what it must have been like for you."

Anna felt her face burning. She couldn't think, couldn't reason. All she could do was shake her head. He dropped his hands to her shoulders, gripping hard to hold her in place because she couldn't seem to stand still.

"I'm sorry, Anna, for all those years that I judged your behavior without ever understanding the reason for it. I finally realized what you were fighting, how hard you worked to stand up to her."

Anna brought her hands to her head, struggling to think and coming up against the same awful idea. He knew. He knew her most carefully guarded secret. "What e-exactly d-did she tell you?"

"After she attempted to bribe me, you mean?"

Anna rolled her eyes at that. "Of all the stupid… I mean, like that was going to work. You're a Chatam, for goodness' sake."

"I'm a Leland," he corrected dryly, his grip on her shoulders intensifying, "and the Lelands don't actually have any money."

"What difference does it make?" Anna asked, shrugging his hands away with thoughtless impatience. "It's not like you care about that."

"No," he said rather cheerfully, "I don't." Grinning, he leaned forward and said, "And neither do you."

She looked up at him, tired of this runaround. She had to know. "What did Tansy say to you?"

Reeves smiled sympathetically. "About the, um, crush, you mean?"

Wincing, Anna squeezed her eyes closed. Maybe she didn't want to know, after all. Maybe she ought to just crawl under the car and stay there until he either went away or she died of starvation, whichever came first. Too late.

"She said she found notebook paper," he told her softly, "that you'd written some names on. Anna Leland. Anna and Reeves Leland."

"Oh-oh-oh." Anna reeled, coming up hard against the side of her car.

Talk about stupid! How many sheets of paper had she filled with that drivel? *Mrs. Anna Leland. Mrs. Reeves Leland. Anna Miranda Leland. Reeves and Anna Leland...* And she'd thought she'd been so clever, tearing the pages into tiny pieces, hiding them in closets and under floorboards, while Tansy undoubtedly had known all along.

And now Reeves knew. Probably his aunts, too.

Moaning, Anna covered her face with her hands and did her best to disappear. After a long moment, she heard shoe soles scrape against the pavement, and then something brushed against her hair.

"Anna?" he queried softly.

"Go away," she choked out.

"No."

She balled her hands into fists. "Please just go away."

"Not until you listen to me."

Here it comes, she thought, the useless dismissals. She could already hear them. *It wouldn't have worked out. We're too different. I was heading off to college. It wasn't real love, just a silly schoolgirl crush.* All the things she'd told herself a countless number of times, he would now tell her. Maybe they would finally work. Maybe, after all these years, she could finally just get over it.

She dropped her hands and opened her eyes, ready for the volley, ready to take the truth right in the heart.

"I can't have you thinking ill of my aunts," he said. "They only wanted to try to derail your grandmother. I think they feel responsible for having discussed among themselves that you would be a wonderful mother for Gilli."

Anna blinked, a rush of warm surprise flowing through her. "They said that?"

One corner of his lips quirked. "A number of times. That seems to have given Tansy the idea to get us together, and we may have added fuel to the fire ourselves."

"Last Sunday at church."

"Mmm. Hypatia hoped that they and I and you together could make Tansy see that…" He seemed momentarily at a loss for words, but he shifted his stance slightly and went on. "That she's driven you away with her obsessive need to control your life."

"Fat chance!" Anna huffed, folding her arms.

"Yeah," Reeves said, "she's nothing if not determined, this grandmother of yours, and she obviously has her own agenda for this dinner. *Her* agenda," he reiterated, "not ours. I propose that we just don't play her game."

"As if I ever have."

He grinned and tapped her on the end of the nose. "Exactly."

Narrowing her eyes at him, she cut him an incisive glance. "What are you suggesting?"

"For starters, that neither of us show up for dinner. The aunties will understand, and it'll throw a spoke in Tansy's wheel. Then…" He shrugged. "We'll figure it out."

Anna wondered what was left to figure out, but she didn't ask. She was still trying to reason through Reeves's behavior. He hadn't said a word about her ridiculous crush. Maybe he figured it was too silly to bother about, water under the bridge, over and done with years and years ago.

Suddenly he asked, "Do you know where my house is?"

Taken off guard, she simply nodded.

"Good. I'll meet you there in an hour, less if I can manage it. Okay?"

She opened her mouth, but so many questions crowded her tongue that she couldn't sort through them to get at the right one.

He shook her gently. "Okay?"

She blinked and gave him the answer he seemed to want. "Okay."

Beaming a smile at her, he hurried back toward the store. "Less than an hour, I promise. Then we'll talk."

Anna hugged herself, watching him dart through traffic back toward the building, his tie flapping in beat to his movements. Even after he disappeared through the automatic sliding doors, she stood there, slightly dazed by the emotional upheaval of the past few minutes. Finally, she pulled her keys from her pocket and let herself into the car. Slumping down behind the steering wheel, she tried to gather her thoughts.

What, she wondered, did he expect to talk about? Her embarrassment at Tansy's highhandedness? *His* embarrassment at Tansy's high-handedness? *Not high school and all that, please God.*

On the other hand, what if he wanted to just talk, period, about...whatever normal people talk about? Was that possible?

He'd apologized for judging her. If she apologized for having made his life a misery all those years ago, that would be a start toward...friendship, at least. Wouldn't it?

There was only one way to find out.

* * *

Reeves let himself into Chatam House via the side door, as usual, carrying the retrieved packet of tea in one hand. The sound of running footsteps greeted him perhaps two seconds before his daughter launched herself at him out of the gloom of the hallway.

"Daddy!"

He caught her up and parked her on his hip, hugging her close. "Hi, sugar." She smelled fresh and sweet and wore clean clothes, a matching set of royal blue knit top and pants. "You look pretty."

"Anna's coming."

"Ooh, I don't think so," he told her, carrying her through the house, "but you and I are going to see her, instead."

She tilted her head, caramel curls bouncing. "Can Special come?"

"Uh, no. Special will have to stay here."

Sighing, Gilli spread her hands in a gesture of helplessness. "I ha'fa stay wif her."

"Gilli, you can't stay with that cat all the time."

"I promise her, Daddy, 'cause Aunt 'Patia say she gots to stay in the kitchen for our dinner party."

"Yes, I know about the aunts' dinner party," Reeves said absently, turning down the central hall.

"No, I mean in the kitchen, me and Chester and Hilda and Carol and Special."

Ah, so that was Hyaptia's plan, a very clever one that would effectively keep Gilli and the cat out of the way. "I see. Well, if that's what you want to do, then I'll give Anna your regrets."

Gilli screwed up her face. "What's grets?"

"*Re*grets. It means that I'm sorry I won't be able to join you."

"Oh. That's 'kay." She patted him as if accepting his apology.

Reeves grinned and carried her into the parlor, where he paused to set her on her feet before addressing the others gathered there.

"Hello, everyone." He moved from spot to spot, kissing cheeks until all three of his aunts had been greeted, then stood before Tansy and acknowledged her with a nod that was almost a bow. Ignoring Tansy's wide smile, he turned back to Hypatia and dropped the box of tea into her lap. "As requested."

"Thank you, dear."

"You're welcome. Unfortunately, I won't be around to enjoy your special tea this evening. In fact, I'm afraid I won't be able to stay for dinner, either."

Behind him, Tansy barked, "What?"

Hypatia looked troubled. "That is a shame."

He grinned. "Sorry, I have other plans." He bent to hug her in sheer gratitude for the lovely, godly woman that she was. "Don't count on Anna, either," he whispered.

"Oh?"

He straightened with a wink. "Mmm-hmm. I hope that's all right with you."

Hypatia smiled. "Of course. God's plans always supercede our own."

He grinned at her. "Couldn't agree more." Maybe this was all part of God's plan. Maybe God had been the real matchmaker all along. If so, He wouldn't let Tansy scuttle things. "I hope it's okay if Gilli stays here. I understand there's a dinner party in the kitchen that she doesn't want to miss."

Hypatia lifted her eyebrows. "I insist that Gilli stay. She's our only hope for a peaceful meal."

Laughing, Reeves turned with an expansive sweep of his arm to take his leave of the others. "Enjoy, my lovelies!" With that he bounded from the room, feeling ridiculously pleased. He couldn't have arranged things better himself.

As he moved toward the stairs, he heard Tansy hiss, "Make him stay!"

"He's an adult," Hypatia returned firmly. "We can't and wouldn't try to *make* him do anything."

Grinning, Reeves climbed the stairs two at a time. He didn't know why he felt so ebullient, and just now he didn't care. Thinking of Anna, he quickly changed into jeans, a black long-sleeved T-shirt and casual shoes before grabbing a denim jacket and heading back downstairs, where he kissed his little girl—and at her insistence, her cat—goodbye. He figured he came away with his face intact merely because Gilli was holding the vicious thing at the time.

Ten minutes later, he pulled up in front of his house to find Anna waiting for him, dressed exactly as before in jeans and a double T-shirt but with the addition of a snug little cardigan. Leaning against the fender of her pathetic coupe with her arms folded, she frowned solemnly; yet he smiled, absolutely delighted to see her.

This woman, he realized, was not just his friend, she was his best friend, someone to be admired, someone who deserved regard and kindness. She had enriched his life and that of his daughter in ways that he could not have imagined. He shook his head, hardly able to believe it.

The brat had become one of his greatest blessings, and very possibly, he realized with a jolt, the answer to his prayers.

Chapter Thirteen

They dined on pizza at Gilli's favorite restaurant, though Gilli had elected to stay at home with her cat. Anna smiled at Reeves's animated account of Gilli's dedication to her pet and Tansy's outraged disappointment as his defection. She listened carefully to his frank description of his encounters—two, as it turned out—with Tansy, and felt a certain sense of vindication at what he said afterward.

"I knew she was difficult, but I figured it was just a quirk of her personality, a first impulse sort of thing. I never realized how far she would go to try to dictate to you or why you would rebel so blatantly. I just want you to know, I get it now."

Anna nodded then shrugged, still troubled by a sense of Tansy controlling her. "She always manages to set it up so she gets her way. Like right now."

"How do you mean?"

Spreading her hands, Anna stated the obvious. "She wanted to get us together, and here we are."

"On our terms," Reeves pointed out, "not hers."

"Still, Tansy gets what Tansy wants."

He reached across the table and captured one of her hands. "Anna, you've got to stop this," he said. "It's about what *you* want and what's best for you, not what Tansy wants or thinks is best. If the two should happen to be one and the same, you can't let the fact that it pleases Tansy mess up everything. I thought you got that when you showed up at church. Don't confuse standing up for yourself with displeasing your grandmother. They aren't mutually exclusive ideas. If we want to be friends, we'll be friends. It's up to us, not Tansy."

Anna glanced at him, sitting there with his dark hair rakishly tousled, looking so handsome and solid and good, every woman's dream. Well, not every woman's, obviously, but hers. Definitely her dream. And he had just offered her some sort of friendship. That was better than nothing. Was she going to let Tansy take it away from her? Reeves was right about doing what was best for herself, and she would, just on her own terms. As soon as she figured out how exactly to accomplish that.

In the meantime, this evening was the closest thing she'd ever had to a date with Reeves, and it might be as close as she ever got to one. She intended to enjoy it.

They talked for hours. When they finally discussed the dossier he had given her, she found herself admitting that she was a bit uncertain about sticking her neck out.

"Dennis is at least a known quantity," she pointed out. "How do I know the next situation will be any better?"

"You just have to have faith."

He told her about the disaster of his marriage, bringing Anna to conclude, "Marissa wasn't who you thought she was."

"Believe me, I realize that," he said. "The thing is,

how do you trust your own judgment again after you've made such a mistake?"

"Someone recently told me that you just have to have faith," Anna answered.

"Ouch. Coming back to bite me." He grinned and slid toward the edge of the booth. "Well, now that we've cleared that up, I have a house to inspect tonight. Come on, I'll give you the ten-dollar tour."

"You'll have to put it on my account," Anna quipped.

Reeves laughed as he stood. Curious and reluctant to let the evening end, she followed suit. She just hoped Tansy didn't find out that she'd spent this time with Reeves; otherwise, she'd never hear the end of it. Tansy would forever remind her how she'd blown her one chance, however remote, to have her dreams fulfilled. She would never understand that it was as much her own fault as Anna's. Then again, what did it matter? Her relationship with her grandmother had never been what she'd wanted it to be anyway. It was too late, surely, to do anything about that now.

It was nearing ten o'clock when Reeves once again pulled into the driveway of his house. A motion detector set off a light that illuminated the drive and walkway out front, all the way to the mailbox on the street, reminding him that he hadn't checked the mail yet. Having called Chatam House earlier to say good-night to Gilli and been assured by Aunt Mags that all was well on their end, he felt no need to rush. In fact, he felt a great reluctance to let the evening end.

He had never talked so easily with anyone else or felt so…not comfortable exactly. Some of his thoughts and impulses about Anna were becoming increasingly uncomfortable. Yet, tonight with her he'd felt a certain rightness, a kind of confidence about himself and his personal life that had been missing previously.

Funny, he'd never had any trouble when it came to business and his career, but when it came to his personal relationships, he'd always been somewhat uncertain. That ought to come as no surprise, considering his parents' history. He realized now that he couldn't know what he hadn't been taught, but God had provided some very valuable lessons of late, and he meant to put them to good use.

Punching the button overhead, he waited for the garage door to lift, then pulled the sedan inside before hurrying around to hand Anna out on her side.

"Hang on a minute, will you?" he said by way of excusing himself.

Leaving Anna standing, he loped out to the curb, where he drew a handful of papers from the dark interior of the mailbox. He glanced over them on his way back up the drive, finding an electric bill among the advertising circulars, along with a letter. Looking at Marissa's name on the return address, he sighed inwardly, but the old familiar burn of failure did not come.

He didn't realize that he'd halted his steps until the motion detector clicked off the decorative lamp affixed to the brick on the corner of the house, leaving only the light from the garage to illuminate the envelope in his hand. This, he told himself with surprising serenity, was his past. Looking up at Anna, the thought occurred to him that there might well stand his future, and suddenly he wanted to run toward it. Her. Them. Yes, them. Him and Anna. Together. If only she didn't let Tansy get in the way.

Setting off with long, sure strides, he slid Marissa's letter and the other mail into his jacket pocket. Anna had been studying the bare, half-empty interior of his garage with probing intensity, as if the trash cans, tools and lawnmower in the corner might tell her what she would find inside the house. As he drew near, she looked around at him.

He'd kissed her before and had wanted to since then. Something must have warned her, for she drew back a step, asking, "What?"

"This," he said. Taking her beautiful face in his hands, he drew her to him even as he stepped closer to her and bent his head.

He risked everything on that kiss, blending his lips with hers in gentle urgency banked with a need far deeper than he'd realized and a joy he had not even suspected.

Yes, he thought. Yes. Yes. Yes.

Oh, but he could be a slow, foolish man! All these years, not to realize who and what he had in her.

He did a very thorough job with the kiss. When he had made all of it that he could, he wrapped his arms around her, holding her close to his heart, while it pounded and he got his breath back.

"Thank You," he whispered, eyes shut tight.

"What for?"

The light had gone off, the timer having run out, so that they stood in the dark now. He chuckled and turned her face up with a hand spread beneath her chin, trying to make out her expression.

"I wasn't talking to you." The whites of her eyes gleamed, widening. He felt the urge to kiss her again but didn't, knowing that it would not be wise, and he wanted to be wise this time, very, very wise. He loosened his embrace, turning her toward the door in the back wall. "Come on."

Turning on lights as they went, they entered the house through a short passageway open on one side to the kitchen, with the laundry room off the other and the master bedroom at the end. He led her there by the hand. Moving swiftly in through one side of the room, they peeked into the spacious master bath and large closets, then went out the other door into another hallway that soon opened onto the large living area of the great room. She admired the free-standing fireplace that separated living and dining spaces, as well as the study that opened off the opposite wall through glass-fronted French doors. Nearly everything had been covered and taped in preparation for painting, giving the place a ghostly, unreal quality.

He showed her Gilli's frilly pink gingham room and the nanny's room, along with two other bedrooms before pulling down the attic stairs and climbing up to poke his upper body through the opening and take a look around. The place looked clean and new. The ceilings had all been replaced, along with the insulation atop them, and everything below had at last been taped, bedded and plastered. Only some sanding and the painting remained to be done. It was as if the honeybees had never invaded.

They walked around past the dining area, with its gleaming brass chandelier hanging shrouded over the center of the canvas-draped table and on to the formal entry. It was nothing so grand as Chatam House, of course, but the architect had carved out space enough for an exquisite Louis XVI console table, along with a matching bench and framed mirror, which had been the aunties' wedding gifts to him and Marissa. It was only here, in this forward space, where the ceiling had not had to come down, so the furnishings remained uncovered.

Anna ran a hand over the marble top of the table, sighing with pleasure. "I've always loved old things. Guess it has to do with growing up in an old house."

He considered a moment then asked the question now uppermost in his mind. "Think you'd like living in a new house, say, this house?"

She shot him an uncertain look, folding her cardigan close. "This is a wonderful house," she answered carefully. "You can't imagine how far beyond my dinky old apartment it is or you wouldn't even ask me that."

"We both know that's not what I'm asking."

He leaned a hip against the table and pressed his hands to his thighs. Why wasn't his heart pounding? he wondered. It had pounded like a big brass drum every time he'd broached, however obliquely, the subject of a possible future with Marissa. How could he now feel so calm, after the spectacular failure of his marriage to Marissa and his initial opinion of Anna?

Anna-Miranda-the-Brat-Burdett.

The old refrain sang through his head, childish voices chanting. As if she'd heard them, too, her head came up, her gaze meeting his. Wide and troubled, her sky-blue eyes had never seemed so sad. She shook her head.

"If you'd said anything like that even a couple days ago, I think I'd have jumped over the moon."

He didn't know if that was a good start or a bad one. Draping an arm across her shoulders, he pulled her around to lean beside him. "And now?" She shook her head again, looking away. "It's not Tansy, is it?" he asked.

"You tell me."

"You can't think this is about her money."

"No, but something's put this in your head."

"You," he said. "It's you.

Sighing, she let him see her worry. "That's just it, Reeves. I'm not sure I know how to live a normal life. My whole life's been about fighting Tansy. I don't know how to do anything else."

He tugged her closer. She leaned her head on his shoulder. It was a nice feeling, a good feeling, a *right* feeling.

"We've been living normal lives, Anna, both of us. This is what the world offers. I think it's time we started living the lives God means for us to have." He laid his cheek against the top of her head. "Let's give it some time, see what He has in store for us. The auction is weekend after next. Let's get through that and see where we are then? Okay."

For answer, Anna shifted and slid both of her arms around his waist. They stayed there like that for several long, sweet moments, until at last she whispered, "Why couldn't Tansy stay out of it?"

"Just put Tansy out of your mind," he told her with some exasperation. "Now, about the auction. Parking's going to be a premium. I could send the aunties' car for you, but I have the feeling Chester is going to have his hands full. Why don't I—"

She pulled back, frowning. "What are you talking about? Why would you send a car? I'm not going to the auction."

"Of course, you're going. How could you not go?"

"I'm not on the guest list."

"That doesn't matter. I didn't get an invitation, either,

but I've already had my tux dry-cleaned because I know that my aunts would never forgive me if I wasn't there."

"That's different."

"No, it isn't."

"You're family," she pointed out.

He couldn't believe this. Surely she realized how much his aunts adored her. They would definitely want her there. He wanted her there. He had, in fact, intended to take her as his date, but he could see that would not do. Tansy would undoubtedly be in attendance, and that in itself would give Anna enough reason not to accompany him. Folding his arms, he took the only tack available to him.

"I can't believe you would intentionally offend my aunts this way."

"You know that's not—"

"Hypatia in particular will be very hurt. She already thinks you blame her and the other aunts for Tansy's manipulations."

"I never said that."

"What else are they to think?" He demanded, throwing up his hands for good measure.

Looking resigned, she sighed. "If you really believe I should go..."

"I know it."

She made a face. "All right. I'll put in an appearance, at least."

"That would be best," he told her, somehow managing to keep a straight face and not break out in a relieved grin.

"But I'll get there under my own power," she informed him smartly. Shooting him a resentful glare, she muttered, "Now I have to find something to wear."

He almost told her to be sure to wear those classy heels but bit back the words at the last moment.

"If you'll excuse me," she said, acid dripping from every syllable, "I have to go look through my closet now."

Hiding a smile, he let her out through the front door and walked with her to her coupe at the curb, where he offered her the briefest of goodbyes. Standing back, he watched her get in and drive away. Only when the red glow of her taillights disappeared from sight did he turn back to the house, grinning widely.

It was a nice house, he thought, looking up at the brick and stone facade, but it would be nicer still with her inside it. He could only pray that, whatever happened next, she would eventually feel the same way.

The invitation arrived at the print shop the first thing Monday morning, hand-delivered by the Chatams' houseman and driver Chester. With it came a second invitation and an apologetic note from Hypatia, saying that the extra invitation was for Dennis and his wife. Well, Anna thought, that ought to appease her cranky boss a bit. She still wasn't happy about having to attend the fund-raiser, partly because she'd had to come up with an outfit to wear but mostly because Reeves and Tansy would be there. She could already feel Tansy watching her every move. Every word, every gesture, ever glance would be watched and weighed, especially if Reeves was involved, and he would be.

She'd spent two sleepless nights thinking about Reeves's *suggestion.* She wouldn't think of it as an almost-proposal. She'd go mad if she allowed herself to imagine, even for a moment, that he might have been sincere. He couldn't be. He just could not be. She didn't know how to deal with the possibility that he might.

More than once, she'd tried to pray about it, but something stopped her. It was as if something blocked her, something at which she didn't want to look too closely. Perhaps that was because she knew that what was stopping her from taking her problems to God did not come from Him. Something in her got in the way, something she couldn't bring herself to face even now. Facing Reeves again, while she wasn't looking forward to it, seemed easier by comparison. Facing Tansy, well, that was just same old same old.

Surprisingly, Tansy had not shown up on her doorstep over the weekend to complain about her dinner plans going awry, but she would do so. It was just a matter of time. Of much more concern was the echoing silence from the direction of Reeves Leland. A girl could be excused for thinking that a guy who *suggested* to the point of almost proposing would call, couldn't she? Even if she had almost turned him down.

If only he had beat Tansy to the punch, if he'd come to his "understanding" of her before Tansy had tried her heavy hand at matchmaking, if he'd given her any indication that he might actually love her, then she would be the happiest woman in the world. But once again, Tansy had ruined it. Yet, Anna could not prevent herself from hoping and waiting for that phone to ring. When it finally did on Saturday morning, Reeves was not the one she heard.

"Anna?" Gilli's piping little voice was unmistakable. "Me and Special miss you."

Anna's heart turned over. "I'm sorry, sweetie."

"Ever'one's too busy to play," Gilli complained.

"They got swings and slides at the park," she added hopefully.

Reeves took the phone then. "Sorry to put you on the spot," he said to Anna, "but it's a madhouse over here. Gilli's hoping you'll meet her in the park, get her out of the way for a while."

What could Anna say but, "Of course. I'd be delighted."

"Is half an hour too soon?" The poor man sounded desperate. No doubt the Chatam sisters had him running himself ragged with preparations for the fund-raiser.

"Not at all. In fact, I'm leaving now."

Gilli cheered when he related that news to her. Anna grabbed her keys. Not fifteen minutes later, she parked her car near the playground down the hill from the century-old Chautauqua building, where the community supported cultural activities such as plays, chamber music concerts and the occasional ballet performance and art show. Reeves and Gilli had already arrived and were walking across the grass toward the graveled playground, where several other children ran and laughed in the cool spring sunshine. Hailing them, Anna ran down the hill to sweep Gilli into an exuberant hug.

"What do you want to do first?"

"Swing!"

They ran to the swings hand in hand. Anna helped Gilli get situated and started her moving before turning to Reeves. He looked achingly handsome in jeans and a creamy tan pullover. She was prepared to tell him that she'd have Gilli back to the house before her nap time, but instead of heading off toward his car, as she'd expected, he ambled close enough to say, "Thanks for coming. I didn't think I'd ever get her out from underfoot. Didn't want to leave her cat. I had to bribe her with you."

Anna blinked as he stepped around her and gave Gilli a little shove that had her giggling with glee. "Don't you have to get back?" Anna asked him.

"Nope. Not until after lunch. Where were you thinking of eating, by the way?"

"I wasn't—" Anna began, only to be interrupted by Gilli yelling, "Pizza!"

"No pizza," Reeves said flatly, giving Gilli another shove. She put her head back and laughed as the swing flew a few feet higher. "How about that new deli on the square?" he asked Anna. "I hear they have good sandwiches and salads. Have you been there yet?"

"Uh, no, but—"

"Let's do that, then." He turned his attention back to Gilli, saying, "Hold on tight, sugar. This one's going to touch the sky."

He pushed her hard enough to elicit a squeal of delight. When he refused to go any higher, however, she quickly decided that it was time to hit the slides.

"Come on, Anna," she cried, racing off as soon as her feet touch the ground.

Anna glanced at Reeves then followed, and so it went until Reeves declared it time for lunch. Even with her stomach growling, Gilli resisted until Anna promised, "We'll come back soon."

"She'll remember that, you know," Reeves warned, taking Anna's hand, "and if she doesn't, I will."

Anna didn't know what to say to that, so she merely smiled, her heart swelling. There was some reason why this was not a good idea, but she couldn't for the life of her remember what it was until they were leaving the deli nearly an hour later and ran into a friend of her grandmother's. The speculation in that older woman's eyes told Anna that Tansy would know about this outing before she could even get back home.

She waited all day, after taking her leave of Reeves and a yawning Gilli, for that knock on her door, but it never came. Bucking up her courage to attend church again the next day, she told herself that Tansy would surely confront her there. Once more, however, she missed her guess. Tansy did walk by after Reeves sat down on the pew beside Anna, but she literally turned her head away without saying a word. Certain this was some new tactic of her grandmother's, Anna could barely concentrate on the sermon for trying to figure out what her response should be. Noticing her distraction, Reeves asked if she wanted to go somewhere and talk after the service, but Anna feared that was the last thing she should do. She couldn't think with him standing so close and smiling like that.

"I—I'm sorry. I can't."

A look of disappointment on his face, he took her hand in his, sweeping his thumb across her knuckles. "You won't stand me up next weekend, will you, Anna? My aunts want you at that auction, and they'll be so disappointed if you're not there."

"I'll be there!" she promised, but he called almost nightly to make sure, and more often than not, they wound up talking for hours.

She learned about his work and his company, his many siblings—six kids spread about among five parents!—and how responsible he felt, as the oldest, for the difficulties that divorce had caused them.

"And here I am repeating the same mistake," he said with a sigh.

"That's not your fault," she told him.

"Of course, it's my fault," he refuted softly. "I picked Marissa, for all the wrong reasons, but I've learned my lesson, believe me. I'll get it right next time."

Anna blanched to think of him marrying some other woman, but she quickly changed the subject. That didn't keep her from thinking about it, though, and when Saturday finally came, she took more pains with her appearance than she ever had before. Let Tansy crow. For once, Anna just didn't care.

Chapter Fourteen

Reeves paced the foyer impatiently. The soft strains of music, produced by a piano and harp, blended with the clink of flatware as the temporary staff put the final touches on the tables in the ballroom. Where was she? A good many guests had arrived already, and Anna had promised to be early. He should have insisted on picking her up.

Stationed in front of a narrow window, Chester opened the door. Reeves whirled and saw Tansy Burdett, decked out in matronly gray silk, enter.

She smiled thinly. "Not arrived yet, has she?"

Reeves took a stranglehold on his temper. "Stay away from her, Tansy. Just give her some room tonight, will you please?"

"I know my part in this," she huffed, marching toward him.

"That's just it. You have no part."

To his surprise, her chin wobbled. "I'll always have a part in my granddaughter's life," she insisted in a trembling voice, "even if it's from a distance. She's all I have."

Before Reeves could follow up on that, Chester announced, “She’s here, Mr. Reeves.”

Tansy marched away at double-time. His mouth dry and palms damp, Reeves faced the door. He gave his French cuffs a tug and rolled his shoulders beneath the black satin-trimmed jacket of his tux. With a black bow tie and a white cummerbund against a white shirt, he suddenly felt colorless and trite. Chester swung that door open, and Reeves ceased to think at all.

It was just a long, slim midnight-blue skirt of some slinky knit, slit to the knee on one side, and a sleeveless, fitted, purple lace top worn beneath a length of sheer dark blue fabric draped over her shoulders and arms, but it looked as fine on her as any ball gown. She’d tucked her hair behind her ears and clipped rhinestones—or whatever they called faux diamonds these days—to her dainty lobes. A matching string encircled her slender neck and one wrist. On her feet were those delightful shoes. Wow.

Summoning up what he hoped to pass off as charm and wit, he stepped forward and shook his head, saying, “Oh, this is not good.”

She looked down at herself in alarm. “What?”

“How will anyone concentrate on the auction items with you in the room?” She laughed, taking the arm he offered. “You’re stunning,” he told her softly, “beautiful, and if you get farther than three feet away from me tonight, I won’t be responsible for my actions.” She laughed again, a bright, crystalline tinkle that sounded like happiness itself.

They strolled toward the ballroom, passing half a dozen flower arrangements on pedestals. “Where’s Gilli?” she asked.

"Oh, she's around here somewhere. I told her she could mingle until dinner started, provided she's on her best behavior. Then Carol will take her to the kitchen for a private party with Special. We can slip off and put her to bed afterward."

Anna nodded and squeezed his arm. "I'd like that."

The aunties were at their stations, Odelia at the door to greet, Mags directing guests to the proper seats, Hypatia handing out catalogs and pointing out items displayed on the rectangular tables that lined the room. The round tables, decorated in layers of white and gold, that stood in the center of the floor were for dining. With flickering candles on every table and an abundance of flowers, the room resembled a fairy glade, an impression enhanced by the smattering of light reflected upon the ceiling and the faint, ethereal lilt of the music.

He knew a moment of tension when Anna spied Tansy bending over one of the bid sheets on the display tables. As if sensing her presence, Tansy straightened and looked straight at them, but then she went back to penning in her bid, and Anna turned away. Reeves said nothing, smoothing a hand over her back until she relaxed.

The evening progressed smoothly from that point. He and Anna made the rounds of the auction tables and dutifully made bids on various items. One of them, a trip to the Bahamas donated by a local travel agency, was proving extremely popular, but Reeves made a generous bid anyway, imagining Anna and himself on the beach. She chose small, inexpensive items and made modest bids, which he upped at every opportunity in hopes of being able to present one or more of them to her.

Every chair was filled by the time dinner was served, and the bid sheets, according to his aunt's whispered progress reports, were nicely covered. They were on track to raise a record-breaking amount for the scholarship fund.

Reeves recognized Anna's corpulent boss and his equally bountiful wife seated at another table across the room, as requested, but after a single wave, Anna paid them no more mind, nor they her. It was just as well. If he had his way, Reeves would keep her entirely to himself tonight.

The aunties had provided their guests with filets mignon, creamy scalloped potatoes with asparagus and a dish of sweet shredded carrots cooked with currants. For dessert, they were presented with chocolate mousse and a "nut mélange in a caramel glaze." If that didn't open wallets, Reeves didn't know what would. As soon as he was finished eating, he made a dash over to place one more bid on that Bahamas vacation, then he grabbed Anna by the hand and swept her from the room. It was time to put Gilli to bed. Chester met him in the hall, however, a grave, apologetic look on his face.

"You're needed in the parlor, Mr. Reeves, and I think the misses will want to be there, too."

"Is it Gilli?" Reeves asked, but Chester was already moving into the ballroom. Glancing at Anna, he clasped her hand tighter and tugged her swiftly toward the front of the house. Striding into the room, Anna at his heels, he swept it with his gaze, and came to a frozen halt.

Marissa sat on the settee, clad in a strapless, red spandex sheath that hugged her curves and ended at her ankles, where the straps of her black spike-heeled sandals began. Her legs crossed, she bobbed one foot impatiently. Gilli, dressed in ruffles and petticoats, perched on the very edge of the cushion beside her. They had the same hair, Reeves noted inanely, though Marissa had tamed her curls into bouncy waves that framed her face and tumbled about her shoulders.

The aunties arrived at about the same instant that Gilli let her feet slide down to the floor. “Hello, Daddy,” she said with false cheer, her mouth curved into the parody of a smile. “Hello, Anna. Look who come.”

The sly look on Marissa’s face made his stomach turn over. Knowing that this sudden appearance could not be good, he mentally kicked himself for not having bothered to read that letter upstairs, though he doubted it would have made much difference in the end.

He started forward grimly, intending to haul Marissa out of there for a private conference, but the moment he stepped off, Gilli said, “She my mommy.”

Reeves stopped immediately, realizing that the last thing his daughter needed was another ugly scene. He made himself relax and almost at once felt the steadying touch of Anna’s hand just above the small of his back. As if in ugly parody, Marissa reached over and slid a hand down Gilli’s fragile spine. Smirking, she looked up at him, the light of challenge in her hazel eyes.

“Sugar,” Reeves said, smiling at his daughter, “why don’t you check on Special? I’m sure he’s missing you.”

“Okay, Daddy,” she said, skipping around the table as if on her way to play.

“And while you’re at it,” he added, “take the aunties with you. They have guests to see to.”

Marissa pursed her mouth, and smoothed a hand over her skirt. Reeves suspected that she had expected to be invited to join the gala evening. She had enough nerve to pull off something like that.

The aunties hustled out after Gilli, throwing him sorrowful, worried glances as they disappeared. Anna's hand never left his back. Somehow, he had not expected it to. Marissa folded her arms and did a lazy perusal of the antiques in the room. He could almost see the numbers clicking in her head as she judged their value. At the same time, he sent a prayer heavenward.

Help me, Lord. Whatever You're doing now, help me get my part right, for my little girl's sake.

"I thought I'd find you here in the lap of luxury," Marissa said with a smirk. "I notice you still haven't moved back into our house."

"My house," he corrected.

Ignoring that, she pointed her chin at Anna. "Who's this?"

He answered succinctly. "Anna. Why?"

Marissa shrugged. "Can't help wondering if she's after my home, that's all."

"You lost all right to that house when you walked out on me and our daughter," Reeves said flatly. "It says so in the divorce decree."

She looked around pointedly. "Mmm, yes, well, you obviously have no need for it. I made a mistake not fighting for my fair share. I just felt so bad at the time." She slanted a smug look at Anna. "Breaking your heart like that and all."

A bark of laughter escaped him. "I kinda got over it."

"You won't get over losing your daughter," she snapped, her expression hardening.

Anna gasped and stepped up beside him. Reeves shifted his weight toward her, both as a warning and a comfort. He knew what Marissa wanted, and it wasn't Gilli, though she was not beneath using the child against him. Strangely, he was not afraid.

"Marissa," he said conversationally, "are you threatening to sue for custody of my daughter if I don't hand over my house to you?"

She picked at an invisible piece of lint on her skirt. "I'm told, by an attorney to whom I'm *very* close, that mothers almost always win in court."

So she had a new boyfriend, a lawyer. Reeves smiled, refusing to be rattled. "Is that so?"

Marissa sat back, folding her arms. "So, which will you give me, your daughter or the house?"

Before Reeves could say a word to that, Anna exclaimed, "The house! We'll give you the house."

Reeves looked at her in stunned wonder. Did she even know what she'd just said? "We?"

"A family is worth more than brick and stone," she argued, and the agonized look in her eyes said that she, above all others, knew it only too well. "Besides," she went on desperately, "it's not like she's going to live in it. She only wants to sell it."

Marissa sniffed. "Live in that pedestrian little bungalow? I don't think so. Even you had sense enough to move in here. Still, it will bring a pretty penny on the market."

Reeves didn't look at her. He was smiling at Anna, who was revealing her heart to him, all unknowing. "But where will we live, sweetheart?" he asked deliberately. "Your apartment's not big enough for the three of us."

"I don't know!" Anna exclaimed, grabbing fistfuls of his shirt. "I don't care. We'll live in a cardboard box, if we have to, but we can't put Gilli through a custody battle, no matter how it comes out in the end."

Reeves thought his heart would burst from his chest,

if his face didn't split first. "You know you just agreed to marry me, don't you?"

"What? No! I—I mean…" She gulped, her eyes widening, and then she squared her shoulders and said, "Yes."

Cupping her face in his hands, he laughed, and said, "I love you, Anna Miranda Burdett."

She blinked. "You do?"

"You and Gilli matter more to me than anything else in this world," he told her, "certainly more than a heap of brick and mortar. But what about your grandmother?"

Anna looked up into his eyes and smiled tearfully. "I'd already decided that I couldn't let her get in the way of this. I've been in love with you for too long! Since high school, at least!"

Reeves beamed. "I know." Wrapping his arms around her, he pulled her close. "If only I'd known it at the time."

"Can't imagine how you missed it, Stick," she burbled against his chest. "What other girl went around gluing your keys to your locker?"

They looked at each other and burst out laughing.

Cupping her face, he put his forehead to hers. "Praise God," he said. "Finally, I got it right."

"How touching," Marissa remarked sourly.

Reeves pulled his gaze from Anna's, dropped his hands, slid his arm about his beloved's waist and looked to his glowering ex. "You can have the house," he told her, "under one condition." She raised an eyebrow, waiting for it. "You will allow Anna to adopt Gilli. Barn door's closed, Marissa. No more coming back to the trough."

Narrowing her eyes at him, she rose languidly to her feet. "Fine." But she couldn't resist sweeping her gaze over Anna and sneering, "I figured you'd go for the kid. You have that mousy housewife look about you."

Anna, to her credit, simply smiled. "What do you think, darlin'?" she asked him. "Do I look like your wife and Gilli's mother?"

"Oh, yeah. Most beautiful thing I've ever seen."

She kissed him, once, hard, on the lips.

Marissa tossed her head and slinked across the room, sniping, "I'll have my guy contact you."

"You do that," Reeves said, "but you get zip until those adoption papers are signed." He grinned down at Anna. "From now on, Gilli's going to have a real mother."

"And you are going to have a real wife," Anna promised softly.

Just then, Gilli burst into the room, the cat dangling from the crook of her arm. Marissa, who was near the door, shot Reeves a look of pure spite then bent to bring her face near Gilli's.

"I'm so sorry, Gilli," she droned, "but I won't be your mommy anymore. Your daddy—"

Before she could complete whatever malicious statement she'd been about to make, Gilli shoved her, declaring, "I don't want you!" With that she ran, not to Reeves, to Anna. "Wanna hold my cat?" she asked, gazing up at Anna adoringly.

Anna, fortunately, knew better than to even try such a thing. "I'd rather hold both of you," she said, scooping up Gilli, cat and all. Gilli giggled and reached out a hand to cup Reeves's cheek, letting him know that she approved of what was happening.

As Reeves turned his head to put a kiss in the center of that little palm, a throat cleared. He looked around to find Marissa gone and his aunts standing abreast in the doorway. Mags snuffled and wiped her eyes on her sleeve, while Auntie Od blew her nose into a lacy hanky. Even Hypatia's eyes sparkled with moisture, but she merely lifted her chin.

"There will be no cardboard boxes," she pronounced, shamelessly revealing that they had eavesdropped every word. "Not so long as Chatam House can offer the barest refuge."

Smiles and laughter erupted as the aunties rushed forward, babbling about weddings and what beautiful children they expected Anna and Reeves to make. Grinning, Reeves encircled his family with his arms, cat and all, his chest to Anna's back. With his chin snugged against her temple, he let the three most wonderful old dears in existence tell him about God's will for his life, just as if he didn't already hold it in his arms.

"Thank You," he whispered.

Anna put her head back and smiled before she lifted her gaze heavenward. "Me, too," she said. "Me, too."

Epilogue

Hypatia watched Anna dip a finger in icing then dab it onto the tip of Reeves's nose, laughing.

"Brat!" he growled over the fork with which he was trying to feed her a bite of their wedding cake. She was still laughing when he poked the cake into her mouth. With the other hand, he swiped the icing from his nose, and then, while Anna chewed, he smeared the remnants across her mouth. Swooping down, he kissed it away, to the applause and laughter of the guests gathered in the ballroom of Chatam House for the wedding reception.

Hypatia sighed. As beautiful a bride as Anna made in a floor-length, long-sleeved closely fitted sheath of Brussels lace, Reeves had never looked finer. He was not just the most handsome groom she had ever seen, he was also the happiest, most relaxed and confident. Gilli looked like a confection in her flower girl's dress, even with Special trotting at her ankles and trying to rub off the pink bow tied around his neck. In a break with tradition, Myra had served as ring bearer, with the rest of Reeves's siblings performing various other duties.

To everyone's relieved puzzlement, Tansy had not

taken a large role in planning the event. She had, however, insisted on paying the cost of the hastily thrown together wedding. One could never tell with Tansy, though, which was why Hypatia stiffened when she saw the other woman march up to the happy couple with her shoulders back and her chin high.

"I have a gift," she announced, shoving a fat envelope into Reeves's hands.

Glancing warily at Anna, he opened the flap and took out the papers, unfolding them to study. After a moment, he looked up at Anna. "It's the deed to Burdett House."

Tansy lifted her chin higher still, ignoring Anna's gasp. "It's not Chatam House, but it has a long and gloried history." She fixed Anna with a steely gaze, adding, "And room enough for a large family."

Hypatia could see the war going on inside of Anna, and so could Tansy. "I've bought a little house on the other side of town, and I've already moved in. Burdett house would be yours one day, anyway," she told Anna. "Who else would I leave it to? You're all I've got." Her chin wobbled, but she went on gamely. "I know I've been hard on you, too hard, maybe, but it's because I was so soft with your father. After my husband died, I indulged Jordan. I made every excuse in the book for him." She squeezed her eyes shut and her voice cracked when she said, "I'm the reason he died of a drug overdose. He thought life was one long party, and I let him think it." Gulping, she looked at Anna. "I vowed not to make the same mistake with you. So instead I made others."

Anna bit her lip and looked to her husband of some two hours. Would moving into the house give Tansy a way to control them? Then again, would a man who hadn't blinked an eye at Tansy's money allow such interference? Anna apparently knew the answer to that question.

"It is a wonderful old house," she said with a slow smile.

Reeves folded the papers and stuck them back in the envelope. "The antiques that my aunts have given us would look good in it," he allowed, sending a pointed glance at Hypatia. She sent another back to him. No, she had not known what Tansy was planning, but she could find no grounds for objection to Tansy giving her house away, especially as it seemed to signal a great turnaround in Tansy's relationship with her granddaughter.

Reeves stashed the envelope in a pocket of his tuxedo and addressed Tansy, one arm pulling Anna close. "Thank you."

To everyone's surprise, Tansy's face crumpled and she began to cry. "Thank you!" she wailed. "All I've ever wanted is for her to be happy, and now she is!" She looked at Anna, tears sliding down the crevices in her face. "I knew how badly I'd messed up when you almost let him get away just to keep from pleasing me!"

Reeves and Anna exchanged looks, and then, as one, stepped forward to lightly embrace and pat Tansy. Gilli rushed over then, that confounded Special now clutched in the bend of her elbow. She tugged sharply on the tail of Tansy's stylish silk suit jacket.

"Wanna hold my cat?"

Tansy actually bent down to comply, and wonders of wonders, Special complacently allowed Tansy to drape him over her shoulder. Gilli followed them to a quiet corner, where they petted the cat and chattered happily.

Hypatia laughed, gazing with satisfaction at her

nephew and his lovely wife. Just look, she thought, at all that God had done.

And just think of what He would yet do.

* * * * *

A MATCH MADE IN TEXAS

"Honor your father and mother"–which is the first commandment with a promise–"so that it may go well with you and that you may enjoy long life on the earth."

–*Ephesians* 6:2–3

To Susan (aka Janis Susan May), my sister in so many ways that we were almost surely separated at birth!

Love,
DAR

Chapter One

She couldn't help being impressed. As a nurse, Kaylie Chatam had encountered many patients whose physical conditions sadly diminished them, but not this time. Not even the bulk of the casts protecting his broken bones deflected attention from the big, commanding presence asleep on the high, half tester bed. Tall and long-limbed yet brawny, with an air of intensity about him even in sleep that his shaggy blond hair and lean, chiseled face did nothing to diminish, he emitted a potent force, a larger-than-life aura.

Kaylie lifted a petite hand to the heavy, sandy-red chignon at the nape of her neck, wishing that she'd secured it more firmly that morning when dressing for church. She'd have preferred to conduct this interview in the shapeless scrubs that she always wore when working, her long, straight hair scraped back into a tight knot. Instead, here she stood, wearing skimpy flat mules with big silver buckles on the shallow toes, a straight knee-length skirt and a frothy confection of a white blouse, her hair slipping and sliding, tendrils hanging about her face.

Turning to the man crowded next to her in the doorway of the bedchamber in one of the second-floor suites of Chatam House, the antebellum mansion owned by her three delightful aunties, Kaylie felt at a distinct disadvantage. Stocky, blunt-featured and of medium height with short, prematurely gray hair, a practiced smile and a pricey, light grayish brown suit, Aaron Doolin had identified himself as the patient's agent.

"Who is he exactly?"

"Who *is* he?" Doolin parroted, obviously shocked. "Who *is* he? Why, that's the Hangman." At her blank look, he went on. "Stephen Gallow. Starting goalie for the Fort Worth Blades hockey team." He glanced at the bed, muttering, "At least he was before the accident."

A hockey goalie? Here at Chatam House? She knew little about the game beyond its reputation for violence, but that was enough to make her wonder what the aunties had gotten themselves into now. More to the point, what had they gotten *her* into? Provided, of course, that she decided to take on this patient, which she could not do in good conscience without at least nominal approval from her father.

"What happened to the bed hangings?" she asked Doolin, gesturing toward the massive headboard of the bed. One of her aunts' prized English antiques, it stood a good seven feet in height. Even the square footposts were taller than Kaylie, though at a mere five feet in her stocking feet, that wasn't saying too much.

Doolin just shrugged. "I don't know from hangings."

"The curtains at the sides of the front of the bed."

"Oh!" He waved a hand, the sapphire on his pinky flashing in the midday light. The edges of his ever-present smile frayed. "Well, during the excitement last night—" he churned his hands then shrugged sheepishly

"—they sort of came down in the scrum. Your aunts thought it best to get them out of the way."

Kaylie analyzed that and came to the conclusion that whatever had happened the night before had involved a certain amount of violence, which explained why the original nurse had walked out and why she was here at Chatam House, staring at an injured, sleeping *hockey player*. The idea still did not quite compute. She tilted her head and wondered what was so compelling about this particular patient.

That he was handsome could not be denied, despite the faint slanting scars on his chin and high on his right cheek. Thick, pale gold hair formed a shaggy frame for a rectangular face with large, even features, the eyes set deeply beneath the slashes of incongruently dark brows. The sooty shadow of a beard that hadn't seen a razor in some days colored his square jaws, cheeks and chin, calling attention to wide, surprisingly soft lips that might have looked feminine in a less aggressively masculine face.

How was she, a pediatric nurse, supposed to deal with a man like this?

Kaylie almost turned around and walked away right then, but her aunts would not have asked this of her if the need were not acute. They had approached Kaylie immediately after worship service that morning, asking her to stop by the mansion at her earliest opportunity. Some tinge of desperation in that request had made Kaylie drop off her father at his—*their*—house and drive straight here. Only then had she learned of the aunts' guest and his need for nursing care. She had been shocked, to say the least.

Known for their good works, the Chatam sisters, triplets in their seventies, often opened their historic antebellum mansion to family and family connections, but this was the first time in Kaylie's memory that they had ever taken in a complete stranger. His situation must be desperate, indeed. She turned to Aaron Doolin once more.

"What is his condition?"

"Drugged," he replied flippantly.

Kaylie just looked at the man. Of course Gallow was drugged. Obviously so. It was nearly one o'clock in the afternoon, and the man was sleeping as soundly as if two people were not standing in his room talking. She understood that the doctor had been called in during the night to sedate the patient. Such a heavy dose indicated that the poor man had been in great physical distress.

Doolin cleared his throat and got serious. "You want to know about his injuries. Uh, let's see. Stevie broke his leg and arm. The arm was pretty bad. That and the ribs is why they've strapped it to his chest that way, and naturally it had to be his left arm because he is left-handed." Doolin grinned and added proudly, "One of the few truly left-handed goalies in the league."

"Is that good?"

The agent goggled at her. "Good?" Shaking his head at her obvious ignorance of all things hockey, he sent her a pitying look. "That, Miss Chatam, is a very good thing, indeed. Especially if said lefty is a big brute with reflexes quick as a cat and the eyesight of an eagle."

A brute. His own agent called him a brute. She could just imagine how her father, a retired pastor, would feel about that. Hub Chatam considered his youngest son's participation in pro rodeo barbaric. Chatam men, he asserted firmly and often, were called to higher purposes than mere sport. Chatam men were lawyers and pastors, doctors and professors, bankers and titans of industry who used their wealth and talents for the good of others in the name of Christ. That Chandler chose to dismiss his father's convictions was a great bone of contention within the family. No doubt, Hub would hold an even less favorable opinion of a pro hockey player, though of course a boarder and patient wasn't the same thing as a son.

"Sorry," she muttered to the agent. "Not much of a sports fan. My field is medicine."

"Medicine. Right. Gotcha. About his condition... Let's see... Broken bones. Two in the right leg, two in the left arm, four ribs, collarbone. I think that's it. Internally, there was a lacerated liver, a bruised pancreas, busted spleen..." Doolin tsked and shook his head. "I don't know what all."

Kaylie nodded in understanding. "Concussion?"

"Um, unofficially, he got conked pretty good."

Unofficially? "Was there brain damage?"

Aaron Doolin reared back. "No way! He's sharp as ever!" The agent smiled. "Mouth certainly works. He's singeing my ears regular again, but hey, that's what I get paid for. Right?" He chuckled, only to sober when it became obvious that she wouldn't join in with anything more than a weak smile.

Stephen Gallow sounded like both a brute and a bully, but who was she to judge such things? Her one concern should be the health of the patient. "What about his lungs?" she asked. "Were they punctured?"

"Nothing said about it."

"They would have mentioned something like that," Kaylie told him. "Trust me."

Nodding, Aaron looked to the bed. "Kid's got plenty to deal with as it is."

No doubt about that, Kaylie mused, thinking of her father, who had suffered a heart attack some six months earlier. Compared to all this man had been through, that seemed almost minor, though Hub continued to behave as if his life remained in immediate danger. She wandered closer to the bed.

Stephen Gallow moaned and twitched, muttering what sounded like, "Nig-nig."

Doolin slid his hands into his pants pockets. "Must think he's talking to Nick."

"Nick? Who's that?"

"Uh, old buddy."

"He's dreaming, then."

"Yeah, yeah. Does a lot of that since the accident." Doolin churned his hands again, in what seemed to be a habitual gesture. "The trauma of it all, I guess."

"He's suffered some very serious injuries," Kaylie murmured.

"You're telling me! Man, I thought he'd bought it, you know?"

"How long ago was the accident?"

"Nine, ten days." He looked at his client, and for the first time the mask of beaming bonhomie slipped, showing genuine concern. "Ask me, he oughta be in the hospital still."

Kaylie smiled to herself. Patients and family were often of that opinion, but home could be a safer, more restful environment than the hospital.

"But you know how it is," Doolin went on. "A big sports star draws attention that hospitals don't particularly appreciate, and when said sports star is trying to keep a low profile… Well, that's why we're here, obviously."

Kaylie furrowed her brow at that. "You mean he's hiding out here at Chatam House?"

The agent licked his lips warily before admitting, "You could say that."

"From who?"

"The press, mostly."

"But why Chatam House? How did he wind up here?"

"Oh, that." The pinky ring flashed again. "Brooksy arranged it."

Brooksy? "You mean Brooks Leland? *Doctor* Brooks Leland?"

Doolin's gray head bobbed. "Yeah, yeah. Me and Brooksy, we went to college together. We were fraternity brothers, and hey, once a frat bro, always a frat bro. Right?"

Frat bro. A smile wiggled across Kaylie's lips. She'd remember that and give her older brother's best friend—that was, *Brooksy*—a hard time about it later. Obviously, Doolin had called Brooks about his patient's need to keep a low profile while recovering from his accident and Brooks had contacted the aunts, apparently Aunt Odelia specifically. Finally, this situation was beginning to make some sort of sense.

"So what do you think?" Aaron Doolin asked. "Can you do it? He just mainly needs someone to help him get around and manage his pain, meds and meals." He eyed her warily. "You think you can make him take his medicine?"

Make him? Kaylie lifted a slender eyebrow at that. She thought of her father again. At seventy-six, Hub Chatam was twice widowed and a retired minister. As the youngest of his four children and the only daughter, she'd taken a leave of absence from her job after his heart attack in order to move into his house, take care of him and help him adjust to the new lifestyle necessitated by his health realities. Six months later, he still wouldn't take a pill that didn't come from her hand. He claimed that he couldn't keep them straight, but let ten minutes pass the appointed time for one of his meds and he was demanding to know when she was going to dispense it.

Before she could answer the agent's question, Gallow's eyes popped open. Startled by their paleness—they were like marbles of gray ice—Kaylie registered the panic in them. She instinctively started forward just a heartbeat before he bolted up into a sitting position. Roaring in pain, he dropped back onto the pillow. A blue streak of profanity rent the air, then he gasped and began to writhe.

Though taken aback, Kaylie instantly realized that he was doing himself damage. Stepping up to his bedside, she bent over him and calmly advised, "Be still. Take slow breaths. Slow, shallow breaths." For the first time he looked at her. Confusion, anger and pain poured out of those eerily pale eyes, but as he stopped moving and gradually controlled his breathing, lucidity took hold of him. Impulsively, Kaylie brushed a pale gold lock from his brow, smiling encouragingly. "Slow…slow… That's it."

His pale gaze skimmed over her with acute curiosity even as he followed her instructions. After a moment, he swallowed and rasped, "Who are you?"

"Kaylie Chatam. Hypatia, Odelia and Magnolia Chatam are my aunts."

"Kaylie's a nurse," Aaron Doolin put in helpfully.

"How about that? The old biddies, er, our *hostesses* had one in the family. Go figure."

Gallow's gaze abruptly shifted to his agent. Kaylie shivered. Had she been the recipient of that suddenly furious, frigid, accusatory glare, she'd have ducked. Doolin just ratcheted up his grin and spread his hands.

"Hey, Stevie! That's my boy. How you feeling there, huh?"

"How do you think I feel?" Gallow gritted out. "And don't call me Stevie."

"Sure. Sure. Doc says you reinjured those ribs last night. Must be killing you."

Literally baring his teeth, Gallow revealed a pair of spaces on the right side where his upper and lower second molars should be. Something about those empty spaces pricked Kaylie's heart. He was no longer the impossibly handsome sports figure or the angry brute but a mere man at the mercy of his own injuries. Until he snarled.

"Reinjured my ribs? You think? That ba—" He slid a gaze over Kaylie. "That bozo ball of lard you hired to take care of me threw himself on top of me! *That's* what reinjured my ribs."

Doolin lifted his hands as if to ward off a blow. "Hey, calm down, will you? How was I to know the guy would do that? I mean, he's a nurse, right? He said you were all over the place and that he was trying to pin you down so you wouldn't fall off the bed."

"He was trying to pin me down, all right, and enjoyed every second of it, until I kicked him in the—" Gallow broke off there and gave Kaylie an irritated look.

Doolin chuckled. "You gave him an anatomy lesson he didn't get in nursing school, that's for sure."

Kaylie stepped back and folded her arms, appalled. This man was a powerhouse of lithe physical strength and jagged emotion that ranged far beyond her personal experience. Stephen Gallow sent her a cool, challenging look. She felt frozen and singed at the same time. A sense of foreboding shivered through her as she watched him take his agent to task with little more than a glare and growl.

"Where's the bozo now?"

"Fired him last night."

"And you think he's going to keep his mouth shut after this?"

"He signed a nondisclosure, and I sent the attorney to remind him of that in person this morning, along with a check for his trouble."

In other words, Kaylie thought, shocked, *they'd paid off the man!* Whether to keep him quiet or forestall a lawsuit, she didn't know. Most likely both. Obviously she had stumbled into a situation that was well beyond her depth.

Gallow dropped his eyelids, his right hand sliding lightly over his left side. Kaylie could tell that he was still in great pain, and the nurse in her could not stand by and watch it, no matter how rough and tough a character he might be. She looked to Doolin.

"Where is his pain medication?"

The agent reached into his coat pocket and drew out a prescription bottle. "Brooks says anything stronger has to be given by injection, and that requires a professional," Doolin said pointedly. "Until we hire another nurse, this is the best we can do."

She took the bottle and read the prescription before going to the bedside table, where a crystal pitcher of water and matching glass stood. She poured water into the glass, uncapped the pill bottle and shook two huge tablets into her palm.

"These should give you some relief, but you'll have to sit up to take them. Will you let me help you?"

Gallow ignored her, demanding of Doolin, "What have you told her?"

Aaron shrugged. "Just what she needs to know."

"Will you let me help you?" Kaylie repeated.

Gallow slid her a dismissive glance. "I don't like being knocked out all the time."

"Taking the meds regularly is the best way to prevent that. Regular doses will keep your pain under control while allowing you to gradually build up a resistance to the narcotic effect. Take them irregularly and they'll knock you out every time."

He glared at her for a moment, but then he held his breath and slowly pushed up onto his right elbow. Kaylie quickly pressed the first tablet between his lips and lifted the glass. He gulped, tilted his head back and swallowed. They repeated the process with the second tablet before he collapsed once more upon the pillow, panting slightly.

Kaylie heard his stomach rumble. Setting aside the glass, she began to reposition the pillow and smooth the covers, trying to make him comfortable until the medication kicked in. As she worked, she spoke briskly to Doolin.

"Please go down and ask my aunts to have Hilda prepare a breakfast tray."

"Okay. Sure. But I thought the staff had the day off."

"They do, but she'll fix something anyway." The aunties took care of their own meals on Sundays, but Hilda had always been a compassionate woman.

Kaylie smoothed the covers over Stephen Gallow's feet with gentle hands. They were enormous feet. Not even Chandler had feet the size of these. She tried to imagine the size of the skates that he would need.

Stephen rumbled out an order. "Coffee."

"Oh, that may not be possible," Kaylie interjected apologetically. "My aunts don't drink coffee, but maybe they'll have some in the kitchen anyway."

Gallow grimaced as Aaron scuttled out of the room. Kaylie told herself that she had done all she could for the moment. It was time to go. And yet, she lingered, oddly reluctant to leave the injured man alone. Brute he might be, but to a nurse an injured man was an injured man. Period. At least that's what she told herself.

As soon as Aaron had gone, Kaylie Chatam started tidying up the place. Stephen had dropped a towel on the floor the evening before, along with a trio of little pillows that had decorated the bed. Too weak to retrieve them, he'd simply left them where they'd fallen and collapsed, exhausted after the drive from Dallas, the climb up the stairs and a cursory scrubbing. Nurse Chatam folded the towel and laid it atop the upholstered bench at the foot of the bed. The pillows she moved to one of a pair of window seats with gold-on-gold-striped upholstery, both of which overlooked the front of the house. Stephen followed her every movement with his wary gaze.

Petite and gentle, with big, dark brown eyes and thick, straight hair a shade somewhere between sandy brown and red, she was pretty in a painfully wholesome way.

That put her a far cry from his usual type, beautiful and somewhat flamboyant. After all, if a guy was going to put up with all that female nonsense, Stephen figured that he ought to get something flashy out of it, something noticeable.

This Kaylie Chatam didn't even appear to be wearing makeup, except perhaps mascara, as her lashes were much darker than her delicate brows, and a touch of rose-pink lipstick. He couldn't help noticing, however, that the creamy skin of her slender oval face seemed almost luminous with good health. He noted that she shared with her aunts a high forehead and faintly cleft chin. That little dip in her almost pointy chin somehow called attention to the plump, rosy lips above, not to mention those enormous eyes. They were so dark they were almost black, startlingly so with her light hair. He wondered just how long her hair was and what she'd do if he managed to pluck the pins from that loose, heavy knot at the nape of her slender neck. More to distract himself from that line of thought than for any other reason, he broke the silence.

"Aaron explain about the press?"

"He said you're hiding from them."

"I'm not hiding!" Stephen frowned at the notion. "I'm keeping a low profile."

"Ah."

"It's necessary," he grumbled defensively, rubbing his right hand over his prickly jaw and chin and wishing he could shave. "You wouldn't understand."

"No, I guess not."

Something about those softly spoken words irritated him, and he barked at her. "Your aunts swore they would protect my privacy, and I made a hefty contribution to some single parents' charity to guarantee it."

She gave him a look, the kind she might give a little boy who stretched the truth. It made his cheeks and throat heat. He mentally winced at the thought of the curse words that he'd spewed earlier.

"My aunts never swear," she told him with the absolute authority of one who would know. "But if they said they would protect your privacy, then they will. And any donation you may have made to one of their charities has nothing to do with it. Trust me. They may have promised, but they didn't swear."

"What's the difference?" he wanted to know, sounding grumpy even to his own ears.

"'But I tell you,'" she quoted softly, "'Do not swear at all: either by heaven, for it is God's throne; or by the earth, for it is His footstool; or by Jerusalem, for it is the city of the Great King.'"

Stephen gaped at her. Had she just quoted the Bible to him?

"It's from Matthew, chapter five, verses thirty-four and thirty-five."

She had quoted the Bible to him!

"So what are you," he demanded, scowling, "some kind of religious nut?"

Folding her small, delicate hands, she regarded him serenely. "Yes, I suppose you could say that, if 'religious nut' is code for Christian."

Realizing that he'd insulted her, he deepened his frown, muttering, "No offense."

"None taken," she replied lightly, smiling that smile again.

He had the distinct impression that she felt sorry for

him and that it had nothing to do with his physical condition.

"Guess your aunts are religious, too?"

"Yes, of course."

Disconcerted, he said nothing more on the subject, just lay there frowning at her. What on earth, he wondered sourly, had he gotten himself into now?

Aaron had touted Chatam House as a bona fide mansion, a posh throwback to an age of bygone opulence, owned and maintained by three dotty old maids with more money than sense, a trio of do-gooders so far out of the loop that they wouldn't know a juicy news item if it bit them. He had seemed right on the money, going by yesterday's brief impressions. In truth, Stephen had been so exhausted and in such pain from the nearly fifty-mile trip from the Dallas hospital down to the smaller city of Buffalo Creek in Aaron's luxury sedan that he'd barely registered the old ladies' names or faces. Before making the laborious climb up the curving staircase behind Chester, their balding butler, they had informed him that he was to be installed in the "small suite," so called because the sitting room was the smallest in the house.

Stephen supposed Chatam House was opulent enough, provided one admired antiques and crystal chandeliers, but he missed his own place and especially his spacious private bath, complete with sauna, walk-in shower, television and music system. This room didn't even have a closet, for pity's sake, just an enormous antique wardrobe, not that he had many clothes with him, just baggy shorts and sweatpants and cut-up T-shirts to accommodate his injuries. Now he learned that he'd landed smack-dab in the middle of a pack of *"godsdien-*

stige ijveraars," as his stepfather would say, otherwise known as "religious zealots."

Stephen had been acquainted with other Christians, of course, his American grandmother, for one. She'd died after his parents had divorced when he was eight and his mother had taken him back to Holland with her to live. Some of his friends back in Groningen, where they had lived with his mother's parents before her remarriage, had been professing Christians, but they'd never talked about it much. Even some of the guys on the hockey team were Christians, but none of them had ever gone so far as to quote the Bible to him! The most any of them had done was invite him to church, though he'd never gone.

He had enough problems now without finding that he'd landed in the midst of a bunch of religious eccentrics. In fact, he'd say that the very last thing he needed right now was to land in the midst of a bunch of religious eccentrics.

The thing was, he didn't have anywhere else to go. Any hotel large enough to accommodate his needs would also leave him open to the sharp eyes of the press. He had considered convalescing at Aaron's house, but that, too, was under constant surveillance by the local sportswriters. Plus, Stephen couldn't quite bring himself to impose on the newlyweds. Chatam House had seemed like the answer, with Buffalo Creek being close enough to allow Aaron easy access but far enough from the Dallas/Fort Worth Metroplex area to keep the press off his scent.

At this point, his only hope was that the press would not make a big deal of the circumstances of the accident that had knocked him out of the playoffs so that management of the Blades hockey team would not feel duty-bound to activate the good conduct clause of his contract and cut him from the team.

That alone would keep him where he was here in Chatam House, *godsdienstige ijveraars* or not.

Chapter Two

Kaylie Chatam walked around the bed and gathered up the other pillow, saying, "You'll need to sit up a bit in order to eat."

"Yeah, yeah," Stephen muttered on a sigh, grateful for something to think about besides his predicament. He began struggling up onto his right elbow again.

Kaylie swiftly moved back around the bed, her flats slapping lightly against the gleaming hardwood floor. She reached his side and wedged the pillow beneath his head and shoulders, but it still wasn't enough to allow him to eat without decorating himself with his food.

"Let me help you move up on the pillows a little more."

Leaning across him, she slid her hands into the crevices between his torso and arms. He was surprised at the wiry strength that allowed her to actually be of help. After he got settled again, she briskly straightened his T-shirt so that it didn't bind his shoulders and neck. Next, she spread the towel across his chest. Embarrassed by his helplessness, Stephen mumbled, "Thank you."

"You're welcome."

Her soft, rather husky voice sent an odd shiver through him.

"Would you like for me to examine your incisions?"

He shook his head, his right hand going to the spot on his right side where they'd opened him up. "The doctor took a look last night. Said everything seemed fine."

Nodding, she seemed to cast about the room for something more to do. Stephen's gaze followed her.

Despite the lack of certain amenities, he decided that this was really a very elegant room. The cool creams and warm golds, set against a milky brown background, showed off the expensive antiques, rich brocades and matching stripes to perfection.

From where he lay, he could look straight through the open doorway to the gracefully proportioned, brown velvet sofa, placed squarely in the center of a large, truly beautiful cream-on-gold rug positioned in front of an ornate plastered fireplace. He recalled an armchair upholstered in striped satin and a writing desk of some sort, as well as crystal lamps and gold-framed paintings.

It was all a little Victorian for his personal taste, but he couldn't deny the beauty of it. His own home was as sleek and modern as it was possible to be, all shiny blacks and bright colors. It seemed rather cold and pedestrian in comparison. Maybe he ought to rethink that. Be easy enough to make some changes while they were rebuilding the place. Just the thought of what had to be done to make his house on the west side of Fort Worth habitable again—and how it had come to be in need of repair—pained and exhausted him, so he shoved it out of mind.

Thankfully, Aaron returned just then with a laden tray, announcing gaily, "Hey, they got a dumbwaiter.

Imagine that. Comes up out there on the landing. It's like an elevator for food, but Hilda says she sends the laundry up that way, too. Pretty slick, huh?"

Stephen nodded and shrugged. "There's one in my stepfather's flat in Amsterdam, where the houses are very old. It works on a pulley."

Kaylie took the tray and placed it on Stephen's lap, asking, "Older than this place? Chatam House is almost a hundred and fifty years old, you know."

He smirked at this. "My stepfather's flat is in a converted *herenhuis* built in 1632."

She blinked. "My, that is old."

"Sixty percent of the houses in Amsterdam were built before the eighteenth century," he muttered, mentally cataloging the contents of the tray. He identified orange juice; eggs scrambled with parsley and diced onion; toast with butter and strawberry jelly; four slices of crisp bacon; a baked apple sprinkled with cinnamon and swimming in cream; and what appeared to be a cup of strong black coffee.

"Mmm," he said, inhaling appreciatively.

Kaylie smiled. "You'll find the fare at Chatam House on an entirely different plane than that of most hospital food."

"No kidding."

He picked up the ridiculously delicate china cup from its matching saucer and touched it to his lips for a quick sample, then made a face. Hot tea. Yuck. He'd never developed a taste for it, and his mother had not pressed him to. He set the cup back onto the saucer and reached for the orange juice instead.

Kaylie chuckled and said to Aaron, "There's a chain coffee shop down on North Main, about a block south of the highway. They have a drive-through window, but I'm sure that if you pick up his favorite grind, Hilda will be happy to make it for him."

"All right," Aaron said, digging into his pocket for his keys. "Be right back."

"I have to be going, too," Kaylie said, swinging toward the door.

Both Aaron and Stephen spoke at the same time.

"What?"

"Where are you going?"

"Home," she answered, turning to face them.

"B-but what about Steve?" Aaron asked, waving a hand toward the bed.

"I don't know. Who stayed with him last night after you fired the nurse?"

"I did," Aaron answered.

"Well, then…"

"I've got a brand-new wife at home!" he exclaimed, twisting to throw Stephen a pleading look.

Kaylie's eyebrows rose at that, but she said only, "I'm sorry, but I'm not prepared to stay at this point. Aren't there any family—"

"None close," Stephen interrupted tersely, frowning.

"Mom's in Holland," Aaron explained. "Dad's in Lubbock. No siblings."

"Friends?"

Stephen sighed richly. Yeah, like his hard-partying friends would take turns sitting at his bedside. Besides, the team was busy. This was their first year to make the playoffs, and the last thing he wanted was to become more of a distraction to them than he already was.

Aaron rubbed his chin. "Cherie, maybe."

"Who's Cherie?" Kaylie asked.

Aaron waved a hand. "Aw, that's Stephen's girlfriend-of-the-moment."

"Aaron," Stephen scolded, glaring a warning that his agent completely missed.

"The female du jour," the social lummox blathered on, "flavor of the month. Matter of fact, unlike you, she's a not-so-natural red—"

"Aaron!" Stephen shouted forcefully enough that Aaron actually closed his mouth. Finally. Stephen muttered, "Cherie's just a team secretary." A team secretary who liked to style herself as his girlfriend whenever it seemed convenient for her.

A shop-made redhead, with a store-bought figure and trendy "bee-stung" lips, the only things real about Cherie were her hands and feet. Even her fingernails and eyelashes were fake, not to mention her cheekbones and chin. That penchant for plastic surgery and high-end beauty salons hadn't seemed like any big deal to Stephen; now it suddenly seemed a little…tawdry, and he didn't want her anywhere near the Chatams. Truth to tell, he didn't want her near, period. He just didn't have the energy to play her game right now.

"Ah. Well, someone's going to have to bring him his supper. We've already imposed on Hilda enough for one Sunday," Kaylie was saying to Aaron. "After he's eaten, if you just make him comfortable, he should sleep through until morning."

"But what about the night?" Aaron began. "Someone has to be here in case he hurts himself again."

"If she doesn't want to help us, she doesn't want to help us!" Stephen barked.

"I didn't say that," Kaylie insisted. "It's just not a decision I can make instantly."

Aaron sighed, shoulders slumping. “Okay, okay. I’ll sack out in the other room.”

“Don’t strain yourself,” Stephen muttered, picking up a heavy silver fork and attacking his eggs with his right hand.

“Stevie,” Aaron said placatingly, “it’s not me. It’s Dora.”

Aaron’s bride of some three months was given to pouting if Aaron neglected her, which, Stephen admitted silently, happened too often. Still, what was he supposed to do without help? Didn’t the small fortune that he paid Aaron count for something?

Kaylie stepped backward. “Well, I’ll leave you to your meal.”

“But you’ll let us know about the job soon, right?” Aaron pressed.

“I’ll let you know tomorrow.”

She whirled and hurried away. Stephen dropped his fork and fixed his agent—and, in truth, his friend—with a glare.

“Now what?” he demanded, suddenly weary again. For once, Aaron had no glib response. “That’s what I thought,” Stephen muttered morosely.

Hurrying down the gracefully curving marble staircase, her hand skimming the gleaming dark wood of the banister, Kaylie pondered the situation. Stephen Gallow was unlike any man she’d ever encountered. She wasn’t at all sure, frankly, that she liked him, but her like or dislike was not the issue. Part brute and part little boy, he presented a problem: she didn’t quite know how to deal with him. How could she? The men in her life were calm, solid, accomplished, erudite, polite…in short, gentlemanly.

Her father, Hubner Chandler Chatam, Jr., was a retired minister. Bayard, her eldest brother by more than three decades, was a banker, and Morgan, at forty-two, a history professor. Even her third brother, Hubner Chandler Chatam III—known as Chandler or Chan and twenty-nine to her twenty-four—had a degree in agricultural engineering, though to her father's disgust, he made his living mainly in pro rodeo competition. Of all the men she knew, Kaylie supposed that Chandler had most in common with Stephen Gallow, but he never snarled, lost his temper, behaved rudely or, God forbid, cursed. At least, not as far as she knew. And Chandler was a believer, a Christian. Stephen Gallow was obviously not.

Moreover, Gallow was a little crude, or as her father would put it, rough as a cob, though not lacking in all sensibility. He had moderated his language, with some difficulty, on her behalf. None of that, however, changed the fact that he had been gravely injured. He needed help. He needed a nurse. He needed her—far more than her father did, certainly, which made her wonder if this was God's way of showing Hubner Chatam that his life was not over.

It was not time for Hub to stop living, and so, in her opinion, it was not time for him to stop ministering. The man whose spiritual strength had for so long guided countless others had somehow gotten lost in his own physical and emotional pain, and though her heart went out to him, Kaylie knew that she had to somehow help him find his way again. Was that God's purpose in bringing Stephen Gallow into their lives? Would Gallow's condition and her attention to him help Hub realize that he should and could reclaim his own life?

She paused in the grand foyer at the foot of the stairs to gaze through the window at the side of the bright yellow door with its formal black trim to the boxy little red convertible that was her one extravagance in life. It was the only thing she had not given up when she'd quit her job and moved from her apartment into her father's house to care for him after his heart attack. She'd sold every stick of furniture that she'd accumulated in her twenty-four years, such as it was, and even gotten rid of the contents of her kitchen because the one in her father's small, two-bedroom frame house did not have room for her things. At the time, she'd told herself that it was necessary. Now, with Hub constantly comparing her to her aunts, who had cared for their own widowed father until his death at the age of ninety-two, she feared that she had made a big mistake.

Lately, as if sensing her dissatisfaction with the situation, Hub had taken to regularly remarking that not all of God's children were called to marriage, implying that she had been called to follow in the footsteps of her maiden aunts. He even quoted Paul on the subject, choosing selected verses from I Corinthians 7. Kaylie had heard them so often that she could recite them from memory.

Now to the unmarried and the widows I say: It is good for them to stay unmarried.... An unmarried woman or virgin is concerned about the Lord's affairs: Her aim is to be devoted to the Lord in both body and spirit...

But hadn't Paul also said that every man should have his own wife and every wife her own husband, that man should leave his parents and cleave unto his wife?

Kaylie shook her head. She knew that Scripture did not contradict itself, that it only appeared to when certain verses were taken out of context, but that did not help her determine what God intended for her specifically. She had dated little, too caught up in school and the demands of her family, faith and career to pay much attention to anything else, but she'd always assumed that one day she would marry and have children. Then two years ago, her mother had died at the age of fifty-six after a brief bout with cancer, and six months ago her twice-widowed father had suffered a massive heart attack. Kaylie's father and three older brothers had all assumed that Kaylie would drop everything and take over Hubner's care. So she had.

Now, she feared that had been a mistake for both her and her father. Perhaps God's answer to that dilemma occupied the half tester bed upstairs. Unless presented very carefully, however, her father would see this job as her abandoning him. She did not wish to deceive or disrespect him, of course. He was her father, after all. She certainly did not want to go against his express wishes, but if God willed that she take this job, then she must. The question was, what did God will in this matter?

Kaylie heard the clink of a silver spoon stirring tea in a china cup. The aunties would be in the front parlor, taking tea after their lunch. The aunties "ate simple" on Sundays, so that the staff could have the day off, just as God commanded, but that did not keep them from indulging in their one great mutual joy: a hot cup of tea. Their parents, Hubner, Sr. and Augusta Ebenezer Chatam, had spent their honeymoon of several months duration in England back in 1932, returning as staunch Anglophiles, with a shipload of antiques and a mutual devotion to tea. They had passed on that passion to their eldest daughters.

Just the thought of her aunts made Kaylie smile. They were darlings, all three of them, each in her own inimitable fashion.

Kaylie turned and walked across the golden marble floor of the foyer toward the front parlor. The aunts called out an effusive welcome as she entered the room.

Though chock-full of antiques, Tiffany lamps, valuable bric-a-brac and large, beautiful flower arrangements, the parlor was a spacious chamber with a large, ornately plastered fireplace set against a wall of large, framed mirrors, including one over the mantel that faced the foyer door. The aunts sat gathered around a low, oblong piecrust table, its intricate doilies hidden beneath an elaborate tray covered with Limoges china. Odelia and Magnolia sat side by side on the Chesterfield settee that Grandmother Augusta had brought back from her honeymoon trip, while Hypatia occupied one of a pair of high-backed Victorian armchairs upholstered in butter-yellow silk.

Though triplets, they were anything but identical personality-wise. Hypatia had been the reigning belle of Buffalo Creek society in her day, as elegant and regal as royalty. It was largely thanks to her that Chatam House had endured into the twenty-first century and adapted to the modern era with its dignity and graceful ambience intact. That she had never married, or even apparently come close to doing so, puzzled all five of her siblings, including her unmarried sisters.

Magnolia, on the other hand, had never evinced the slightest interest in romance, at least according to Kaylie's father, Hub, Jr., their older brother. Mags had a passion for growing things and spent hours daily in her cavernous greenhouse out back. A tomboy as a girl, she still had little patience with the feminine frills that so entranced her sister Odelia.

Secretly, Kaylie was most fond of Odelia, who was affectionately known by the vast coterie of Chatam nieces and nephews as Auntie Od. With her silly outfits and outlandish jewelry, she always provided a chuckle, but it was her sweet, softhearted, optimistic, almost dreamy approach to life that made her the epitome of Christian love in Kaylie's mind. Odelia also seemed to be the only one of the sisters who had ever come close to marriage.

"Kaylie, dear, how is the patient?" Hypatia wanted to know as soon as Kaylie sank down upon the chair opposite her.

"Handsome, isn't he?" Odelia piped up. She'd still wore her Sunday best, a white shirtwaist dotted with pink polka dots. The dots easily measured two inches in diameter, as did the faceted, bright pink balls clipped to her earlobes. Her lipstick mimicked the pink of her dress, creating a somewhat startling display against the backdrop of her pale, plump face and stark white, softly curling hair. Like her sisters and the majority of the Chatams, including Kaylie herself, she had the cleft in her chin.

Kaylie chose to answer Hypatia's question rather than Odelia's. "He's resting now and should do so until dinner. I've told Mr. Doolin that he'll have to bring in something for his dinner. Please thank Hilda for the breakfast tray."

"Of course, dear," Odelia crooned. "You know that our Hilda is ever ready to perform charitable acts. Poor man."

"You don't have anything else to tell us?" Magnolia asked, eyes narrowing. As usual, Mags wore a dark, nondescript shirtwaist dress, her long, steel-gray braid curving against one shoulder. On any day but Sunday, she might well be shod in rubber boots. Instead, in deference to the Sabbath, she wore penny loafers.

Kaylie knew that she was asking if Kaylie would come to their rescue by agreeing to provide nursing care for their unfortunate guest, but Kaylie was not yet prepared to commit to that. She could not make any promises until she had prayed the matter through and discussed it with her father. The aunts had to understand that.

"It wouldn't hurt if you checked in on him from time to time this evening," Kaylie said softly, answering Magnolia's question as deftly she was able.

"I'll be glad to look in on the poor boy," Odelia said brightly.

Hypatia, however, was not so sanguine. She even displayed a little annoyance. "Of course we'll look in on him, but that young man requires nursing care."

"He does," Kaylie admitted, then she took pity on them, adding, "I've promised an answer by tomorrow morning."

Hypatia dipped her chin. Slimmer than her sisters and still clad in the handsome gray silk suit that she'd worn to services that morning, her silver hair coiled into a smooth figure eight at the nape of her neck and pearls glowing softly at her throat, she might have been bestowing favors—or demerits—at court. Kaylie had to bite her tongue to keep from proclaiming that she would take on Stephen Gallow's care at once, but she knew too well what her father's reaction to that would be.

"I suppose we'll see you in the morning, then," Hypatia said primly.

"As soon as Dad sits down to his breakfast," Kaylie confirmed with a nod.

"Your father used to make his own breakfast," Magnolia pointed out with a sniff.

"Yes, I know." Her father used to do a lot of things that he seemed determined no longer to do. "Now I must get home." She rose and moved toward the door.

"Thank you for coming by, dear!" Odelia chirped. "Tell brother we'll have him to dinner soon, why don't you?"

"I'll do that," Kaylie replied, rushing through the foyer. "See you tomorrow."

She closed the door behind her with a sigh of relief before starting across the porch and down the steps to the boxy little red convertible that waited at the edge of the deeply graveled drive. She really needed some time alone. Her father had no doubt fed himself from the roast and vegetables that she'd left in the Crock-Pot that morning, and her own stomach was too tied in knots to allow her hunger to plague her. The sooner she took this matter to God, however, the sooner she would have her answer. And the sooner God's plan for them all, Stephen Gallow included, could come to fruition, for a plan He must have. The Almighty always did.

"Such a darling that girl is," Odelia said with a sigh. "She reminds me a good deal of you, Hypatia."

"Nonsense," Hypatia said, sipping from her teacup. "I would never have allowed Hubner to get out of hand as he has."

Well, that was true, Odelia had to concede. Hypatia

never let anything or anyone get out of hand, while Odelia, conversely, seldom had things in hand. Like now. She'd only wanted to help, though. Perhaps she and Kaylie were more alike than she'd realized. Kaylie always sought to please everyone around her all the time. She had allowed Hub to take advantage of her to the point that she hardly had a life of her own anymore. Odelia bit her bright pink lip.

"Feeling sorry for himself, at his age," Magnolia grumbled about their brother. "We don't sit around feeling sorry for ourselves."

"Oh, but we have each other," Odelia pointed out.

"Our brother has four adult children, three granddaughters and two great-grandsons," Hypatia pointed out.

"And he's been blessed with love twice," Mags added.

"That's right!" Odelia said with a happy giggle. Trust her sisters to put everything into proper perspective. "Perhaps he'll even be blessed a third time!"

"At his age?" Mags snorted, recoiling.

"What has age got to do with it?" Odelia wanted to know. Surely Magnolia wasn't hinting that romantic love had forever passed them by. Why should that be?

"I hardly think," Hypatia interceded sternly, "that Hubner will find a third wife in time for Kaylie to decide she isn't needed by him so she can help us with our…guest."

Problem, she had been about to say. But not *their* problem. Oh, no, Stephen Gallow was more rightly Odelia's problem. Squelching a sigh, she put on a wobbly smile.

"I'm quite sure it will all work out for the best."

"God willing," Hypatia inserted. "Be that as it may,

it was not well done of you, Odelia, obligating us to take in this…this…"

"Hockey player," Magnolia supplied, her tone leaving little doubt that she considered the man a ruffian of the worst sort. Last night's unhappy contretemps had only confirmed that opinion.

Odelia bowed her head in contrition. Hypatia was right about her obligating the sisters unfairly. But what was she supposed to have done? There she was, sitting in Brooks's waiting room, having made an appointment for her yearly physical, when suddenly she'd been swept into his office and told about this poor, injured man who hadn't a place in the world to go and hardly anyone to care for him. It had sounded so reasonable the way Brooks had explained it all, and when he'd asked it as a personal favor, well, what could she do but say yes? And the payment they'd offered!

Well, of course, the Chatams never accepted payment for kindness, but there was the new single parents' ministry at the Downtown Bible Church to consider. She'd thought that worthwhile project would welcome a hefty contribution. Still, the sisters had barely settled back into their normal routine after their nephew Reeves had moved from Chatam House, with his bride, Anna, and daughter, Gilli, before along came Mr. Gallow. If only he had not so quickly proven to be such a *presence* in the house.

"I'm sure God will work it all out for the best," Odelia offered meekly. "If Kaylie does decide to help us, even Hub will benefit, don't you think? He'll have to take up his life again, then. Yes?"

"You could be right," Hypatia said after a moment.

"I agree," Magnolia added reluctantly. "But just so

you know—" she glared at Odelia "—whatever happens, I, for one, will *not* be emptying any bedpans."

Odelia felt the color drain from her face. Oh, dear. Surely it wouldn't come to that. No one could expect them to… Quickly, she set aside her teacup and held out her hands.

"Sisters," she said earnestly, "I feel the need to pray."

Chapter Three

Clasping her hands together, Kaylie bowed her head over the evening meal. "Father God, we thank You and praise You on this, Your Sabbath Day," she prayed. "You have restored Dad's health and given us lives of comfort and security. Bless Bayard and his family, Morgan and Chandler, the aunts and all our Chatam kin. Turn our minds ever to Your service, Lord, and let us not forget that we serve You only by serving others—which reminds me, Father, of that poor Mr. Gallow whom the aunts have taken in. Heal him, Lord, in such a way as to bring glory to Yourself, so that he is forever aware of Your love and power. Direct our paths, Father, and make Your will known to us, and finally, bless this food to the nourishment of our bodies. These things we pray in the name of Your Holy Son, Jesus the Christ. Amen."

"Amen," Hub Chatam echoed.

Dressed simply in black slacks and a white shirt, Hub unbuttoned and rolled back the cuffs of his sleeves before picking up his fork. His thinning hair, a mixture of light brown and ash-gray, seemed at odds with his bushy white eyebrows and dark brown eyes. Pushing up his bifocals with the tip of one finger, he trained those dark eyes on his daughter.

Kaylie had turned the remnants of his lunch into a hearty beef stew for their dinner, serving it with buttered bread and prepackaged salad. She kept her gaze carefully averted, applying herself to her meal. For several moments, silence reigned in the cozy, outdated kitchen, broken only by the clink of flatware. Kaylie could feel the comment coming, however, and finally it arrived.

"You waxed eloquent this evening, Kaylie."

She smiled. "Did I? Guess that's what comes of spending time praying."

"That's what you were doing this afternoon, sitting out in the backyard in the lawn chair? You were praying?"

Nodding, she scooped up a bite of stew. "Spring is a wonderful time to talk to God out of doors. I couldn't resist."

"Little warm for mid-April," her father muttered.

"Mm. We could be in for a hot summer."

"When have we not?"

Kaylie chuckled. "True."

Conversation lagged for a few minutes, and finally they got to the crux of the matter. "Who is this Mr. Gallow you mentioned? I assume he is the reason you dumped me after church and raced off to answer your aunts' beck and call."

Kaylie sighed mentally. Her father never used to be snide and self-centered. As a pastor, he had been one of the most caring, giving, selfless men she'd ever known, working long hours in the service of others. He had built Downtown Bible into a thriving, growing community of believers with vibrant worship, Scripturally sound doctrine and effective ministry. After choosing about a decade ago to allow a younger generation to lead the church into a new era, he had stepped aside as senior pastor, but neither the membership nor the new administration had been willing to truly let him go.

At their urging, he had assumed the position of Pastor of Congregational Care. The church's ministry to the homebound and marginalized had expanded significantly under his tutelage. Part of the job had been organizing teams to check on, visit and minister to those sometimes invisible members, but Hubner Chatam had never been a mere administrator, and he'd often spent five, even six, days of every week in the field.

Then her mother, Kathryn, had died, and Hub never quite seemed to recover from her loss, perhaps because he had been widowed once before. The mother of Kaylie's two older brothers, Bayard and Morgan, had died of an accidental blow to the head when a hammer had fallen from a tall shelf. After losing his second wife, Hub had lost his zeal for ministry—and his zeal for life along with it. Chandler, her only full sibling, maintained that their father had grieved and resented his way into his heart attack. Kaylie only knew that he had become a very unhappy man, so she let go the remark about her "dumping" him.

"The aunts have taken him in as a favor to Brooks," she said, knowing that the doctor was one of Hub's favorite people. The good doctor had also lost a wife, to an inoperable brain tumor, and that seemed to have formed a bond between the two men.

Hub put down his fork thoughtfully. "Dr. Leland is not one to impose."

"No, he isn't."

"What's wrong with this Gallow?"

Kaylie sipped water from the tumbler beside her plate and said, "He was seriously injured in an accident."

"What sort of accident?"

Kaylie wrinkled her brow. "I don't think anyone ever said."

Hub clucked his tongue and shook his head, muttering, "Gallow, Gallow, unusual name. Don't believe I know any Gallows. Where is he from?"

"Actually," she answered with some surprise, "I believe he's originally from the Netherlands."

"The Netherlands! You don't say! Dutch then, is he?"

"You wouldn't know it to hear him speak," Kaylie said.

"What about his relatives? Surely you spoke with them."

Folding her hands in her lap, Kaylie shook her head. "Aren't any. At least, none near enough to help out."

"Ah. So your aunts, at the urging of Brooks Leland, have opened the family home to him," Hub deduced, "and now they find him more of a burden than they expected."

Kaylie nodded. "I'm afraid so."

"And because you're a nurse they expect you to deal with him."

"I do seem the logical choice," Kaylie pointed out.

Hubner waved a hand in agitation. "Do they not realize the level of your responsibilities?"

"I would say that the 'level of my responsibilities' is extremely light," Kaylie told him. "I've been thinking, in fact, that it might be time for me to go back to work at the hospital."

Her father sat back, clearly appalled. "But that would

require shift work! You'd be gone all hours of the day and night."

Kaylie had considered that, and now she quite shamelessly used it. "Hm. Yes, I suppose that's true. Taking care of Mr. Gallow would be much less time-consuming. His injuries are serious, and his meds must be administered by a professional, but he's well enough to leave the hospital, at least. A couple hours in the morning, a couple hours in the afternoon and evening… I'd be home every night, free to get you your meals and your pills."

Hub considered, frowning at her, but eventually he accepted the obvious. Neither of them could, with a clear Christian conscience, say no. Hub grimaced.

"I blame my sisters for this. Once again, their 'project' means work for others."

"Dad!"

"You know it's true. Oh, I'm sure their hearts are in the right places, but never do their good works consist of labor only for them." He tossed up a gnarled hand. "Whatever they take on, it always requires teams of volunteers and committees of…committees! They're never satisfied until the whole of Buffalo Creek is involved. I suppose I should be thankful that we don't live any closer to Dallas. Imagine what causes they could get embroiled in there."

Kaylie bit back a smile, partly because he was right. Somewhat. The aunts did tend to take on huge schemes like raising funds for the Buffalo Creek Bible College and the local free clinic. Lately their pet project was one that Hub had once championed himself, ministries and services aimed at single-parent households. The aunts were preparing, as Hypatia put it, to take that initiative to a "whole new level."

"Maybe Mr. Gallow is more than they can manage on their own," she said, "but this time it's just me involved, and I expect to be paid for my expertise."

"Oh, yes, throw money at the problem," Hub said, "as if the Chatam well will never run dry. Your brother Bayard has warned them time and again."

A staunchly conservative banker, Bayard constantly harped on the idea that the aunts, now approaching their mid-seventies, *could* outlive their inheritance, as if they lived profligately. The aunties and most of the rest of the family, including Hub until recently, pretty much just tuned him out.

"You misunderstand. The aunts aren't paying me, Dad. Mr. Gallow is."

"Oh. Well, I suppose that if he's getting free room and board, he can afford to pay for private nursing care."

Kaylie supposed that he could pay for a lot more than that, but she didn't say so. Why open the door for questions that she would rather not have to answer? Like where Stephen Gallow's money came from, for instance. Having run out of reasons for complaint, at the moment, Hubner went back to his meal, and Kaylie turned her silent thoughts to how best to serve her new patient.

"Good morning."

Stephen opened his eyes to the now familiar sound of the gentle, slightly husky but decidedly feminine voice. He'd been awake for some time, actually, the throbbing in his bones keeping him still, while he worried about his situation with the team.

The playoffs were now officially under way, and though he had been the goalie to get the team there for the first time in their short history, he had been out of the pipes for nearly two weeks now, with weeks more to go before he could even think about starting rehab. He wasn't going to see ice time again this season, so should the team actually win the Stanley Cup—a long shot but feasible—his part in the triumph could well be forgotten. Of course, it was entirely possible that, given the good conduct clause in his contract, the team might cut or trade him regardless of what happened in the playoffs, especially if his backup, Kapimsky, proved able to get the job done.

Stephen had expected Aaron, bleary from a night spent in a strange bed, to be the first person he saw this morning, and though he would never admit it, Stephen dearly wanted his agent's reassurance. Instead, he would have to settle for the ministrations of the new nurse. At least he hoped that she had decided to take the position. He turned his head slightly to find Kaylie Chatam regarding him serenely from the open doorway.

He smiled, for two reasons. One, the petite nurse's soft red hair hung down her back in a thick, straight tail of pure silk at least as long as his forearm. Secondly, she was dressed for work in shapeless pink scrubs with surfing penguins printed on them.

"In the Netherlands," he told her, "they say *'Goedemorgen.'*"

"Gude morgan, then."

He tried not to correct her pronunciation, covering his amusement by saying, "Penguins?"

She plucked at the fabric of her loose top, looking down at a penguin tumbling through a cresting wave. "Best I could do. No skates, but at least they're creatures that are comfortable on the ice."

He laughed. And regretted it. Squeezing his eyes shut

against the sharpened pain, he hissed until it subsided to a more bearable level. When he opened his eyes again, Kaylie Chatam was standing over him, pill bottle in hand.

"Mr. Doolin's gone down to ask for your breakfast tray. Let's get these into you so you'll be up to eating when it's ready. All right?"

"Fine," he grumbled. "But then I need to get to the bathroom."

She dropped the pill bottle into one of the cavernous pockets on the front of her smock and slid her small but surprisingly strong hands beneath his arms, helping him into a sitting position on the side of the bed. He tried to bite back the groan that accompanied the action, but the pain was breathtaking. It eased as soon as he was still again. She quickly gave him the pills. After swallowing a pair of them, he was ready to go forward. He shoved up onto his good leg, jaw clamped.

Moving effortlessly into a supportive posture, Kaylie slid her arm up over his back to his shoulder, her own shoulder tucked neatly beneath his arm. Hopping and hobbling, he inched toward the bathroom door. Small bathrooms, he mused a few minutes later, had their good points, as the close confines allowed him to manage for himself. Afterward, the little nurse made a very welcome suggestion.

"Maybe you should eat your breakfast in the sitting room."

Stephen looked into the sitting room and smiled. Comfortable as it was, the bed had already begun to feel like a prison to him.

"If it's any inducement," she went on in a teasing voice, "there's a large cup of coffee in there."

Stephen eagerly slung his arm around her shoulders. "Lead me to it."

Chuckling, she eased him forward. By the time they reached the near end of the sofa, some three or four yards, his head swam. Bracing her feet wide apart and gripping his one good arm, she helped him lower into a sitting position in the corner of the comfortable couch before fetching a small, brocade footstool for his injured leg.

"How's that?"

He waited until the pain subsided enough that he could get his breath. "Guess I'll live. What about that coffee?"

While she went to the small writing desk standing against one wall and retrieved a tall, disposable cup with a cardboard sleeve, Stephen looked around him. Oddly elegant paintings that featured game birds, dogs and tools of the hunt from a bygone era covered the walls of the room. In contrast to the antique artwork, he noted, with relieved satisfaction, a flat-screen television hung over the mantel. The old girls didn't have their heads entirely buried in the past, then. The screen was nowhere near as large as the one in his media room back at the house in Fort Worth, but it would do for watching the playoff games.

Stephen took the coffee container from Kaylie with his good right hand, turning it with the aid of the fingertips of his left to get the drinking slot in the plastic top adequately positioned. Taking a careful sip, he sighed with satisfaction.

"I have cream, if you'd like," she said, reaching into her pocket once more and drawing out the tiny containers.

"Black is fine."

Nodding, she parked her hands at her slender hips and glanced around before snapping her fingers and hurrying back into the bedroom. "Hang on."

Like I'm going anywhere, he thought wryly. She returned an instant later with one of the bed pillows and a bath towel.

"We'll have to keep using this as a lap tray until I find one," she explained, placing the pillow across his lap. She covered both it and his chest with the towel.

He slugged back more of the coffee. It was still hot but thoroughly drinkable, and he moaned in delight as the silky brew flowed down his throat.

"Wonderful," he said, using his thumb to tidy the corners of his lips. "This is the best cup of coffee I've had in weeks. Thank you."

"My pleasure," she said, smiling down at him, and oddly enough, he thought that it just might be. She actually seemed pleased that he enjoyed the coffee. Something about that struck him as… Well, it just struck him.

He had little time to puzzle over the matter as Aaron carried his breakfast tray into the room just then. Despite being rumpled and unshaven, Aaron whistled cheerily as he crossed the floor.

"It's a good thing I'm a married man again," he said at his jocular best, "or else I'd have to take that Hilda away from poor old Chester. That woman can cook! Mmm-mmm."

At the word *again,* Stephen saw Kaylie's eyebrows rise ever so slightly. Silently amused, he glanced innocently at Aaron as Kaylie moved aside so he could deposit the tray on the pillow across Stephen's lap.

Belgian waffles, still steaming from the iron, sliced

strawberries, maple syrup, ham and—Stephen couldn't believe his eyes—*gele room.* Kaylie touched the rim of the fluted cup of thick, sweet, golden cream with the tip of one finger.

"Clotted cream, a bit of England right here in the very heart of Texas." Her dark eyes twinkled merrily. "My aunts are devoted to all things English."

Stephen had no idea why that might be, but he didn't care. Setting aside the coffee, he picked up his fork with his left fingers and his knife with his right. It was awkward, and he got cream on the edge of his jacket sling, but he managed to cut up the waffle. Nurse Kaylie watched intently, but she did not offer to cut up his breakfast for him. He liked her for that.

Aaron took his suit jacket and tie from the desk chair and began putting them on, chatting happily. "Our darling nurse has given me a shopping list, Steve-o. I'll just make a quick run into the picturesque town of Buffalo Creek, and then it's home to the little bride." He clapped a hand on Stephen's shoulder. "I leave you in capable, if dainty, hands." He bowed over one of those dainty hands like some sort of old gallant, saying grandly, "I'd kiss your pretty little pink toes, darlin', if I wasn't married."

"Again," Kaylie chirped, looking a bit startled with herself, as well as amused.

"Hey," Aaron quipped good-naturedly, "third time's the charm, right?"

He waved and strode happily from the room. Kaylie pressed a hand to her chest and looked at Stephen.

"Has he really been married three times?"

Stephen nodded, going to work on his ham. "Never knew the first one, but anyone could have told him that was a no-go. She was, er, an exotic dancer. The, um, second wife," he went on, "used him as a stepping stone to the bigger things."

"Bigger things?"

Putting down his knife, Stephen took up his fork with his right hand, though he still had some difficulty eating that way. "Aaron's second wife left him for a hockey player," he told Kaylie bluntly, "after Aaron negotiated a six-million-dollar contract for the guy." He gave her the name, but since it obviously meant nothing to her, he added, "The creep's a starting center on the East Coast now."

"Ah."

"I think Aaron maybe got it right this time," Stephen went on. "I think Dora loves him. She sure acts like it. Behaves as if he's the cleverest, wittiest thing she's ever met." He shook his head.

Nurse Chatam slid her small hands into her big pockets. "He is kind of funny."

Stephen chuckled and forked up another bite. "He is, really, especially when you get to know him. Fact is, Aaron's a good guy."

"But you give him a hard time anyway," the little nurse remarked softly.

Stephen stilled. He did. He really did give Aaron a hard time. He wondered why. But then he knew. He gave Aaron a hard time because Aaron did not give him one when he clearly deserved it. Suddenly chilled, tired and irritated, Stephen dropped his fork and tugged at the neck of his T-shirt, the armhole of which had been slit to accommodate the cast on his left arm before the jacket sling went on. The back of the sofa had tugged it askew, and the stupid thing was choking him.

Seeing the problem, the little nurse leaned close and

reached behind him to pull up the fabric of his shirt, loosening the pressure on his throat. She smelled clean and sweet, like the air after a spring rain, and Stephen felt a sudden longing. In some ways, that longing made him think of his boyhood and his mother, but the feeling was in no way childlike. He suddenly wondered just what the next several weeks might hold. Who was this petite, Bible-quoting lovely, anyway, and why did she make him feel clumsy and ignorant?

Waiting until she straightened, he turned a bland face up at her and asked, "What should I call you? Nurse seems a bit impersonal."

"Kaylie will do."

"All right, Kaylie. And I'm Stephen. Or Steve, if you prefer."

"But not Stevie," she said, a quirk at one corner of her lips.

"Not Stevie," he confirmed. Stevie had been a boy whose parents had tugged him this way and that between them, an innocent who had ceased to exist decades ago, mourned by no one, not even him, though he had been that boy. "So, Kaylie," he said, changing the subject, "tell me something about yourself."

"Not much to tell. What do you want to know?"

He really wanted to know if she was married or involved with anyone, but he had more game than to ask outright. "Well," he said, pondering his options, "so, um, where do you live exactly? I know you don't live here."

She shook her head. "No. No, I don't live here. I live with my father, about three miles across town."

With her father? Interesting. Odd, but interesting. What woman her age lived with her father? That brought up another question.

"And, uh, how old are you?"

"Twenty-four."

That was about what he'd figured, despite the air of inexperience about her.

She leaned forward, her hands clasped behind her back, to ask, "And you?"

"Twenty-eight." Felt more like eighty-two of late. He put on a smile and said, "I take it you're not married. I mean, since you live with your father."

"Uh, no, not married."

"Engaged?"

"No."

"Dating?"

She blinked at him, tilting her head. "Forgive me, but I don't see how that is relevant."

Feeling thwarted and a tad irritated, he waved a hand. "Sorry. Just making conversation. I can't help being a little curious, though, since you live with your father still."

"Not *still,*" she said pointedly. "Again." He waited for her to go on, and after a slight pause, she did. "My father is seventy-six years old and suffered a heart attack a few months ago. I moved in to take care of him."

"What about your mother?" Stephen asked.

"Deceased." The way she said it told him that the death had been fairly recent.

"Sorry to hear that."

Lifting her head, she beamed a soft smile and said, "Thank you."

That smile took his breath away, rocked him right down to the marrow of his bones. The sincerity, not to mention the beauty, of it was downright shocking. No one in his world was that open and genuine.

After a moment of awkward silence, she glanced

around the room, before blurting, "My brothers expected it of me."

Knocked back into the conversation, Stephen cleared his throat and marshaled his mental processes. "They, ah, expected you to take care of your father, you mean?"

She nodded. "They're all older, and I'm the only girl, and a nurse, too."

"I see. What if you hadn't wanted to take care of him, though?"

"I did!" she exclaimed quickly.

"Did?"

"Do!" she corrected. "I do want to take care of him."

"But?" he pressed, certain that some caveat existed.

She bit her lip then fluttered her hands. "You have to understand that he's been widowed twice over the years, and since he left the church, he's been at loose ends."

"Left the church?"

"Retired, I should have said. Retired from the church."

Carefully, to prevent any misunderstanding, Stephen asked, "He worked for the church?"

"He's a minister," she said, confirming Stephen's worst fears. "Or was a minister. *Is* a minister," she finally decided with a sigh. "He just isn't active in ministry right now."

Stephen's mind reeled. So she was not just a Christian, she was the daughter of a Christian minister! "With three brothers, no less." He hadn't realized that he'd muttered that last aloud until she addressed the comment.

"Yes, well, two are half brothers, to be precise, and a good deal older. Bayard's fifty-five, and Morgan's forty-two."

"Fifty-five!" Stephen echoed, shocked. "My mother's only fifty-three."

"My mom would be fifty-eight. She died two years ago."

"So your dad was nearly twenty years older than her."

"Yes. It just didn't seem that way until she got sick. He aged a dozen years during the weeks of her illness, and he hasn't been the same since."

"My father hasn't been the same since my parents' divorce," Stephen said, to his own surprise. Realizing how personal the conversation had become, he quickly changed directions. "What was it you sent Aaron after?"

She ticked off a list of items. "Hand sanitizer, antibacterial soap, lip balm, sterile gloves, syringes… The doctor called in a new prescription, by the way, injections that should help you control your pain better."

Stephen let that go without comment, but he was desperately tired of all these drugs. He felt as if he was sleeping—and dreaming—his life away. The dreams, unfortunately, were not pleasant ones. Kaylie, he noticed, tapped her chin, staring at him as if trying to read his mind.

"I wonder if I should have asked for leverage straps?"

"Leverage straps?" Stephen parroted. "Whatever for?"

"To get you up and down more easily," she explained. "I'm not very big, you know, and you're—"

"Six foot four," he supplied, "and over two hundred pounds."

"Exactly."

"Still," Stephen pointed out, "we've managed pretty well so far, and I'm only going to get better, you know."

"Hmm, I suppose." She continued tapping her chin, the tip of her finger fitting nicely into the tiny cleft there. More a dimple, really, Stephen had begun to think it a charming feature. "Maybe I should've asked for a lap tray, too," she murmured, staring down at the remnants of his breakfast.

"Now that I'll go with," Stephen said. "Why don't I call Aaron and add that to the list? No, wait. I don't have a cell phone any longer." His had been destroyed in the accident, along with his car and half his house.

"You can use mine," she said, producing a small flip phone from those seemingly bottomless pockets.

"Better yet," Stephen said, "let's text him. Then he has it in writing."

"Oh," she replied casually, "my phone doesn't text."

Stephen's jaw dropped. "You're kidding." Stunned, he stared up at her. "You're not kidding!" Who, in this day and age, didn't have text?

Kaylie, of the dark, bottomless eyes and heavy, light red hair, tilted her head. "Is that a problem?"

"Yeah, it could be. Like, what if I need you in the middle of the night or something?" He ignored for now the fact that he didn't have a cell phone himself. "Do you want me waking up the entire the household by shouting or even by ringing you? Or would you rather I sent you a nice quiet text message?"

"Oh, I won't be staying the night here," Kaylie told him calmly.

"Won't be staying—" Stephen broke off, momentarily dumbstruck. "But I thought you were taking the job!"

"I am. I just won't be here at night—or whenever you're sleeping."

"B-but what if something happens?"

"Such as?"

Such as nightmares, he thought, dreams that tormented him until he woke writhing and screaming, memories about which he could not bring himself to speak. He hated the weakness and guilt that allowed the horrific dreams to flourish, and the second accident seemed to have brought back the memories of the first one in all its horrific detail, details he'd give almost anything to forget.

"I don't know!" he snapped in answer to her question. "You tell me. You're the nurse."

She patted his shoulder consolingly. "Now don't worry. The aunts will look in on you, and there's always the staff. Hilda, Chester and Carol have been taking care of Chatam House and its occupants for over twenty years, you know. They do, however, have Sundays and Wednesdays off."

"You mean the cook, and that old bald guy I met when I first got here?" Stephen protested.

"Chester's not old," Kaylie argued with a smile. "Why, he's just barely sixty!"

"But what if I fall out of bed or trip on my way to the bathroom?"

Kaylie Chatam folded her arms, looking down at him with the patience and authority that a particularly wise adult might reserve for an unreasonable child. "You'll be fine as long as you don't try to get up and about on your own too soon. I'll make sure you're properly settled in before I leave, and I will, after all, be just a phone call away."

A phone call and three miles, he wanted to snarl. Well, if that's the way she wanted to play it, he would make doubly sure of her availability. He held out his hand, instructing, "Give me the cell phone."

Frowning, she produced the phone and dropped it into his palm. Stephen flipped it open and punched in the numbers with his thumb before hitting the send button and lifting the tiny phone to his ear. After several rings, Aaron answered. Stephen interrupted his effusive greeting and got right down to business.

"You're going to have to make another stop or two. Seems Kaylie would like to add a lap tray to her shopping list, so I don't have to eat off the bed pillows. Then I need you to do something for me. I want two cell phones with texting, Internet access, global positioning and anything else you can think of. One for me, one for our Nurse Chatam, who will not, as it turns out, be working full-time."

"Even full-time is not around-the-clock," she pointed out, parking her hands at her slender waist.

"For the money we're paying you, it ought to be!" Stephen snapped. Then he barked into the phone, "Just do it, Aaron," and hung up.

He passed the phone back to her, glowering. He didn't know why he was so upset, really. Just last night, he'd argued that Aaron didn't have to stay, and truth be told, the fewer people who knew about his nightmares, the better. Yet, he found that he'd been looking forward to having Kaylie Chatam around. She seemed to bring a certain serenity with her, an assurance that, temporarily at least, banished his worries and made him believe that he could put yet another stupid, ugly episode behind him.

But who was he kidding? Some things could never be gotten over. Some decisions, some disasters, could not be left in the past. They could only be lived with, one torturous day at a time.

So be it, he decided angrily.

His past had left him with enough pain to go around, and he was suddenly in the mood to share.

Chapter Four

Stephen Gallow, Kaylie decided, was as much child as adult. Honestly, the way he pouted! Then again, she should be used to it by now, for his behavior really was not much different from her father's. Men! What was it that made them such impossible patients? Either they were too macho to give in to disease or, once overwhelmed by it, they wallowed in black despair and petulant behavior.

She thought of her mother and how patiently and cheerfully that dear woman had endured her own swift decline: dizziness so acute that she couldn't stand without retching, vision so blurry that she could neither read nor watch television, pain so intense that there were whole days she could not lift her head from her pillow. At the end, she could not swallow even her own saliva, but she had smiled with gratitude every time someone had wiped her mouth for her. When relief had finally come, she had passed into the next life with the most peaceful expression imaginable. And Hubner Chatam had been angry ever since.

Why, Kaylie wondered, was Stephen Gallow angry?

For angry he definitely was, so much so that she probably ought to tell him to keep his job or find someone else more to his liking. But she didn't. Instead, she remained mute, for what if she offered him her resignation and he took her up on it? After all, if taking the job was God's will for her, then she had no business resigning it.

If that explanation did not entirely satisfy, she chose not to search for another.

Stephen expressed a sudden weariness, so she got him to his feet and helped him hobble back to the bed, his rapidly failing strength burdening both of them. Doolin came in just as they reached the bed, his arms laden with bags.

"Are you sure we didn't forget something?" he quipped, dumping the bags on the chest at the foot of the bed. "I could've bought a nice gurney while I was out or a coffee plantation in Brazil. Hospital, anyone? I hear there's a good one in Galveston, right on the beach. Palm trees, sun and sand."

"Hurricanes," Stephen growled, easing down onto the edge of the bed.

"Always looking on the bright side," Aaron joked, digging into the bags. "Got those phones," he said to his client, "and just in the nick of time. You'll never guess who called. Okay, you will, because she's been calling ever since you drove your car through your house."

Kaylie gasped. "Is that what happened?" She looked at Stephen. "You drove your car through your house? But how is that possible?"

They both studiously ignored her questions. Instead, Stephen glared at Aaron. "You did *not* give her my new number. Tell me you did not give her my new number."

"I didn't give her your new number," Aaron said

dryly, huffing slightly as if Stephen had questioned his loyalty. "That way she can keep calling me and pleading to speak to you."

Stephen looked away. "Tell her I'll talk to her when I'm better."

"I've been telling her that. She says if she doesn't speak to you soon, she's coming over here."

Stephen seemed to dismiss that out of hand. "She doesn't know where I am."

"She knows where I am," Aaron pointed out. "She knows where the arena is and the team offices."

Stephen's head jerked around, an appalled look on his face, but then he sighed. "I can't deal with this now, Aaron. Find a way to put her off. Now, give me the phones."

Aaron threw up his hands and went back to pawing through the bags. "I'm just saying..."

Confused and curious, Kaylie helped Stephen into a prone position.

"Get me the other pillow, will you?" he mumbled, his gaze averted. "I've spent enough time flat on my back."

"All right."

She went to do as requested, aware of Stephen and Aaron speaking quietly together in the next room. She returned with the second pillow and, after making Stephen comfortable in a semi-reclining position, she distributed the goods about the room, placing each item where it would be most handy. Meanwhile, Aaron and Stephen discussed the phones and their functions. Eventually, they called her over, and Aaron explained what amounted to a miniature handheld computer with a touch screen, camera, microphone and speaker. The thing was amazing and must have cost a fortune. She turned over the sleek contraption in her hand and looked to Stephen.

"This really isn't necessary, you know."

"I think it is," he said dismissively, failing to meet her gaze.

Aaron jumped in, using his "good buddy" voice. "I've programmed in Steve's new number, mine and the doc's. The roll-up keyboard works like this." He demonstrated, adding, "Makes it easier if you're not used to phone-pad texting. This way you just type."

"Okay," Kaylie said, pocketing the sleek new gadget. "If you say so."

"One thing," Stephen insisted, deigning to look at her. "I want your word that you'll keep that with you at all times. Understood?"

Kaylie just barely refrained from rolling her eyes. "I'll keep it with me at all times. And when you don't need my assistance anymore, I'll return it."

Stephen bobbed his head in a curt nod. Aaron split an uncertain look between the two of them and clapped his hands together with forced joviality. "Okeydoke. I am off to see the little woman." He walked backward toward the door. "Either of you need anything, you give me a shout." He paused in the doorway long enough to point a finger at Stephen and say, "I'll see you in a day or two, kid. You behave yourself and let nurse darlin' take care of you. Understand?" He winked at Kaylie and blew her a noisy kiss, exclaiming, "Angel of mercy!" With that, he turned and hurried from sight.

Stephen put his head back and closed his eyes, dismissing her as effectively as if he'd turned his back on her. Unfortunately for him, she'd had a good deal of recent experience in dealing with hardheaded men. Leaning a shoulder against the bedpost at the foot of the bed, she folded her arms and regarded him thoughtfully. Kaylie very much wanted to ask Stephen about the "she" whose phone call to Aaron Doolin had so obviously upset him earlier, but she had no plausible professional reason for doing so. She didn't see anything to be gained by taking him to task for his attitude, but the accident, on the other hand, seemed well within her purview, her personal curiosity aside.

"It might help me to know about your accident," she said after a long moment of silence.

He opened an eye and peered down his nose at her. Closing that eye again, he settled more comfortably. She assumed that would be the end of it, but just as she dropped her arms and started to straighten away from the bedpost, he spoke.

"I accidentally drove my car through the garage wall and into my house. What else do you want to know?"

Horrified, she shook her head, grasping the bedpost with both hands. "How on earth did such a thing happen?"

Sighing richly, he opened both eyes and stared up at the ceiling. "Some friends had driven my car and left it parked outside with the top down and a storm threatening." Kaylie winced. "Worried that the storm would ruin the interior, I rushed out to move the car into the garage, but when I should have hit the brake, I accidentally hit the gas pedal."

"Oh, my, and in a convertible, no less."

"A very expensive convertible with a powerful engine. Powerful enough to propel me through two walls and right into a free-standing fireplace."

"Goodness!"

"Nothing good about it," he said sourly. "Not only was the car ruined, the house all but came down."

"No wonder your injuries are so serious!"

He lifted a hand to his head, as if holding down the top of it. "Nothing I don't deserve for being so incredibly stupid. *Idiotic dwass,*" he muttered.

She didn't need to know Dutch to understand the gist of that. Her heart went out to him. He might be a spoiled sports figure, but he was also a seriously injured man whose pride had obviously been as battered as his body.

Her father had his faith and his family to help him overcome his loss and his health issues, but what or who did Stephen Gallow have? Only himself and his sports agent, as far as she could see.

Was that why God had brought him here to Chatam House? Of course it must be. She'd already considered the possibility that Stephen Gallow's sudden presence in her family's life had to do with a loving God's plan for her father, but God continually reached out to all of His creation. She must not forget that fact. It was as if God's love for Stephen Gallow imbued her in that moment. Instinctively, she reached out a hand to him.

That hand fell upon the covers blanketing his foot, his huge foot. That foot would make two of hers, and yet, she sensed that deep inside he was as lost and troubled as any little boy alone in the world. He might be a gladiator on the ice, but here and now he was a wounded patient in need of a kind, caring hand.

"Can I get you anything?"

He shook his head.

"Are you in pain?"

"No more than usual." He flattened his mouth then said, "Not as much as earlier."

Accepting that she could do nothing more for him at the moment, she nodded and moved toward the door, saying, "I'll just take your breakfast tray down, then." Pausing, she looked back at him. "I could bring you a book. The aunties have quite a library, you know."

He lifted his eyebrows at that, but then he shrugged. Kaylie smiled and went out. She was halfway down the stairs, having left the tray in the dumbwaiter, when the new phone in her pocket dinged and vibrated. Surprised, she dug it out and peered at the screen.

It read, "Sports. Thrillers. Sci-fi. Westerns."

She understood that he was telling her what sorts of books he preferred, most likely in the order that he preferred them. Awkwardly, she typed out a return message, pecking at the tiny keyboard with the tip of her forefinger. "See what I can find."

She watched as the message went on its way, then she went on hers, shaking her head. How odd that Stephen seemed to find it easier to reveal his tastes in a text message rather than in person. That seemed to say something important about him, something sad.

As Kaylie had told Stephen, Hilda Worth and her husband, Chester, along with Hilda's sister, Carol Petty, had been taking care of Kaylie's aunts and Chatam House for decades. The aunts considered them family, and since they lived in what had been the carriage house, they were ever-present fixtures about the estate, as much a part of it as the magnolia tree on the west lawn, the rose arbor on the east and the priceless antiques that comprised the majority of the furnishings. None of the family would treat the staff with less consideration than they would allow each other, which was why Kaylie went straight to the kitchen to clean up after her patient.

That was exactly where Aaron Doolin found her, up to her elbows in the enameled, cast-iron sink. She rinsed the last dish and set it in the folding wooden dish drainer next to the sink before drying her hands on a towel and turning to face him.

"I thought you left."

"Yeah, I thought I had, too, then I remembered to do what I'm paid to do." He waved a sheaf of papers at her.

"What are those?"

Doolin trained his practiced smile on her. "We never discussed salary and what all." It was the "what all" that made her narrow her eyes. Aaron rubbed hands together. "How does a thousand dollars a day sound?"

She laughed, thinking it was a joke. "Ridiculous."

He grimaced. "Okay, eleven hundred."

Oh, now, this was absurd. No wonder Stephen had expected around-the-clock availability. She parked her hands at her waist. "You can't be serious. What were you paying the last person?"

"Nine hundred," Aaron said, poking a finger at her. "What? You think we're trying to go on the cheap now, pay you less than the last guy? I can show you the canceled check, if you want."

It took several seconds for her to conclude that he meant it, and when she did, she could only shake her head. "Wow, did he ever see you coming. You can hire a private nurse at half the cost from any agency in the Metroplex area."

Aaron's salt-and-pepper brows shot up, but then he rubbed his chin, watching her as if she was some alien life form. "Did I forget to mention the nondisclosure contract? You can't talk about any of this, you know. Nada, nothing. Not a thing that has to do with Steve or his care."

"All medical personnel are forbidden by law to discuss their patients. Didn't they explain that to you at the hospital?"

Aaron looked perplexed. "Well, yeah, but the other guy said that only applied there."

"The 'other guy' was unscrupulous, then," she told him.

Doolin shrugged and declared, "Who knew! He came to me, said we'd need someone discreet. I'm no health professional. How was I supposed to figure out this stuff?"

Frowning, Kaylie folded her arms. "I'll be glad to give you an address where you can report him, if you like. I'm sure the hospital would be eager to know that one of their employees is soliciting private jobs, too."

Aaron cleared his throat and said, "Ah, maybe the less said there, the better. I mean, we're the ones trying to keep a low profile, right? So, um, what would you consider a fair daily fee?"

She told him, and he seemed dumbfounded for a moment. "Really?" he asked weakly.

"Really. Just don't expect more than eight hours a day from me. As I've already explained to Stephen, I won't be spending nights here."

Doolin frowned warily. "Are you sure he'll be okay?"

"As long as he behaves sensibly."

"Good luck with that."

"Look, I'm not a babysitter. I'm a nurse." He opened his mouth to argue the point, but she cut him off. "All right, all right. That'll work itself out. Let's concentrate on one issue at a time. How about we do it this way? How about you pay me by the hour, then if the job requires more time than I think it will, we're all happy."

Doolin nodded. "Yeah, yeah, we'll keep track by phone. You send a text when you arrive and when you leave. I'll verify it with Stevie and write the check. What hourly rate were you thinking of?"

She told him, and the deal was at last struck. Evidently pleased with himself, Aaron beamed then scowled very sternly. "But you still have to sign the nondisclosure agreement. That's just how we roll on this."

Kaylie fought a smile. She could almost see him trying to negotiate a multimillion-dollar contract, all steely-eyed and tough one minute, happy as a puppy with a new ball the next. The man was less agent than actor. She quite liked him, and she liked Stephen Gallow for employing him.

"Whatever you say."

He went back to beaming, and she went back to trying to keep a straight face.

"Great! Don't mean to pressure you, but I have to protect my boy," Aaron prattled, clearly relishing the act. "He's got enough problems with the team as it is. We can't have anyone blabbing to the press."

"I don't blab to the press or anyone else, Mr. Doolin."

"Aaron," he corrected. "A woman of few words. I knew I liked you." He plopped the papers down on the enormous butcher-block work island in the center of the homey, brick-and-plaster room and produced an ink pen. "Now, if I can just get your John Henry..."

She dutifully signed the documents, which Aaron witnessed and dated. Stowing the ink pen with one hand, he gathered up the papers with the other, kissed them and stuffed them into a pocket of his coat. "Now I can get home to the missus."

"I, uh, just have one question for you," Kaylie said quickly, surprised at herself, though not for the first time that day.

"Sure. What's that?"

"What sort of problems does Stephen have with his team exactly?"

Aaron clapped a hand to the nape of his neck uneasily. "Why do you ask?"

The answer came to her only as it was falling out of her mouth. "So I can pray for him. An informed prayer is often more powerful than a vague one."

"Huh. I wondered just how that worked," Aaron said. "I mean, isn't God supposed to know everything already?"

"Absolutely, He does. Prayer is not for His sake. It's not as if we have to remind Him about what's going on in this world," she explained. "Prayer is for us. It's a tool for our benefit."

Aaron Doolin nodded his head, his lips curling up at one corner. "Okay, I can get behind that. So, lay it on the Big Guy, if you want. Most specifically, you can ask Him not to let the team cut or trade our boy. Not that I think they will for sure. It's just that there's this good-conduct clause in his contract, see, and, well, if they wanted to be sticklers about it…" He sighed, braced himself with a hand placed flat atop the work island and crossed his feet at the ankles. "It's like this, see. About five years ago, when he first came into the league, there was this drunk-driving accident."

"Oh, dear," Kaylie said, dismayed. She almost wished she hadn't asked.

"Hey, Stevie was young and celebrating the fact that he'd finally made the big league. Anyway, he learned his lesson, a stiff one. Truly. Only the club insisted on the clause, and technically..."

"He was drunk when he drove his car through his house," she surmised softly.

"Technically," Aaron repeated with some force. "I mean, he was drinking, but he had a couple of buddies drive him home that night, which was the responsible thing to do. Right? If they hadn't left the car out with the top down and a storm hadn't blown up all of sudden it wouldn't have happened." Aaron spread his hands. "Steve was just parking the car in the garage, not driving. Not *really* driving."

Kaylie sighed. If her father ever got wind of this... She didn't even want to think about it. One of his chief complaints about her brother Chandler's chosen occupation was the abundance of alcohol surrounding the sport of rodeo. Still, she didn't want to have to defend Stephen Gallow to her father or even to discuss him at all if she could help it. She didn't want to have to choose between her father's approval and taking care of Stephen—mostly because she didn't know, at this point, which she would, should, choose.

She managed a smile for Aaron. "I understand."

"Hey, it's like I keep telling Stevie. As long as the press doesn't make a big deal of this, it'll blow over. In the meantime, I'll be there reminding management just who it was that got the team to the playoffs in the first place." He smoothed a hand down the front of his shirt, apparently forgetting that he wasn't wearing a tie, and added, "Little insurance wouldn't hurt, though. I mean, he could use somebody up there looking out for him, you know?"

She knew. Oh, yes, she knew. But she doubted that Stephen did.

"Thank you for confiding in me, Aaron."

"Aw, you're part of the team now, right? The Gallow team."

Kaylie let her smile speak for her. Flipping her a wave, Aaron sauntered away. Kaylie's smile faded to a frown of concern as he disappeared from sight.

The Gallow team. What neither Stephen nor Aaron seemed to understand was that it was much more important that they were all on God's team.

She heard a ding and felt a vibration. Rolling her eyes, she dug into her pocket for the new phone. This time the message read, "Where r u?"

Shaking her head, she typed a simple reply. "Kitchen. You ok?"

"Bored," read the message he sent back. "Hurry."

Electing to simply drop the phone into her pocket, she went to find a few books that might, hopefully, appeal to him. Technically, entertaining him was not her job, but representing Christ to him certainly was. She just hoped that she didn't regret letting him foist this phone on her.

Being in constant contact with Stephen Gallow was bound to turn her world upside down.

The stack of books stood almost a foot tall. Some hardbacks, some paperbacks, Kaylie had chosen them with as much care as her patient's incessant texting had allowed. Using his one good hand, Stephen went through the offerings skeptically. They included a baseball biography, a mystery, a couple of lawyer/suspense novels—

he pointedly yawned at those—a nonfiction account of the historical exploits of a fellow named Joseph Walker and four books from a fiction series about the Second Coming of Christ.

"Those ought to keep you busy," Kaylie said in a satisfied tone.

"Or put me in a coma," Stephen grumbled, dumping the last book on top of what was now a jumble on the bedside table. As soon as she'd entered the room, he'd announced that he'd already checked the hockey news via the internet on his new phone and scoped out some interesting downloads. Apparently, several games were being installed on the amazing little contraption as they conversed. He checked the progress of the installation and sighed.

"Oh, come on," she cajoled, waving a hand at the heap of books, "something there has to interest you."

He glanced once more at the bedside table before determinedly turning his head away. "I'm too tired to read right now."

"Then sleep for an hour or two," she suggested lightly.

His pale gray eyes instantly turned to ice. "Why? So you can disappear on me?"

Kaylie ignored that, making every effort to retain her patience. The man, after all, was in pain. As opposed to just being a pain. Glancing pointedly at her utilitarian wristwatch, she noted the time.

"I'll leave a few minutes before eleven to make Dad his lunch. Be back here just after noon to help with yours. You might want to clean up after that. Then I thought we might wrap your ribs, give you a little more stabilization in your torso so you can move more easily. The jacket sling helps, but it's not the best thing for your ribs." Aware of his deepening glower, she forged on. "By that time, you'll probably be needing another rest. I have some errands to run later this afternoon, but I'll return in time to give you dinner and meds. Can I bring you anything? Maybe some puzzles or a—"

He rolled his eyes, but before either could say more on the subject, they were interrupted.

"Yoo-hoo!"

Recognizing the voice, Kaylie turned toward the door. "Aunt Odelia?"

Footsteps clattered across the sitting room, then Odelia's stark white head, topped with a big floppy yellow bow, appeared around the edge of the doorway. Wearing too much rouge and pale orange lipstick, she beamed a smile before hopping out from behind the door and fully showing herself with a happy "Ta-da!"

The effect was… Well, it was daffodils. Odelia had dressed, head to toe, in daffodils, including heavy gold-and-enamel daffodil earrings that looked as if they weighed a ton and a white, daffodil-dotted dress worn over an equally voluminous orange shift. Backless yellow shoes with plastic daffodils standing two inches high on the toes completed the outrageous ensemble.

It was all so breathtakingly Odelia.

Refusing to be embarrassed for her dear aunt, Kaylie embraced Odelia and affectionately declared, "You look positively floral today, Auntie."

Odelia giggled as happily as any girl. "Thank you, dear. I love your penguins." She waved a lacy handkerchief in Stephen's direction, saying, "Looks like we both dressed in honor of our guest today."

Kaylie shot Stephen a desperate, pleading look. A

moment passed, during which he gaped, before he realized what she wanted from him.

Proving that he had manners enough to be nice, he said to Odelia, "Uh, thanks. Very…clever."

"That outfit certainly puts you in mind of Holland," Kaylie supplied helpfully, "which is so well-known for its beautiful flowers."

"Oh, right," he managed, "especially tulips."

"Well, daffodils aren't tulips," Odelia said with a laugh, holding out her filmy white skirt, "as Magnolia pointed out to me at breakfast. And she would know." Leaning closer, the daffodil-clad Odelia confided to their guest, "She's a self-trained horticulturist, my sister is, almost a botanist, really. Loves her garden and greenhouse." Odelia smiled and turned to show off her finery. "But they're almost tulips, aren't they? Very like. And it's not as if there's a tulip dress in every closet, is it?"

Stephen opened his mouth but apparently found nothing to say in reply to that and so wound up simply shaking his head.

"Can we help you with something, Aunt Odelia?" Kaylie asked quickly.

"Oh, no, dear, not at all. Just checking on our Mr. Gallow. How is the dear boy?"

Biting her lip, Kaylie telegraphed an apologetic look to him then indulgently said to her aunt, "As well as can be expected. How kind of you to see about him."

"Kind," Stephen echoed, but he didn't fool Kaylie. She knew exactly what he was thinking. Kind of weird. Kind of ridiculous. Maybe even kind of loony.

"I'm going to be out later this afternoon," Kaylie said to Odelia, telling Stephen with her eyes that this was payback. "Maybe you could check in on him then."

Even while Stephen glared daggers at Kaylie, Odelia clapped her hands, hanky fluttering. "I have a lovely idea! Perhaps we'll take tea here with Mr. Gallow this afternoon."

Jerking, he looked for a moment as if he would spring off the bed and flee. Kaylie indulged in a smirk. As if he could outrun Odelia, even in her flip-flop daffodil shoes. Kaylie did have some pity for him, though. She knew how much he hated tea, and he was recovering from serious wounds, so she let him off the hook.

"I think the tea will have to wait until he's stronger."

"Oh, of course. Of course. Poor thing."

He did look terribly weary.

"I think we ought to let him rest now," she told her aunt.

"Well, I'll leave you then," Odelia said, turning away. "Just sing out if you need anything, Mr. Gallow."

"Yes, ma'am," he said. "Thanks. But it's Stephen, please. Or Steve, if you prefer."

Looking back at him over her shoulder, Odelia batted her eyelashes at him. "Stephen. Such an elegant name."

Elegantly named Stephen appeared to have a touch of dyspepsia. Odelia frilled her hanky at him in a coquettish wave and clacked away in her daffodil shoes.

Stephen and Kaylie looked at each other in silence until the clattering faded, at which point Stephen drolly observed, "There's a word for her in Dutch. It's 'kooky.'"

Kaylie flattened her lips in a flat, scolding line to keep from laughing. "That's not very nice."

"How about *zonderling,* then?"

She narrowed her eyes at him. "Meaning?"

"Eccentric."

Zonderling. Kaylie had to bite her lip to hold back a

smile. "Why do you think we call her Auntie Od?" she said softly.

Stephen grinned. "Well, if the name fits…"

"She's also a complete sweetheart who cares about everyone and everything," Kaylie hastily defended, "and the reason you're here, by the way."

"She's the reason? How's that? I thought Dr. Leland arranged this."

"Brooks asked Aunt Odelia to open Chatam House to you, and she did, but of course he knew she would. That's why he asked her in particular, I'm sure."

"And I suppose it had nothing to do with the very generous sum of money we offered," Stephen retorted.

"Which went to charity," Kaylie reminded him, leaning a shoulder against the footpost of the bed.

"Right," he said. "I support a lot of charities."

Kaylie smiled, strangely delighted to hear it. "Really? Which ones?"

"Whichever ones the team tells me to. It's in my contract. Pain in the, ah, you-know-what most of the time." He made a little shrug. "But that's how it is. Comes with the territory."

Deflated, Kaylie bowed her head. "That's nice." For a moment there, she'd thought she'd stumbled onto something that her father might appreciate about this man. Glancing at her wristwatch again, she saw that she was running late and pushed away from the footpost, saying briskly, "I have to go. Don't get up unless there's someone here to help you. All right?"

"Fine," Stephen muttered resentfully, laying his head back on the pillow.

He let out a gusty sigh. Kaylie paused for an instant, worried that he might be in more pain than she'd supposed, but then his eyes drifted shut and his big body seemed to relax. She realized that he would be asleep within moments.

Tiptoeing from the room, she pulled her keys from the pocket of her smock and headed downstairs. As she slid behind the wheel of her beloved convertible some minutes later, she shook her head. Imagine driving through the walls of a house and into a fireplace. The wonder that was Stephen hadn't been killed.

She thought of her father, waiting for her at home. No doubt, he would behave as petulantly and spoiled as the man she was leaving behind for his sake. It struck her suddenly how alike the two were. Stephen had survived a horrendous accident and would ultimately be none the worst for wear. Hub had survived a massive heart attack without damage to his heart muscle. Except for the medication that he must take to control his cholesterol and blood pressure, his life should have been little changed. Both had good reason to praise God; yet, both behaved as if God was picking on him. How could it be, she wondered, that two such different men—one of them an elderly retired Christian minister, the other a fierce, young, physical competitor—had so much in common?

"Are You trying to tell me something here, Lord?" she asked softly. *Is this my true calling, then?* she went on in silence. *Am I made to nurse fractious, unreasonable men? Or am I missing something?*

She wanted to help. She truly did. She wanted to help her father, and she wanted to help Stephen Gallow.

"Show me, Lord," she whispered. "Please show me what to do."

Chapter Five

As much as he disliked her being away from his side, Stephen had to admit that Kaylie proved as good as her word. She arrived back at Chatam House just after noon and brought up his lunch. Despite his nap, however, she wisely judged him too weak to make the trek back into the sitting room. She was right. He felt like a limp dishcloth; much as it grated, he dined in bed after only a token argument.

Later, she helped him clean up somewhat and change into fresh clothing, but he simply did not have the energy to shave. She decided to forego wrapping his ribs for the time being. For one thing, he wasn't likely to be doing much more moving around today. For another, his incisions were still sore to the touch. Eventually she dosed him with painkiller that he did not want but desperately needed. After disappearing into the bowels of the house with his lunch tray, she must have left again a short time later, for she was gone when he awakened in just over two hours.

Her aunts popped in and out during the afternoon,

thankfully one at a time and sans tea tray. Stephen found them surprisingly entertaining.

Hypatia was the first. Graceful and slight, she put him in mind of the beloved queen of the Netherlands, Beatrix. She seemed to simply appear in the chamber, giving Stephen something of a start. He looked up from playing a game on his phone and there, without warning, she stood. Almost terrifyingly proper, she had him actually speaking in perfect syntax during their brief interview, as if he expected to be graded on his grammar. It didn't take long for him to realize that Hypatia reigned as the undisputed authority at Chatam House.

He was bored enough to have picked up a book when Magnolia clumped in bearing two vases of flowers, one of which she left atop the dresser in his bedroom. The other stayed in the sitting room. Frumpy and a tad on the stocky side, she seemed more than a little suspicious, sniffing the air as if checking for gas leaks. When he politely asked about the flowers, however, she eagerly told him more than he'd ever wanted to know about the various blossoms. How could he not describe the incredible tulip fields of Holland and the massive international flower market in Amsterdam for her? Afterward, to his disgust, he drifted off to sleep again, despite becoming surprisingly but thoroughly engrossed in a mystery novel with a floral theme, of all things.

Odelia woke him when she brought up his dinner, a succulent baked chicken breast and yams, with asparagus and pickled beets. Kaylie sailed in while they were trying to get situated and took over, allowing Odelia to leave in a flutter of lace and daffodils. Stephen gobbled down everything, including the beets, relieved to find his appetite strong and ridiculously glad to see Kaylie with her sweet smile and her hair windblown, tendrils escaping her ponytail to waft about her face. She admired the flower arrangements and teased him about Magnolia taking a liking to him. Frightening thought.

She helped him take care of his personal needs then stayed to hold a small mirror while he used the electric razor that Aaron had supplied him at the hospital. She asked questions about the book he was reading and surprised him by saying that she would have to take a look at it herself once he had finished with it. Then she made him comfortable, administering his meds and straightening his bed with brisk, easy, efficient motions. Her placid smile remained fixed but somewhat impersonal.

That irked him for some reason, and the fact that he could not bully himself into staying awake long enough even to check the scores of the night's hockey games did not help. As the drug and his own exhaustion pulled him under, he thought unhappily that he should be playing tonight and instead may have tanked his career. To add insult to injury, his pretty little nurse apparently did not like him. God clearly felt the same.

Carrying such thoughts into sleep with him, he should not have been surprised that his rest was uneasy. Yet, when the nightmare came in the dark of the night, it took him unaware. One moment he floated in a vast, black sea of oblivion, then suddenly he found himself behind the wheel of the sleek, low-slung, midnight-blue sports car that had been his signing gift to himself. He had bought the vehicle as soon as the ink had dried on his first pro contract and couldn't wait to show it off. The valet at the club where he and Nick had stopped in for drinks earlier that evening had gushed about what a sweet ride it was when he'd delivered it to the curb that night and traded Stephen the keys for a generous tip.

Adrenaline pumped in Stephen's veins as he put the car through its paces. It sped through the night, wind whipping through the open windows, Nick whooping it up in the passenger seat. Pleased with life, Stephen laughed and stomped the gas pedal. Nick braced an arm against the dash, howling with glee as the car shot forward.

Suddenly headlights appeared. Stephen knew with sickening dread that he was dreaming and exactly what was coming, but he could do nothing.

"No! No!" he cried. "Wake up! Wake up!"

He tried everything, from trying to rouse himself from the dream to yanking and pounding the steering wheel, but nothing prevented the bone-jarring crash. Then they were rolling, banging around the interior of the car as it tumbled. Unbelted, Nick slammed into him more than once, tossed about like a rag doll. Stephen knew that the car would come to rest on the passenger side and what he would see then.

Blood. Shattered glass. Crumpled metal. Nick, twisted and broken.

Howling in grief, Stephen clawed at his own safety restraints. Abruptly, the colored lights of emergency vehicles flashed macabre shadows across the scene, but Stephen knew it was too late. Still, he struggled, sobbing and screaming, desperate to reach the dearest person in his world. Nick could not be gone. He could not, for how could anyone possibly live in a world without Nicklas?

The call came on the house phone, not the expensive mobile unit that Stephen Gallow had insisted she must have. Somehow, though, even as she reached for the receiver on the low chest beside her bed, Kaylie knew that it had to do with him. Hearing Odelia's trembling voice on the other end of the line only confirmed that assumption.

"Kaylie? Can you come? He's fallen, and the pain is terrible. We don't know what to do."

"I'll be right there," she answered without hesitation, throwing off the bedcovers.

Her father tapped on her bedroom door as she pulled on her scrubs. "One moment!" Reaching for the doorknob with one hand, she stuffed a pair of socks into a pocket with the other.

"What's going on?" Hub demanded, yanking a knot in the belt of his plaid robe. "I heard the phone ring, and it's not even 5:00 a.m."

"Stephen has fallen," she told him, stomping her bare feet into athletic shoes.

"Who is Stephen?"

"Mr. Gallow."

"Your new patient?"

"That's right."

Hubner rolled his eyes. "I knew this job would turn into a terrible imposition."

Kaylie tried to hang on to her patience as she stuffed her wallet into her pocket and grabbed her keys. "I don't have time to discuss it, Dad."

Pushing past him, she moved down the narrow hallway and into the living room. Hub padded along behind her in his house slippers.

"When will you be back?"

"I have no idea."

She skirted the room, with its comfortably worn furnishings and fieldstone fireplace. Just as she reached the opening to the small foyer, a lamp snapped on and her father spoke again.

"What about breakfast?" he asked, the faintest whine in his voice. "Will you be back in time to get breakfast, do you think?"

Exasperated, Kaylie rounded on him. "I don't know, Dad. Thankfully, you can feed yourself."

Something dark and troubling flashed across his face, but Kaylie's worry for Stephen pushed all other considerations away just then. She whirled and rushed out, telling herself that she would apologize later. As she raced toward Chatam House, her only prayer was for the injured man who had put that tremor into her auntie's voice.

Locking his jaw, Stephen held still as Kaylie injected medication into his upper right leg. Red-hot pain radiated up and down from the thigh, knifing up into his hip and down into the plaster cast below his knee, all the way to the ankle. Add to that the intense throbbing in his ribs, and it was all he could do retain consciousness.

Nevertheless, as soon as Kaylie recapped the syringe, he insisted through his teeth, "I do not need an ambulance!" For all the good that did him. She had already made the call to 9-1-1.

Ignoring his desires entirely, she turned to address those crowded into his bedroom. She surprised him, this small, wholesome, quiet woman; he might even have been fascinated by the cool, competent manner in which she had taken control and created order out of chaos within moments of her arrival, had she not ignored his every wish and order.

"Carol, would you go down and watch for the emergency vehicle, please?" she directed briskly. "Hilda, I think everyone is going to need a hot cup of tea soon."

Carol, in her messy ponytail and hastily donned slacks and blouse, nodded. Dressed in a threadbare caftan, her elder sister, Hilda, did the same. Her straight, thin, gray-dulled yellow-gold hair flopped about her double chin.

"I'll heat some cinnamon rolls, too." She went out with her younger sister.

Chester, wearing black pants and a white undershirt with bare feet, watched his wife and sister-in-law leave without comment, then looked to Kaylie for his own assignment.

"Thank you for helping to get him back into bed," she told the older man.

Stephen grunted in agreement. He wouldn't have believed that the old guy could manage it, but somehow he had, though at the time Stephen had thought the transfer from the floor to the bed would kill him. He'd have bitten off his own tongue before he'd have admitted it, of course. He was a hockey player, for pity's sake, toughest of the tough.

Kaylie dispatched Chester to move the sofa in the sitting room so the paramedics could get a gurney into the bedroom. He went out to rearrange furniture in his bare feet. That left just the aunts and Kaylie herself.

"What can we do, dear?" Odelia asked, looking like a runaway from the circus, with pink foam rubber curlers in her white hair and a ruffled, knee-length, red satin robe zipped over a floor-length yellow nylon gown. Stephen would have laughed if he hadn't been so busy trying not to whimper like a wounded dog.

Magnolia, her long braid intact, wore a flannel robe

over flannel pajamas, while Hypatia, her silver hair clubbed sleekly at her nape, appeared ready to receive visitors in tailored navy silk with white piping. Her silent, intelligent gaze contained a good deal of concern, along with a measure of speculation that unnerved Stephen. She had been the first to arrive after his fall, and he sensed that she at least suspected the cause.

He closed his eyes to escape that acute amber gaze and heard Kaylie say, "Just pray for him. I'm pretty sure he's broken another bone above the leg cast and dislodged the old break."

Stephen felt the terrible urge to cry, partly because the leg screamed and partly because a really bad break could mean the end of his career. If so, he—and only he—could be blamed. He had done some stupid, stupid things in his life and would never, apparently, quit paying for them.

While silently berating himself, he felt the gentle touch of several hands on his shoulder and chest. He looked up to find the Chatam sisters standing over him, their heads bowed and eyes closed. A glance at Kaylie, who hugged the footpost of the bed, showed that she, too, stood in an attitude of prayer. Before he could digest the amazing notion that they were actually going to pray over him at that very moment, Hypatia began to speak.

"Father God, we entreat You, on behalf of this poor man. You know his great pain, Lord. You know the reasons for it. Give him comfort now, Father, please. Heal him inside and out. Let him feel Your great love and power. You have brought him here to this place for a reason, Lord, and we trust that it will work out for his best and Your great glory and honor. Make us blessings to that cause, Sovereign Father. These things we pray in the name of Your Holy Son and our Savior. Amen."

Stephen lay dumbfounded for several seconds before realizing that, to his utter shock, the pain seemed to have subsided to a manageable level. Oh, but surely that had more to do with the injection that Kaylie had administered moments ago than any prayer. Didn't it? If so, it would be the fastest working injection he had ever received, but then his sense of time was surely skewed.

Carol shouted up the stairwell that the ambulance had arrived, and Hypatia immediately went into action, herding her sisters from the room. "We had best get out of the way now. Kaylie can manage this." She paused at the bedside long enough to look down on Stephen again. "We will be praying for your swift return to us, Stephen dear. God bless."

Stephen dear. It felt suddenly as if he had unknowingly crossed some divide and managed to plant himself in the bosom of the Chatam family. Nameless emotion swelled his chest. Unaccustomed to such feelings, he attempted to turn it off with an icy glare, but for once his game face failed him. A tight smile curling up one corner of her mouth, Hypatia patted his shoulder comfortingly and followed her sisters from the room. Kaylie instantly took her place, bending low to sweep a lock of hair from his forehead and address him softly.

That absurd, nameless yearning swept through him again. Why, he wondered, did the slightest display of tenderness from this woman reduce him to a maudlin nostalgia for something he had never known and could not even describe? She was not his mother. She was not his girlfriend. She was not even his type. She was a paid nurse, an employee, an uptight little holy-roller with as much disapproval as pity in her big, dark eyes. Yet, something about her made him want more than simple professional comfort from her.

"Stephen, listen to me. I need to know how it happened."

A great clattering and thumping on the landing snagged his attention. "They're here."

"I know. Quickly. How did it happen? Why did you fall?"

He shook his head, unwilling to say. Hypatia might suspect, but she didn't *know,* and she wouldn't if he could help it. This was his issue, his secret shame. But then Kaylie gently cupped his face with her small, delicate hands, as if it, he, were somehow precious to her. He could not have denied her anything at that moment.

"It's important, Stephen. Please."

"Nightmare," he admitted tersely, shifting his gaze from hers.

"It's not the first, is it?" she whispered, her voice a sweet, soft zephyr of compassion. Her hands stroked his face, creating an island of bliss in a sea of pain and angst.

Men and material suddenly crowded the room. Kaylie left him to sweep all of his medications from his bedside table into the pockets of her smock and answer questions from the emergency medical technicians. Two of them moved into position and quickly transferred him from the bed to the gurney, an excruciating experience that Stephen endured with a clenched jaw.

The trip out of the suite, down the stairs and into the ambulance was every bit as painful as he'd expected. He gulped and gritted his teeth, training his gaze on the frescoed ceiling above, a painting of blue sky, fluffy cloud and feathers. Suddenly a large, ornate crystal chandelier blocked the peaceful scene.

Stephen closed his eyes and attempted to blank his mind, only to find Hypatia's prayer whispering inside his head. *Give him comfort now, Father, please. Heal him inside and out. Let him feel Your great love and power.* Before he knew what he was doing, Stephen was adding his own plea to Hypatia's prayer. *I know I don't deserve it, but please, please help me.*

He felt an odd sensation sweep through him, a chill that was not cold, a wind that did not blow. Then suddenly the EMTs were loading the gurney into the ambulance. To his horror, Stephen heard a man's voice say, "Good grief. That's Hangman Gallow. What's the star goalie of the Blades hockey team doing here in Buffalo Creek?"

Stephen groaned. So much for prayer and keeping a low profile! The news of his whereabouts would likely be splashed all over the DFW Metroplex by evening, and speculation about his accident would soon run rampant. Team management would probably be screaming in Aaron's ear before week's end. As if reading his thoughts, Kaylie clambered up into the ambulance with him, clasped his good hand with hers and spoke into his ear.

"Don't worry. These are medical personnel bound by privacy laws, but I'll speak to them myself just to be sure that nothing slips out."

He doubted that it would make any difference. He was going to lose it all anyway. Deep down, he'd always known it, but he'd keep fighting to the very end, because that's what he did, he fought. Always.

"Never give up," he muttered.

Drugs, weariness and pain all weighed on him, pushing him down toward oblivion, but he struggled to stay awake, to stay in control.

ZZd.

"It's all right," a voice whispered. "Just relax."

For a moment, he was confused. Was that his mother's voice? Aunt Lianna's? No, of course not. She hadn't spoken to him since Nick's death.

A man's deep voice said, "Doesn't look like he's been doing too well."

Stephen roused, wondering when his father had come. "I'll do better," he vowed. "I'm not a pansy," he insisted, shaking his head. "Not a mama's boy. I can do it."

"Yes," said that sweet voice in his ear. "You can do it. You are doing it. Rest now. Just rest." Gentle hands pushed him down. Relief swept through him.

Rest. He could rest now. Tomorrow was soon enough to get back on his skates. Tomorrow he would prove himself. Again. But first, he would rest. Gratefully, he sank into unconsciousness.

When he woke again—it might have been minutes or hours later—they were off-loading him from the ambulance, and Kaylie Chatam was there, her small, delicate, feminine hand clasping his.

"I was dreaming," he muttered.

The smile that she rained down on him warmed every tiny corner of his heart.

"I know," she said sweetly. "I know. We're going to do something about that."

A pair of shapeless green scrubs and a working knowledge of the local hospital granted a gratifying amount of access in a process that might otherwise have relegated Kaylie to the role of distant observer.

Instead, she'd been allowed to accompany Stephen in the ambulance. His mutterings had broken her heart, but she didn't have time to really think about what they had revealed.

As promised, she spoke to the EMT crew before they departed for their station, making it clear how important confidentiality was in this instance. They joked that they would avoid risking their careers for the price of autographs.

"Sure, sure," Stephen responded groggily. "Game tickets even."

"But later," she insisted to a quartet of smiling male faces. "We'll be in touch."

Thankfully, no one questioned her right to stay at Stephen's side. The emergency room physician was too concerned with Stephen's physical condition to care about such things. He was not someone Kaylie knew well, but he seemed to accept her presence without question and allowed her to provide the necessary information pertaining to previous injuries and prescription drugs.

No one said a contrary word when she accompanied Stephen to X-ray, not even when she squeezed into the lead-shielded operations niche with the technician or studied the developed pictures. Every time she returned to Stephen's side, his hand groped for hers, and she always gave it to him, understanding well that she had become, by sheer default, his lifeline in this situation.

While they waited for the doctor to report his findings, Stephen blearily asked her to tell him what to expect. She could have put him off with medical mumbo jumbo or disclaimers about her personal expertise, but she chose instead to give him the truth.

"I think you're looking at surgery, Stephen. There's

a new break above the cast, and the old break appears to have been dislocated. It looked to me like you have some fragmenting there. That sometimes means a shortening of the bone."

What color remained in his face drained away, and the grip on her fingers became almost punishing. "So it really could be the end of everything," he rumbled.

"Of course it's not the end of everything," she told him firmly. "Many people naturally have one leg that's slightly longer than the other. Most don't even know it. Few doctors even try to treat it if the discrepancy is less than three centimeters."

"Three centimeters," he echoed hollowly. "As little as three centimeters and I might never skate again. Oh, God."

"At least you're looking in the right direction for help," Kaylie told him, bending close and smiling indulgently. She was discovering that the man beneath the tough exterior had fears and concerns like any other and that he responded to a compassionate touch with a silent, secret hunger that clutched at her heart. "Would you like to pray about it?"

His gray eyes, foggy and bleak now, plumbed hers. "I—I don't think I know how. I have tried. I even learned a prayer once, but…"

"What is it? What prayer did you learn?"

He stared at her for a moment then squeezed his eyes shut and whispered, "Our Father, Who art in heaven."

"Hallowed be thy name," Kaylie joined in, repeating the familiar words of the Lord's Prayer with him. At the end, she added her own. "Please, Lord, if it can be within Your will, spare Stephen the loss of his skating. Surely You have given him the talent and desire to play hockey for a reason. Show him what that reason is, to Your glory. Amen."

"Amen," he whispered.

A throat cleared, and Kaylie turned to find that the doctor had once more entered the cubicle. She gripped Stephen's hand and waited for the verdict.

Surgery. Kaylie was right about that.

Please, God, Stephen thought, *let her be right about everything else.*

He almost laughed at himself. Praying at the drop of a hat now, was he? As if God had ever listened to him! The Chatams, on the other hand, when Kaylie or her aunts prayed, it was as if they summoned the very presence of God into the room, as if that Power drew close and cloaked them in peace.

Stephen knew that he had clung to Kaylie all that morning like a toddler clinging to a security blanket, but he couldn't seem to help himself. Thankfully, she didn't appear to mind. More than likely, she considered it a part of her job, so he hesitated only a moment before asking if she would be there with him during the surgery.

She tilted her head, her long, sleek, dusky red hair sliding freely about her face and shoulders. He caught his breath. With her hair down around her clean face and those big dark eyes glowing with concern, she looked too beautiful to be of this earth. Only the presence of the doctor and the entry of another nurse into the room kept Stephen from foolishly reaching up to clasp the nape of Kaylie's neck and pull her down to him for a kiss.

"I'm sorry," she told him softly. "The operating room is one place I cannot go, but I'll be right here, praying for you."

Stephen gulped and nodded. Then, as if aware of that longed-for kiss, she bent and pressed her lips to the center of his forehead. A sense of peace and well-being filled him. It flowed into the all the dark, lonely crevices of his soul, bringing light and something else along with it, something he had a difficult time identifying.

Hope, he decided woozily.

Not the hope for any one thing, but the mere chance, the opportunity, that something in his life might finally go right, that it might all somehow come together finally.

The feeling was almost embarrassingly intimate and, at the same time, comfortingly ordinary. It somehow set him apart from, yet united him with, all humanity. It elated and terrified. In an instant, the whole world and his perspective of it shifted from one of disappointment and struggle to one of teeming possibilities. He couldn't bear the thought that it might be imaginary, ethereal, fleeting, and in his clumsy way he attempted to grab on to it.

"Hey," he teased, swirling a finger around his forehead, "let's skip the meds from now on and just go with that. What do you say?"

Kaylie laughed and stepped back. Only then did he realize that he was about to be wheeled away. An orderly and an orthopedic surgeon had been summoned and an operating room cleared for immediate use, he was told.

"A smaller hospital sometimes has its benefits," Kaylie said.

Stephen nodded and reached out to her as he rolled past. She brushed his fingertips with hers.

"I know Dr. Philem personally, and he's one of the best orthopedists around," she assured him, keeping pace with the head of the gurney as it traveled down the gleaming corridor. “Don’t worry about a thing,” she went on softly, “not even the nightmares. I think we can even take care of those.”

Nightmares.

With that one word, she destroyed the first truly bright moment he had known in years. The nightmares unlocked all his horrors, all his failures, all his fears. All his guilt. As her face receded from his view, the all too familiar black pit of despair, disappointment and shame opened inside him, swallowing whole his momentary joy.

For what could possibly ever “take care of” the fact that he had killed his best friend?

Chapter Six

Rubbing her arms lightly, Kaylie studied the displays on a variety of machines surrounding Stephen's bed.

"So how is he?" Aaron asked, nervously jiggling the coins in the pocket of his light gray slacks.

"He's fine. They used a temporary nerve block so he'll probably feel better than he has in some time once he comes out from under the anesthesia."

Aaron had arrived just after the surgeon had given Kaylie the post-op summary. Brooks Leland, at the behest of the aunties, had contacted the personable sports agent, something Kaylie should have thought to do herself. Instead, for nearly two hours she had sat in the waiting room with her head bowed and her hands clasped, beseeching God on Stephen's behalf and thinking about what he had said in the ambulance and the way he had prayed with her before they'd taken him into surgery. That prayer had pricked her heart, a heart already softened by his physical suffering, mindless mutterings and the way in which his hand had repeatedly and continuously clasped hers. Perhaps Stephen was not a believer, but she had to believe that God was moving in Stephen's life.

Kaylie felt genuine delight at that, but she felt only sadness about what his words in the ambulance had revealed. Someone, she very much feared, had taunted Stephen as a child, called him a pansy and a mama's boy. Was that, she wondered, why he had chosen such a violent, punishing sport?

"What kind of cast is that?" Aaron asked, indicating the black casing that covered Stephen's leg from the hip to the ankle, leaving the sole of his foot bare.

Pulled from her reverie, Kaylie explained that in a few weeks the temporary cast, along with the screws that the surgeon had inserted to stabilize the bone, would be removed and replaced with a cast that would allow Stephen to walk, or at least get around on his own somewhat. The recovery-room nurse—a brisk, plump, forty-something woman whose name Kaylie could not recall—breezed into the curtained cubicle while Kaylie continued to answer Aaron's questions about this latest mishap and the doctor's prognosis.

After a moment, Kaylie heard the woman say, "Mr. Gallow? Mr. Gallow, can you hear me?"

Steven cleared his throat just as Kaylie turned back to the bed. "Yes," he croaked. "Where'm I?"

"You're in recovery, Stephen," Kaylie answered.

His eyes popped open, and he looked straight up into Kaylie's face, smiling crookedly. "'Lo, beautiful."

Instantly, his lids dropped closed again, and he went off on a sigh. Her heart lurching, Kaylie stepped back as the nurse went about checking his vital signs. Kaylie prayed that her face did not show the thrill that she had felt at his slurred compliment. The man was drugged, for pity's sake, and probably used to flirting with every other woman he saw. That's what sports stars did, wasn't it?

"Can you cough for me?" the nurse asked Stephen. His head rolled on the pillow, but he obliged, opening his eyes again.

"The two of you should go on up to his room now," the nurse said to Kaylie and Aaron. "We'll bring him to you as soon as he's ready."

"Wait, wait," Stephen mumbled, reaching out his good hand to Kaylie. "My leg. How many cen'meters?"

"None," she assured him, resisting the urge to clasp his fingers. Somehow, with her heart still tripping, it did not seem wise just then. "You lost no bone. The doctor was able to stabilize everything. It's going to take several weeks longer to heal than it might have otherwise, but it will heal."

Stephen breathed out a huge sigh of relief, dropped his head back on the pillow and mumbled, "Keep th' prayers comin', *liefje*."

Aaron chuckled. "You just do what this nurse tells you. *Liefje*. See you up in your room."

Stephen looked around in surprise at the sound of Aaron's voice. "Hey," he said through a big, goofy grin. "What're you doing here?"

"Looking at a trussed turkey." Aaron waved a hand in jocular farewell and turned away with Kaylie to start down the wide aisle between the rows of beds. "What am I doing here? As if I haven't always been here for him. Is he really going to be all right? He hasn't done himself in this time?"

"He's going to be just fine," Kaylie said, smacking a big round button on the wall that opened the wide mechanical doors at the end of the aisle. Her relief, however, was tempered by an uncomfortable feeling of having wandered onto dangerous territory.

As they ambled through those doors and into a bright corridor, Kaylie told herself that comforting the man and becoming emotionally involved with him were two different things. She would do well to remain as personally aloof as possible for a number of reasons. For one, the man was obviously self-destructive. For another, he did not share her faith. Thirdly, his lifestyle was utterly foreign to her. Spurred by that, another thought occurred.

"What does *liefje* mean?" Kaylie asked after a moment. She'd first thought that Stephen had merely mangled her name due to his drug intoxication, but then Aaron had repeated the word back to him in that teasing manner of his.

Aaron shot her a knowing, lopsided grin. "Sweetheart. It means sweetheart."

Sweetheart. Kaylie's heart thunked. She felt a disturbing shiver of delight, which was pure foolishness, of course. It meant nothing to him, and should mean nothing to her.

"Hey, I've picked up a lot of the Dutch, you know," the bluff agent went on, swaggering a bit.

"I'm sure," Kaylie muttered with a limp smile.

"I'm pretty good at stuff like that," he bragged. "Stevie, now..." Aaron wagged a finger at her. "Stevie's good at two things—hockey and hockey. Everything else, like life, for instance, well, he just never has seemed to get the hang of it."

Kaylie felt her heart sink. It was no more than she had suspected, of course. Mentally shaking her head, she sternly told herself to get her mind back to business.

What was wrong with her anyway? She had allowed the mutterings of a drugged patient to set her thoughts on a path that they would never have wandered down otherwise. She chalked it up to exhaustion. Losing several hours' sleep plus several hours of stress must have scrambled her brain.

She suddenly wanted to go home. And why shouldn't she? Stephen was out of surgery and would be spending the next twenty-four to forty-eight hours in the hospital. Aaron was here to lend support; she was no longer needed. Pushing aside memories of how Stephen had clutched her hand earlier, she walked Aaron to the elevator, where she checked her watch. The time was just after 11:00 a.m.

"Listen," she said, punching the up button for him. "I'm going to swing by and give my aunts a brief report on Stephen, and then I have to get home to make lunch for my father."

Aaron blinked, obviously surprised. "But you're Steve's nurse."

"Aaron, he's in the hospital. He doesn't need a private nurse in the hospital."

"Uh-huh. Well, I have this sneaking suspicion that he's going to expect to see you, anyway."

"Tell him I'll be by tomorrow to check on him," she decided, backing away.

Aaron raised both eyebrows. A ding signaled the arrival of the elevator. Aaron spread his hands as the doors slid open. "Okay, then. Say hello for me to the old…uh, your aunts."

Kaylie nodded and made a little wave before turning and swiftly walking away. Stephen, she told herself, would be just fine, and she would be…

Safe? From what? Temptation?

Obviously, she would do well to keep her distance for now. Tomorrow, she would reestablish a professional relationship, and that would be that.

Meanwhile, her father undoubtedly needed mollifying. She regretted now the manner in which she had left him that morning. He had come to depend on her, after all, and she had impatiently blown him off. Yes, the situation had been an emergency, but now the crisis had passed.

It was time to get back to her real life and let God work in both situations—without her silly overreactions getting in the way.

"You really didn't have to come," Stephen said to Aaron, settling into the bed. *Another day, another bed,* he thought with a sigh. He was heartily sick of this state of affairs, but at least he wasn't in pain. Oddly, the leg throbbed but it didn't hurt. How weird was that?

"Hey, I had to be sure my meal ticket didn't get punched," Aaron said, shaking a finger at Stephen. "I've still got a few more meals in you."

"Right," Stephen drawled. It was a little late for Aaron to pretend that his only interest in Stephen was financial. "I appreciate it, man. I really do, but Kaylie says it's going to be all right, so you really didn't have to come all this way. Kaylie will take care of things here."

Aaron hunched a shoulder, a grim look on his face. "Yeah, well, she's going to be taking care of them from a distance then."

"What do you mean?"

"She ran along home to daddy. He needs his lunch."

Stephen frowned then told himself not to be ridiculous. “She’ll be back after she gets him fed.”

“I wouldn’t count on it,” Aaron told him. “She said to tell you she’d see you tomorrow.”

“Tomorrow?” Confused and sluggish, Stephen shook his head. She hadn’t left his side all morning, and she had to know that he’d already come to depend on her. “I don’t get it.”

Aaron brushed back the sides of his suit jacket and grinned, his hands parked at his waist. “Couldn’t have anything to do with ‘beautiful *liefje.*’ Nah.”

“Huh?”

“You don’t remember calling her beautiful or *liefje?*”

He did, actually, but it had seemed perfectly natural at the time. Using his good hand, he rubbed the top of his head. “No big deal. I—I was dopey. Right?”

“Right. Don’t worry about it,” Aaron advised, still grinning. “I’m just gigging you. Nurse Dear isn’t exactly your style. Right? Besides, it’s like she said, you don’t need a private nurse in the hospital.”

That had not been Stephen’s experience. The longer he’d been hospitalized before, the greater difficulty he’d had getting the nurses to respond to him, but he said nothing. No reason to give Aaron more ammunition.

“Say, speaking of Kaylie, she tells me that the paramedics who brought you in are expecting autographs,” Aaron said.

Stephen nodded. “Yeah, I, uh, may even have promised them game tickets.”

“Hey, if it’ll keep them quiet…” Aaron shrugged.

Stephen agreed. Kaylie had said they wouldn’t talk, that they were bound by privacy rules the same as her, but it didn’t hurt to be accommodating. Besides, he owed them.

"I've got some autographed pucks out in the car," Aaron went on. "I'll bring some in before I leave. Okay? It's not like you can sign anything with your writing hand in a cast, after all."

"Always prepared," Stephen said with as much smile as he could muster. "So how did it go with the team last night?"

Aaron jingled the change in his pocket. "They lost, five to four."

Bad news. Or good, depending on how he wanted to look at it. He had a hard time thinking of it as good, even if it might mean that the team was missing him. "How's Kapimsky doing?"

Kapimsky was his replacement in the net, the young, untried backup goalie for the Blades.

Aaron shrugged. "Like you'd expect, stiff and nervous."

That would change, Stephen knew, with experience. The pressure-cooker of the playoffs was a tough place to get that experience, though. Winning the Stanley Cup was the goal of all thirty NHL teams, the be-all and end-all of pro hockey. For a team to advance to the Stanley Cup series, they had to win four of seven games in each of three rounds of finals. The two teams not eliminated at the end of those three rounds, one team from each division, would then battle for the cup with another series of seven games.

If the Blades advanced, management might start thinking young Kapimsky could handle the job and exercise the clause in Stephen's contract that allowed him to be cut. On the other hand, if the team lost, they might blame Stephen for not being in the net when they needed him most. Either way, it looked like a lose-lose proposition for him.

Still, he had gotten the team to their first playoff position. The franchise was only four years old, and he'd been guarding net for them for three. That had to count for something. If not, at least the possibility existed that he would be able to play elsewhere next season.

He wondered how much Kaylie's prayers had to do with that, but then he turned off that line of thought. He didn't want to think of Kaylie or her God just now. Her absence smarted in a way that he didn't want to examine too closely. It would pass. In all likelihood, it was nothing more than a result of his debilitated condition, anyway. That didn't keep it from stinging, a circumstance he found completely unacceptable.

After everything else that had happened, he knew better than to open himself up to that kind of disappointment. Especially now, with all he was currently going through and his future hanging in the balance, the last thing he needed was an emotional involvement. All he needed was a nurse. And peace. What, he wondered, made him think that he could have both in one small, wholesomely pretty woman?

"Aunt Hypatia, I'm sorry, but I'm bound by ethics and regulations. I can't discuss any specifics concerning my patient. I just wanted to let you know that Ste… Mr. Gallow's injuries and pain have been addressed."

"Well, of course, they have," Hypatia said with a sniff, waving her teacup at the other occupants of the sunroom. "That's what hospitals—and nurses—are for, and I understand that you have professional limitations, dear. My question is about his nightmares. *Do* you have any idea what is behind them?"

Kaylie shifted uncomfortably on the round seat of the high-backed, barrel-shaped rattan chair. "Ah, it's possible that the cause relates to his medical care."

Actually, inducing nightmares was a known side effect of at least one of Stephen's—Mr. Gallow's—pain medications. She probably should have mentioned that possibility to the doctors today, but it hadn't seemed as important as making sure that Stephen received the proper diagnosis and treatment for his injuries. If she had stayed, she most definitely would have asked that a notation to that effect be put in his chart, but tomorrow would surely be soon enough to mention it. The staff at the hospital, who had a complete list of his medications, would not give him the suspect drug while he was using intravenous painkillers anyway, so she really had no reason to feel guilty for leaving him. Yet, she did.

Hypatia set aside her teacup, making an uncharacteristically unladylike snort. "The cause relates to some trauma in that young man's past."

"Rooted in an unhappy childhood, no doubt," Odelia said, clasping her hands together, a lace hanky caught between them. "Oh, that poor dear boy." She was dressed almost solemnly today in a double-breasted, royal-blue pantsuit with gold buttons and earrings the size of small saucers. Kaylie could imagine demitasse cups sitting in their centers. Still, for Odelia, this was positively funereal, especially as compared to the backdrop.

The sunroom at the rear of the house was a large, glassed-in space right next to the kitchen. Filled with pieces of bamboo and wicker furniture upholstered in a vivid floral pattern, it was a bright, restful space. A ceiling fan rotating lazily overhead stirred the fronds of palms and ferns scattered artfully about the room in large pots.

"There is more," Magnolia pronounced thoughtfully, munching on a gingersnap, "to our young Stephen than meets the eye."

Smiling wanly, Kaylie said nothing, glad that professional strictures prevented her from mentioning to her aunts what Stephen had said in the ambulance. It would only confirm their assumptions. On the other hand, their concern for him was genuine.

Hypatia sighed. "We'll just have to continue praying for him as best we can."

"I'm sure he'll appreciate that," Kaylie said, rising to her feet. "Now I'd better get home. Dad is probably anxious. I just wanted to check in with you."

"And when will you see Stephen again?" Odelia wanted to know.

"Sometime tomorrow."

"Give him our very best wishes," Magnolia said.

"And tell him," Odelia chirped, "that his room here is waiting for him."

"I will. It shouldn't be long before he's back," Kaylie assured her. "Day after tomorrow at the latest, I imagine."

"Yes, they don't keep anyone in the hospital very long these days," Hypatia said disapprovingly.

Kaylie let that go and passed out farewell kisses. "In case I haven't told you," she said, on her way out of the room, "I admire what you're doing for Stephen."

"Oh, we're thrilled to do it," Odelia trilled, causing her sisters to aim very pointed looks at her. Subsiding into a meager smile, she waved her hanky at Kaylie, who went out mentally chuckling to herself.

She marveled that the sisters had agreed to take in an injured professional hockey player who was a complete stranger to them, but surely the whole thing had been directed by the caring hands of God.

"This is no good to me!"

Kaylie heard Stephen's voice raised in anger even before she pushed through the heavy door to his room early the next morning. A dark-haired nurse in violet scrubs straightened from a bent position and turned. She had a folded newspaper in her hands and an exasperated expression on her face, a face that Kaylie knew well.

"Hi, Linda. Problems?"

Linda Shocklea was an old schoolmate and a fine nurse. She rolled her eyes at the bed, flourishing the newspaper. "His Highness asked for a newspaper. I brought him a newspaper."

"There are no hockey scores in that local rag!" Stephen snapped. "I need a *real* newspaper."

Linda slapped the offending paper under her arm, saying, "I have explained that the local paper is all we get delivered up here and I cannot leave my post to go downstairs to find him a Fort Worth or Dallas paper."

Stephen ignored her, gesturing heatedly toward the television mounted high in one corner of the room. "They don't even have a sports channel on the TV!"

Kaylie smiled apologetically at the other nurse. "I've been hired to care for Mr. Gallow. Leave this to me."

Heaving a relieved sigh, Linda pulled open the door. "Gladly."

Obviously, Stephen had been making a nuisance of himself. Kaylie turned to face her employer, her hands linked together at her waist. For a long moment, he would not meet her gaze, just sat there in the bed fuming.

And to think, Kaylie mused, *that I had such a difficult time staying away last night.*

It hadn't helped that her father had been in such a surly mood. He had started out sounding concerned and solicitous, his earlier pique ameliorated by his delight that she had returned home in time to see to his lunch. He had even asked about Stephen's condition. She had answered as well as she was able, mindful of Stephen's privacy concerns. The problem had come when her father's queries had turned to Stephen himself, or, more to the point, when she had answered them, particularly the question about Stephen's age.

"So young?" her father had said, frowning. "I thought Mr. Gallow to be an elderly individual."

She had been somewhat taken aback by that, but even more so by her father's rapidly darkening mood. By dinner, she had resorted to keeping out of her father's way, and she had quickly found herself thinking that she could serve better at the hospital. But she had stayed at home, judging it the wiser action. Evidently, she had been right to come this morning, however, rather than wait until the afternoon.

"I'll go down and get you a paper," she told Stephen quietly.

He folded his arms mulishly. The gesture lost something due to the fact that his left arm was already bent at the elbow, set in a cast and strapped to his chest. She disciplined a smile. Suddenly his hand shot out.

"Forget the paper. Give me your phone. I'll look up the scores on the internet."

"No," she said calmly, "you can't."

His face, already shadowed with two days' growth of beard, darkened. "Why not? I bought that phone. I can use it if I want."

"Cell phone use is strictly forbidden in patient and treatment areas, no matter who owns the phone."

He glared at her, slapped the heel of his hand against his forehead and literally growled. "Raaaaagggh!"

"I'll go now so I can get back before the doctors make their rounds," she said.

"Fine," he snapped. "Go. Go! You're good at that."

That hit home. Obviously, he had missed her yesterday. She didn't know whether to be pleased or troubled. Ducking her head, she quietly slipped from the room. Hurrying down to the gift shop, she picked up both the Dallas and the Fort Worth papers, then swiftly returned to Stephen's room. He seemed somewhat mollified when she handed over the newspapers. At least he didn't bite her hand.

Digging through the pile, he found the sports section of one paper and clumsily began spreading it out on the bed. Kaylie stepped in and turned the pages for him until he found what he wanted. Then she folded the paper, with the story exposed, and placed it in his good hand. He read earnestly for several minutes. Finally, he closed his eyes and let his head fall back on the pillow.

"You're pleased," she said, smiling as a warm glow filled her chest. It seemed ridiculous to feel so delighted at evidence of his pleasure, but she couldn't help herself. He thrust the paper at her. Taking that as an order to read it, she did so.

From what she could gather, the team had lost the first game of a series, despite some excellent penalty killing and other things she didn't understand. Finally, she hit upon the paragraph that she thought might have so pleased Stephen.

"Most said it would be enough for this young team to make it to the playoffs for the first time in their short history," she read aloud. "Today, despite this loss out of the starting gate, expectations are building. The one flaw in that scenario is the position of goalie. Abel Kapimsky, 24, is a promising young goaltender and shows flashes of pure brilliance, but he's no Stephen Gallow. Then again, who in this conference is?"

She went on to read in silence how Gallow's goaltending had lifted the general level of play for the whole team and been instrumental in winning that first playoff berth. The writer noted that the mysterious injury which had taken Gallow out of the lineup could have also taken the wind out of the team's sails. That, to the team's credit, had not happened. After the loss, the team captain had, in fact, admonished his team to go out there and win the next one for the Hangman.

Smiling, Kaylie tossed the paper onto the bed. "Well," she said blithely, "that ought to lighten your mood."

Those gray eyes tried to freeze her where she stood. "I have good reason for my mood."

"Mmm, and I suppose the same goes for your attitude," she ventured softly. Those icy eyes narrowed, but for some reason Kaylie found herself smiling.

"What's wrong with my attitude?"

"Oh, please. A little honesty, now."

"Meaning?"

"Has no one ever told you that you can catch more flies with honey than vinegar?"

"Has no one ever told you that you look better with your hair down?" he sniped.

Kaylie's hand went automatically to the heavy twist of hair at her nape. She almost always confined it when she was working. Otherwise, it got in the way. Self-consciously, she dropped the hand, dismayed to find that her first impulse had been to dig out the pins and clips that maintained the chignon. She didn't know what was worse—that he thought her unattractive with her hair confined or that she cared what he thought about her looks.

"Sorry," Stephen muttered, having the grace to shoot her a sheepish glance. "You look fine. I only meant that you have gorgeous hair. How you wear it is none of my business."

He thought she had gorgeous hair! Her hand once more sneaked up to touch the offending chignon, and she quickly turned away, unwilling to let him see how much his opinion affected her. "Thank you," she murmured, trying not to feel too pleased.

"I said I'm sorry, all right?" he grumbled.

Nodding, she bent to check the drip rate on his intravenous unit. "No problem."

"Arrrgh!"

She turned to find him beating his fist against his forehead. Alarmed, she asked, "Are you in pain?"

He dropped his hand, glaring at her. "No, I'm not in pain. Not much, anyway. I am in a foul mood. I admit it. Okay? I hate hospitals, and I hate not being able to get out of this bed! I'm bored out of my gourd and I'm worried—" He broke off.

"Worried about your career," she surmised.

"Wouldn't you be?" he shot back.

Kaylie didn't bother answering that. Instead, she sent up a silent prayer as she sifted through the second newspaper on the bed. Finding the sports section, she thumbed through it until she came to the hockey report. Quickly scanning the article, she saw that this reporter was not nearly as sanguine about the loss and the team's chances, for one pertinent reason. Reading aloud from the article, she pitched her voice to a strong, authoritative level.

"As thrilled as the fans may be at the team's long overdue entry into the playoffs, the hope of the Blades began and ended with goalie Stephen Gallow, who has had his problems off the ice in the past but rarely on it. Hurry back, Hangman! We need you."

She looked up in time to catch a look of raw emotion on his face. It was an expression of relief and pride and abject longing. Understanding struck. In an instant, she saw what Stephen Gallow would likely never admit even to himself, that like everyone else in this world, deep down, he needed to be needed. That's what playing for the Blades was really about for him. He just wanted someone to need him. She, who had felt the needs of so many and counted them a burden, felt suddenly ashamed.

Chapter Seven

Folding the paper neatly, Kaylie passed it to Stephen for his own perusal. He seemed to soak in every word. A faint smile curved his lips, but the face that he presented to her clearly showed concern.

"This helps, but sports writers and team management are not the same."

"No, they're not," she agreed, "but neither one is God. Why don't you leave the future to Him and concentrate on getting well?"

"Easy for you to say," Stephen muttered, looking at the article again.

"Yes," she said meaningfully. "Yes, it is." When he made no response to that, she changed the subject. "When's the next game?"

The frown came back to Stephen's face. "Tomorrow night." He glared at the television in the corner. The folded sheet of newspaper dropped to the bed. "You think there's any chance I can get out of here before then?"

Kaylie smiled. "We'll see what the doctors say."

"It helps that I have you, right?" he pressed, sitting

up a little straighter. The pillow slid down behind him, and Kaylie reached around to pull it back up. "I mean, you can take care of me at home, uh, Chatam House, so why stay here? Yeah?"

"We'll see," she repeated, smiling.

Stephen leaned back. "I need you, you know." Kaylie blinked, more than merely surprised. "No, really. Yesterday, for instance. What would I have done without you?"

"Someone would have called an ambulance," she told him.

"Yeah, maybe, but who would have held my hand throughout one of the worst days of my life?"

She said nothing to that, but when he held out his hand, she placed her own in it.

"I need you, Kaylie," he said softly. "That's why it's so tough when you cut out on me."

Warmth spread throughout her chest, radiating from her heart. "I'll do my best for you, Stephen," she told him, "I promise you, my very best. But I do have other obligations, you know. My dad needs me, too."

His smile flattened. "Sure," he said, letting go of her hand. He glanced around the room. "So what now? We stare at the walls until the docs show up?"

Sighing, Kaylie gathered up the newspapers. "Why don't we start by taking a look at the news?"

"Oh, that'll cheer me right up," he grumbled, but he lay there and listened to her read, commenting from time to time and offering reasoned, if sometimes sarcastic, arguments when she disagreed with him. In truth, they agreed more often than not, and Kaylie found some of his comments to be surprisingly insightful, informed, no doubt, by his life on two continents.

His foul mood seemed to lighten considerably, and

his pain level remained low. The nerve block administered by the surgeon would wear off sometime in the next thirty-six to forty-eight hours, and his pain would return to previous levels, but she trusted that they could manage it successfully. Though mercurial, Stephen in a better mood and not in pain was a delightful experience, and it pleased her to be responsible for that in some small way.

Perhaps it pleased her too much.

"In the Netherlands," Stephen pointed out in response to an article on highway gridlock, "if you live more than ten kilometers from your job—that's just over six miles—your employer must provide you with a bicycle."

"A bicycle!" Kaylie exclaimed. "Oh, yeah, that would work. I can just see it now, bicycles fighting all those pickup trucks for space on our freeways. Yikes!"

"The bicycles don't go on the freeways," Stephen pointed out. "They go on the city streets, which have special bike lanes, and that frees up space on the highway."

"Bike lanes aside—and I've never seen a bike lane on a Texas street—what about heat stroke? We get triple-digit summers here, not to mention other extreme weather."

"The weather's not the issue. They get freezing weather in the Netherlands. The issue is distance. Here, everybody lives an hour's drive from work."

"Not everyone can live where they work," she argued.

He started to reply, but just then the door swooshed open and Brooks Leland strode into the room. Tall and fit with a touch of distinguished gray at his temples, a stethoscope about his neck and a white, knee-length lab coat in place of a suit jacket, the general practitioner was both genial and handsome. Stephen had liked Leland from the first moment they'd met only days earlier, but the instant the other man's eyes lit on Kaylie, Stephen knew the good doctor's likeability was about to take a nosedive.

The plummet began when Kaylie hopped up from the bedside chair and rushed toward Leland, calling out, "Brooks!"

It dropped like a rock when the doctor grinned and opened his arms. "There's my favorite nurse."

The two didn't just embrace, they hugged, rocking side to side in their exuberance.

"Kaylie darlin'," Brooks Leland drawled, pulling back slightly to gaze down at her, "it's been too long."

"That's what you get for being such a stranger," she scolded playfully. "Why don't you ever come by anymore? Dad would love to see you."

"I'll make a point of it. Soon."

"You better."

The door opened again, bumping Leland in the back, and another white coat slipped into the room. Stephen recognized the orthopedic surgeon, Dr. Craig Philem. So did Kaylie. Worse, he recognized her.

"Kaylie, Kaylie, Kaylie," he admonished with mock censure, reaching out an arm toward her. "Don't you know that our Dr. Leland makes time with *all* the best-looking nurses?"

"None of whom will give Craig here the time of day," Leland said with a wink, one arm draped casually about Kaylie's shoulders.

"You wish," Philem smirked, as Kaylie, to Stephen's disgruntlement, laughed and reached out to slide her free arm around the young surgeon's waist so that the three of them stood linked.

Both shorter and thicker than Leland, with receding sandy brown hair, the orthopedist was, nevertheless, an attractive man. His eyes alone commanded attention, being a bright, intense blue. Stephen glumly supposed that some women might find those dimples adorable, too.

Kaylie said something clever and chummy, no doubt, but Stephen tuned it out, wondering sourly if she was on hugging terms with every doctor in the hospital. Targeting the two physicians, he decided that it was past time to get down to business.

"If you two are through pawing my nurse, I'd like to get out of here."

"Great!" Philem exclaimed. "How does tomorrow morning sound?"

"Right now sounds better."

"Not happening, champ," Leland said, strolling forward and lifting his stethoscope from around his neck. "Maybe if this was the first or only broken bone we had to worry about… As it is, though, I have to agree with Dr. Philem." Waving Stephen into silence, he popped in the earpieces of his stethoscope and slipped the bell beneath Stephen's T-shirt. After several seconds, he motioned Stephen forward, shifted and listened to his back. "Lungs are clear," he finally announced.

Philem stepped up, lifted the bedcovers and checked the color of Stephen's toes. "How's your pain level?"

"Eh," Stephen said with an unconcerned shrug of one shoulder.

Philem chuckled and glanced at Kaylie. "These hockey players are tough cookies. But seriously, is the leg bothering you?"

"Only when I move it," Stephen said.

"It'll get worse as the nerve block wears off," Philem warned. "But we'll do our best to get on top of it and stay there. Isn't that so, Kaylie?"

"Yes, sir. I just have one concern," she said, smiling at Stephen. "He's been having nightmares."

"Kaylie!" Stephen snapped, appalled.

"That's why this happened," she went on, ignoring him. "He broke the leg again when he fell out of the bed." She shifted her gaze to Brooks, adding, "I suspect that's what led to his rib injuries the other night, too."

"Kaylie!" Stephen barked again.

"Is that right?" Leland asked him. Then, without waiting for an answer, he shook his head. "I should have picked up on that."

"Those are some pretty violent nightmares," Philem noted.

"What happened to my right to privacy?" Stephen demanded. To his surprise, Kaylie turned on him.

"What are you talking about? I haven't breached any confidentiality. These are your doctors. They need to know how the drugs are affecting you."

"The drugs?" Stephen echoed uncertainly.

"She's right," Leland agreed, consulting a PDA that he'd drawn from a pocket. He rattled off several familiar-sounding drug names. "In combination, any two of those can, in some cases, induce nightmares. In a small number of patients, one of them can even cause hallucinations." He drew a prescription pad from a pocket, produced an ink pen and began to scribble. "Let's change the anti-inflammatory and the oral analgesic." After a few moments, he tore off the top sheet and handed it to Kaylie. "You can adjust the injections, too. May take a little tweaking, but I trust you to keep him comfortable without producing side effects."

Kaylie slid the prescription into her own pocket and nodded at Stephen. "I'll take care of him."

"Lucky stiff," Philem cracked. He launched into a series of instructions that Kaylie probably didn't need to hear and Stephen ignored.

Instead, he watched her, the classical lines of her profile drawing him like a lodestone. He understood now what she'd meant yesterday when she had mentioned "taking care of" his nightmares. He understood, too, that she had become indispensable to his well-being. When he'd said earlier that he needed her, he hadn't been exaggerating. Maybe he had been trying to schmooze her a bit, but the truth was that he didn't see how he could do this without her now.

Truth be told, Philem was right. He was lucky to have found her, and every instinct he possessed dictated that he hold on to her, which was why he didn't like watching these two white-coated mashers drool over her. Not that he was jealous or anything. It was just that, well, she was *his* nurse. That meant she was with *him*. Right? He was determined to make that clear to her at the first opportunity.

Her thoughtfulness and kindness touched and soothed him, and selfish as it might be, that was not something he meant to forego. She didn't need to know that his nightmares were all too real, though, so real that no drug in the world could possibly make a difference.

Predictably, Stephen's mood had soured again. Kaylie felt his disappointment at this new setback and sensed his need to be up and moving around. When she suggested that he take a ride in a wheelchair just to get out of the room, however, his horror was almost laughably palpable.

"I'm not getting into any wheelchair!"

"Oh, I do fear that you are," she said calmly. "How do you expect to get around otherwise?"

He glowered. "The same way as before."

She shook her head. "You can't put an ounce of weight on that leg until you get the walking cast, and I think you'll find that the length of this one changes your center of gravity so that even hopping around on one leg will be very difficult. Trust me on this. You aren't going farther than a few feet unless it's in a chair."

Stephen rolled his eyes. "Great. That's just great."

"It won't be forever," she pointed out, but he heaved a sigh and looked away.

Searching for some way to lighten his mood again, she made small talk and scrolled through the channels on the TV, none of which elicited more than a grunt of disdain from him. Then inspiration struck. She walked over to the bedside table and picked up the receiver of the telephone there. After checking the note in her pocket, she punched in a number and waited for the call to be picked up on the other end. A male voice answered almost immediately.

"Carter."

"Hello, Carter. It's Kaylie Chatam. Just thought I'd let you know that today would be a good time to stop by."

"Great! We've finished our shift, but I think the guys are all still around. I'll get them together, and we'll head over to the hospital. What's the room number?"

"Three-thirty."

"Give us fifteen minutes."

"Looking forward to it," she told him. Aware of Stephen's glower, she hung up, cocking an eyebrow at him in silent question.

"So now you're arranging dates on my time?" he demanded.

"What?"

"It's not enough that my doctors fall all over you? Now you've got to set up meetings with your other boyfriends when you should be taking care of *me?*" He stabbed a finger downward.

Kaylie gaped at him. Was he jealous? She laughed in answer to her own silly question. Jealous? Of little old her? No. The man was spoiled. He wanted her there to wait on him hand and foot. That was all. She parked her hands at her waist.

"You don't know what you're talking about."

"Don't I?" He tossed out a hand. "I'm not blind. I saw with my own eyes how they greeted you. Leland especially seems to think he has some claim on you. Isn't he a little too old for you?"

She couldn't help rolling her eyes. "Brooks Leland is my older brother Morgan's best friend, if you must know. He's like a member of the family, another brother almost."

"Oh." Stephen pondered that for a minute, his frown easing, but then the frown deepened again. "What about Philem? And don't tell me he's like a member of the family because I saw the way he looked at you."

Kaylie felt heat blossom in her cheeks. "We're friends."

"Baloney. There's something going on between you and Philem."

"We're not dating, if that's what you're implying."

Stephen's eyes narrowed thoughtfully. "But he's asked, hasn't he?" Suddenly, he grinned. "He asked, and you shot him down. Ha!"

"I didn't 'shoot him down,'" she insisted. "My father was very ill," she added defensively, "and I didn't feel I could be away from him."

Stephen's grin grew. "It's because Philem's going bald, isn't it?"

"It is not! I told you—"

"Yeah, yeah, Daddy was too sick at the time. And what's your excuse now?"

Kaylie blanched. "And now, we're friends," she told Stephen firmly, "*not* that it's any of your business."

The truth was that she and Philem had dated for a while, and she had liked him very well—still did like him—but when he'd kissed her, she'd suddenly found herself wanting to run in the opposite direction. After her father's heart attack, she'd used his physical condition to allow the relationship to wane. They had remained on friendly terms, but that's as far as it had gone. And as far as she would allow it to go.

"It is my business if you're making dates for three-thirty in the afternoon when you should be working for me!" Stephen insisted.

Kaylie went to the door and pulled it open. Pressing it all the way back, she stood against it, her arms folded, while he glowered in confusion. Finally, she pointed to the two-inches-high gold letters affixed to the door. Three-three-zero.

Stephen's eyes nearly popped out of his head, but then he recovered enough to accuse, "You gave my room number to someone." She nodded, a tad smugly perhaps. "Who?" Stephen demanded.

For once, Kaylie decided to get back a bit of her own. "Guess you'll find out when they get here." With that, she spun and left the room, the door smoothly swinging closed behind her.

"Kaylie!" Stephen yelled, but the door muffled the sound.

Ignoring him, she stepped far enough away that she couldn't hear. The nerve of the man, jumping to such conclusions, acting as if he owned her! Far worse was the unmistakable thrill that she felt because of it.

Dismayed, she reached out to the Lord of her life.

Father God, why him? Why couldn't Craig Philem make her heart trip? Or Brooks, even! Anyone else, anyone who could fit into her world. Anyone who shared her beliefs and lifestyle. Anyone her father might approve of. *Lord, I don't understand myself. Surely I'm just feeling sorry for him. Help me put these feelings into perspective. In the name of Jesus, help me.*

Linda Shocklea walked by with another nurse, took one look at Kaylie's face and stopped, nodding at her workmate, who went on her way. "The bear bit you, did he?"

Kaylie sighed. "Let's just say that I'm giving my patience a breather."

Linda chuckled. "It's a pity, isn't it, that such a good-looking guy is such a grouch?"

"Well," Kaylie said, feeling unaccountably protective of him, "he's been through a lot, and he still has a lot to get through."

"Mmm." Linda cut a knowing gaze in Kaylie's direction. "Honey," she drawled, "a man that handsome, if he was all healed up, I might let him bite me, too." She grinned and sauntered off, leaving Kaylie alternately gaping and sputtering laughter.

A moment later a male voice softly called her name, prompting Kaylie to turn in the opposite direction. A quartet of male smiles greeted her. As the four drew near, one of them asked, "How's he doing?"

"See for yourself," she said brightly, leading the way.

You gave my room number to someone. As if she would ever do anything to hurt him. She only hoped that she wasn't foolish enough to let herself get hurt.

"You may not remember these guys," Kaylie said as four young men crowded into the room. "They transported you to the hospital."

"I remember." Stephen acknowledged the paramedics with nods.

Having one leg in a cast made it difficult to kick one's self, but he would have dearly liked to do so. Barring that, he'd have been pleased for the floor to open up and swallow him whole, adjustable bed and all. As it was, he could only smile and shake hands all around. It was bad enough that he'd made a fool of himself over her and the doctors, but he should've known that she wouldn't give his room number to anyone who could or would harm him. To make matters worse, at least one of these fellows, Carter, was a real fan.

"Man, I saw your last shutout. Amazing game! One of the best I've ever seen."

Stephen gladly recapped that game with the guy. It kept him from having to look at Kaylie. Eventually, he sent Carter to the drawer in the beside table where the autographed pucks were stored and saw them handed out.

"My agent's working on those game passes," Stephen

told them. "I hope a game next season is okay. Playoff seats are just so hard to come by."

"Oh, hey, I'd rather see you play, anyway," Carter assured him. The others murmured agreement.

"Not that we'd turn down playoff tickets," one was quick to add.

Stephen chuckled. "I hear you. I'd sure rather be there than here myself."

Kaylie stepped in and put an end to the visit at that point. "Better let the patient get some rest, boys."

He did feel a little ragged, but when she glanced at her watch, he suddenly felt even worse. She was going to leave him here on his own again. It was nothing less than he deserved, of course, but he didn't like it. Still, he could not let her go without apologizing and at least trying to explain his behavior.

The paramedics dutifully filed out, waving and thanking him for the pucks.

"No, no," Stephen protested. "Y'all took good care of me. I appreciate it."

Carter was the last out the door. He smiled at Kaylie, waggled his puck at her and winked. Stephen felt a kick in his chest and an instant spike in his temper, and that's when it hit him that she was right, after all. He *was* jealous! Terribly so.

The knowledge took his breath away. For the first time in his life, he was actually jealous, and he didn't like it, not one little bit. The question was, what could he do about it? What should he do about it?

Helplessly, he watched her check her watch again, and the next thing he knew, he was pleading with her.

"Wait. Don't go yet. Just wait a minute, will you?" Well, that was another first: Stephen Gallow pleading with a woman. Usually, they threw themselves at him and he occasionally allowed himself to catch one. None of them had ever affected him as Kaylie did, though. "I—I have something to say."

Standing all the way across the room, Kaylie looked down at her toes, rocking back on her heels and folding her arms. He held his breath until she looked up again. Heart pounding, he held out his hand. She hesitated for a long moment, but finally she moved forward. Once she drew near, she put her hand in his. A ridiculous smile broke out on his face. It was insane, but he couldn't help a surge of nervous relief and sheer joy, especially when he gave her a tug and she came unresisting to the side of his bed. Looking down at her much smaller hand in his, he swept his fingers across her knuckles and spoke with blunt honesty.

"I've been unreasonable at times, even unbearable, and I apologize."

"No apology necessary," she told him softly, all forgiveness and generosity.

"I know that it's selfish of me to want to keep you to myself," he went on, squeezing her hand, "but it's so much easier when you're here."

"I understand," she said.

He shook his head. "I don't think you do. I'm not sure I understand it myself. When you're with me, I feel so…comforted, peaceful…hopeful, even, but it's more than that. It's…"

"It's what?" she asked, tilting her head.

He looked up into the purity of her face, her deep, dark, open gaze filling him with warmth. Her kindness and sweetness and patience enveloped him. A fierce yearning shook him to his core. Instinctively, he reached up, and then he was pulling her down, his hand clamped around the nape of her neck beneath the heavy weight of that crazy, looping bun that he hated simply because it kept her hair contained. She didn't have far to go. He surely stood more than a foot taller than she did, but he was partially sitting in a high bed, and she was already bending close. It seemed like an eternity, but no more than a heartbeat passed before their lips met.

What happened next could not be explained.

The room and everything else seemed to spin away. Sensation electrified every nerve ending in his battered body. At the same time, Stephen's mind clarified. He saw the stark reality of his own life.

He had been living, existing, in a kind of desert—a dry, cold, barren, lonely place where he didn't want to be anymore—and Kaylie was his first, perhaps his only, chance to escape it. She was warmth and shelter, companionship, contentment, peace—and much too good for the likes of him. She obviously knew it, too, for she suddenly wrenched away and fled the room.

Stephen collapsed back against his pillow, closed his eyes and prayed that he hadn't totally blown it. He suddenly did not see how he could do this, how he could put himself back together again and overcome this latest fiasco without her. He wasn't even sure that he wanted to try.

As the morning passed into afternoon and then into an interminable evening, he began to fear that he might not have a choice. His kiss might well have driven her away for good.

Chapter Eight

"Stupid, stupid, stupid," Kaylie murmured, pacing the hospital hallway the next morning. She still could not believe what had happened, what she had allowed to happen, the day before. That kiss had made her positively giddy—until she'd realized the implications.

She was not the sort of female that Stephen Gallow seemed accustomed to, and she certainly did not kiss her patients. What he must think of her now! She hadn't been able to face him after that kiss, and so she'd run. She'd stayed away because he was the last man with whom she ought to be getting involved. Her father, and very likely even her brothers, would disapprove. Why, *she* disapproved! She'd always assumed she'd find some quiet, bookish fellow with a clear calling to service, something they could share and work at together. Stephen Gallow was so far the opposite of her imagined mate that she couldn't think why she felt so drawn to him. But drawn to him she was, and so she'd cowardly stayed away.

That had been possible yesterday. The man was in the hospital, after all. Today he was supposed to go home to Chatam House, and that changed everything. Still,

Kaylie had prayed long and hard before she'd decided to come here this morning. The inescapable facts were that, no matter how foolishly she had behaved yesterday, she was still a nurse, and he was still her patient. She had an obligation to Stephen Gallow.

Now that she was here, though, she couldn't bring herself to go into his room—not alone anyway. Thankfully, Craig Philem breezed into the corridor right on schedule.

"Good morning, Kaylie. Ready to take your guy home?"

Her guy. Gulping, Kaylie nodded and waved toward the door, inviting the doctor to go in. Ever the gentleman, however, Craig reached around her and pushed the door open, standing back so she could enter first.

"Kaylie!" Stephen exclaimed, his voice imbued with relief and concern.

Guilt stabbed her. He had been worried about her. She hadn't expected that. In fact, she'd assumed that he would be angry and petulant. For some reason, she'd rather have faced his anger than his concern. Fearing that he would immediately begin apologizing, explaining or cajoling in front of Craig, she sent him an imploring look, but he didn't even notice. He was too busy frowning at the doctor.

Craig, thankfully, did not seem to realize that anything might be amiss as he went about checking Stephen's vital signs. As he did so, Stephen sat quietly in the bed, his gaze on Kaylie. He seemed sad. Alarmed, she wondered if anything had gone wrong during the night.

"Heartbeat's a little rapid," Craig noted, stuffing his stethoscope back into his coat pocket. "You that anxious to get out of here?"

"More than anxious," Stephen said, looking directly at Kaylie. She couldn't quite manage to hold his gaze. Hers went skittering to Craig.

"How'd you rest last night?" Craig asked Stephen.

"Well enough, when they let me."

Craig chuckled. "Yeah, we slap you in here, tell you to rest, then we send the nurses in every couple of hours to hassle you. It's our way of keeping you from getting too comfortable."

"No worry on that score," Stephen muttered.

"You'll be glad to know, then, that I'm letting you go home."

"About time," Stephen said, closing his eyes and sighing.

Craig let them know that the nurse would be in shortly with discharge papers and written care instructions. "Not that you need them with Kaylie on the job. Strictly protocol."

Kaylie smiled and nodded in acknowledgment of the compliment.

"I've been told to ask you, though," Craig said to Kaylie, "when you might return to pediatrics." He slid his hands into his coat pockets. "Seems I'm not the only one missing you around here."

"Oh, I, uh, really couldn't say," she stammered. "Dad still depends on me."

"I thought your father's condition was stable."

"Well, yes, but his age and…" She waved a hand ineffectually.

Craig glanced at Stephen, nodding. "Mmm. I see. Other responsibilities."

She didn't know how to respond to that. On one hand, he seemed to have made a completely erroneous assumption. On the other, he was entirely correct. Suddenly she realized that he was about to leave her alone with Stephen.

Noting that Stephen's breakfast tray still rested on the rolling bed table, which had been pushed to one side, she rushed to snatch it up, saying, "I'll just get this out of the way."

Craig looked at the tray. It had barely been touched. Doctor and nurse spoke at the same time.

"Not eating much."

"You didn't drink your coffee."

Stephen shrugged. "Never found runny eggs and raw bacon appetizing. And that's not coffee. I think someone accidentally drained their crankcase into my cup."

"I'm sure Hilda will have something more appetizing for you," Kaylie told him. "Meanwhile, I'll run downstairs and get you a decent cup of coffee." That would keep her busy until the discharge nurse joined them.

Stephen shrugged listlessly again. Newly concerned, Kaylie followed Craig from the room, deposited the tray on the wheeled rack in the hallway and fled downstairs to the cafeteria, where she bought two tall coffees from a specialty vendor, her own disguised with French vanilla flavoring, sweetener and a goodly dose of cream. As shields went, it wouldn't provide much protection, but she cravenly prayed for distraction, at least, anything to prevent a repeat of yesterday's lunacy.

To her profound relief and surprise, Aaron Doolin was in the room, along with the nurse, when she returned. Apparently, Stephen had already made his own arrangements for transportation. Kaylie did not mention that they could have called on Chester. He would gladly have brought the aunties' town car for Stephen's use.

Stephen accepted the fresh coffee with placid pleasure and set about downing it as activity swirled around him. Kaylie's own concoction went barely tasted as things moved apace. She listened patiently to the nurse's discharge instructions, and then Aaron informed her that he called her aunts to let them know to expect Stephen shortly. As Stephen's legal rep, Aaron signed the papers then helped Stephen dress in loose burgundy sweatpants and a yellow-gold jersey from which Aaron's wife, Dora, had cut one of the sleeves. Kaylie slipped clean white socks onto Stephen's feet, marveling again at their size.

Just under an hour later, a nurse wheeled Stephen out to Aaron's waiting car. Kaylie was stunned to find out that Stephen had instructed Aaron to purchase a wheelchair for his use. That chair was already tucked into the trunk of Aaron's luxury sedan.

Kaylie saw Stephen settled onto the backseat of Aaron's car, then followed behind it in her own vehicle. When their little caravan arrived at Chatam House, they found Chester at the side entrance beneath the porte cochere, putting the finishing touches on the old wheelchair ramp that Grandpa Hub had used. Chester had pulled it out of storage and bolted it into place at Aunt Hypatia's instruction.

The ramp covered the redbrick walkway and steps and extended out onto the drive, forming a small, flat base where the chair could be positioned atop the deep gravel. The wood-and-metal structure needed a fresh coat of white paint, but that did not distract from the colorful beauty of the flowers that frothed beneath its railings and tumbled in brilliant disarray from the enormous terra-cotta pots flanking the bright yellow door with its austere black framing. Spiraling green topiaries stood sentinel next to the mounds of shrubbery that softened the stark, white-painted, quarried stone from which the great house was built.

As Kaylie waited for Aaron and Chester to take the wheelchair from the trunk of the car, she felt the full glory of spring surround her. Air as soft as cotton, sunshine as clear and bright as crystal and temperatures hovering in the seventies combined to sooth the soul. Brilliant green carpeted the expansive lawns of Chatam House, delighting the eye. Kaylie could even see a few small, creamy white blossoms peeking out from the waxy, dark green leaves of the enormous magnolia tree on the west lawn. She wondered if Aunt Mag's roses were blooming in the arbor on the east side of the house and couldn't believe that she hadn't even thought to check as she'd come up the drive earlier. Her thoughts then had been consumed with problems. Yet, here was proof of God's omniscience and care.

She stood aside and bowed her head, silently praying as Chester and Aaron eased Stephen out of the sedan and got him into the chair.

Forgive me, Father, for wallowing in my own angst. I know that You are with me every moment and that You will show me what to do and what to say if only I am brave enough to pay attention and obey. Help me, then, to help Stephen and, above all, to open his eyes to You. Amen.

She looked up straight into those solemn gray eyes, but Stephen quickly looked away. He had been unusually quiet all morning. In fact, an air of gloom hung over him. He sat silently while Chester attached a support sling to the chair for his broken leg. Troubled, Kaylie lightly touched Stephen's broad shoulder.

"Are you feeling okay?"

He glanced up, nodded and looked down again. Apprehension shivered through her. She did then what any nurse might have done; she laid her wrist against his forehead to check for a temperature. He jerked back as if she'd burned him. Feeling a tad scorched herself, despite discerning no telltale fever, she tucked her hands behind her.

A moment later, Chester maneuvered the chair around and pushed it up the ramp, remarking how he'd used to do this for old mister Hub senior. Aaron joked that the old fellow probably hadn't compared size-wise with a polar bear, implying that Stephen did. Stephen's lack of retort seemed to worry Aaron, who looked askance at Kaylie as he stood aside to allow her to enter the house ahead of him. She could do nothing more than wordlessly share his concern.

The darkness of the back hall embraced them, redolent with the aromas of old wood, beeswax, brick, tea and, unless Kaylie missed her guess, Hilda's fabulous gingerbread muffins. The old house seemed to take them into its arms, as comforting as one of the aunties' hugs. As they moved between the vast kitchen, butler's pantry, formal dining room and back parlor, Kaylie thought, as she often did, of the generations of Chatams who had called this house home over the past century and a half. In addition, this place had provided temporary sanctuary for countless other individuals, Stephen being just the latest.

Why, her cousin Reeves Leland and his adorable moppet Gilli had spent weeks and weeks here this past winter after discovering that honeybees had invaded the attic of their own place. Reeves had recently married

Anna Miranda Burdett. They lived at Burdett House now, a lovely old Victorian just a few blocks away.

The aunties had hosted their wedding reception in the ballroom, and it had been a lovely, poignant, yet somehow lighthearted, affair that had made Kaylie wonder if she would ever know such joy. Conversely, after Reeves's wedding, her father had become adamant about her being called to remain single. Kaylie had struggled with the idea all along, but never more so than lately. She didn't even want to think why that might be.

Their group reached the end of the corridor and turned into the west hall, one of a pair that flanked the massive central staircase, which terminated in the south-facing foyer. Chester wheeled Stephen past the ladies' "withdrawing room"—the gents' opened onto the east hall between the library and the ballroom—and one of Kaylie's favorite chambers in the old house, the cloakroom. Though now a storage facility for galoshes, umbrellas and overcoats, Kaylie imagined it filled with everything from fur-lined capes, swirling great coats and top hats to fringed leather suede, ankle-length dusters and cowboy hats. The cloakroom had probably seen them all at one time or another.

Kaylie was not surprised when Chester turned Stephen's chair into the front parlor. She saw at once that the aunties had subtly shifted the furnishings to make way for the wheelchair. The sling supporting Stephen's right leg straight out in front of him complicated matters, however, and it took some maneuvering to bring him near the tea tray, especially with all three of the aunties directing traffic. Finally, things were arranged to their mutual satisfaction.

"Thanks," Stephen murmured to Chester, who nodded and went out.

Hypatia reclaimed her usual wingback chair and directed Aaron to its twin, while Magnolia sank down on one end of the settee and Kaylie assumed a seat next to Stephen on an English mahogany side chair brought forward for the occasion. Odelia, however, continued to hover over Stephen, waving her lacy handkerchief and fluttering the bell-shaped sleeves of the filmy white blouse that she wore with a brown fringed skirt, white moccasin-style loafers and clusters of turquoise beads that dangled almost to her shoulders.

"Welcome home! Welcome home, Stephen dear. You poor darlin'." In her enthusiasm, she bent and embraced him, her hands cupping his head, her earrings swinging in his face.

He shot Kaylie an amused glance that eased a small measure of her concern. "Thank you, ma'am."

"How you've suffered!" Odelia clucked. "We're so happy to have you back again." She patted his good hand. "Don't you worry a bit. We're going to get you well, no matter how long it takes. Isn't that so, Kaylie dear?"

Kaylie didn't even have time for a limp nod before Hypatia said, "For pity's sake, Odelia, sit down." Her tone could not be construed as anything but an order.

Unperturbed, Odelia trotted over and dropped down beside Magnolia, her sweet smile in place. Hypatia then turned to Stephen, offering him a more formal welcome.

"It is good to see you again, Stephen dear. May we offer you a refreshment?" She leaned forward, reaching for the teapot. "Cream or sugar?"

"Uh…" Stephen shook his head. Taking his response

as a repudiation of the condiments, not the tea, Hypatia began to pour. Meanwhile, Ophelia popped up and piled a trio of dark, fragrant muffins on a delicate Limoges china plate, along with a slice of cantaloupe and a delicate silver fork. She handed him that plate just as Hypatia passed him a cup of black tea on a matching saucer. Stephen tried to accept both, but the muffin plate wound up in his lap.

Kaylie lurched forward and caught the plate and the muffins. The fork and cantaloupe hit the floor. Aaron laughed, but Ophelia went into paroxysms of apologies and reassurances.

"Oh! Oh, oh, oh! How clumsy of me! Your fruit!" She grabbed a heavy linen napkin, hiked her skirt and gave every evidence of intending to drop to her knees. Kaylie managed to head her off.

"Here, let me." Placing the muffin plate on the seat of her chair, Kaylie took the napkin from Odelia, bent and swept up both fork and cantaloupe slice, setting them aside on the tray.

"Kaylie to the rescue," Aaron chortled. "Getting to be a habit, huh, Stevie?"

Stephen winced but made no reply.

Magnolia shoved a plate of muffins, sans fork and fruit, into Aaron's hands as Hypatia reached once more for the teapot, asking in a strained voice, "Cream or sugar?"

Oblivious to any awkwardness, Aaron took both. Hypatia managed to prepare his tea while shooting daggered glances at Odelia, who returned meekly to her place on the settee. Magnolia tsked and helped herself to a plate of goodies while Auntie Od bounced numerous regretful looks around the room. Kaylie selected another slice of melon for Stephen, spearing it with a clean fork. She placed it on his plate that way and returned the plate to his lap, within easy reach. She then filled another plate and passed it to Odelia with a sympathetic smile.

Subsiding back into her chair, Kaylie took Stephen's saucer from him, allowing him to use his good hand to handle his tea. He gave her a slight nod in thanks but failed to meet her gaze as he raised the cup and sipped. A muscle quivered in the corner of his eye, but his face remained expressionless, even as Aaron exclaimed, with a full mouth, over the muffins and slurped his tea. The muffins, Kaylie knew, were delicious, so she offered Stephen the saucer. He placed his teacup on it, and she set both aside as he reached down to take a muffin from the plate on his lap.

"Kaylie, dear, would you like a cup of tea?" Hypatia asked.

"Yes, thank you."

"And muffins?" Magnolia suggested, passing her a fresh napkin.

Considering that she only had two hands, Kaylie declined. "I'll share with Stephen."

Stephen smiled at her and bit off a hunk of a muffin. An instant later, bliss relaxed the muscles of his face and widened his eyes. "Mmm." He chewed and swallowed. "Wow. Even my *oma*'s gingerbread isn't this good."

Kaylie snatched one of the muffins from his plate as the aunties erupted into expressions of delight at Stephen's praise. The sugar-crisped crust protected the moist insides, rich with golden raisins and pecans. While Kaylie nibbled and Stephen gobbled, the aunties explained in minute, and often conflicting, detail how Hilda prepared the luscious treat.

The subject quickly exhausted itself, at which point Odelia smiled at Stephen and said, "Perhaps Oma would like Hilda's recipe."

"She might," Stephen replied with a tired smile.

"And who is Oma, dear?" Magnolia asked. "Your cook?"

"My grandmother. *Oma* is Dutch for grandmother."

"How lovely!" Odelia exclaimed. "What's the Dutch word for aunt?"

"Tante."

"Tante. I like that. *Tante* Odelia."

Stephen polished off his second muffin and went to work on the melon, holding the slice suspended on the fork. He put it down without finishing it, and Kaylie noted the signs of fatigue in the droop of his shoulders and eyelids.

She interrupted a chummy discussion between Aaron and the Aunties to say, "I think Stephen should get upstairs now."

That presented a problem that Kaylie had mulled over off and on for the past two days. Grandpa Hub had depended on Chester to carry him up and down the stairs, but Chester had been a decade younger then, and at ninety-two Grandpa had been little more than skin and bones. Aaron honed in on the issue at once.

"Hey, next time I'll bring along some of your teammates," he joked to Stephen. Looking at the aunties, he explained, "The Blades have a couple of Swedes and a Russian who make Stephen look like their baby brother."

"Maybe Chester and Mr. Doolin can get Stephen up the stairs by turning the chair backward," Odelia suggested.

Kaylie didn't see how that would be possible, given

the fact that Stephen's leg stuck straight out and blocked access to the front of the chair so no one could lift from that side. She doubted that anyone could lift Stephen up so many stairs, anyway. Nevertheless, they would likely need Chester's assistance. Magnolia went to get him while Kaylie maneuvered Stephen's chair to the foot of the stairs. They both looked up that broad, gracefully curving staircase and knew that he was getting up there only one way.

"Do you think you can do it?" she asked him quietly as the aunts and Aaron arrived to offer support.

He snorted. "Do I have a choice?"

"We'll take it slow, rest along the way."

He nodded grimly. Chester arrived, and without any further discussion Stephen pushed up to his feet, or rather, foot.

"You sure about this?" Aaron asked, realizing what Stephen was about to do. "Maybe we could rig some sort of ramp." It would take a team of oxen to pull Stephen up such a steep slope, and everyone knew it.

"Just get over here and give me a hand," Stephen ordered.

Aaron pushed past Kaylie and slipped his shoulder under Stephen's good arm. The aunts worried aloud, but Chester merely remarked that he would take up the chair. Hoisting the contraption, he began to climb the stairs with it. Behind him, Stephen hopped up onto the bottom step, his bad leg held out at an awkward angle. Kaylie rushed to lend what aid she could.

It was a grueling, lengthy process that brought Kaylie to tears and both Stephen and Aaron to the brink of exhaustion. By the time Stephen dropped down into the chair again, he was moaning, Aaron's chest pumped like a bellows, and Kaylie had to surreptitiously wipe her eyes. She quickly wheeled the chair along the landing, through the sitting room of Stephen's suite and into his bedroom, where she, Aaron and Chester got him into bed.

While Chester went back downstairs and Aaron sagged against the bedpost, Kaylie quickly administered an injection of painkiller.

"And I thought I was tough," Stephen murmured, his eyelids sagging.

"You are unbelievably tough," she told him softly. "I don't know another man who could have managed that, not even my brother Chandler."

His light gray eyes opened, delving deeply into hers, and he whispered, "I was afraid you wouldn't come back."

"Of course I came back."

His eyelids drifted down again, and he breathed the words, "I need you to come back."

"I did," she said. "I will." She realized then just how true that was. "I'll come back for as long as you need me."

How, she wondered, as Stephen's hand sought and gripped hers, could she do anything else? She supposed it meant that they would have to discuss that kiss, but oh, how she wished they could pretend that it had never happened.

Aaron's cell phone rang just then, and he dug it from his jacket pocket, looked at the caller ID and winced before showing it to Stephen, who moaned low in his throat.

Kaylie glimpsed the photo of a mature, smiling woman with a long face and straight, shoulder-length, pale blond hair just before Aaron put the phone to his ear and exclaimed, "Hannah! How is *mijn favoriete meisje?*"

Even Kaylie knew that his accent was deplorable, though she had no idea what the phrase even meant. That it was Dutch, however, she did not doubt.

"Yeah, well, there have been a few developments," Aaron said reluctantly, glancing at Stephen. "Fact is, we just got our boy back here to the mansion from another little hospital stay." He emphasized the word *mansion.*

He listened for several moments before saying, "Uh, right, right! Thing is, I guess we were just too busy to think of it, little issue with his leg." Then, "Naw, naw, it's gonna be fine. Surgery was a complete success."

He glared at Stephen and pointed at the phone, but Stephen shook his head adamantly, turned away and closed his eyes. Aaron bowed his head, balancing his forehead against the palm of his free hand, his arm wrapped around the bedpost. "Yeeaah," he drawled, "the thing is, see, he's asleep. His nurse gave him a shot, and he went out like a light, let me tell you." He straightened, looked at Kaylie and pointed to the small phone nestled against his ear, as if to ask that she confirm his assertion.

Kaylie spread her hands, glanced at Stephen and shook her head, silently indicating her confusion and reluctance to get involved.

Aaron smoothly shifted gears, his jocular mien sliding over him like a second skin. "Hey, you ought to see this place. It's really something, an honest-to-goodness antebellum mansion. They've got a dumbwaiter out on the landing, murals on the ceilings and enough crystal hanging around to bury a fellow if it should fall. Why, your boy's resting on rare antiques, or so I'm told."

He suddenly stood upright, eyes wide. "Uh, uh, let's

wait on that a few more days." Turning to Kaylie, he churned his hand, silently asking her for help, but what help? "U-until the, um, doctors o-okay him for visitors." Grimacing, he showed his teeth to Kaylie. "No, really. It's j-just a precaution. Yeah, yeah, of course I'll tell him you called." Aaron laughed in that practiced way of his and went on. "Now, don't worry about him. He's in good hands, and I'm sure he'll be well enough to speak to you in, uh, soon."

After a few more seconds, Aaron ended the call and slumped against the bedpost once more. "Whew! Thought for a minute there that she was about to jump a plane."

"She'd better not!" Stephen growled, flopping onto his back.

Kaylie parked her hands at her hips and demanded, "What is going on? Who was that?"

Stephen clamped his mouth in a hard line, but Aaron seemed surprised that Kaylie didn't know. "Hannah Scherren, Stevie's mom."

"His mother!" Kaylie bent toward the bed. "You don't want your mother here? Why ever not?"

Stephen rubbed a hand over his face. "I just don't, that's all."

"But she's your *mother*."

"Listen," Aaron said suddenly, "I gotta run." He started off, then paused and turned back to shake a finger at Stephen. "The thing is, if you would just talk to her, it might do you both a world of good."

"Stay out of it, Aaron."

Aaron sighed. "Been four years since you last spoke to any member of your family, Stevie."

"I said to stay out of it!"

"Not since the funeral."

Kaylie gasped. "What funeral? Whose? What are you talking about?"

Aaron shook his head and made for the door again. "You want to know that, you gotta ask Steve."

Kaylie turned back to the bed, but Stephen's glare warned her not to press the issue. "Don't," he said when she opened her mouth.

Curiosity and concern burned within her, but she knew that it would be a mistake to become further involved with Stephen Gallow's personal life. She closed her mouth and sat down in the wheelchair next to the bed. Stephen closed his eyes, and after a moment, his hand groped for hers. Kaylie did her best not to reach out, but somehow their palms met, and their fingers intertwined. She sat with her head bowed, asking herself what she was doing with this man, until the pressure of his fingers slowly eased. Finally, she slipped free and left him sleeping peacefully.

Moving out into the sitting room, she lifted a hand to the back of her neck and then turned her eyes heavenward. The mystery of Stephen Gallow had just deepened, and the differences between them had never been more painfully obvious, and yet…and yet…

"Show me Your purpose in this, I beg You."

A man who would not even speak to his own mother could not be for her.

But could she be for him?

Chapter Nine

Alone again.

That was Stephen's first thought when he woke. Alone and in pain, considerable pain, more than he'd expected, but nothing he couldn't manage until Kaylie came again.

I'll come back for as long as you need me.

He had carried her whispered promise off into exhausted, thankfully peaceful slumber, but he couldn't forget now how appalled she had been that he wouldn't speak to his mother. How could he tell her why? She would likely despise him then, as his family must.

I'll come back for as long as you need me.

Yet, she'd thought that he hadn't needed her in the hospital, and she had stayed away. Now she had to know that there was much wrong in him. Would she break her promise? Or would she simply go away for good?

The sound of her voice came to him, growing louder as she crossed the sitting room toward his bedchamber.

"I'm sorry, Dad. I know I've been gone more than usual today, but this is a special case."

Pleased and surprised, Stephen opened his eyes and strained to hear every word.

"You know that he just got out of the hospital."

Pushing up onto his elbow, Stephen looked into the sitting room, listening shamelessly, but Kaylie must have come to a stop just out of sight.

"I'm sorry you had to make your own lunch, but I came home as soon as I could to put a casserole in the Crock-Pot, didn't I?"

A pause followed, then, "I can't be sure when he'll wake up, but don't feel you have to wait to eat until I get there." And finally, "Okay, fine. I'll come as soon as I can. I promise. Bye."

Stephen eased back down on the bed, calling out, "Kaylie?"

Just as expected, she stepped into the doorway, her old flip phone in her hand, a smile on her face. "You're awake! You must be hungry. You slept straight through lunch."

"Did I?"

He licked his lips, aware now of his hunger and thirst. As if she could read his mind, she walked to the bedside table, pocketed her phone and poured him a glass of water, saying, "I brought this up fresh just a little while ago."

Turning onto his side, he took the glass in his good hand and managed a long drink before collapsing back onto his pillow. "Thanks."

"You're welcome. So how do you feel?"

"Like I've been beat up."

"The leg's starting to ache, isn't it?"

"How'd you know?"

"I'm surprised the nerve block hasn't worn off already," she said, smiling down at him. "Do you want something for pain before I go down to get your meal?"

He shook his head. "I don't want to go back to sleep. What time is it, anyway?"

"Nearly four."

He nodded, and she turned away, but he called her back. "Kaylie?"

"Yes?"

"Thank you for staying."

"I wasn't here all the time."

"I know, you went home to put on dinner for your dad, but you were here most of the time, weren't you?"

She looked down at her hands. "I thought you might need me."

"I do."

She said not a word to that; neither did she meet his gaze.

"Will you stay while I eat?" he asked tentatively.

She nodded. "Someone has to take down your tray when you're done."

"Thanks," he said, but then before she could get out of the room, his big mouth got the better of him and he halted her again. "Kaylie?"

She stopped and turned her head, gazing at him over her shoulder. "Yes?"

He was having second thoughts, but the idea had been uppermost on his mind since she'd walked into his hospital room that morning, and the sooner it was out, the sooner they could honestly address it. And the sooner he would know where she truly stood on the matter. Last night he'd thought she was done with him; then she'd walked into his room this morning. He tamped down his misgivings and said, “I hope you don’t regret that kiss. Because I don’t.”

She froze for several heartbeats, but then she turned, her body pivoting at the end of her neck, and calmly asked, “Why won’t you speak to your mother?”

He must have looked as if he’d been poleaxed, because that’s how he felt. She flipped around and walked out of the room. He stared at the empty door for several long seconds, but then he had to smile, even as his stomach sank.

Oh, man. Talk about giving as good as she got! Her message couldn’t have been more clear. If he tried to discuss the one subject, she would insist on discussing the other, and that was the last thing he wanted. The very last thing. Mercy, his gentle little nurse had just backed him into a corner and forced a standoff. These, he understood perfectly, were the conditions under which they would proceed: the kiss hadn’t happened, no estrangement from his mother. He supposed he’d just have to live with that, whether he liked it or not.

She returned in less than twenty minutes with his lap desk and a dinner tray. Hilda had outdone herself with a dish that Kaylie called “drover’s pie,” consisting of tender bits of beef in a thick, dark gravy presented in a nest of mixed vegetables surrounded by a hearty helping of mashed potatoes and topped with a flaky biscuit crust. It beat by a mile the bland, anemic meal that the hospital had served him the night before. Add to that bounty a huge dish of banana pudding that was to die for, and Stephen wound up stuffing himself. Thoroughly sated, he leaned back against the stack of pillows behind him and sighed.

"I may just have to steal that woman away from your aunts when I leave here. Man, can she ever cook."

Kaylie chuckled. "If you want to see what damage three little old ladies on the warpath can do, you just try that."

He laughed. "Yeah, I can just image your aunts coming after me with hoes and pitchforks. Hypatia, of course, would be wearing pearls and pumps, and all the more terrifying for it, while Magnolia sported galoshes and heavy gardening gloves."

Kaylie snorted behind her hand. She had brought the desk chair in from the other room and sat with her legs crossed at the knee, watching him pack it in. Oddly, she'd seemed to derive some sort of pleasure from watching him eat. His mother had done that when he'd been a little boy. Kaylie, however, was not his mom, and he was no boy now.

"And Aunt Odelia?" she asked, a smile wiggling on her lips.

He considered and decided, "Viking gear, complete with finger bones dangling from her earlobes and a horned helmet."

"Except she'd tie bows on those horns," Kaylie said, giggling.

He laughed at the thought of it, but then he shivered. Odelia would probably use his intestines to tie those bows. Still, that Hilda was some cook. It might be worth the risk.

"I don't know how you could pass up that drover's pie," he mused. It was the wrong thing to say.

"I promised Dad I'd have dinner with him," Kaylie murmured. She checked her watch then hastily rose and took the tray from his lap desk. He was really starting to hate that watch of hers. "How's your pain level?"

"I'll live," he muttered, though the leg had started to throb pronouncedly.

"Let me send this down to the kitchen, then we'll address that."

She went out, supposedly to send the tray down to the kitchen via the dumbwaiter, and returned a few minutes later. Moving to the bedside table, she picked up several small prescription bottles there and began to go through them one by one.

"I had these filled earlier on my way back here." She went through them one by one. "Anti-inflammatory. You take it after you eat. Nutritional supplement. Aids in repairing the bone. Antibiotic, twice a day for the next four days. Just a precaution. Pain med. One shouldn't knock you out. Two might, but not likely. You'll definitely feel them, though. The new injection obviously puts you on your back, so we'll save that for bedtime and extreme instances." She uncapped and shook out pills from all four bottles, then dumped the pills into his palm and handed him the water glass from the bedside table. "Bottoms up."

He dutifully swallowed the collection of capsules and tablets and drained the glass.

"Now let's get you in and out of the bathroom before those hit you. Okay?"

"Yes, please."

She carried the desk chair back into the sitting room and pushed in the wheelchair, but it quickly became obvious that the positioning of his leg would make the chair useless in such close confines. He didn't mind. It meant that he'd have his arm around her while he hopped to and from the bath.

They went through the laborious process, him hopping on one foot, Kaylie steadying and supporting him. He was relieved to find that he could still do pretty well for himself once he actually got where he was going. His left leg was apt to be twice as strong as the right before this was over, though. He made a mental note to have Aaron speak to the team kinesiologist first thing tomorrow, then he had to stop and think what day this was. Thursday, he decided. Yes, definitely Thursday. The team was playing tonight.

By the time he got back to Kaylie, he was aching all over. Nevertheless, he insisted that she put him in the wheelchair and push him into the sitting room so he could watch the pre-game show and the hockey game to follow. She did so reluctantly and only after explaining the functions of the chair and showing him how to operate it. Wasn't much to it. As it was all hand-operated and he had the use of only one hand, he wouldn't be going very far in the thing by himself, anyway.

She fetched his phone from his bedside table and gave it to him, along with a slip of paper that she pulled from a pocket. "This is the telephone number here at Chatam House. If you need anything, call the phone here and Chester will come up."

"But I can still call you, right?"

"Of course. It's just that Chester's closer and can take care of most of your needs. I'll be back later to give you your injection. Okay?"

"Okay, but that's hours from now."

"True. So, in the meantime, if you need anything call on Chester."

He shoved his hand through his hair. "Surely you see that I have greater need of you now than I did before this cast covered my whole leg. Besides, you have no idea how boring it is being stuck here with nothing to do and no one to talk to."

"Well, you have the TV," she said, plucking the remote from the mantel, "and there are books on the bedside table. Plus, you have your phone."

He rolled his eyes and snapped, "Fine. You weren't hired to keep me company. I get it."

"It's just that I have other responsibilities," she said a tad defensively, "and I've already been here more today than I expected because I had to be sure how the new meds would affect you."

"Whether they'd give me nightmares, you mean."

"Yes, among other things."

He had not, fortunately, dreamed at all—not that he remembered, anyway. In fact, now that he thought of it, the nightmare hadn't come since the doctors had changed his prescription. The lack of nightmares didn't change the reality, however.

He averted his gaze, shrugging. "Guess I'll see you later then."

"Yes. See you later."

She handed him the television remote and went out. Loneliness swamped him the instant she left his sight.

Appalled, he shook his head. It wasn't that he was actually lonesome. Of course it wasn't! He'd been living alone for the better part of a decade now. Good grief, could he not be alone in a suite of rooms in a house full of people without becoming maudlin about it?

He toyed with the idea of calling Aaron and getting him down here to watch the game with him, but Aaron had already made that onerous drive once today, and Stephen really couldn't, in good conscience, ask him to make it again. He wondered whom else he might call and thought of his mother. Suddenly the need to hear the sound of her voice welled up in him, but the next instant Nick's face wavered before his mind's eye. Gulping, Stephen pushed away that vision, along with any desire to contact his mother. What other choice did he possibly have?

Ten minutes later, he was pecking out a text message to Kaylie, informing her that the game would be over by ten.

"It's ready, Dad," Kaylie said, setting the casserole dish on the cast-iron trivet in the center of the kitchen table next to a tossed green salad. "Will you bring the bread?"

"It's not right," Hub rasped, continuing with a theme that he'd been harping on since she'd gotten home. "You should be able to eat undisturbed at a decent hour."

It was forty minutes past their usual dinnertime, a mere forty minutes, and they tended to eat early, but Kaylie said nothing. It would help if Stephen would refrain from texting her every half hour or so. Still, she couldn't help thinking of the way Stephen had enjoyed Hilda's drover's pie tonight.

She smiled to herself, remembering the appreciative sounds he'd made and the expressions of bliss on his handsome face. It had been thoughtful of Hilda to cook a dish that he could eat with one hand and to have it ready early. Otherwise, they would have had to find something to tide him over until the aunties' normal dinner hour, which was about twenty minutes from now. Hilda had said she'd done it because Stephen had missed lunch, but Kaylie suspected that it was a combination of Hilda's compassion and Stephen's complimentary remarks regarding her gingerbread muffins. Kaylie's own cooking did not receive such high marks from her father.

"And we ought to be able to count on a decent dinner," Hub went on, carrying the loaf of whole wheat bread to the table from the kitchen counter by its plastic sleeve, "not these hastily thrown together, one-dish concoctions that are all you have time for now. Your mother would have laid a proper table and provided a balanced meal."

Kaylie let her exasperation show, placing one oven-mitted hand on her hip and gesturing toward the table with the other. "What is wrong," she asked, "with place mats, dinner plates, napkins, forks, knives, spoons and drinking glasses? Isn't that an adequate table setting? And where do you think I got the recipe for this casserole? From Mom, that's who! I'm sorry she's not around to serve it, but that's not my fault."

Hub reared back as if she'd struck out at him. "So, you think it's *my* fault?"

"Of course not!"

"Will you blame God then?"

"Never! It's no one's fault. Sometimes life just is what it is, and we have to deal with it as best we can."

"We were dealing very well, I thought, until you took this job," Hub grumbled, pulling out his chair.

"Were we?" Kaylie asked, divesting herself of the oven mitts. "Were we really dealing well?"

He set his jaw mulishly. "What's that supposed to mean?"

Kaylie sighed, pulled out her chair and sat down, choosing her words carefully. "Lately I've realized that we've been locked away inside this house for too long. We still have ministries to perform."

Hub took his seat, his mouth a thin, severe line. "I devoted my life to ministry."

"Dad, you speak as if your life is over!"

"That part of my life is, given my age and health."

"You could live another twenty or thirty years. Just look at Grandpa Hub. He was ninety-two when the Lord took him home and still overseeing his investments and charities from his wheelchair."

A look of such bleakness overcame her father that Kaylie wanted to weep. She reached for his hand. Though gnarled and pale, it still felt strong to her. Only his spirit, it seemed, was weak.

"You may be content to putter around your garden and sit in your chair for the next twenty years, Dad," Kaylie said softly. "You are certainly entitled to, but I am young and healthy, and the only thing I know without any doubt about myself right now is that I am called to nursing."

"But are you called to nurse this particular man?" Hub asked, gripping her hand hard.

"Yes," she answered without hesitation, a little shocked that she did not have to mull that over first, especially considering her mixed feelings and many hours of prayer on the matter.

Hub released her. "I am not so sure. You're alone with him too much. He's too young and pushy. We know nothing about him. He—"

"He's gravely injured and cannot manage on his own," Kaylie interrupted, folding her hands in her lap and bowing her head. "Will you pray over our food or shall I?"

Hub cleared his throat, and Kaylie prepared herself for a long, sermonizing monologue of the sort to which Hub had only rarely resorted during his career as a preacher. Instead, he quickly asked for a blessing on the food and left it there. Grateful for that, Kaylie tried to be as pleasant as possible throughout the meal and into the evening, though her mind never wandered far from Stephen and how he might be doing.

She felt terrible guilt for leaving Stephen there on his own—and terrible guilt at the idea of leaving her father to go and check on Stephen. Reminding herself that her father truly would be alone, whereas Stephen could call upon her aunts and the staff at Chatam House, she forced herself to remain at home. She had texted Stephen that he should call when he was ready for bed. When that happened, she would go to him.

But Stephen did not call, and it was not duty that finally drove her to make her excuses to her frowning father and rush over to Chatam House. She didn't know what it was exactly, but it felt horribly like longing, and so she whispered a prayer before she started the engine of her car.

"Lord, guide me. I am so confused, so torn. I'm not sure how to help either Stephen or Dad. I want Your will in all things, so I ask You please to reveal Your will to me in unmistakable ways. I know I should be able to discern and decide, but I don't trust myself to know what is best. I don't even know what *I* want!"

That brought her to a shocking halt, for it was a blatant lie. She did know what she wanted. She wanted to fulfill her calling as a nurse. She wanted to marry and have children. She wanted her father to find joy in this final stage of his life. She wanted to spend time with Stephen—not just see to his medical needs, but to spend time with him.

"But are those the right things to want?" she asked her Lord.

Dashing a tear from her eye, she laughed at her own confusion, opened her heart to God and just let it be for the moment.

Some ten minutes later Kaylie parked her convertible with the top up under the porte cochere at Chatam House and let herself in via the side door. Though not yet ten o'clock, the house was quiet. She walked the darkened hallways with an odd sense of anticipation, turned through the foyer and climbed the stairs without seeing another soul. As she moved along the landing toward the front of the house and Stephen's suite, her way was partially lit by the gray light of the television emanating from his open doorway. She was halfway there when he roared in apparent anguish.

"Aaarrrgh!"

She broke into a run, swinging through the door and into the sitting room, just in time to see Stephen pound his good right fist on the arm of his wheelchair.

"Forty seconds!" Stephen howled, glancing over his shoulder at her. "He lets them go ahead with forty seconds left to play!"

Kaylie slumped against the back of the sofa, one hand splayed over her heart and gasped, "You scared me."

"We were tied," Stephen barked at her, "and Kapimsky let them score!" He raised a hand and made a grasping motion at the television screen, as if he might pluck this Kapimsky off his skates. "Forty seconds from overtime."

Suddenly, his demeanor changed. Sitting forward, he lifted his fist at the TV. "Go, Smitty, go. Deke left, deke left. No! Left. Aw, man. Their goalie's a strong right, so he always expects a shot from the left. You fake left, then you shoot right." A buzzer sounded, and Stephen threw up his hand.

"I take it they lost," Kaylie said, starting around the sofa. Her heart still hammered. In those few seconds before she'd entered the suite, she'd imagined him on the floor in pain, having reinjured himself yet again, and the guilt had been heavy indeed. For whose fault would it have been except her own?

Stephen muted the television and curtly nodded for her to sit on the couch. "They lost," he confirmed, "in the last *forty seconds!* Unbelievable." He shook his head.

Kaylie gladly dropped down onto the cushions. "So is it over for them?"

He shook his head. "Naw, this is a seven-game series, but we're down two-to-one now." Sighing, he rubbed his forehead and shifted in his chair. "I should have been in the pipes tonight. I should be there for my team!" He smacked the arm of his chair with his palm, punctuating his words. "I deserve to be cut after this. Stupid. Stupid. Stupid."

"Well, yes, it is stupid for you to think like that," Kaylie said bluntly.

Stephen looked up in some surprise then shifted again, saying, "Look, I did this to myself, okay?"

"Okay. That doesn't mean you deserve to be cut from the team, especially for what happened tonight. That's on them." She swept a hand, indicating the casts on his arm and leg. "This is on you, and you've suffered mightily for it. Still are, judging by the way you keep fidgeting in that chair."

Stephen sighed and pointed the remote at the television. "I just want to hear the post-game—"

"Uh, no," Kaylie said, taking the remote from his hand.

What was it with the men in her life lately? One insisted that his life was essentially over, and the other seemed determined to beat himself up even more than he already had.

"You need rest and medication." She pointed the remote and shut off the television, tossing the small, rectangular black box onto the sofa, then moved behind his chair. The fact that he didn't argue confirmed her diagnosis.

"Watch the drinking glass," he mumbled.

"Hmm? Where?"

He reached down and came up with a tall crystal tumbler. "Your aunt was good enough to bring me a glass of apple juice earlier."

"Ah." Kaylie smiled to herself. She took the glass from him and carried it to the desk, where she left it, intending to take it downstairs with her later. "Odelia, I presume."

He held up a finger. "That's *Tante* Odelia."

Kaylie laughed, moving back to grasp the handles of his chair. "Can you get the brake?" He leaned forward and flipped the lever that freed the wheels. She rocked the wheelchair back and then shoved it forward. "So Odelia's styling herself as your *tante* now, is she?"

"Something like that."

"Look out," Kaylie teased, swinging the chair around in order to back through the door. "She'll be adopting you into the family if you're not careful."

"I wouldn't mind," he said after a moment, a wistful tone in his voice.

"I expect your mother would," Kaylie pointed out softly.

"I doubt it," he replied, shaking his head, "not after everything that's happened." He quickly changed the subject then. "My father certainly wouldn't. He washed his hands of me long ago."

Kaylie brought the chair to a halt beside the bed and set the brake with her foot. "I—I can't imagine such a thing."

He shot a wry look over one shoulder. "We're a pair, huh? Your father doesn't want to let go of you. Mine doesn't give me the time of day."

"H-how do you know that? About my father, I mean."

Stephen shrugged, not looking at her. "Little things you've said. A phone conversation I overheard. The fact that you still live at home."

"Not still," she said, knowing that she sounded defensive. She walked around to stoop and adjust the foot and leg rests so he could stand.

"Right. *Again,*" Stephen acknowledged dryly. "You're living at home *again*. And your father likes it that way."

"Is there anything wrong with that?" she asked, straightening and backing away.

"I don't know," Stephen said, putting his good foot on the floor. "Is there?" Pushing up with his good arm, he levered his weight onto his foot. Kaylie moved into position to assist him, using the need to do so to forestall answering his question. He didn't press it. Nevertheless, she felt compelled to answer him. He motioned toward the bathroom, and she helped him take two hopping steps in that direction. Grasping the door frame with his good hand, he prepared to move inside on his own, and Kaylie suddenly found herself blurting the truth.

"He thinks I shouldn't marry, just stay home and take care of him."

Stephen leaned against the door frame, twisting so that he could face her, one eyebrow cocked.

"Some are called to remain single," she defended, lifting her chin. "Just look at my aunts. None of them have ever married—though I've heard that Auntie Od and Mr. Copelinger down at the pharmacy might have if…" She shook her head over the irrelevancy of that. "It even says it in the Bible."

"You're kidding. I thought the Bible was all for marriage."

"Well, yes, except for certain circumstances, then it's better not to marry."

Stephen studied her for several seconds. Abruptly, he turned away, hopping through the door.

"Sweetheart," he said, shaking his head, "if ever I've met a woman meant to be a wife, it's you."

He hopped around to catch the edge of the door and push it closed, but her hand came up, seemingly of its own volition, and blocked it. Cocking an eyebrow, he waited.

"Wh-what makes you say that?" Somehow, she just had to know.

Stephen tilted his head and leaned down, bringing

them nose to nose. She saw that he was trembling and feared that his strength had played out, but she waited breathlessly for his reply anyway.

"Because," he said, the very lightness of his voice heavy with meaning, "you're the first woman I've met that I would even consider marrying."

Chapter Ten

Because you're the first woman I've met that I would even consider marrying.

The words echoed inside Kaylie's head. Stephen would consider marrying her. She was the first woman whom he would consider marrying. Consider. Marrying.

Suddenly she found herself reliving that kiss. She felt the connection again, the surprising excitement and rightness of it, the unfamiliar warmth and yearning. It was the last that had frightened her so, causing her to jerk back. Blinking, she was astonished to find that Stephen had pushed the door closed in her face.

She comprehended two facts simultaneously. One, several moments had passed. Two, she was in grave danger of losing her heart.

The hopelessness of the situation swamped her.

Her father was already convinced that she had been called to remain single, but even were he not, he would certainly never approve of her marrying a man like Stephen Gallow. Should she do so, she might well find herself more at odds with her father than her brother Chandler was, even estranged from him. Hub disapproved of Chandler's lifestyle, finding the sometimes hard-drinking, hard-partying, often brutally dangerous atmosphere of the pro rodeo circuit unsupportive of a Christian lifestyle, despite the Cowboy Church "phenomenon," as he called it. Would Hub think any better of hockey?

She couldn't imagine that he would, and she had always strived to honor her parents with her choices and decisions. How could she abandon that now, and was that not what a romantic involvement with Stephen would require? Suddenly she wanted to run for the hills again, to get as far away from this temptation as she could. Blindly, she started for the door, only to stumble into Stephen's wheelchair—and the realization that she could not leave him.

The man could barely get around with assistance; on his own, he was trapped. She was bound by duty, both as a nurse and a Christian, to help him. His physical condition was still serious, but his spiritual condition might well be even more acute. No, she could not abandon him, and if her duty to her father came into conflict, well, that was her problem alone. Stephen was weak and in pain and…lost.

As exasperating as her father could be, as sad as her mother's passing had been, Kaylie had never doubted that she was treasured by them. Thanks to them, she had grown up grounded in the surety of God's love for her and the absolute belief that nothing could ever separate her from such love, not time or space or even death. But what surety did Stephen have? She sensed genuine friendship between him and Aaron, but how certain could Stephen be about that when Aaron depended on Stephen for income?

It seemed to her that Stephen really had no one. And how unnecessary that was when Jesus stood waiting with open arms!

Lord, she prayed, *please let Stephen see You in me and my family. Let him turn to You and find the love that You bear for him. And please, Lord, teach my heart how to love Stephen as You would have me love him. To Your glory.*

The door opened behind her, and she turned to find Stephen sagging against the frame once more. He looked haggard and weary, his jaws unshaved and his pale eyes sunken. Her heart turned over. She quickly pushed the wheelchair out of the way and went to help him.

"Let's get you off your feet."

"Foot," he corrected with a crooked grin, his arm sliding across her shoulders.

"All the more reason," she said, mindful of his battered ribs and collarbone as she attempted to aid his progress.

At last, he sank down on the bed, and she briskly went about setting the covers to rights, something she should have done while he was in the bathroom. He smiled faintly as she tugged and tucked and smoothed, then dutifully swallowed his meds and submitted himself to an injection. As he settled onto his pillow again, his gray eyes sought hers.

"Will you stay with me for a while?"

"Of course," she said, after only the briefest hesitation.

Nodding toward the wheelchair, he said teasingly, "Your turn."

Laughing lightly, she pulled the chair close to the bed and sat. She waited for him to choose a topic of conversation, even as she feared what it might be. Instead, he reached down for her hand and closed his eyes. Sometime later, she realized that he had drifted off to sleep. Still, she stayed, her hand in his, until her own drowsiness drove her to her feet and at last sent her home.

Because you're the first woman I've met that I would even consider marrying.

The words floated into Stephen's consciousness, and for that stupid remark, he silently called himself every derogatory name in the book: fool, idiot, lunatic, dimwit. When he ran out of English versions, he switched to Dutch: *dwass, krankzinning, stom,* even *hersenloos.*

How he could have been so brainless as to say such a thing he could not imagine. In truth, he had fully expected her to be gone when he'd hobbled out of the bathroom, to run as she had after that kiss, but she'd surprised him yet again. Not only had she been there, she'd smiled so benignly that his worst fears had evaporated and the treasured peace that she seemed to bring had settled around him.

He had allowed her gentle bullying and fussing, meekly swallowing her pills, suffering her injections and putting up with a tuck-in routine that a five-year-old would find insulting.

Oh, who was he kidding? He enjoyed every quiet order that came out of her mouth, every smile that curved her rosy lips, every delicate sweep and light pat of her fingertips. He reveled in them, truth be told. Such caring and tenderness had been absent from his life for far, far too long, so long that he hadn't even realized how much he had missed them until Kaylie Chatam had begun caring for him.

Relieved of every discomfort and disgustingly exhausted, he had craved sleep but he also craved connection with Kaylie. Intending to make conversation, he'd teased her into staying. When she'd willingly complied, he'd availed himself of her hand, marveling anew at its daintiness, but instead of conjuring conversation to keep her with him, his mind had turned to blankness. Now, once more, he would awake alone.

He didn't understand why that mattered so much all of a sudden. After Nick had died, Stephen had known that he was truly alone, forever separated from his family by loss and guilt. He had learned to live with it. Until now.

Now, he wanted to think that Kaylie cared for him, as opposed to "took care of him." The difference was significant. The first implied an emotional connection; the second, a simple, professional one. He wanted that emotional connection badly, craved it with a desperation that frightened him.

For a moment, Stephen wondered if his concussion had addled his brain worse than the doctors had assumed. Since losing Nick, he had eschewed all but the most basic emotional connections for years, telling himself that was safer all the way around. Besides, he was too busy establishing his career. His game could not afford such distractions.

He had shut out everyone and everything not essential to his concentration on hockey and his performance on the ice. When he indulged in social occasions, it was most often at the behest of team management, in the interest of team morale or just to shut up Aaron. All work and no play, as the saying went. Even his "romantic" relationships had been brief, shallow and selfish on both ends.

He hadn't realized just how selfish he could be,

though, until he'd taken Kaylie's hand in his last night and wished Kaylie's father would disappear so that Kaylie herself might not.

He opened his eyes, and to his everlasting surprise, Kaylie was there, sitting in a patch of bright sunshine that poured through the window next to the bed. Wearing lime-green scrubs, her hair in a ponytail, she sat quietly in his chair sorting pills into tiny cups arranged in a small plastic tray on her lap. He caught a pleased, energizing breath, and she looked up. Smiling, she quickly dispensed several more pills before speaking.

"Good morning. I was just organizing your meds for the next few days. How do you feel?"

His stomach growled as if in response, and she laughed, tucking the tray into the drawer of his bedside table. "We can take care of that."

Atop the table stood a tall, disposable cup of coffee in a foam rubber insulation sleeve. Rising from his chair, she removed the cup from its protective holder, clasping it between her palms.

"Not hot but warm enough, I think. Breakfast will be up in a few minutes. Meanwhile, you can work on this."

He used his elbow to dig his way higher in the bed while she took out a paper-covered straw, peeled it and slid it into the opening in the top of the coffee container.

"You're not just beautiful, you're a genius," he said as she passed him the cup. She ducked her head as he tentatively slurped up the fragrant brew. Not hot by any measure but drinkable.

"It's just that you're so easy to please," she murmured.

He yanked up his gaze. "Hah! Easy to please? Me? As if!" He shook his head, laughing, and went back to sucking up that dark ambrosia. "Then again," he said, pausing, "with you, maybe I am easy to please. Or maybe it's just that *you* please me. I don't really know." What he did know was that he felt absurdly, ridiculously happy.

"And maybe," she said, blushing furiously as she drew her phone from the pocket of her smock, "being gravely wounded has changed your perspective."

He'd give her that. Such experiences were life altering, as he knew only too well. But his wounds weren't what made him glad to be alive for the first time since—he faced the thought squarely—for the first time since he had killed Nick. To his surprise, the pinch of grief and regret did not change the facts.

He was happy. For this moment, he was truly happy.

Suddenly, in a rush of jumbled sensation, he remembered all the other happy moments in his life. The sheer number of them shocked him, things like trying to rope a tumbleweed while his father shouted advice and the west Texas wind blew it first here then there, or crouching low at his mother's side to watch the winding path of a snail in his *oma*'s garden. He felt his father clapping him on the shoulder after a big win, his grandmother's yeasty hugs, his mother ruffling his hair, the dry west Texas breeze and the misting North Sea rain. He could almost close his hand on the satisfying smack of a puck into his mitt, knowing that the net stood empty behind him, and puff his chest with pride as he signed his name to an actual NHL contract. He heard the sound of his own laughter mingled with Nick's and felt his heart trip at the appreciative glance of a pretty girl.

So many happy moments, and somehow they were all embodied in a slight female with big, dark eyes and hair the color of light red sand. Awesome.

By the time Kaylie informed Hilda that he was ready

to eat, he had swigged down three-fourths of the coffee and felt the urge to be moving. With her usual careful efficiency, she helped him through his morning routine then wheeled him out into the sitting room and went to get his breakfast from the dumbwaiter.

Stephen found himself talking as he gobbled, his aches and pains easy to ignore. Such was not the case by the time he had cleaned up, changed his clothing and collapsed back onto the bed, even though Kaylie had poked pills down him beforehand. Still, despite the physical complaints, he schooled himself into cheery acceptance when she announced that she must go but would return in time to bring him his lunch.

To his gratification, she seemed to dither about it for a bit, asking, "What will you do with yourself while I'm gone?"

He randomly reached for a book from the stack on his bedside table. "Oh, I'll read, play with my phone, whatever."

"No moving around on your own," she warned. "If you have to get up, call Chester."

Snapping her a smart salute, he squared his shoulders. "Yes, nurse *liefje*."

A smile wiggled her lips. She went out saying, "I'll have Odelia bring you something to drink."

"Juice!" he called out. "Not tea!"

Her laughter was the only promise he got. It was the only one he needed, the only one he wanted, and he'd put up with almost anything to have it. He'd even share her with her greedy father.

Their days took on an easy routine. Aaron popped in and out. On Sunday, he brought his wife with him. Dora was a plump, curvaceous, stylish blonde, with green eyes and a breathless way of speaking that made her seem helpless and none too bright, but in the little time that Kaylie spent with the woman, she learned that the opposite was true. Dora had a witty sense of humor and shrewd judgment. She quickly sized up the situation and voiced her assessment of it.

"Why, Stevie," she breathed, curled up next to her husband on the sofa, "I haven't ever seen you this relaxed."

"Yeah," Aaron joked, "I may need a list of those drugs you're taking."

"It's not the drugs, sugar," Dora corrected, leaning heavily against him. "It's the ambience. Just feel this place." She let her gaze sweep languidly around the room and come to rest on Kaylie, adding, "Of course, I'm sure the company has a lot to do with it."

Kaylie shifted uncomfortably from foot to foot. Still dressed in her Sunday best with her hair held back by a simple headband that left it streaming down her back, she felt like a schoolgirl allowed to sit quietly in a room with the adults—until Stephen smiled up at her and clasped her hand. Suddenly she felt…claimed. And thrilled by it.

Determined to resist such temptations, she quickly made her excuses and escaped to her father. When she returned later, dressed in scrubs, her hair ruthlessly scraped into a bun, it was as if nothing had occurred, and so it remained.

In midweek, Aaron brought one of the team trainers to see Stephen. An earnest, fit, fortyish man with a shaved head, he gave Stephen a careful examination under Kaylie's watchful eye, made some astute observations and asked some penetrating questions.

"You'll be out of that jacket in another few days," he told Stephen, then looked to Aaron. "I'll want to see his X-rays, but if what Miss Chatam says is correct—and I have no reason to doubt her—we may want to tap this Dr. Philem, especially if the facilities down here are adequate."

"Oh, they are," Kaylie was quick to assure him, excited to think that Craig might reap some formal connection with the Blades out of this.

The trainer cocked his head. "We'll see. The situation has some real positives. Buffalo Creek is far enough from the Metroplex to escape some of the harsher scrutiny but still within easy driving distance. Worth looking into."

That's where it was left, until Brooks called on Friday morning to report that the team had asked him to provide a reference for Craig Philem, who was thrilled. He also said that he'd be stopping by as early as possible to check on Stephen. Kaylie was about to head home to prepare her father's lunch when he finally strolled into the sitting room with Odelia on his arm and Chester trailing along behind. Chafing a bit with the inactivity today, Stephen had elected to spend the morning on the sofa with his cast propped on the footstool. He looked up and smiled.

"Hey, Doc! You're just in time for lunch."

"Well, of course, I am," Brooks said. "Exactly as I planned."

"That's not what you told me," Kaylie retorted, folding her arms.

"You're right," he admitted glibly. "I'd hoped to make it in time for breakfast. Lunch is plan B."

Odelia giggled, setting her earlobes to jiggling. Since she was wearing earrings that resembled globs of purple gummy worms, the effect was a little scary. She'd have looked like a walking bait shop if not for the optically disconcerting white spirals printed on her purple cotton sheath, which she wore with white sandals. The wide straps of the sandals and neat, clean lines of the short-sleeved dress lent an odd air of demureness to the otherwise crazy costume. In other words, it was pure, quintessential Odelia.

"In honor of Brooks's visit," she announced gaily, "we're having a garden party." She slipped free of their visitor and went to bend over Stephen, adding, "And Brooks says you may join in, if you feel up to it, Stephen dear. Would you like that?"

"*Tante* Odelia," Stephen said with a grin, "I would love it."

"Are you sure?" Kaylie asked, biting her lip with worry. She couldn't help thinking of the ordeal that the stairs presented.

As if reading her mind, Brooks stepped forward. "I think we can make it a little easier for him." Gently nudging Odelia aside, he began to pull the straps free on Stephen's jacket sling. "For starters, let's get rid of this."

Kaylie helped Brooks carefully maneuver the confining, vest-like object over Stephen's head. Brooks then lifted Stephen's shirt, revealing tautly sculpted muscles, and performed a three-fingered tap along the twin ladders of his ribs. Stephen winced lightly from time to time but never lost his smile.

"Sore but much improved," Brooks pronounced. "Ready to try it without the jacket?"

"Absolutely."

Brooks looked to Kaylie. "Let's get him a simple sling. That'll keep the weight of the cast from stressing his clavicle and shoulder muscles and still let him lift his arm and start moving a little more fluidly."

Stephen eased back on the sofa with an "Aaahhh," and Kaylie smiled, promising, "I'll take care of it this afternoon."

After a few questions and a check of Stephen's pulse and eyes, Brooks stuffed his tools back into the pockets of his suit jacket and offered his arm to Odelia. "I hear Hilda's apple-chicken salad calling me."

She laughed, and they swung toward the door. Chester and Kaylie helped Stephen back into his chair, then the trio started off after Odelia and the good Doctor Leland with Kaylie pushing and Chester again trailing along behind. At the head of the stairs, Stephen rose, balancing his weight on one foot. Kaylie and Odelia went down with the chair while Chester and Brooks took positions on either side of Stephen beneath his arms. Had he been a few inches shorter, they could have carried him. As it was, he hopped lightly from step to step until he reached the bottom and sank once more into the wheelchair.

Odelia hurried ahead, chattering merrily about May Day being the perfect day for a garden party. Stephen tilted his head back, gazing up at Kaylie with wide eyes.

"Good grief. Is this the first day of May? I've lost track."

"It is," Brooks answered for her. Bending low, he

murmured to Stephen, "No dancing around the Maypole for you, though."

Kaylie smacked Brooks lightly on the arm with the back of her hand. "Or anyone else, you pagan."

"Hey, I'm an anti-pagan. I firmly believe that Christianity should co-opt every festival and holiday, despite its origins, and make it exclusively our own."

Kaylie couldn't argue with that.

Reaching the end of the east hall, she turned Stephen's chair and backed him down the slight slope into the sunroom. Chester split off and went into the kitchen, while Brooks sprinted ahead to the end of the room near the cozy brick fireplace and opened one side of the French door for Odelia. He threw the other side wide as Kaylie approached with Stephen in the wheelchair. Once more the aunties had rearranged their furniture to accommodate Stephen, a fact he immediately grasped.

"Bright room. Odd furniture groupings." He leaned his head back, smiling. "All for little old me?"

"All for great, massive you," she grunted, shoving his chair over the threshold. He laughed as they gained the outdoors.

The expansive brick patio looked like a spring wonderland, with flowers spilling from a dozen knee-high pots and hanging from graceful wrought-iron stands. The aunties had pushed together two square, redwood tables for their party, creating a space in the center large enough to accommodate Stephen's outstretched leg. The arrangement came with the added benefit of a pair of tall, rainbow-striped umbrellas that rose from holes in the redwood tabletops.

As they reached the table, Stephen sucked in a deep breath, spreading his arms as wide as the cast immobilizing his bent elbow and lower arm allowed. "Now this is my idea of paradise." He nodded toward the figure of a man moving near the greenhouse set back at some distance and asked, "Who's the gardener?"

Everyone looked at Magnolia, who beamed and said, "His name is Garrett Willows. Hired him almost a month ago. Two green thumbs." She turned up her own two in tacit approval.

"Oh, I know him," Kaylie remarked, setting the brake on Stephen's chair. "Or of him, anyway. Isn't he the older brother of Bethany Willows Carter?"

"That's right," Hypatia said, spreading a starched linen napkin across her lap. As usual, she looked regal in apricot silk, especially next to Magnolia's simple print shirtwaist.

Brooks pulled out the wrought-iron chair beside Stephen for her, and Kaylie absently dropped down into it, musing aloud, "Wasn't there something significant about Garrett?" It hit her suddenly. "Wasn't he sent to—"

Odelia shoved a basket of rolls at her, reaching across Brooks as he took a seat between her and Kaylie. "Have some bread, dear."

"Yes," Magnolia echoed, cutting her eyes meaningfully at Hypatia. "Have some bread."

"Oh, for pity's sake," Hypatia scolded, "as if I don't know the man has been in prison. The two of you act as if I sit in some ivory tower, completely cut off from the rest of the world while you drag in your strays—no offense, Stephen dear. Well, I know what goes on. I remember perfectly that Garrett Willows pled guilty to assault for beating his stepfather half to death."

"Pity he didn't finish the job," Brooks muttered. He cleared his throat when Hypatia shot him a quelling glance. "Sorry. It's just that Garrett went to prison for trying to protect his mother from her husband, and even after that, she stayed with the man. Less than two years later, he killed her."

Kaylie remembered the whole ugly story now, how Bethany herself had used to come to school with bruises and scratches that she'd tried to hide. Garrett had been in his early twenties and Bethany, who was Kaylie's age, about seventeen when he'd taken a baseball bat to their stepfather. Bethany had been newly married when her mother had died, and Kaylie remembered that at the funeral Bethany had sobbed that it was her fault for leaving her mother alone with her brutal stepfather.

Stephen let his gaze sweep around the patio once again in an obvious attempt to lighten the mood. "Don't know this Garrett, but I'm inclined to believe Magnolia when she says that he has two green thumbs. I suspect that makes four in total."

Magnolia blushed, indicating the level of his success in diverting the conversation. "Why, thank you, Stephen dear." She literally batted her eyelashes at him. Intentionally frumpy Aunt Mags! It was enough to make Kaylie gasp when Aunt Mags cooed, "Are all hockey players so silver-tongued?"

Stephen and Brooks both burst out laughing.

"I think you have me confused with my agent," Stephen said, and that sent Brooks off into a chain of stories about Aaron Doolin's college days that kept everyone at the table laughing merrily for some time.

When Carol placed a plate filled with chicken salad, apple slices, fresh greens and sliced hardboiled egg before Kaylie, she regretfully shook her head. "Oh, no. I can't stay. Dad will be expecting me at home." Checking her watch, she hastily pushed back her chair.

"Nonsense," Hypatia decreed. "Hubner can take one meal alone. We'll make it up to him by inviting him to dinner tomorrow evening. How will that be?" Without waiting for an answer, she looked to Carol, saying, "Bring me a phone, will you, dear?"

"Oh, allow me," Brooks said, pulling his mobile phone from the pocket of his suit jacket and handing it across the table. He shared a conspiratorial smile with Kaylie, who understood perfectly that seeing Brooks's name on the caller ID would add weight to Hypatia's plea.

Kaylie told herself that she should just get up and go, not let the company, food and the beauty of the day seduce her away from her duty. But it was just one meal, after all. Just one. Hypatia made the call, saying that they had coerced Kaylie into staying for lunch because Brooks had arrived and inviting Hub and Kaylie to join the sisters for dinner the following evening. No mention was made of Stephen until Hypatia passed the small phone back to Brooks.

"We'll expect you to join us, too, of course, Stephen dear," she said in an amiable tone that allowed no refusals.

He smiled wryly and inclined his head. "My pleasure."

"And you, as well, Brooks," she went on in a somewhat lighter vein.

He lifted a hand. "Sorry as I am to say it, I have a prior commitment. It's my evening at the free clinic."

"In that case, will you honor us now by praying so that we may eat?"

"Delighted to."

Everyone bowed their heads as Brooks offered simple but eloquent praise and thanks for the company, the surroundings and the meal. Carol reappeared with tall, frosty glasses of iced tea garnished with lemon slices and mint leaves. To Kaylie's surprise, Stephen took a long drink of his.

Lifting his glass, he said, "I've tried telling my friends in the Netherlands that this is how you're supposed to drink tea."

"Hear, hear," Brooks agreed, eliciting a number of politely indignant arguments from the aunts.

Finally, Odelia sat back, smiled indulgently and declared, "Oh, you wretches. You're teasing us!"

Stephen and Brooks just smiled, saying nothing, while the aunts twittered with amusement. Kaylie bit her lip and sent Stephen a laughingly censorial glance from beneath her brow, but he refused to look at her, most likely for fear of giving himself away. One thing she knew about the man was that he could not abide hot tea. Actually, she mused, she'd come to know a good deal more about him than that.

She knew that he could be cross, arrogant and demanding but also thoughtful, sweet and charming. Tough as nails and boyish at the same time, he could display a remarkably selfish nature and then a poignantly needy one as if they were two sides of the same coin. She knew that he was not a believer but that he was respectful enough of her beliefs to discipline his language and behavior so as not to offend. She also knew that his kiss could make her heart explode, his tender touch could curl her toes and his joy could make her positively giddy, all of which seemed to war with the purpose for which God had brought him here, or purposes, as the case might be.

His lifestyle and her own felt at odds, and too many mysteries remained for her comfort, mysteries she increasingly longed to uncover. She thought of this Cherie with whom he was supposedly involved and wondered why she had not put in an appearance by now. Were Stephen her own boyfriend, even if they were just casually dating—and she suspected there was nothing casual about it—Kaylie knew that she would not be so inattentive. She knew, too, that he was a man of whom her father was not likely to approve. Perhaps, she mused, if her father came to know him as she did…

Oh, but what was she doing? Building castles in the air. Forgetting her purpose. Yielding to temptation.

She looked at Stephen, smiling with undisguised delight, and knew that her heart, and perhaps even her faith, was very much at risk.

Chapter Eleven

Despite Kaylie's private misgivings, lunch became a relaxed, drawn-out affair. Brooks was the first to leave, but the aunts lingered until the heat, rising into the nineties, drove Hypatia and Odelia indoors. Mags always seemed oblivious to the temperature and trundled off to the greenhouse. Kaylie didn't find the temperature uncomfortable, either, but she was surprised when Stephen suggested that they sit out on a pair of chaises near the fountain.

"Are you sure? It's not too warm for you?"

"No, I love the heat."

"But you spend so much time on the ice."

"Maybe that's why I like it warm the rest of the time. Spending half my life on sixteen-degree ice has given me an appreciation for the other end of the spectrum."

"Sixteen degrees!"

"Yeah, that's why I have to keep moving back there even when the puck's in play on the other end of the court. It's not all that cold, frankly, if you're actually skating. That's why hockey gear is designed to wick away sweat and why I like a little heat."

"All right," she conceded, "we'll stay, but not too long. The last thing you want to do is get a sunburn on top of everything else."

"True."

She pushed him over to the nearest chaise and held the chair while he managed the transfer.

"Ah," he sighed, stretching out. "Most comfortable position I've found in quite a while." He caught her hand as she claimed the second chaise and lifted his face to the sun. "The Dutch love to bask in the sun, you know. Swim, too."

"Really? I thought it was very cool there."

"Most of the time it is, but they do get a little summer, and at the very first sign of it, they hit the water." He chuckled, as if remembering. "It's funny when I think about it. My dad lives out in dusty west Texas where you'd think they'd crave water sports, but the only time I can remember seeing him in a bathing suit he was wearing boots and a cowboy hat."

Kaylie smiled at the mental picture. Curiosity swelled, and she gave in to it, quietly asking, "Why don't you see your father now?"

Stephen blew out a breath through his nostrils. "Well, you have to understand how it was with my parents. Mom was an exchange student at Texas Tech when she met my father. When she got pregnant, he insisted on marrying her or having custody of me. I think he was afraid of exactly what happened, that she'd run back to the Netherlands with me. She was never really happy in the marriage, and she hated west Texas. She and I traveled back and forth between the Netherlands and Texas for years, until we were spending more time there than here. They used to have terrible fights about it. Finally, when I was eight, they divorced. My dad begged me to stay with him, but…"

"She was your mom," Kaylie supplied simply.

Stephen nodded. "They both wanted me, you know? And that was great, but it was also a kind of burden. I couldn't be with them both at the same time, and Holland was more my home than Lubbock by then. My father and I had almost become strangers."

"He berated you, didn't he?" Kaylie asked gently, indignant on Stephen's behalf. "Called you a mama's boy and a sissy."

"What?" Stephen looked over at her in surprise. "No! Where'd you get that?"

"From what you said in the ambulance." She tried to recall his exact words. "Something about not being a pansy, a mama's boy."

"Oh, that," he said, shrugging dismissively. "That was the best thing my dad ever did for me."

"I don't understand."

"Look," he said, shifting slighting over onto his left side in order to face her, "when I was sixteen I came back to the States to play triple-A hockey. It was my first step toward the pros, and my dad arranged it all for me. He drove to Colorado and convinced a coach there to give me a tryout, flew me over here, hired me a private trainer to get me ready and shelled out a fortune in fees."

"You obviously made the team," she said, and he nodded.

"I did, but it was tough sledding that first year. We practically lived on a bus, playing and practicing in different towns all over Canada and the U.S., but nowhere near Lubbock."

"Not surprising," Kaylie commented.

"More than once I called my dad to come and get me," Stephen went on. "The first time, he did. Drove all the way to Minneapolis. Within a week, I was begging him to take me back. After that, whenever I'd call, he'd, well, he'd say whatever it took to keep me fighting for my spot on that team. Some of those phrases he used became my private mantra. Two years later, I won a full scholarship to college in Wisconsin. From there, I got picked up by the AHL and a year later signed with the Blades. My dad opened the door to all that for me."

"Your father may have opened the door, but you did the hard work," she pointed out.

"True, but I'm not sure I'd have stuck it out if he hadn't egged me on that first year."

"So why the estrangement now?"

Stephen shifted over onto his back again. "It's just that there's always been this distance between us. We haven't spent more than a couple weeks at a time together since I was eight. Then, when I went off to college and he was no longer paying the bills..." Stephen rubbed his forehead, admitting, "It was my fault. Mom didn't like letting me come back to the States, and she expected me to spend my summer and holidays with her, and I wanted to hang with my buddies, you know? Team becomes everything when you're a kid on the road like that. There just didn't seem enough of me to go around, and Dad felt I chose Mom and Nick over him."

"Nick?" Kaylie asked, immediately latching on to that name. It was as if a shutter came down.

"My cousin," Stephen said, sitting up and swinging his legs over the side of the chaise. "Guess it's warmer out here than I thought, and I've got that climb up the stairs to face. We better go in."

"Right. Okay." She got up and brought around the chair. Once he was settled, she pushed him inside. Before they left the sunroom, she stopped. "Let me get Chester." Hurrying through the butler's pantry, she stuck her head inside the kitchen and asked Chester for his help.

It took two trips, one for her and Chester to help get Stephen up the stairs, another for Chester to get the chair up to them.

"We need two chairs," Stephen decided, waiting for Kaylie to get the sling in place once more. "It's too much work this way. I'll call Aaron."

"Oh, don't bother him with it," Kaylie said. "If you really want a second chair, I'll take care of it."

"Do," he told her. "If you don't have to lug this chair up and down the stairs, I won't feel so guilty for insisting you lug *me* up and down every day from now on."

Kaylie grinned and shared a look with Chester. "I see. Created a monster, have we?"

"Nope. Just gave him a little room to roam. I'd kiss you both for it if I wasn't afraid Chester would break my other arm."

"Good call," Chester quipped blandly, sending Kaylie and Stephen both off into gales of laughter.

They soon calmed down and solved the problem by renting a second chair, a chore accomplished by Stephen himself over the phone. Chester volunteered to go and get it, along with the new sling that Kaylie also ordered, and leave the chair parked in the cloakroom downstairs until needed. This arrangement allowed Stephen a new level of freedom that obviously lifted his spirits and signaled that he was truly on the mend.

Kaylie's own delight was tempered by the knowledge that their time together was growing ever shorter, but she resolutely refused to dwell on tomorrow evening's planned dinner. She would not take hope in it, would not let her imagination flit off on flights of fancy. Her purpose in Stephen's life was to represent Christ to him. His purpose in hers was to help her father regain some perspective on his own life. Anything more would cause a rift between her and her father, and that surely could not be within God's will. Could it?

Later, at home, she brushed off her father's queries about the abruptness of the invitation and even rebuffed a question about Stephen's progress with a bland reminder that she was not allowed to discuss a patient's medical condition.

"Hmm," Hubner said. "Well, I expect I'll be able to judge for myself soon enough. I will be allowed to see him, won't I?"

"Oh, yes," Kaylie replied casually. Why she didn't tell him that Stephen would be joining them for dinner, she didn't know. It may have been the cold, hard weight of dread in the pit of her stomach. Or the hot flutter of guilty hope in her chest.

Stephen felt pretty much as he had the night of his first date—a little sick to his stomach, a little intrigued, a lot hopeful. That first real solo date had come later for him than it did for many young men.

His experiences as a young teen in the Netherlands had revolved around group activities, not that he'd had much time for friends. Hockey had usurped a large portion of his life even back then. After he'd moved to the U.S. to play triple-A at sixteen, he'd had even less time for socializing. It was the summer before college when he'd found himself on the receiving end of a surprising amount of female attention and had finally taken advantage of it.

Or it had taken advantage of him. He'd never been quite sure which. He still remembered that pretty blonde's eagerness and the secret heartache and tawdry disappointment he'd felt when she'd casually moved on to the next guy. He'd kept it light ever since. Concentrating on hockey had seemed the saner course for a lot of reasons. He found nothing light or casual about his feelings for Kaylie Chatam, though—and the two of them were so far from dating that it was sadly laughable.

He looked at himself in the bathroom mirror, critically taking his own measure. Teeth clenched, he smiled and turned his head to check the false teeth filling the upper and lower gaps in the side of his mouth to be sure that they looked natural. Getting one's teeth knocked out was a given in hockey. Cosmetic dentistry loved the sport.

Having managed to shave himself from his chair earlier, with the hand mirror propped against a stack of books, Stephen now tackled his hair with a damp comb and the minimal use of his left hand.

The hair was a problem. He simply had too much of the stuff. It was so thick that he had long ago developed the habit of shaving his head at the beginning of every season and then at the end of it visiting the barber for a good styling, which he kept neat until the beginning of the next season. That way, he didn't have to make time for visits to the barber during the season itself. Several other players used the same system, including a few on his own team. This year, however, the entire Blades lineup had decided, as a gesture of unity, to hit the ice for game one as bald as chicken eggs and not to cut their hair again until the season ended. Like him, they were all looking pretty shaggy about now. He solved his problem by combing the whole mess straight back from his brow and allowing the ends to curl at his nape. That, he decided, tweaking his open collar, would have to do.

Aaron had obligingly driven down that morning with a change of clothing for him, the result being softly pleated, slate-gray trousers and a loose, pearl-gray silk dress shirt that perfectly matched his eyes. With the cuffs left open and rolled back, the sleeves of the shirt were loose enough to accommodate the cast on his arm, but the outside seam of the right leg of his slacks had been carefully split to the knee by Dora. He wore these with dark gray socks and a matching leather belt.

Hobbling back to his chair, a task made surprisingly easier by the absence of the jacket sling, he wondered if anyone would appreciate all the trouble he had gone to in an effort to make himself presentable. Chester said not a word one way or the other as he pushed Stephen to the head of the stairs. Leaving the chair there, they managed the descent, Chester under Stephen's left arm and Stephen supporting himself with his right hand on the stair rail.

He sat in the massive front parlor with the Chatam triplets, flirting shamelessly with all three of them when Kaylie and her father arrived. His heart pounded with ridiculous fervor at the sound of the opening door in the foyer. Two voices called out.

"Sisters?"

"Everyone?"

"In here," Odelia trilled, fluttering her hanky as if they might spy it through the wall. She was dressed this evening all in ruffles, from the creamy pale pink of her soft blouse and skirt to the garish hot-pink of her shoes and earrings. Where she got such outlandish earrings he didn't know, but these resembled quarter-sized leather buttons, each surrounded by a stiff leather ruffle, the whole being the size of a silver dollar.

Kaylie led the way, her step brisk as she entered the room. Her hair, Stephen noted immediately, hung down her back in a straight, silken fall. Only belatedly did he realize that she wore saddle-brown leggings with a sleeveless turquoise-blue tunic, the neckline cut straight across the shoulders. Neat drop earrings, each composed of a single turquoise stone the size of a thumbnail, and simple turquoise-colored flip-flops completed the ensemble, the most fetching, in Stephen's opinion, that he'd seen her wear. He barely had time to take it all in when her father stepped into the room, paused as if to get his bearings and blatantly zoned in on Stephen.

This Chatam was a slender, gangly, pot-bellied older man of medium height with absurdly white, bushy eyebrows and thinning, light brown hair heavily infiltrated with ash-gray. He wore oversized, steel-rimmed glasses, calling attention to penetrating eyes the same dark brown shade as the dress slacks that he wore with heavy black dress shoes, a matching belt and a stark white polo shirt. Stephen nodded in greeting and watched the elder Chatam's sagging face harden around a frown, his shoulders pulling back as those dark eyes took Stephen's measure. The wheelchair, Stephen saw, was dismissed as inconsequential. When a bland expression of dignity smoothed over the older man's frown, Stephen took it as a sure sign that he had been found wanting.

The weight of that felt shockingly heavy. It hurt more

than Stephen could have imagined, and given his past that was saying something.

Since Nick's death, Stephen's life had evolved totally around hockey and those who paid attention to such things. When he'd wanted to impress someone, he'd done it on the ice. Unfortunately, Kaylie's father didn't look the sort to be dazzled by a deadly sweeping paddle-down or lightning-fast half-pad butterfly save.

Stephen had known, of course, from the very beginning that money and status counted for nothing here, either. The cachet of old money clung to these Chatams like perfume clung to a rose, though by all appearances Kaylie and her father were of modest means. Judging by the condition and amenities of Chatam House, the old girls themselves controlled a considerable bankroll, but Stephen seriously doubted if any of the three had been shopping for anything more than necessities in decades. In this family, money just did not seem to matter beyond the good that it could do. Otherwise, he would not have donated a handsome sum to some single parents' ministry for the privilege of recuperating within these hallowed walls.

As for status, according to yesterday's table conversation, the Chatams were as apt to take in convicted felons as pro sports figures, which put him in his place quite firmly. Still, Stephen could not complain.

The fact was, these Chatam women were the most generous, caring people he'd ever met. The jury remained out on the men, but with women like these, Stephen couldn't blame the guys if they were more careful and protective than the average father or brother. He even thought that he might be a little offended on behalf of Kaylie and her aunts if such was not the case, all of which meant he had a problem, one he didn't quite know how to handle.

With skill, money and status out of the equation, that just left Stephen with himself, which he knew was sadly lacking.

"Brother!" Odelia gushed, coming to her feet as Kaylie and her father approached. "Come meet our special guest." Hanky fluttering like a bird desperate to escape her plump hand, Odelia made the introductions. "Stephen dear, this is our eldest brother, Hubner Chandler Chatam, Jr."

Stephen resorted to a silent nod by way of acknowledgment, managing to keep perfectly still otherwise. "Hub, this is Stephen." She broke off and turned blinking amber eyes on Stephen. "I'm afraid I don't know your full name, dear."

Leave it to the Chatam sisters to stand on ceremony.

"Oh, um, it's Stephen George Radulf Landeberht Gallow." He made himself smile, though he couldn't remember the last time he'd even spoken his cumbersome moniker.

Odelia beamed. "How delightful!" She turned to her brother. "Hubner, this is—"

"I heard." He thrust his hand at Stephen. A little surprised, Stephen shook it. Sort of. He'd barely begun the motion when Hubner took his hand back, turned and greeted his sisters.

"So how have you all been?" He glanced at his daughter, adding, "Kaylie's brought home surprisingly little news."

The sisters traded looks before putting on their smiles. While Hypatia ably guided the small talk, Odelia and Magnolia doing their parts, Stephen noticed that Kaylie wandered the room, first going to stand by the massive fireplace. She ran her fingertips over the ornate plasterwork before turning away to smell the huge flower arrangement standing atop a tall, three-legged table in the center of the space. From there, she ambled over to a heavy lamp with a colorful stained-glass shade. She was standing by the front window, gazing out over the long, looping drive, when Carol appeared in the doorway to remark that dinner could be served anytime the sisters were ready.

Only then did Kaylie come near Stephen. She walked over to release the brake on his chair and grip the handles in preparation for wheeling him to the dining room. They went last. Hypatia led the way, followed by Magnolia, Hubner and Odelia, in that order. For a moment, it seemed that Odelia and her brother would engage in a mini standoff as each insisted that the other take precedence, but then Hubner sent a pointed glance at Kaylie and went ahead, leaving Odelia to sparkle in their direction, flutter her hanky and prance off after him. Kaylie held a moment longer before backing the chair around and pushing it forward. They had almost reached the doorway when she finally spoke.

Leaning forward, she remarked softly, "You look nice."

Stephen's smile flashed. "You look more than nice."

"Please don't mind my father," she went on anxiously.

Before he could make any sort of reply, she turned the chair into the dining room.

In his opinion, it was the dreariest room in the house. The woodwork had all been stained a black-brown to match the long, rectangular table and towering sideboard. An enormous rug, gold and black figures against an ivory background, did little to break up the darkness. Neither did the dingy wallpaper, yards and yards of it printed with regimented rows of tiny flowers, all seeming to march in lockstep. The only true splash of color in the room came from a bunch of flowers arranged in a long, low crystal epergne with brass feet in the center of the table.

A chair had been removed from the center of the near side of the table, leaving a space between the supporting columns. Odelia needlessly pointed them to it.

"Stephen, you're here, and Kaylie, of course, is beside you."

"Hubner, you can take the head of the table," Hypatia said, giving Stephen the clear impression that this was normally her seat. "I'll sit between you and Stephen." That left Odelia and Hypatia on the other side of the table, with Odelia directly across from him. Smiling at Stephen, she shook out her heavy dark green napkin and spread it across her lap, saying, "I love these intimate family dinners."

Family dinner, he thought, surveying with some amusement the array of dishes and silver in front of him. He wondered hopefully if this made him an honorary member of the Chatam family. Not, he imagined, if Hubner had anything to say about it.

Chester and Carol came in through a door in the end of the room, carrying bowls and platters. Hilda followed with a silver basket of puffy hot rolls. Chester placed a platter of meat surrounded by cooked cabbage directly in front of Hubner, saying, "Your favorite, Pastor Hub."

Hub Chatam rubbed his slightly protruding belly with both hands and looked to Chester's wife. "Hilda, you are a jewel among women." He cast a look at Kaylie, adding, "I haven't had eye-of-the-round roast since I last ate it at this table."

In addition to the beef, cabbage and bread, there were bowls of roasted potatoes, carrots and a dark, rich gravy that had Stephen licking his chops. Without invitation or comment, Hub spoke an elaborate blessing that Stephen frankly had trouble following. The "amens" of the others caught him off guard, causing his own to lag a syllable behind. It was the only word that he spoke of his own accord throughout the entire meal, though the sisters did their best to draw him out with questions and comments. He was polite, of course, and as pleasant as he knew how to be, but Kaylie's careful silence naturally fed his own, while Hubner Chatam's heightened his unease exponentially.

By dinner's end, despite the wonderful food, Stephen longed for the privacy of his sitting room, so when the Chatam sisters suggested that the group gather in the family parlor, Stephen at first declined.

"I—I think I'll just head back upstairs, if you don't mind." He'd have been fine if he'd stopped there, but no, he had to add, "There's an important hockey game on TV that I need to watch."

"Oh!" Odelia squealed. "How lovely! We've been wanting to learn more about the game, haven't we, sisters?"

To his horror, both Magnolia and Hypatia agreed. Desperately, he looked to Kaylie for rescue.

"Are you in pain?" she asked softly. He opened his mouth to lie, but then she checked her watch. "Mmm, not time for your next meds yet."

That's when Hubner Chatam got to his feet and tossed

down his napkin, declaring, "Yes, by all means, educate us, if you will, Mr. Gallow."

Caught like a rat in a trap. Kaylie placed a comforting hand on his shoulder, observing softly, "You're going to watch it anyway, and the TV in the family room is larger than the one in your suite."

Sighing inwardly, Stephen put on a smile and nodded.

A mixture of modern furnishings and antiques gave the windowless family room a comfortably casual feel. A pair of overstuffed sofas upholstered in a floral pattern and a trio of comfortable chairs made the space feel homey if a bit crowded. The television was, as promised, a larger version of the one in his suite. At least fifty inches in size, the flat screen hung on the wall adjacent to the obviously well-used fireplace. Under other circumstances, Stephen would have been delighted to watch the game in such surroundings. Unfortunately, watching hockey with the elderly Chatams was every bit as bad as Stephen had feared it would be.

The sisters asked more questions than a roomful of cheeky third-graders, and their brother harrumphed over every answer and explanation. The tactics of the other team didn't improve Stephen's mood any, either. By midway through the second period of play, Stephen was so aggravated that he forgot himself and shouted at the television.

"Come on, Ref! How many times are you going to let them interfere with my goalie?"

"*Your* goalie?" Hubner Chatam scoffed. "Why do sports fans always claim a form of ownership? It's not as if you have some actual financial interest in the team, is it?"

Stephen required a moment to fully ingest that seemingly foolish assertion. "Other than the fact that they pay my salary, no, but it's my team, so he's my goalie."

"You *work* for the Blades?" Hubner asked pointedly, his dark eyes going wide behind the lenses of his glasses.

Stephen spread a glance among the women. The sisters seemed as confused as he. Kaylie, however, looked stricken, her cheeks blotched with pink.

"I—I don't guess I ever mentioned that Stephen is the starting goalie for the Blades," she said to her father.

"Was," Stephen corrected, "until I landed here." He smacked the arm of his chair with his palm. Glancing at the TV, he added softly, determinedly, "Won't be in this chair for much longer, though, boys."

Hubner Chatam suddenly catapulted himself to his feet with much more speed and agility than Stephen would have judged the old fellow capable of. "You're a professional hockey player!"

It sounded oddly like an accusation.

"Yeah," Stephen admitted, his patience beginning to fray. "What's wrong with that?"

The feisty right-winger of the Blades chose that moment to take exception to a cheap shot by an opposition defenseman and dropped his gloves.

"Why'd he do that?" Magnolia asked, pointing to the TV as the two skaters warily circled each other. Abruptly, the players erupted into roundhouse punches.

"Fighting with the gloves on will get you fined," Stephen muttered. "They're hard to protect the hands from flying pucks, so they do too much damage in a scuffle."

"It's all right to fight like this?" Hubner demanded.

"They'll both be penalized," Stephen said offhandedly, "but sometimes it's necessary."

"Necessary!"

"The refs can't be everywhere, see everything. Sometimes the only way to stop something is to let the other team know you're not going to take it anymore."

"It's pointless, barbaric violence!" Hub pronounced. "I've seen enough."

Every head in the room turned to watch him stomp away. He was well out of sight when he bellowed, "Kaylie!"

Moaning, she closed her eyes, but then she rose and hurried after him. At the door, she paused to stammer thanks for the dinner. Then her troubled gaze met Stephen's and she mouthed the words, "I'm sorry."

He could only shake his head. She disappeared, and Stephen reluctantly turned back to the aunts.

Hypatia sighed and lifted her chin. "I apologize, Stephen dear. My brother's viewpoint has become increasingly narrow in the last few years."

Odelia shrugged and said rather sheepishly, "It is a bit shocking to old ghosts like us, this fighting. Exciting, though."

Magnolia just wanted to know, "Did we win?"

Stephen glanced at the screen. The other team's guy was bloody and headed for the locker room, while the Blades' skater sat in the glass-walled penalty box, grinning.

"Yeah," Stephen said. "Looks like it."

"Good." She nodded decisively.

Less than a minute later, the Blades scored the first goal of the game, and all three aunts cheered with Stephen, though Hypatia was quick to clear her throat, lift her chin and lapse into silent dignity. Too distracted to fully enjoy the moment, Stephen kept one eye on the game and another on the door.

There wasn't much to see in either case. No one scored in the third period, so the game ended with the Blades winning one-zip, and still Kaylie had not returned. The sports commentators lamented the lack of action in this second round opening game, while the aunties clucked over the time and Kaylie's continued absence. Stephen made light of it, suggesting that Chester be called to help him upstairs.

"There's really not much I can't do for myself once I'm back in my room."

It was true. While he ached in half a dozen places, his overall pain had faded to easily manageable levels, and Kaylie had organized his meds so well that he merely had to check the times she had written on those paper cups and toss back the pills. He could pretty well dress and undress himself and lever himself on and off the bed. Managing his meals and getting around would still be a challenge, but he could always call on Aaron or Chester or hire another nurse.

He didn't want to do any of those things, though.

He wanted Kaylie. That he didn't deserve her simply did not matter. His heart wanted Kaylie Chatam.

And he very much feared that tonight had somehow set her forever out of his reach.

Chapter Twelve

Kaylie argued until she was blue in the face—or rather, red—for she had never been so angry with her father. It took every bit of her self-control not to shout at him, for he was being ridiculously unfair.

"It's a sport like any other."

"Sports have their place," Hub said, "but they're not worthy of a grown man's occupation."

"Pro sports are a business."

"What has that got to do with anything? There are many businesses in which I would not want to be involved."

"But that's you. The world does not agree that pro sports is a bad thing."

"The world! Ah, yes, but we are called to stand apart from this world."

"Many Christians, probably *most* Christians, would disagree with you!"

"Fist fighting!" Hub exclaimed, as if that alone explained his objections. "What other sport do you see that in?"

"Football, basketball..."

"Rarely! And never sanctioned. Why, prizefighting is less brutal."

"They clear the benches to fight in baseball," Kaylie pointed out. "Soccer is infamous for brawling."

Hub shook his head stubbornly. "I don't like it! I don't like it because you lied to me, Kaylie."

"I did not! You never asked what—"

"You let me think he was a broken shell, an older man, no temptation."

That last word rocked her because it summed up Stephen Gallow for her perfectly. Temptation. He tempted her to womanhood and affection, to laughter and kisses, to a different life than she had ever imagined and a desperate, hopeful longing. He tempted her to want more for herself than her father wanted for her, and that realization hurt on several levels. He tempted her to love him, to risk even her relationship with her father for that love. It seemed unfair for her father to throw that at her now when she had struggled so to get it right, to do the right thing for everyone, the godly thing. Perhaps she had left out some of the details, but she had done so because she had known that he would overreact. So perhaps she had already dishonored her father. And perhaps that wasn't all her fault.

"I think I had best go before we say things we'll both regret," Kaylie decided softly. "Good night, Dad."

"Kaylie!" he admonished, but for once she ignored him.

She was an adult, after all, fully capable of and fully responsible for managing her own emotions. And she still had a job to do, a job she felt compelled to do. Just how to do it and honor her father, she did not know any longer. She didn't even know what she was supposed to do, what God meant for her to do.

The dilemma became even more confusing when she arrived at Chatam House, let herself in the side door and made her way up the stairs to find Stephen sitting on the edge of his bed in gym shorts and a sleeveless T-shirt, poking around a pill cup. He looked up, seeming unsurprised to see her standing there, and lifted the little paper container, balanced on the tips of the fingers of his left hand.

"This is right, isn't it?"

Nodding, she came forward and took the cup from him, dumping the pills out into his hand. Then she poured him a glass of water from the carafe on the bedside table. He swallowed the pills and set aside the glass.

"Tired?" she asked, noting the shadows about his eyes.

He nodded, but he didn't lie back. Instead, he met her gaze, asking gently, "Has it all changed somehow, Kaylie? I guess I thought we had something going on, something meaningful." He shook his head and asked, "Is that over?"

She folded her arms, feeling chilled and a little lost. They had never spoken of any personal feelings between them, but she wouldn't pretend that such feelings did not exist.

"I don't know. He's my father, Stephen, and my faith teaches me to honor him. I have to consider his opinions, his wishes, his needs, even his fears."

"I don't know what to do. I'm a hockey player, Kaylie. It's all I have, all I am."

"No. No, it isn't. There's more to you than hockey, but I would never ask you to give up hockey just to please my father. That would be like asking you to stop being you, and I'm not sure I could bear that. Unfortunately, Scripture doesn't say to honor your father unless he's completely unreasonable."

"I wouldn't ask you to dishonor him."

"Of course you wouldn't."

Stephen wrinkled his brow. "Isn't there anything I can do?"

She tilted her head. "Pray. We can both pray."

Stephen nodded but was clearly unsatisfied with that answer. "It just seems like there ought to be something more I could do." He reached out with both hands and pulled her to him, the cast on his left palm hard against her waist. "Would it help if I kissed you again?"

"No," she whispered, allowing her regret to imbue her voice, "that would only make it worse."

Gulping, he nodded and put his forehead to hers. "Prayer it is."

She slipped her arms around him. "It's been known to work, you know."

"It's been known not to," he said soberly, pulling back, and then he told her about the night his cousin and best friend, Nick, died.

"I'm that one-in-a-million Dutchman who can't hold his liquor," Stephen admitted wryly, doing his best to keep his resentment at bay. "We drink beer for breakfast in the Netherlands. Oh, not me. Two beers, and I'm done, useless. All my friends know, all my family. Nick used to tease me."

Stephen chuckled softly, hurting right down to the marrow of his bones, but he didn't let that stop him. He told her everything, how he'd sent for Nicklas to come and keep him company in the U.S. They were like brothers, he and Nick, the siblings neither had ever had, his mother's only sister's only child. Just months apart in age, they had practically lived together after Hannah had taken Stephen back to the Netherlands. His aunt Lianna had been like a second mom to him, and it had been the same with Hannah and Nick. So naturally, when Stephen had called, Nicklas had come, and naturally, Nicklas had insisted that a celebration was in order when Stephen formally signed with the Blades.

"A single beer and a glass of champagne was what I had that night," Stephen recalled, "but Nicky, he was tossing them back so fast. We didn't stay long. I preferred to be driving my new car. All that horsepower, all that flash…"

He shook his head and told her what he remembered of the accident, how they'd been fooling around at night on a vacant street in a newly platted neighborhood when a cement truck had suddenly appeared. Stephen had swerved his car out of the way and hit a curb. The car had tumbled downhill over and over until it came to rest on the passenger side, leaving Stephen hanging by the straps of his safety belt above a crumpled and torn Nick.

"I begged," Stephen admitted, closing his eyes. "I begged God not to let him be dead. I begged not to have killed him."

His neck felt stiff, and he rotated his head, trying to loosen the muscles and banish the memories. That was what he'd walked away from the wreck with, a few strained muscles. Nick had died, and he'd had a stiff neck.

He'd been a madman at the site, fighting the emergency personnel, first when they'd tried to treat him and then when they'd taken Nick away. They'd had to sedate him to get him into an ambulance. As a result, there'd been no alcohol test, but the cops had witnesses who'd seen him drinking at the club. Not that it had mattered. Stephen had pled guilty in open court, expecting, almost hoping, for a prison sentence. They'd given him probation, and the team had written a good-conduct rider into his contract.

"So I skate. And Nick's gone," Stephen said, hating the forlorn sound of his own voice. "And I haven't seen my mother, aunt or grandparents since his funeral."

"That's why you don't take your mother's calls, isn't it?"

Stephen hung his head, admitting, "I just can't talk to her without thinking of Nick, without knowing that she is thinking of her only nephew, without knowing that my aunt Lianna will never see her only child again."

"Was Nick wearing a seat belt?"

"No."

"Why not?"

He shook his head. "Because that was Nick—carefree, living on the edge."

"If he'd worn his seat belt he might have survived. You did."

"I was driving," Stephen insisted, "even though I knew I shouldn't have been. They have to know it, too." He closed his eyes. "I don't deserve to have them in my life any longer."

"But they don't deserve to lose you, Stephen. Don't you see? They've lost Nick *and* you."

"I—I can't face them. Nick is gone, and I can't do anything about it. That," he said bleakly, "is how I know prayer doesn't always work."

Kaylie shook her head at him, her hands lightly framing his face. "Stephen, you can't wait until the worst has happened then ask God to undo it."

"Then what's the point?" he demanded. Her hands fell from his face to his shoulders.

"The point of prayer is to keep us in contact with our heavenly Father, to get to know Him. You can't live your life ignoring God and the things of God and then expect Him to offer mercy on demand," she said. "That's like ignoring the law, then when you're caught, expecting the court to come to your rescue. Prayer is as much guidance as rescue, Stephen, and it starts with a personal relationship with God."

"I don't understand. How do you have a personal relationship with someone you never see?"

She folded her arms. "You just told me that you haven't seen your mother in years and go out of your way not to communicate with her, but you still have a personal relationship with her, don't you?"

He shifted uncomfortably, trying to find fault with that logic. "She's my mother."

"And God is your creator."

Stephen gulped. "I—I don't know how *not* to have a personal relationship with my mother, but how do I *start* one with my Maker?"

"You know who Jesus is, don't you?" she asked softly.

"Sure." At least, he'd thought so, until she explained it all to him.

Stephen's gaze turned inward as he considered all that she'd said, and then she gave him the key to his own salvation.

"Don't let your guilt keep you from forgiveness,

Stephen. Don't deny yourself the very peace for which Christ Jesus gave Himself on the cross."

They each had too much to think about. By mutual, unspoken assent, they put it all aside when together. Kaylie stole as much time as she could. With Stephen's strength returning and his pain subsiding, she should have been able to leave him on his own more. As long as she left the sling in place on the wheelchair and positioned it properly, he could get himself from the bed and into it and even maneuver himself inch by careful inch into the sitting room. But the suite had become a prison to him, and she knew very well that he lived for the moment when she would help him down the stairs to escape the house.

The rose arbor, accessible from the patio via a bumpy path of paving stones, became their favorite idyll. The arched trellis, weighted with frowsy, bloodred blooms, formed a fragrant tunnel and hid a padded bench inside. Dappled gold sunshine filtered through the leafy shelter, and when the breeze was right, the interior remained cool well into the afternoon. As old-fashioned as it seemed, Kaylie had taken to reading aloud to Stephen, who claimed to be absorbed by the history of explorer Joseph Walker, which she supposedly made even more compelling by her intonation.

While they pretended that their time together was impersonal, so did her father. On a daily basis, he inquired politely, almost icily, how "the patient" fared, and on a daily basis she reported that Stephen was mending well and would soon gain more freedom of movement. That happened on the morning of the fifteenth when Chester brought out the aunts' town car to drive Stephen and

Kaylie into town. Stephen had offered to call Aaron to cart him around, but Chester and the aunts would not hear of it. The latter stood waving beneath the porte cochere as they drove away, much like a triune mother sending off a child to the first day of school. Stephen, the big tough guy on skates, waved happily in return through the rear windshield, glad to be going anywhere, even if only to the doctor's office.

Craig Philem greeted them like royalty, and Kaylie couldn't help noticing that most of his approbation was aimed at Stephen this time. Considering that he was now listed among the consulting physicians for the Blades hockey team and busily expanding his office suite to accommodate the honor, she couldn't blame him. He did a most thorough job of X-raying Stephen's broken bones, even those he had not set himself. Pleased, he replaced the initial post-surgery leg cast with a shorter, sturdier version that would allow walking with crutches. To facilitate that, he also shortened the cast on Stephen's upper arm, promising to remove it in another couple of weeks.

They walked out, more or less, side by side, with Stephen swinging lightly on his crutches. Stephen astonished both Kaylie and Chester by insisting upon going shopping.

He bought everything that he could find to fit him at the local men's store, including a suit, though he couldn't even get both arms in the jacket due to the cast. While they waited for the pants to be hemmed, he ambled around the downtown square to pick out gifts for everyone in the house, settling on sunglasses, of all things.

For Odelia he chose gaudy frames ringed in rhinestones, for Hypatia smart pearl-white. Mags wound up with military-green. Chester came away wearing an aviator style, while Hilda and Carol got classic tortoiseshell of different shapes. At Stephen's insistence, Kaylie tried on a dozen pairs or more. In the end, he insisted on a cat-eyed copper frame that cost more than every other pair of sunglasses she'd ever owned. Stephen himself went for a wraparound style in silver with the blackest of lenses.

As a last act of exuberant self-indulgence, he insisted on visiting the local drive-through for milk shakes, ordering one of just about every variety. Later, they all sat around the patio back at Chatam House in their fashionable shades slurping decadently and ruining their lunches, staff included. He was so happy that it hurt Kaylie to think she might actually break his heart. And her own.

She knew what she wanted, but she waited for some sign from God to tell her what she should do.

Stephen felt very proud of himself, at least on one score. He did not attempt to press or seduce or even charm Kaylie. Instead he learned simply to be, with and without her, no artifice or attitude or even thought, taking each moment as it came, living in hope and, oddly enough, praying. The last was harder than he'd thought it would be.

He'd begun simply because she'd asked it of him, but he didn't understand what he was supposed to say to a God whom he did not quite know. In the past, he had made demands or desperate, maddened pleas, but that had not worked out too well, so he did his best just to get acquainted. Telling God about himself, essentially explaining his actions, choices and feelings, seemed foolish. Wasn't God omniscient, all-knowing, all-wise?

Yet, Kaylie had said that prayer must be grounded in a personal relationship with God, so Stephen set about first explaining and then, often, excusing. Or trying to. Funny, but the more he argued his excuses, the less he was able to, and in the process he somehow came to understand himself better. He didn't like everything he found, especially the cowardice and the shame. In fact, some of what he saw in himself brought him to tears and, strangely enough, apology, though he did not quite get why he felt that need. In the end, however, he found a sort of peace with himself. How that could happen, he didn't know, but wanted to. He wanted to understand.

An idea gradually took root, one he'd have scoffed at earlier, and he was trying to find a way to address it when Hypatia did it for him. She made the invitation at dinner on Saturday evening. He had come down for the meal, even though it meant not seeing Kaylie that night. Her father, she had said, required her at home. Stephen didn't like the sound of that, but he couldn't honestly plead a greater need when he was now capable of seeing to himself.

Odelia gushed about how happy they were to see him up and about on his own, and Mags, as he'd taken to calling her, offered to show him around her greenhouse one day early next week. Then Hypatia made her contribution.

"Perhaps, Stephen dear, since you are again ambulatory, you would consider attending church with us tomorrow? It would thrill us to have you there."

He tried to smile and make light of it, as if it were nothing more than taking in a movie or playing a round of golf with his buddies, but the moment felt somber, almost monumental. He couldn't quite pull it off with the necessary insouciance. Instead, he merely nodded and quietly said, "I think I'd like that."

Hypatia patted his hand, Mags beamed, and for a moment he thought Odelia might cry, but then she burst into gay laughter, waved her hanky in the air and all but dived into a particularly sumptuous chicken pot pie.

"You should all know," he said around a bite of that same tasty dish, "that I'm plotting to kidnap Hilda."

The aunts laughed, while he secretly wished that it could be Kaylie, but Kaylie, he had come to realize, would have to be won, and that he could never do on his own, but only by the grace of God.

After dinner the aunts watched the hockey game with him. Ahead two games to one, the Blades lost, allowing their opponent to tie the series. Stephen's disappointment was tempered by the sweet expressions of commiseration that the three old dears heaped on him.

"They'll get 'em next time," Mags offered hopefully, patting his shoulder.

"You'd have beat them!" Odelia insisted, squeezing his face between her hands.

Hypatia merely smiled benignly and advised, "Never doubt that God is in control, Stephen, and working for the benefit of all."

He wanted to believe that with a desperation that frightened him, and that night he besieged heaven from his bed, asking for everything under the sun, from the team winning the Stanley Cup to keeping his position with them, from Kaylie's father's approval to deserving her father's approval, from the strength to win her to the strength to lose her. And finally he found the strength to do something else.

At three o'clock in the morning, he called his mother.

* * *

Daylight found Stephen tired but strangely serene. He dressed himself in the new navy-blue suit pants, a royal-blue shirt and a gray silk tie, black socks and one black shoe. Tossing the jacket over his shoulder, he took up his crutches and made it downstairs in time to share breakfast with the aunties, which they ate at the butcher-block island in the kitchen. As Sunday was a day of rest, the sisters did for themselves, allowing the staff as much freedom from their duties as possible. Chester, however, drove them to church, Hypatia riding in the front seat with him. Mags and Odelia—decked out in bright yellow with huge black buttons, black pumps with yellow bows, a black straw hat with a curled brim and black and yellow beads dangling from her earlobes—rode in back with Stephen. They all sported the latest in sunshades.

To his surprise, Chester, Hilda and Carol all attended church elsewhere, preferring, as Hypatia put it, a less formal evening service. The aunts chose to attend an early one. Chester left them at the main entrance. Odelia fussed over him, helping him into one sleeve of his suit jacket and adjusting the drape of the other side over his cast and sling. He kissed her cheek, and she giggled like a schoolgirl. They walked inside, as strange a quartet as anyone had ever seen, surely, and doffed their sunshades, tucking them into pockets and purses.

A whirlwind of introductions later, Stephen found himself seated at the very front of the soaring white-washed sanctuary with its oddly elegant gold-and-black wrought-iron touches. The aunties kindly left him on the end of the aisle, with space to stretch out his leg and also for another person or two.

He fought every moment not to turn his head to

look for Kaylie, but when another body dropped down onto the pew next to him, he turned with a smile, fully expecting to find her there. Instead, a distinguished-looking, fortyish fellow with medium brown hair and streaks of silver at his temples returned his smile, black eyes twinkling through the lenses of his silver-rimmed glasses. He had a very authoritative air about him, aided by the tan linen vest that he wore with a white shirt, brown suit and red tie. As he possessed the distinctive Chatam cleft chin, it came as no surprise when Odelia leaned close to whisper, "One of our nephews, Kaylie's brother Morgan Charles Chatam."

Before he could take that in, a hand touched his shoulder, and Stephen twisted in his seat to find Kaylie and her father behind him. She beamed as she settled back, but the sour look on Hubner Chatam's face made Stephen's heart sink in his chest. Gulping, he faced forward once more as the small orchestra gathered below the dais began to play. From that moment on, it was a challenge to concentrate, and Stephen found himself, wonder of wonders, falling into silent prayer.

I know I don't deserve her, Lord, or any of the other good things in my life, but I want to. I can't do it on my own, though. No one can truly deserve Your blessing without forgiveness. Isn't that why Your Son took up the cross, that we might be forgiven and forgive in turn? Even ourselves.

With song rising around him, Stephen finally let go of the guilt that had blackened his soul for so long. Afterward, he began to enumerate those good things with which he had undeservedly been blessed. It was a surprisingly lengthy list, not the least of which was the stilted and then progressively cozy talk that he'd had with his mother last night and the three elderly triplets who had opened their home and hearts to him. Somewhere in the midst of it, he got caught up in a prayer being led by someone else, and before he knew what was happening, he was leaning forward to catch every word out of the preacher's mouth.

When the congregation rose for a final hymn, Stephen's mind was racing with all he'd heard and how it supported what he had instinctively learned these past weeks, and then it was over, without him quite being ready. He felt as if he'd been plunked down in a strange place all of a sudden.

This new Chatam, Morgan, stepped out into the aisle and raised a hand to urge Stephen to follow. Without any sort of preliminary, he clapped that same hand on to Stephen's shoulder and addressed him with the familiarity of an old friend.

"Hello, Stephen," he said, his voice deep and resonant, as if it traveled up from a great distance. "Good to see you here. This way." Turning, he led the way up the aisle. Bemused, Stephen slowly followed.

Kaylie fell in beside him as he passed her pew, leaving her father to walk behind with his sisters. "I'm so glad you came," she told him through the brightest of smiles.

For some reason he blurted, "I called my mother last night."

Kaylie gasped and hugged him, nearly knocking him off his crutches. "Oh, Stephen, that's wonderful! How is she? What did she say?"

"She cried," he confessed, "and then she scolded, and then we had a good talk. I promised to visit as soon as I'm able. She's having my houseboat taken out of dry dock for me, in case I decide to spend a few weeks there during the off-season."

"And will you?"

"I think so."

"Oh, Stephen, I'm so proud of you! I knew it. I just knew it. I even told Dad that it would happen."

"You've discussed me, then?"

She wrinkled her nose. "I'm not sure *discuss* is the right word, but yes, we had quite an exchange last night."

Stephen's heart lurched. "And?"

"And," she said gently, "I know God brought us together for a reason. It's in His hands."

Stephen gulped. In God's hands. Nodding, he let her steer him up the aisle, praying that they were moving toward an understanding, a beginning for the two of them. Together.

Chapter Thirteen

Ahead of them, Morgan beckoned, clearing the way through the throng. “Come on, you two,” he called loudly, “or we’ll never get out of the parking lot.”

“I see you’ve met my brother,” Kaylie said, sounding amused.

“I guess you could put it that way,” Stephen replied softly. “Does he have to approve of me, too?”

“Oh, Morgan approves of everyone,” Kaylie said gaily, “but if you want to impress him, you have to love history.”

Stephen sighed.

“I suspect you’re talking about me,” Morgan said good-naturedly, holding one of a pair of heavy, arched doors open for them. Stephen and Kaylie passed through, and Morgan immediately abandoned the post, staying to Stephen, “I assume sis has told you that I’m a history professor.”

“Uh, not exactly.”

Morgan clapped him on the shoulder again. Though shorter than Stephen by several inches, he was a solidly built man and packed quite a wallop. “She hasn’t exactly told me about you, either, but I'm pretty good at hearing what people don't say." He winked at Kaylie, adding, "I hope you like to eat Mexican. Sis always cooks Mexican when the cowboy comes around."

The cowboy? Thoroughly confused, Stephen watched Kaylie throw her arms around her brother, crying, "Oh, Morgan, I love you!"

"Doesn't everyone?" he chortled, hugging her hard enough to lift her feet from the floor. Releasing her, he slung an arm around Stephen's shoulders. "Now, come on," he said. "Let's see if we can stuff you and that leg into my car."

"But—" Stephen glanced over his shoulder at the aunts, who were just now filing into the foyer with Hubner.

"Oh, no," Morgan declared cheerfully, "they can't help you now." He waved, and Odelia fluttered a black hanky at them. Morgan whirled and started off, the sides of his coat flapping.

"But where are we going?" Stephen asked, struggling to keep up.

"Why, to beard the old lion in his den," Morgan answered, never once looking back.

It was a near thing. Morgan drove a decidedly unprofessorial, starlight-blue sports car, and the only way Stephen could get in was to balance on his crutches and slide in legs first, twisting and folding his torso until he was wedged into the seat. Morgan had to open the sunroof and stick the crutches down through the top. Once behind the wheel, he acted like a teenager with a new license, whipping around corners, grinding gears and zipping through tight spaces. Along the way, he explained that things had "come to a head" between father and daughter, and Hubner had "called in reinforcements," meaning Kaylie's three older brothers, to "help the girl see reason."

"As if," Morgan added, "she's ever seen anything else. I think she's a little too reasonable, if you ask me."

Stephen wasn't sure what that meant or if he even liked Morgan speaking of her that way. "She's just trying to do the best she can by everyone."

"Wouldn't be Kaylie if she didn't," Morgan said. "Brace yourself. We're here, and Bayard has already arrived."

Here was an older white frame house with red roof, red shutters, redbrick wainscoting, detached garage and a tree-shaded front yard. Morgan parked on the street at the curb behind a full-sized, silvery green sedan.

Stephen passed the crutches to him through the sunroof and was still trying to get himself out of the vehicle when Kaylie and Hubner turned into the drive in her boxy little convertible. She rushed to help, Hubner grousing that it surely didn't take both Morgan and her to get Stephen out. It did, though, for he had to come out head and shoulders first, literally crawling his way up and onto his feet and then the crutches.

"I'll get Bayard to take you home in his sedan later," Kaylie promised, walking him up to the dark red door. Hubner and Morgan apparently entered through a back way.

"And Bayard is?" he asked as she opened that door, revealing a small, dark foyer screened from the living area by a wall of carved wood spindles.

"My oldest brother."

She slipped past him, pushing the door wide, but he

caught her around the waist, his crutch digging into his already sore armpit.

"Wait. Who's this cowboy you cook Mexican food for?"

"That," said a stern male voice, "would be me."

Stephen looked up at six feet two inches of boots, snug jeans and well-filled-out chambray shirt. His big, thick hands parked at his waist, the cowboy in question lifted a heavy, sandy brown eyebrow, silently challenging Stephen's right to so much as touch Kaylie. Stephen looked at that hard, set face with its dimpled chin and knew he'd finally met his match. All right, he thought, resisting the urge to toss aside his crutches, let the battle begin.

"Chandler!" Kaylie cried, launching herself.

"Hey, sprite!" Catching her up, Chan spun her around before setting her feet to the floor again—as far away from Stephen as possible. Stephen frowned at that.

"I didn't see your truck."

"It's got a four-horse trailer hitched to it, so I had Kreger drop me."

"Kreger is Chandler's partner," Kaylie explained to Stephen, "both in a ranch outside of town and the rodeo arena, where they compete in team roping, among other events." She turned back to her brother. "Are you in town for long?"

He eyed Stephen and rumbled, "Long as it takes."

Stephen smiled and said conversationally, "You know, I'm not as helpless as I look."

"Oh, stop," Kaylie admonished, stepping to Stephen's side and sliding an arm across his back to urge him forward. "This isn't a macho-man contest. Behave yourselves, both of you. Come in, Stephen, and sit down."

Smugly, Stephen allowed her to direct him past Chandler and a dark hallway into a surprisingly large, oak-paneled living room with an impressive rock fireplace. Cushions had been scattered across the knee-high hearth, and it was there that Stephen chose to sit, craning his neck to view the portrait over the mantel. An oil painting of a sweet-faced woman, it had to be Kaylie's mother, given the red hair, bobbed at chin length, and big brown eyes.

Across the room, in front of a sliding glass door that looked out onto a wild, pretty garden, Kaylie's father somberly occupied a brown corduroy recliner, and another man took up one end of a long, matching sofa with an enormous rectangular coffee table parked in front of it. Rather portly with thick lips and a deeply cleft chin, he had stuffed his big belly into an expensive, black three-piece suit and looked like the sort who might sleep in silk ties, so much a part of his daily routine were they. His brown eyes goggled when he saw Stephen.

"Good grief!" he exclaimed. "You're Hangman Gallow. I heard they signed you at three million a year."

"It's not straight salary," Stephen said somewhat defensively. Indeed, once the taxes, annuities and expenses were paid it amounted to much less, but even that figure was ample.

"No, no, of course not," the other man said. "Wouldn't be wise. I'd be glad to look at the structuring of it for you."

"This is my oldest brother, Bayard," Kaylie put in, her smile a tad strained. "He's a banker."

"This is not a business meeting!" Hubner declared hotly.

"No one said it was," Bayard retorted, "but a good businessman always has his eyes and ears open."

"Well, there you have it," Morgan said cheerfully, strolling over to lean with both hands on the back of the sofa. "Bayard votes for Stephen's bank statement. I vote for Kaylie's good sense, and Dad and Chandler, while forever at odds over everything else, especially Chandler's chosen profession, vote for their own convenience."

"I resent that," Chandler snapped.

At the same time, Hubner declared, "The Chatam men have always prided themselves on their decency and refinement. We are bred to boardrooms and pulpits. We put our skills and educations to the betterment of others, not frivolous, barbaric sport! We are ministers and, yes, bankers, professors and lawyers—"

"Shipping magnates and doctors," Chandler went on in a bored voice, "apothecaries and the odd state senator, authors and orators and scientists… Yes, I know, anything but professional cowboys."

"Or hockey players," Stephen muttered.

As one, Chandler and his father turned on Stephen, barking, "You stay out of this!"

"Chatams are good Christian men," Hubner went on, "who embrace their God-given responsibilities with faith and obedience. They are—"

"I believe the word you're looking for is 'snobs,'" Chandler sneered.

"No such thing!" Hubner pounded the arm of his chair. "A Christian man is humble! He doesn't need to beat another, only to do his best in the eyes of God! He is no brute!"

"Was King David a brute when he slew Goliath?"

Chandler demanded. "Was Gideon a brute when he led God's army? Was Joshua—"

"What is going on?" Stephen roared, effectively silencing the room, so effectively that he was a little embarrassed. "You didn't bring me here to watch a family feud," he added sullenly.

"I didn't bring you here at all," Hub grumbled.

"That was me," Morgan admitted cheerily. "Only seems reasonable if sis is going to marry him."

Startled, Stephen swung his gaze to Kaylie, who stood in the center of the room, twisting her hands together. Her face colored, and she wouldn't look at him, but he could have cried for joy. He'd always known that with Kaylie Chatam it would be marriage or nothing. He couldn't bear the thought of nothing, but he'd hardly dared hope for anything else.

"I didn't say I was going to marry him," she refuted smartly. "I only said that I'd marry him if he asked me to."

"He will," Stephen said flatly. "He is." He glared at Chandler when he said it, but the big cowboy was looking poleaxed.

"Sugar, are you sure about this?" Chandler asked, moving forward to cup Kaylie's elbows in his big hands. "He's a hockey player. That's a different world."

"I'm not from Mars," Stephen said dryly. "My father's a rancher in west Texas. Mom's a fashion designer in Amsterdam. My stepfather's a flower broker."

"Flower broker!" Chandler yelped.

"It's big business over there," Bayard put in helpfully. "Largest flower market in the world."

"Well, there you have it," Morgan pronounced. "Big business and big money with a side order of west Texas thrown in. What else could you want?" He wagged his finger at no one in particular, adding, "And you said I shouldn't have brought him along."

"You didn't bring him here," Kaylie said, moving to Stephen's side and sliding her arm across his shoulders. He carefully let out a breath that he hadn't even realized he'd been holding and reached up to grasp her hand. "Not really. God did. I'm convinced of it."

Stephen closed his eyes. *Thank You, Lord.*

"You believe that because you want to believe it," Hub said desperately.

"Yes," Kaylie gently replied, "and you won't believe it because you don't want to, but I love him, and I believe God means us to be together, and that's all there is to it."

"You love me?" Stephen said, as near tears as he could possibly be without sobbing.

"Of course I do."

"And I love you," Stephen hastily supplied, laughing with relief as moisture gathered in the corners of his eyes. He reached across with his right arm, wrapped it around her waist and pulled her down onto his lap. Kaylie's soft smile launched his heart into a whole new stratosphere of delight.

"But what about Dad?" Bayard was demanding.

"If you marry, he'll be alone," Chandler said worriedly to Kaylie.

"I'm alone, Chan," Morgan pointed out, "and so are you. Bay's the only one of us who has his own family."

"But Dad's health—" Chandler began.

"Is better than most men's his age," Kaylie said gently.

Hubner cast a look at that portrait over the mantel, grimaced and turned away. In that moment, Stephen understood a large part of the problem. It was fear, the fear of loneliness and change, but the solution was so simple that he didn't understand why they couldn't all see it.

"Who says he has to live alone?"

"I won't have a babysitter!" Hub declared bitterly. "And I won't be forced into one of those smelly warehouses." He visibly shuddered at the thought. "I won't be foisted onto my sisters, either. They're almost as old as I am, and they sacrificed enough of their lives taking care of our father."

"But you'd have Kaylie do the same thing," Morgan pointed out.

Hubner blanched, muttering, "It's not the same thing. Kaylie has a calling."

"To nursing," Kaylie said, "not to singlehood. The aunts are called to singleness, Dad. I am not."

"You're missing the point," Stephen said, tugging on Kaylie's hand. He smiled up at her, saying, "I have no objection to Mr. Chatam living with us."

Kaylie gasped. "Stephen!"

"I'll take you any way I can get you, sweetheart. Aunts, brothers, fathers, the whole kit and kaboodle, whatever it takes. Besides," he whispered into her ear, "I have a really big house."

She wrapped her arms around him. "Stephen."

Across the room, Hubner Chatam's eyes had widened behind his glasses. "I—I couldn't leave Buffalo Creek," he sputtered, but Stephen detected a note of hopefulness in his voice.

"Why not?" Morgan asked. "Bayard has."

Bayard humphed. "It's a business decision. The bank's in Dallas, but Buffalo Creek is still home."

"Uncle Murdock did and Aunt Dorinda," Morgan went on. "I can name you a dozen others."

"I am not the others," Hub snapped. "I am the eldest Chatam, and the Chatams are Buffalo Creek. We have a responsibility to this town. Buffalo Creek is my home. My…" He paused then finished softly, "My ministry is here."

"Was here," Morgan said gently, "until you abandoned it."

"I didn't abandon it," Hub argued. "Chatams do not abandon their callings." He put a hand to his head. "It abandoned me really, though I prayed that God would take me before that happened."

"Oh, Dad," Kaylie said. "Why don't you see that God still has use for you? Why else would he let you recover so well from your heart attack? And just think what that experience could mean to others in the same condition."

He glanced around guiltily. "Who would listen to an old man whose best days are behind him?"

"I would," Stephen said. "In fact, I—I have some questions that I need answered, if you don't mind. Spiritual questions. Who better to ask than you?"

Hub's eyes went very wide behind his glasses. After a moment, he cleared his throat. "I'm sure we'll have some time to talk after lunch," he muttered.

Kaylie smiled at that and laid her head on Stephen's shoulder. "Thank You," she whispered. "Oh, thank You. Thank You."

Stephen did not assume that she was thanking him, but he would give her all the reason to do so that he could.

"As for leaving Buffalo Creek," he said brightly, "I like it here. No reason we can't find or build a house nearby."

"Not the Netherlands?" Hub asked.

"Kind of a long commute to Fort Worth," Stephen said. "The Netherlands is for vacations. And honeymoons?" he whispered into Kaylie's ear. She tightened her arm around his neck, so he added, "For starters. After that, I was thinking Italy."

"And when were you thinking of taking this honeymoon?" she whispered back.

"I've always wanted to be a June bride," he muttered, and she giggled.

"All right, enough of that," Chandler ordered.

"Not from where I'm sitting," Stephen retorted cheekily.

"Time enough for it later, then," Bayard said, hoisting himself to the edge of the sofa. "When do we eat? I'm starved."

That did it. Smiling broadly, Kaylie popped up and rushed toward the kitchen. "Morgan, add a plate to the table. Chandler, that salsa you like is in the refrigerator. Bayard, you'll have to sweeten the tea yourself. Stephen…"

He grabbed his crutches and got to his feet. "Yes?"

She whirled around, smiling dreamily. "Just… Stephen." With that she danced away, her brothers following. That left him alone with his future father-in-law, who got up and walked to his side. Stephen waited, and after a moment Hub spoke.

"I can't approve of your occupation."

Stephen quoted from that morning's sermon. "'Seek not the approval of man but the approval of Him Who is above man, of God Himself.' I think that's what the pastor said."

Hubner cleared his throat. "Yes, well, I expect you'll grow on me."

Stephen chuckled. "I expect I will."

"Is that so?"

Stephen nodded. "Kaylie's spoken to me about a personal relationship with God through Jesus Christ. I figured you would be the one to explain that to me."

"I—" Hubner's chin wobbled and his face softened. "Yes," he said, thawing, "I would be the one." He cleared his throat again. Sucking in a deep breath, he admitted, "I fear there are some things I need to get off my chest first."

"I've been doing some of that myself," Stephen told him. "Comforting process."

"Yes," Hubner agreed, clapping him on the shoulder and starting him toward the dining room. "Yes, it is. Maybe you can, ah, give me a better understanding of hockey later. One should have all the facts, after all."

"Be glad to," Stephen said. "Lately I'm all about promoting understanding in the family."

"Family," Hubner echoed, bowing his head. "I may be too proud of mine," he admitted.

"Well," Stephen allowed, "it seems to me that you have plenty to be proud of." He glanced over his shoulder at the painting above the mantel. "Beautiful woman, Kaylie's mother."

Hubner's gaze followed his. "Yes, she was."

"Almost as beautiful as her daughter."

Hubner smiled. It was reluctant. It was wan. It was the first sure sign of peace between them but not, Stephen felt sure, the last.

Chapter Fourteen

"Stevie baby!"

Stephen and Kaylie twisted in their seats to wave at Aaron and Dora Doolin.

They weren't the first unexpected guests to stop by the VIP arena box that night. The infamous Cherie and a small coterie of seductively clad "ice bunnies" had flounced in earlier—and then right out again upon Stephen's formal announcement of their engagement. Stephen had seemed sheepishly amused. Kaylie had looked at the ring on her finger and smiled to herself, confident in her beloved and the God Who had brought him to her.

Beaming megawatt smiles, the Doolins plunged into the milling throng of Chatams, paramedics and friends helping themselves to the buffet provided by the arena caterer. Beside Stephen and Kaylie, the aunts, too, greeted the newcomers. Odelia, decked out in the team colors of maroon and yellow-gold, waved her hanky at them, the garish walnut-sized garnets on her earlobes sparkling like disco balls. Hypatia, in pearls and pumps, granted them a regal nod, but Aunt Mags, dowdy as ever, barely glanced their way before turning back to the action on the rink, if the Zamboni reconditioning the ice could be called action.

After two periods, the Blades were trailing in the make-it-or-break-it seventh game of the series, but Stephen seemed to have recently turned philosophical about the outcome and his part in it. Or lack of part in it, if the team so decided. He was through hiding like a guilty child, he'd said. A soon-to-be-married man had to learn to face his failures and responsibilities—and leave the rest to God.

For that reason, he'd met with team management and explained himself as fully as possible, vowing never to drink again. He had also invited his father here tonight, at Kaylie's urging. George Gallow hadn't even replied, but at least, Kaylie told herself, Stephen had made the effort. She was terribly proud of him.

Aaron made his way to the front of the box, towing Dora behind. When they reached the double row of seats overlooking the ice, however, it was Dora who spoke first.

"Lemme see! Lemme see!" Grabbing Kaylie's hand from Stephen's, she gasped at the elegantly simple two-carat, marquis-cut diamond on Kaylie's dainty finger. "Ooh, classic. I'm so happy for you." She smacked Stephen on the cheek, adding, "I'm happier for you."

"Thanks." He and Aaron shook hands, Stephen saying, "I thought you were hobnobbing with team management tonight."

"Oh, yeah, and brother are you going to be happy when you hear my news." Aaron bounced on the pads of his feet.

"What news?"

Aaron leaned close and muttered in a voice audible by everyone in the suite, "Kapimsky's going to Canada."

"No kidding!"

"They're rebuilding up there and need a hotshot young goalie to get 'em into the playoffs." He pounded Stephen on the shoulder and, grinning, added, "They wanted you, but the team won't let you go."

Stephen closed his eyes, hugging Kaylie tight with his right arm. Stephen sighed as if a weight had lifted from his shoulders. He brought his hand around and clapped palms with Aaron. "Thanks, man. That's a great wedding present."

"Speaking of presents, the team's got something for you. Will you come down to the locker room right after the game and bring the better half with you?"

Stephen uneasily shifted in his seat, his cast knocking against the half wall at the edge of the box. "I don't know. It would mean running the press gauntlet, and Kaylie may not be ready for that."

"We'll be there," she said confidently, and Stephen's arm tightened.

"Thanks, babe," he whispered.

Half an hour later, it was all over. The team had lost by a single point, their opponents advancing on to the finals, but no one could expect them to hang their heads. They'd come a long way fast, and the future looked bright. Kaylie and Stephen rose to make their way downstairs, taking their leave of the family with kisses and pats and handclasps.

Hubner came over to squeeze Stephen's shoulder and say, "Next year, son. Next year."

Smiling, Stephen nodded. Kaylie knew that her father

would never be a hockey fan, but he showed signs of becoming a Stephen fan, and that was what counted most.

Aaron returned to run interference for the happy couple, keeping the press from eating them alive and checking the locker room to make sure that everyone was still decent before ushering them inside. Stephen paused, his weight balanced on his crutches. Kaylie's slipped her hand supportively into the curve of his elbow. Instantly, they were swamped by sweaty skaters speaking half a dozen different languages. The team captain called for order and got it.

"These are yours, man," he said to Stephen, producing three battered pucks. "One for every game we won in this series."

Stephen shook his head. "No, I can't. Kapimsky should get those. He—"

Kapimsky stepped forward. "You got us here, dude, and you gave me my shot. Those pucks are yours."

Kaylie beamed as the two shook hands, and Stephen congratulated Kapimsky on his new contract.

"Next year, all the way!" someone called.

A cheer went up. After it died down, Stephen made introductions. The men congratulated him and joked with Kaylie about being the team nurse.

"Well, I have specialized in pediatrics," she quipped. "That ought to qualify me for the position."

Stephen laughed with everyone else. They stayed a few moments longer, then got out so the guys could strip and shower. Monday morning, Stephen said, they'd start cleaning out their lockers, the season finally having come to a close. He seemed at peace with that.

Aaron pocketed his phone, saying, "I called your car around. Head on out back. They'll be waiting for you."

Stephen had hired a series of limos to ferry the family to and from the game so no one would have to worry about getting lost or finding a decent parking place. He passed the hockey pucks to Kaylie, saying, "Can you hold these for me, babe?"

She dropped them into her purse. "I can't imagine they'll be the only ones."

"Let's hope not!" Aaron quipped. "I'll pick them up later and get them into the display case."

The case had been moved to Aaron's office for safekeeping while Stephen's Fort Worth house was being repaired and put on the market. He and Kaylie, meanwhile, had an appointment with an architect for the following week and were already shopping for a small acreage near Buffalo Creek to build on, as well as a house to rent in the meanwhile.

By the time they reached the car, she could tell that Stephen was tired but pleased. He stood back to let Kaylie slide into the long black vehicle through the door held open by the driver, but a voice from the shadows near the arena stopped her.

"Steve."

He turned so quickly that he almost fell. Kaylie's hand flashed out to steady him, but it was another that set him to rights, a big square hand thickened with maturity and hard work.

"Dad!"

George Gallow backed away a step. Shadows carved hollows in the cheeks and eye sockets beneath the hat that he wore, but the resemblance to his son was marked. Tall and lanky with feet and hands the size of small boats, he was a large, vibrant, if quiet, presence.

"I didn't think you'd be here!" Stephen exclaimed. "Why didn't you come up to the suite?"

George shrugged. "You know me, not much for crowds."

Kaylie moved up close to Stephen. He reached back for her, pulling her forward.

"So this is the one, huh?" George said.

"This is the one," Stephen confirmed.

George swept off his hat, smoothed his dark blond hair with his hand and nodded. "Pleased to meet you."

Impulsively, Kaylie stepped up and hugged him. "It's a pleasure to meet you, too. Thank you for coming."

He didn't lift a hand to return the embrace, but he didn't back away, either. "Mmm," he said, "not the first time. Don't s'pose it'll be the last."

"You've been here before?" Stephen asked, clearly shocked.

"Time or two."

"Why didn't you let me know?"

"Wasn't sure you wanted to see me."

"Dad," Stephen said, sounding exasperated, "I've always wanted to see you. I just… I didn't know how…"

George Gallow nodded his understanding. "Okay. It's okay, son."

"I haven't done a very good job of letting you in, have I? I'm sorry for that."

George Gallow shrugged, standing awkwardly, and Stephen did what Kaylie prayed he would. He hobbled forward and wrapped his arm around his father's shoulders. George caught his breath and pushed it out again, then he patted Stephen on the back before quickly pulling away.

"Guess I'll see you at the wedding then."

"Well, I'll be there," Stephen quipped.

George Gallow grinned. "Me, too." He ducked his head, adding, "Better let your mother know."

"Don't worry about that," Stephen said, smiling. "It'll be fine. From now on, everything is going to be just fine."

"Be a nice change," George said, fitting his hat back onto his head. Then he nodded at Kaylie and walked away.

"Well," Kaylie said, laughing.

"Very well," Stephen said, slipping his arm around her waist. "Extremely well."

"I wish it could have worked out for them," Kaylie said with a sigh, "your mom and dad, I mean."

"I know," Stephen said. "I do, too, but they were never a good match. Not like us."

"A Dutch hockey player and a pediatric nurse," she reminded him pertly. "Not many would put us together, I imagine."

"A half-Dutch, half-Texan hockey player."

"It's still a weird match," she teased, leaning into him. "A match that could be made only in Texas."

He laughed and folded her close. "Or heaven."

So it was. A match made in Texas. And heaven.

He laid his cheek atop her head, and she closed her eyes. Silently they praised God. Together.

* * * * *

SPECIAL EXCERPT FROM

Love Inspired®

When a former sweetheart reappears in this widow's life, could it mean a second chance at love?

Read on for a sneak preview of A Widow's Hope, *the first book in the series Indiana Amish Brides.*

He knocked, and stood there staring when a young, beautiful woman opened the door. Chestnut-colored hair peeked out from her *kapp*. It matched her warm brown eyes and the sprinkling of freckles on her cheeks.

There was something familiar about her. He nearly smacked himself on the forehead. Of course she looked familiar, though it had been years since he'd seen her.

"Hannah? Hannah Beiler?"

"Hannah King." She quickly scanned him head to toe. She frowned and said, "I'm Hannah King."

"But…isn't this the Beiler home?"

"*Ya.* Wait. Aren't you Jacob? Jacob Schrock?"

He nearly laughed.

"The same, and I'm looking for the Beiler place."

"*Ya,* this is my parents' home, but why are you here?"

"To work." He stared down at the work order as if he could make sense of seeing the first girl he'd ever kissed standing on the doorstep of the place he was supposed to be working.

"I don't understand," he said.

"Neither do I. Who are you looking for?"

"Alton Beiler."

LIEXP0718

"But that's my father. Why—"

At that point Mr. Beiler joined them. "You're at the right house, Jacob. Please, come inside."

He'd never have guessed when he put on his suspenders that morning that he would be seeing Hannah Beiler before the sun was properly up. The same Hannah Beiler he had once kissed behind the playground.

Alton Beiler ushered Jacob into the kitchen.

"Claire, maybe you remember Jacob Schrock. Apparently he took our Hannah on a buggy ride once."

Jacob heard them, but his attention was on the young boy sitting at the table. He sat in a regular kitchen chair, which was slightly higher than the wheelchair parked behind him.

The boy cocked his head to the side, as if trying to puzzle through what he saw of Jacob. Then he said, *"Gudemariye."*

"And to you," Jacob replied.

"Who are you?" he asked.

"I'm Jacob. What's your name?"

"Matthew. This is Mamm, and that's Mammi and Daddi. We're a family now." Matthew grinned.

Hannah glanced at him and blushed.

"It's really nice to meet you, Matthew. I'm going to be working here for a few days."

"Working on what?"

Jacob glanced at Alton, who nodded once. "I'm going to build you a playhouse."

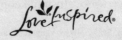

SPECIAL EXCERPT FROM

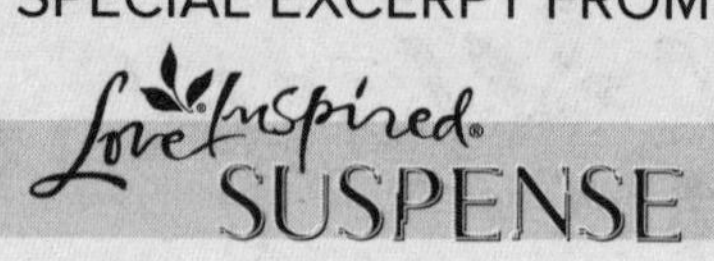

With a child missing and a killer on the loose, Ava Esposito and Oliver Davidson team up to save a life and hunt a killer.

Read on for a sneak preview of Rescue Operation *by Lenora Worth, the next book in the Military K-9 Unit miniseries, available August 2018 from Love Inspired Suspense.*

Ignoring the tilt and rumble of the HH-60G Pave Hawk helicopter about to hoist her down below, Senior Airman Ava Esposito adjusted the sturdy harness sleeves around the black nylon sling holding the sixty-five-pound yellow Lab that was about to rappel with her. Roscoe's trusting eyes followed her while he hovered close to her chest.

"That's right. It's showtime. We've got to find that little boy."

Roscoe wouldn't understand, but they were armed and ready for anything or anyone they might confront in the dense woods that belonged to Canyon Air Force Base. This reserve covered hundreds of acres and could hide a person for weeks if not months. Right now, she had to find a lost little boy and watch her back for a serial killer who'd escaped from prison in the spring and was reported to be back in these woods.

LISEXP0718

Her focus humming on high alert, Ava checked her weapons and equipment one more time. Then she patted the alert K-9 on his furry head. "Ready?"

Roscoe woofed his reply.

Nodding, she scooted to the open side of the chopper and let her booted feet dangle out, Roscoe's warm breath hitting the inch or so of skin she had showing outside of her heavy camo uniform, protective combat vest, knapsack and M16 rifle.

Above her, a crew member adjusted the carabiner holding the pulleys that would hoist both Ava and Roscoe so they could rappel down, each with their own pulley to hold them securely together.

Nothing but heavy woods, scattered rocks and hills. But somewhere out there was a lost, scared little boy.

Something whizzed past her. But even with the chopper's bellowing roar all around her, she heard the ding of metal hitting metal.

And then she saw it. The ricochet of a bullet hitting the fuselage. Someone was shooting at them!

LISEXP0718